TABEA'S STORY

The Memoir of a World War II German Army Nurse

Betty J. Iverson

To Lavonne, have a good read —

Betty J. Iverson

ISBN: 1-4033-8366-9 (e-book)
ISBN: 1-4033-8367-7 (Paperback)

Library of Congress Control Number: 2002095119

This book is printed on acid free paper.

Printed in the United States of America
Bloomington, IN

1stBooks – rev. 01/22/03

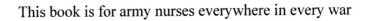

This book is for army nurses everywhere in every war

They are often the unsung heroines.

ACKNOWLEDGMENTS

I want to acknowledge Tabea, first of all, who was willing to share her story, had an incredible memory and was an inspiring woman.

My husband, Ted, who is not only my life partner and faithful supporter, but a computer expert as well who assisted with the technical process of preparing the manuscript for publication.

I deeply appreciate my talented readers who made invaluable contributions, especially Carol Collier, Bill Sumner and Ene Bonnyay.

In addition, I want to thank my family for their support: especially my daughter, Adriene, who scanned the pictures; my daughter-in-law, Wendy, who suggested that history be added for readers like her, who knew so little about the Second World War.

And last, but not least, I thank my friends who encouraged and supported me, especially Jean, Donna and Eva.

CONTENTS

PROLOGUE

Many years have passed since Tabea Springer stepped off a plane in New York city to begin a new life in the United States. She cherished her new county because it symbolized a freedom and tolerance foreign to her Teutonic upbringing. She was never far from Germany, however, in her thoughts and heart. She often shared her exciting war stories with friends and acquaintances.

Her minister encouraged her to jot down her stories. Tabea said she wanted Americans to see in themselves the generosity and compassion which had attracted her and lured her to emigrate.

I had many interviews with her in her mobile home in Marina, California. She led me through her life and painted unique pictures of the Second World War as she experienced it in Poland, Russia and Germany. She revealed little known facets of the war and later the devastating effects of the division of Germany on her and those about her

While I have worked with Tabea for several years in the writing of her story, I am penning the prologue alone because she suffered a stroke in 1981 which affected her speech. Her sisters eventually took her back to Germany to take care of her. Tabea died there on June 6, 1982.

Tabea and I both hope that the book will lead to a greater understanding of the German people and an appreciation for the love of humanity that transcends nationality. This is what she saw in the American soldiers in the Second World War.

Tabea dedicated her story to her parents, Hans and Carla Springer, who not only gave her life but brought her to faith in her Lord Jesus Christ.

Betty J. Iverson

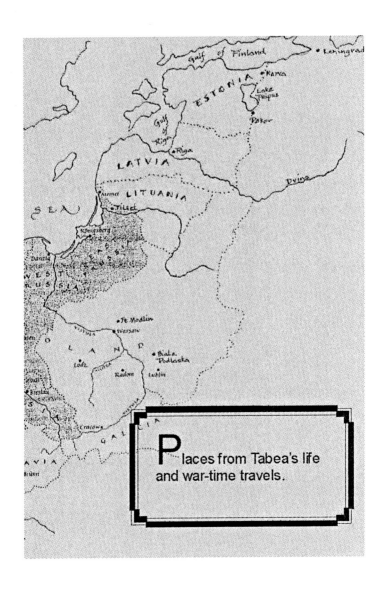

Places from Tabea's life and war-time travels.

PART ONE

Early Years

Betty J. Iverson

CHAPTER ONE: A NEW PLACE

The year was 1912 and Germany was prosperous and at peace, although there was still an uneasy tension in the Balkan nations. Austria and Russia both had interests in this area, and Germany had encouraged Austria to pursue a conciliatory course with its Balkan neighbors.

My father, Herr Pastor Hans Springer, was standing in the hall, doing his best to stay out of the way of the parishioners who had come from Hamburg with their wagons to move us. They were carrying heavy loads of boxes and furniture out of the house. Papa was tall and thin with thinning dark brown hair and a mustache and short beard. My sisters and I scurried about excitedly, watching the men, admonishing them to "be careful" as they hoisted our precious possessions from our bedrooms. Papa appeared excited, too. The call to Hamburg had come unexpectedly, but was welcome. Papa had said lately that he had done all he could do here in Kassel, and he was ready to move on to another challenge.

The church in Hamburg would certainly provide that. It was much larger with over four thousand members, and Papa was grateful to know there would be two younger ministers to assist him. Wherever we lived, Papa always reached out to the community, and he was sure Hamburg would offer him many avenues. As for us, his four daughters, we were certain that the big city of Hamburg would offer many cultural opportunities. I was excited about the move.

I could just imagine the thoughts crossing his mind as he gazed intently at all of us. First there was my oldest sister, Liesel, now thirteen, who hurried past him with yet

3

one more box for the wagon. With her long curly auburn hair and willowy figure, I had been told that she resembled her mother, Elizabeth, Papa's first wife. She was only two when her mother had died and Liesel hardly remembered her. Fortunately my mother, Carla, Elizabeth's younger sister loved her as if she were her own. The family was not surprised when Papa eventually married Carla.

Liesel was becoming a beautiful young woman, who yearned for nice things and admired those fashions and amenities that were part of the upper class. If Papa was concerned about her, he never let on, except for a troubled expression that crossed his brow now and again when he gazed at her.

And then there was me, Tabea, his second daughter, born soon after he married Carla. People often said I was just like him. Although I was only nine, I was a responsible girl, someone who would look after others. My face was long and thin and I felt rather plain-looking with my mousey brown hair. Since mother suffered from asthma, I had to assume a good shareof the household tasks and take care of her whenever an asthma attack struck. She was short and plump with curly black hair that softly framed her face. Although she was often fatigued with her asthma, she did not have a wrinkle lining her porcelain complexion. Even now, I was at mother's side, helping her with all the last minute details to make sure she was not overwhelmed.

I saw Papa look tenderly at Deborah, just five. I could hear him say, as he often did, "Deborah is my little injured bird." A delicate child with scoliosis, curvature of the spine, Deborah was taught at home by a tutor hired by my parents. In Germany in the early 1900's, imperfect children weren't accepted in the regular classroom but instead were isolated in special schools for deformed children. Papa could not endure the thought of his little daughter being teased or made to feel like a cripple, so the decision to tutor her at home had come easily. Deborah demanded very little and was eager to please. She was already showing artistic talent, and Papa hoped that one day she could make this her profession.

And then there was Papa's bright spirit, Esther, everyone's favorite. She was a happy and energetic two-year-old. Papa often told me, "I feel good just being around her." I wondered if my parents weren't spoiling her, but with her sparkling brown eyes, blonde hair, and impish ways, she was hard to resist.

"Hans, Hans!" Mother interrupted my reverie. "Come quickly! Look at what these men have done to my dining room table. They've ruined it." She looked as if she could burst into tears any moment. Papa rushed to the dining room where mother showed him a long scratch along one side where the pad had slipped and the table grazed the doorway.

"Now, now, dear, it's just a small scratch and we can have it repaired in Hamburg," he said soothingly. The young men carrying the table were most apologetic, assuring them that the church would see to its repair. I saw mother breathing rapidly, and Papa helped her to a chair. "You see, Carla? It will be taken care of. Tabea, why don't you take mother in the kitchen and check that everything is ready to be moved out of there?" I quickly nodded and led mother away.

That dining set meant the world to mother. Before they were married, my parents shopped for furniture together. Papa soon learned that a woman who is an interior decorator has distinctive tastes! For their dining room she had chosen this unique set of heavy oak. The table and chair legs were carved lion's feet, and the handles of the buffet drawers were lion's heads. The seats of the high backed chairs were covered with yellow satin. Mother must have known what her future would hold, because she bought a table that would extend to seat twelve. I smiled to myself, as I thought how often that occurred.

After mother had settled down, I went back to the dining room, telling Papa, "She's fine now. I think she's excited like the rest of us. Papa, I can't wait to live in Hamburg. I've heard it has over a million people. I've never seen a city that large. And it's built on the estuary of the Elbe River-will you take us there?" Papa nodded, but hardly pausing for breath, I continued. "And you know what else? This beautiful city is said to have canals, bridges and tunnels (even a pedestrian walkway underwater) that lace the city together like a corset. A lake in the middle of the city has a marina full of sailboats and is surrounded by parks. Doesn't that sound lovely?" I knew I was babbling on, but I was so excited about the prospect of living in Hamburg."

Papa laughed out loud as he said, "I think you've been reading up on Hamburg, Tabea. I've never seen you so enthusiastic. I suspect you'll be the one in our family with the "wunderlust." My cheeks grew warm with embarrassment. I assured him that I would always be around to take care of him and mother. Papa nodded, smiling to himself. "We'll see about going through that tunnel, Tabea."

Papa headed back to his study. I headed outside to see what my sisters doing. When I came back in, I stood at the doorway of the study and watched as Papa packed the last of his books, lingering over a few of his old pharmacy books. They were reminders of both his first profession and the break with his father. Papa told me that he had come to the ministry at a great cost. When I asked what he meant, he told me this story.

His father, Oscar had not only seen to it that all of his children were well educated, but he chose their professions as well. Papa was sent to pharmacy school and then came home to work with grandfather in the family pharmacy. How different things were in those days. There were no pills in bottles or boxes, but rather the pharmacist prepared each medicine by mixing various powders in mortars with pestles, sealing each dose in an envelope. Powdered opiates were weighed on a gram scale. There were bee hives in the orchard, and teas and herbs grown in the teahouse. Grandfather kept twenty pound jars of opiates in the cellar, as well as casks of fine wine. When the doctors stopped in, he enjoyed serving them a glass of wine. Although Papa was always invited, he said he never felt comfortable. Quiet and introspective, his first love was music. Grandfather was annoyed that he could spend so much time composing music or playing his zither or violin.

While Papa found the work in the pharmacy pleasant enough, he felt a growing restlessness. Not only was music his passion, but even more important, he felt a calling to serve people which was not being fulfilled in the pharmacy. When he broached this subject to his mother, telling her that he was considering being a minister, she was shocked. Apparently she knew what grandfather's reaction would be, but being a God-fearing woman, she said simply, "Take it to the Lord, my son and he will guide you."

While grandmother attended church regularly, my grandfather saw fit to make an appearance only now and again on special occasions. If he did not approve of music as an occupation, he certainly would not approve of the ministry! But one starry winter night as Papa walked in the snow pondering his future, he felt more strongly than ever a call to serve the Lord. Although he was an obedient son, who did not want to hurt his father, he made his decision and knew what he must do.

The next morning Papa told grandfather of his desire to enter the ministry. As expected, his father was furious! "What is this nonsense you talk about? The ministry? Bah! I won't have it!" With a sweeping gesture about the pharmacy, Grandfather thundered, "Look around, Hans. All this will be yours one day. This is why I provided a university education for you."

Quietly Papa returned, "Yes, and I'm grateful for what you've given me, but I've thought about this for a long time, father. I don't want to hurt you, but I feel called to serve people in another way–a way that is not being fulfilled here in the pharmacy."

Grandfather shook his head in disbelief.   "You're working for the good of people here, too–and enjoy a social life with the doctors as well. What's wrong with that?" Papa remained as firm and unyielding as his father, even though he knew he was defying the custom of German fathers to shape their children and choose their destiny. When grandfather saw that Papa could not be swayed, he turned aside in hurt and bitterness, never speaking to Papa again until many years later when he lay dying and called for his son to come. Grandfather sold his pharmacy a few years after Papa left, so none of his children would inherit it. Papa left immediately for the University of Tubingen.

I heard Papa sigh as he finished the last of his packing. He glanced up and saw me. "Are we ready to leave the old and start anew, Tabea?" I nodded, wondering what Hamburg would mean for us Springers

CHAPTER TWO: HAMBURG

I was delighted that true to his word, Papa took us on an outing in Hamburg as soon as we were settled. The first thing I noticed were the great crowds of people and the ten story buildings. As we walked along the docks, I was awed by the sight of huge ships arriving. One of the dock hands told us that they came from all over the world bringing coffee, copper, corn, oil, iron ore, just to name a few imports. "You see, girls," Papa said thoughtfully, "our new city is a port as well as an industrial center. And now I have another treat for you today. We're going to the zoo."

His statement was greeted with more squeals of excitement. Esther danced around, not sure what a zoo was, while Liesel couldn't decide whether it would be boring or interesting. I'm sure my eyes shone with excitement, as I grabbed Deborah's hand and told her we were going to see the animals.

I was excited as we walked into the Hamburg zoo because this was the first zoo in Europe to place animals in their natural settings. I was even more astounded to see black people for the first time in my life. There among all the animal displays, were several black families living in a replica of an African village. They were carrying on their usual activities of cooking, carving spears, and occasionally dancing with their spears, all in full view of the zoo visitors. I was utterly fascinated and would have stood there for hours if Liesel hadn't pulled me away saying, "Tabea, it's impolite to stare. Come along." (At the time, I did not think it strange for people to be displayed in a zoo. In later years, when I remembered our trip to the zoo, I was horrified that I saw people displayed in a zoo with the animals)

These early years in Hamburg were as stimulating and uplifting to me as Kassel had been depressing. I wondered if the saying was true, "The people of Hamburg have a touch of the English–very cool, but if you win a friend, he will be loyal to you." Although strands of gray were now streaking Papa's dark brown hair and mustache, he was obviously happy in his ministry here. Mother had a brief respite from the asthma attacks. My sisters and I not only enjoyed our schools but we also enjoyed those outings with the daughters of our family doctor. We had picnics in the park after canoeing on the Alster River, took ballet lessons and went to the opera. At first we were picked up by a horse-driven carriage, but later we were driven by a chauffeur in a shiny black automobile. We felt quite grand as we rode down the street peering through windows framed with green silk curtains.

Deborah did not go to school with us, but continued to be tutored at home and her artistic talent flourished. An art teacher instructed her in pencil and charcoal sketching as well as painting on tablecloths and doilies. A small room was set aside as her studio. She did not pity herself, although one day she confessed to me that she felt Papa was ashamed of her. "Oh no, Deborah," I protested. "How could you feel that way? Papa loves each one of us just the same, and he's proud of your talent and your lovely drawings."

"Oh I know that," she replied. "It's just that I think he's proud of how pretty and smart the rest of you are, while he feels the need to apologize for me and explain."

As she grew, Deborah's curved back became more obvious, and she wore dresses with large collars in an attempt to hide her increasingly uneven shoulders and arms that seemed too long for her body. All the exercises and

11

chinning bar stretches we did with her, as well as the uncomfortable corset she had to wear were to no avail. The curve would have its way. Even though she was well-liked and accepted by the girls in her youth group at church, she was keenly aware that a cripple was commonly thought to be a punishment from God. Fortunately, our parents did not share this view, but rather saw Deborah's deformity as an opportunity for them to be merciful and caring. I tried to be sensitive to Deborah's feelings, because she was a sweet and sensitive girl.

Spring arrived and we went on hikes in the forest, and Papa invented a special game. He would bring along a tuning fork and ask us to guess the notes of the song of each particular bird. "Listen girls," he would say, "to all the melodies in nature: the tumbling brooks, the trilling wren, and the chirping crickets. And look above at the those honking geese? See that big V they form as they fly?" Music was so much a part of his soul, that I wondered that it didn't swallow up the ministry as it had the pharmacy. Perhaps it was the burst of nature in spring that inspired Papa, but one day he came home and announced, "I'm going to lease a small farm in the suburbs."

I looked up from my book and noticed instantly mother's look of horror as she said, "Hans, you can't be serious!"

"Oh but I am, Carla. I think it's time the girls learned how to take care of living things, like plants and animals. And just think, we'll be able to grow our own vegetables." Gently he put his arm around her shoulders and said, "Now don't say you don't like the farm until you've seen it."

Carla turned to face him, asking anxiously, "But Hans, what about the girls' education? They're going to fine schools here in the city."

"I've already looked into that, my dear," replied Papa confidently, "and the girls can continue at their same schools. The train station is about a half hour walk from our home, where they can catch a train into town that will bring them close to their schools." Mother was only somewhat reassured, while my sisters and I adopted a wait-and-see attitude.

Liesel, clearly was not pleased. She said, "This is our home. Why can't we stay here?" Papa just asked her to give it a chance.

The very next day, Papa took us out to see our new home. The house was a rambling two-story frame home on a three thousand meter plot of land. "There are seventy fruit trees, over two hundred berry bushes of various kinds, and twenty strawberry beds," Papa told us as we walked along. "I have personally counted them all." Muttering contentedly to himself, Papa walked about the property like an aristocratic baron on a feudal estate.

Practical concerns were uppermost in mother's mind. She cautiously approached our current housekeeper, Lisbeth, about coming along with us. To her surprise and relief, Lisbeth readily agreed, saying the country air would do her a world of good. Lisbeth had come to work for us at the age of sixteen and was part of our family and always jolly and easy-going. As a matter-of-fact, she was so easy going to a fault-downright slow. This flaw irritated mother, but she put up with it because Lisbeth was obviously fond of us.

Papa took a month's vacation to help us get settled. We met our neighbors almost immediately. On one side lived a professional hunter, who earned his livelihood by selling rabbits and deer in the open markets in October. On the other side lived a farmer with sixteen children, all of whom were like cookies cut with the same cutter: stocky, blonde, and apple-cheeked. This farmer, Gustav, was indispensable to us. We were definitely Greenhorns about farming.

Our new country life was a challenge for my sisters and me. Instead of being chauffeured to ballet lessons and picnics, we were now taking care of the animals Papa had bought: chickens, rabbits, geese, and even a pig. The pig immediately deposited a litter of fourteen piglets with a runt. We took turns bottle feeding the tiny one. Soon our hands were blistered from hoeing in the garden and our backs ached from planting row after row of vegetables. Before long, our cheeks were as rosy as the neighbors. Even Deborah was the picture of health.

Harvest time came and with it the canning of all those fruits and vegetables. Liesel felt it wasn't fair that after all that summer work, we now had even more work. I nodded, as I, too, was growing tired of the routine. "Yet you have to admit," I said, "all those cellar shelves lined with jars of every hue and color look beautiful." Our table never lacked fresh produce from the garden, eggs from our chickens and milk from the farmer next door.

Although we had homework during the school months, we were still expected to keep the garden weeded and the animals fed. We were grateful that our father had hired a gardener to tend to the heavier chores of pruning and plowing. Mother reconciled herself to this new life and actually enjoyed seeing us busy. She was adamant that idleness led to wrong-doing and often said, "If you have nothing to do, rip a button off your coat and sew it back on again." The farm satisfied her work compulsion, but she was probably happier about our lot then we were.

Fortunately life was not all work for us. With sixteen children next door, we did not lack for playmates. They taught us to ride horses bareback, clutching their manes, and initiated us into the farm games where we explored all the nooks and crannies of the barn. Our lives were enriched by watching the wonder of a new life arrive, whether it was a little bunny or a baby chick. I felt secure as I approached the threshold of my womanhood, completely oblivious to the dark clouds that were gathering over Europe. As I look back, we enjoyed such a peaceful content existence. who could have predicted what was coming next?

CHAPTER THREE: CLOUDS ON THE HORIZON

Mother and I were in the garden picking berries one hot August afternoon in 1914, when suddenly we saw in the distance clouds of dust rising from the road and heard the sound of thundering hooves. Uniformed men on horseback gradually came into view as a unit of about twenty-five cavalry soldiers, resplendent in gray uniforms stopped at the gate. They looked so grim, that my heart pounded with fear, until the leader smiled and spoke to mother in a friendly voice.

"Is there anyone staying with you from Serbia?" he asked. "Oh no," Mother answered quickly, shaking her head. "Why are you looking for people from Serbia?"

The officer looked incredulous at her question. "Haven't you heard the news? We're at war with Serbia! A Serb terrorist shot the Austrian Archduke Francis Ferdinand and his wife Sophie while they were visiting Sarajevo in Bosnia on June 28th." Mother appeared stunned by the news. I wasn't sure what it meant.

Austria-Hungary issued an ultimatum to Serbia which granted permission for Austro-Hungarian officials to enter Serbia and punish those persons involved with the assassination. Serbia tried to negotiate this ultimatum, but Austria refused to back down. Serbia's response was then to reject the ultimatum altogether and mobilize their troops. Austria declared war on July 28th. In addition to this conflict, war was brewing between Russia and Germany, who had issued an ultimatum to Russia to cease the military buildup on its borders. With a large Slavic population, Russia had long been sympathetic to Serbia. When their ultimatum was ignored, Germany quickly declared war on

Russia. Like falling blocks, countries quickly took sides, with the Central Powers of Germany and Austria-Hungary facing the Allies: Serbia, Russia, France, the United Kingdom, and eventually Italy. Indeed, because of this assassination in Serbia one day nations would be involved from the United States to Japan and be known as World War I.

However, on this hot August day, none of us standing here in the berry patch had any inkling of what this skirmish would lead to and how drastically it would affect our lives.

The soldiers looked hot and tired, and Mother asked, "Would your men like some berries?" Like all Germans, we adored our army and would gladly give them anything they needed.

The officer turned to his men, saying, "Go help yourselves." Immediately the men dismounted and were soon lost among the bushes as they filled their canteens or helmets with gooseberries and currents. I watched in fascination because I had never been around so many soldiers before. My mind was spinning: War? What did that mean for us? Would soldiers from another country come here?

While the men picked, the officer went on to say that they were on a mission to collect horses from the farmers. "This is a time for all Germans to unite and support their army!" We learned later that our neighbor had given him four of his finest stallions.

Mother and I bade the soldiers a polite good bye and rushed back to the house, as though it were a haven that would keep the stormy world from intruding upon us. "Wars are terrible," Mother said, "and we must now commit our soldiers to the Lord in prayer, and ask Him for peace to come quickly."

Isolated as we were in the country, news came through very slowly, since there were no radios at this time. The newspaper, our main source of news, often reported an event a week or more after it happened. Occurrences outside Germany took even longer to reach us. Another source of news was the Town Herald, a man who ran through the village ringing a bell and announcing important news or posting notices. That evening, we heard his familiar bell and then his cry, "Germany is at war! The Kaiser has mobilized the army and the navy."

We were a fearful family circle as we gathered that evening. Papa was reassuring and told us, "Don't worry, my daughters. We have excellent generals and this war will probably be over in six weeks." He went on to reflect that the Kaiser had ruled Germany for forty-four years in peace. "We're a strong country with one of the best armies and a navy, whose ship, the Europa, has won an award for being the fastest ship on the seas." Like most Germans, he had absolute confidence in his country's invincible might.

By the end of 1914, Germany faced opposing armies from the border of Switzerland to the North Sea, a front of about five hundred miles. The war was in fact a two front war. Very soon, the commitment to win the war had reached every home. As it escalated we realized the war would not end quickly as we had hoped. Visitors from Hamburg told us that food had been rationed, and they had difficulty finding fruit and vegetables in the stores, since produce was allotted first to the hospitals for the wounded. Bread, butter, meat and candy were very scarce. Apples and carrots, when they could be found, were now special treats.

Our school days were now cut back to four hour sessions so the students, both boys and girls alike from eight to fourteen, could work on the farms. We were taken to the fields in buses to harvest the crops. I worked for the farmer next door, often getting up at 5:00 a.m. to harvest potatoes by hand. My sisters worked on our farm, since our gardener, like every able-bodied young man, had left for the army.

The Town Herald posted notices requesting that women knit items such as socks, shawls, knee warmers and ear muffs for the military. They were to bring them to the Buergemeister (mayor) at the city hall. In addition, citizens were asked to donate their copper to the government, which would also be collected at the city hall.

Mother considered it her contribution to peace to donate all her beautiful copper pots and pans, despite the fact that many of them were family heirlooms, centuries old. "If grandmother knew that her copper collection was going to be melted down for cannons, she would roll over in her grave!" she sighed.

For me, this was a bittersweet parting. I remembered the long hours spent polishing all those copper pans, so I wasn't exactly sad to see them go. I did, however, hate to part with an exquisite piece that had been in the family since 1800. This piece was a copper egg cooker, shaped like a large egg shell cut in half, and set on a small alcohol burner. One half cooked the egg soft, while the other half cooked it hard. The cooker was beautiful! When I asked if we couldn't keep just that one piece, Mother shook her head firmly, saying, "We must all make sacrifices for peace." So the copper egg cooker was taken to the city hall along with the rest of the copper pots and pans. I was sure I'd never see it again.

19

A few months later, my sisters and I took a bundle of knitted woolens to the city hall. The first floor housed the offices, while the Buergemeister and his family lived in an apartment on the second floor. A maid answered our polite knock and ushered us into the kitchen while she determined where the woolens were to be stored. As we stood there waiting, I glanced idly around the room until my gaze fastened on the table. There, gleaming in all its beauty like a captive princess, was our copper egg boiler! I poked Liesel and pointed. Liesel gasped and whispered, "Why that's ours!"

I wanted to snatch it up and run home, but didn't dare. Anger rose within me like a brewing tea pot. How could the Beurgemeister take such an item for himself, I thought, while the rest of us are making sacrifices? Liesel and I ran home so fast that Esther and Deborah stumbled just trying to keep up with us. We couldn't wait to tell mother because surely she'd know what to do. Mother listened intently as our story tumbled out and then, in her own soothing way she said, "You know how beautiful that egg cooker is. Perhaps the Buergemeister couldn't bear the thought of destroying it. He probably isn't keeping it for himself, but will return it to us when the war is over." However, mother's kind words did not convince me. Every time I saw the bulky Buergemeister strutting about the town, I pictured our egg boiler setting on his table.

Months faded into years, and the war dragged on like an endless dreary winter. Papa was seldom at home these days, because he visited the many wounded soldiers in the hospitals of Hamburg after his parish duties. Sometimes, I went with him. The sight of young men missing arms or legs or with disfigured faces astounded and repelled me at first. But then compassion overwhelmed me. I wanted to do something to relieve their misery, but there was nothing I could do. I hoped that perhaps one day I could.

"Papa, these men are so young, so terribly maimed and their lives ruined by this awful war." I said after a particularly disturbing visit. The man my father was praying with cried and asked to die, rather than to live without legs. "How much longer can this go on?"

"That isn't ours to say, Tabea. We don't know the reasons for many things, including war." he responded solemnly. "But we do have a God who can bring healing and forgiveness to any situation." Then he sighed, "This war seems senseless to me, too."

Essentials became more scarce. When we could no longer buy grain to feed our animals, probably due to the Allies blockading the ports, we slaughtered them one by one and ate them. We gathered mushrooms in the forest to dry for the winter. Fortunately for us, we could buy milk from our neighbor. When I gathered crops in his field, he paid me with turnips and potatoes, twenty pounds for a day of labor. Turnips and potatoes became our mainstay-gone were the days of a lavishly spread table. Still, we fared better than most, especially when our fruit trees bore in the summer. Friends from the city came often with buckets in hand, since we had invited them to come and share our bounty.

When our coal supply was depleted, we gathered wood from the forest to burn in the cook stove. With the rationing of both gas and electricity, we relied solely on petroleum lamps for light. A glass bowl filled with water was placed in front of the lamps to magnify the light. Fortunately our house was old and already equipped with these lamps, some hanging from hooks on the walls, while one hung suspended from a chain in the living room. With the advent of electricity, these lamps had not been needed until now.

Even though I was just a teenager, I suspected that the newspapers printed more propaganda than news. Often slogans appeared, such as "God punish England", or "On to Paris", and "Germany Over All". We were exhorted constantly to stick together and sacrifice for the glory of the Fatherland. I sensed that the war wasn't going well for Germany when there didn't seem to be as many headlines about victories as there were initially.

Secret weapons such as the Zeppelin, were touted as the ultimate weapon to end the war quickly. Another secret weapon, nerve gas, stirred quite a controversy. Some people were against it and wrote letters to the newspaper protesting its use, even though it wasn't clear if nerve gas had been used. But the rumors continued to circulate that nerve gas was being used experimentally in France and Russia, always justified as a "means to end the war quickly."

I watched my father age overnight. His brown gray-streaked hair faded to white, while his thin face became lined with deep creases. He was often tired, and mother worried about him. Papa's stoic shell had obviously been penetrated by the many deaths and the increasing number of grotesquely wounded men arriving daily from the front lines. Added to this was the affront of seeing those sons of rich farmers and lawyers who avoided military service.

We felt a blow when we heard that the United States had declared war on Germany on April 16, 1917. Papa had spoken often of his regard for the United States because some of his relatives were there. "There's a saying in our family," he said, "that every fifty years a Springer emigrates to America." He had cousins in New York who were publishers and lawyers and others in Kansas who were farmers. He spoke of America as a big country with unlimited possibilities, and that anyone could make a fortune in that great land, even a billion Marks.

"With the entrance of America into the war," he sighed sadly, "We're in grave trouble." He no longer spoke of Germany's great generals, but instead focused on praying for an end to all the suffering. There were seldom, if ever, headlines recounting victories in the newspaper. He was told by the wounded that the American troops were devastating their lines.

Easter that year was indelible in my memory. In the midst of my sadness, the joy I found in Christ came to me in a special way. Papa was away at a conference, but mother promised us an Easter celebration. After church, she filled a picnic basket with a small portion of potato salad, one slice of bread (our family's daily ration) and an egg, beautifully decorated by Deborah. The sun was shining brightly as we walked into the forest. I felt as if we were entering an enchanted world. Massive branches of pine and fir trees joined to form arches, and the birch trees' pale green leaves hung like lacy veils. The violets, in full bloom, spread a purple carpet beneath our feet, as we walked past the crocus and snowbells poking their white heads up through the grass. Here there was no war, only the chirping of the birds, the wind rustling through the trees, and the water tumbling over the rocks in the stream.

We spread our blanket by the stream and Esther picked some pussy willows to adorn our picnic table. Mother took the egg, cradled it in her hands, and prayed, "Dear Lord, bless our meal as Jesus blessed the five thousand. May we know the happiness of Christ's arising." Then she carefully divided the egg into five portions, and the picnic

23

commenced. I was amazed that I felt full even though the meal was small. My heart and soul had been fed as well.

We walked home arm in arm, singing hymns, and Mother remarked, "Isn't this like the two disciples from Emmaus who walked with Jesus after His resurrection and didn't even recognize Him until later?" I nodded, feeling content.

By now the war had gone on so long that any talk of sacrifice for the Fatherland was meaningless. The situation was desperate. People were tired of the loss of men, the food and fuel shortages, and the escalating destruction. Finally, on November ll, 1918, the armistice ending the war was signed. We were relieved for the war to end, but from the outset, we were aware that peace would be a bitter pill for us Germans to swallow. Almost immediately, the headlines reported that Germany had been stripped of its colonies in Africa and the Far East. Alsace-Lorraine was given to France as well as the Saar Basin. (Supposedly for only a fifteen year period.) The state of Poland was enlarged by carving away more German territory, most notably the Polish Corridor that separated East Prussia from the rest of Germany. Further the Treaty of Versailles gave Memel to Lithuania and North Schleswig to Denmark. The hardest blow of all was the designation of Danzig, the crown jewel, as a Free City.

In addition to the loss of land, Germany's military was drastically reduced. The Treaty of Versailles brought other hardships to us. Bankrupt as our country was, we were required to pay reparations to countries such as France and England for war damages. While some people were bitter, Papa was resigned, saying, "We lost–we have to pay for it."

One of the most humiliating things of all for Papa to bear was the abdication of Kaiser William II, whom he deeply admired. When the Kaiser fled to the Netherlands, rather than face trial as a war criminal, Papa considered this a family scandal. For me, all the mixed feelings of shame and futility were gathered up in the memory of that sacrificed egg boiler.

Friends from the city recounted stories of the turmoil in the streets between the radical groups and the police. Some said they were even afraid to venture from their homes because of the fighting between the anarchists, patriots, socialists, and soldiers returning from the war. Germans against Germans meant there was no peace at all.

When Frederick Ebert was appointed president by the Weimar National Committee, a precarious semblance of order was restored to our lives, only to have the galloping inflation make the time of order almost as unsettling as the time of war. Money became worthless. A loaf of bread cost a billion marks, or 25 American cents, while a newspaper was 50,000 marks. I was shocked to see a Frau pulling a wagon full of money to do her marketing. Price tags in the stores often doubled within minutes.

Society returned to its primitive ways, and like our Teutonic ancestors had done, we began to exchange goods and services, rather than use marks. My parents exchanged our family silver, oriental rugs, paintings, and good crystal for food or clothes. I watched sadly as the valuable Persian rug, another family heirloom, was traded to a farmer for a six week's supply of eggs and meat. Mother took her silver candlesticks, bowls, and serving spoons to a shop keeper to trade for clothes for us.

Yet during this time in the early 1920's, it wasn't those farmers and shopkeepers to whom we traded our valuables who got rich. Many of the farmers went bankrupt and were forced to sell their farms to businessmen for very little. The farmers then continued to work the farm for a modest salary from their new landlord. Factories and stores, also bankrupt, would be closed and then taken over by money lenders who became known as the new rich. This class sprang up overnight and the dislike and hatred for them came just as quickly. The war had cost us so much, and now our own countrymen were taking advantage of us. Some, but by no means even a majority, of these new rich were Jewish, yet there were many who focused on the Jews. In addition, there were those who made a fortune manufacturing munitions, the most famous and wealthiest of all being the Krupp family.

There were troubles within our family as well. Liesel had finished at the gymnasium and then enrolled in an interior decorating school in Hamburg. After this, she became a hostess for a wealthy family, eventually securing a position with the family of Thomas Mann, a writer. Liesel had always liked nice things, and now she was in her element among the rich. Hard times were not to her liking. She seldom visited us, but when she did she never stayed more than a day.

I watched uncomfortably on one of Liesel's visits as she stood in the parlor and looked about the bare rooms, now stripped of valuable rugs, the grand piano, paintings and even the lion-footed dining room set. She said, "And how is Papa supporting you on the church's money? I tell you, I know where I'm going and believe me, it will be a better life than this!" She was dressed in the latest fashion, wearing high heels, the first I had ever seen. Liesel loved large, fancy hats and long sweeping skirts in the dark elegant colors of the wealthy, navy blue or dark green. Then her gaze rested on us, her three sisters. I became keenly aware that our simple cotton dresses and flat heeled shoes were modest and certainly not high fashion. "Look at yourselves," she said condescendingly. "You look like country girls with no taste."

My cheeks were burning with shame and anger, and I said, "We like nice things, too, Liesel. Our changed circumstances have not taken that away. Papa is supporting us just fine, and it isn't fair for you to insult him." I got up quickly and left the room as I was close to tears and did not want to give Liesel the satisfaction of seeing me cry.

A flood of memories was unleashed as I mulled over my feelings for Liesel. As children, Liesel had often teased me, pointing out that my nose was ugly, or my face was as "thin as a ruler." When I went crying to mother, she would comfort me by saying that Jesus' love was more important than that of people. But one day I decided that I was not going to run to mother anymore. Liesel and I were in the orchard when Liesel began to taunt me. I grabbed her thick auburn braid, which was Liesel's crowning glory, and yanked it with all my might. Liesel took off, running through the orchard, screaming at the top of her lungs. I scrambled after her, hanging onto that braid. After that, there was an understanding between us and a marked decline in the teasing. I felt that I was now her equal.

I observed my parents' uncomfortable silence with Liesel, as if they didn't know how to respond to her insults and her focus on wealth. Our family had always deferred to the rich, and now Liesel was claiming that niche. Although Papa complained bitterly about Liesel turning her back on the church, I never heard him confront her directly.

However, I soon forgot about Liesel's attitude toward the family, as I became absorbed in my new ventures. I began to write and produce plays and operettas that recalled the glory of the days of the Kaisers and promoted a loyalty to the Fatherland. All those patriotic ideals I'd been taught by my father I now expressed in music.

Deborah, who was now sixteen, still painted, although we could no longer afford a tutor. I had recruited an artist to paint the scenery for the plays, and he let Deborah assist him. Deborah glowed with pride and self-confidence and held her head high in spite of her increasing uneven shoulders. She was a kindred spirit to me.

Esther by now was a happy and carefree thirteen year old, who loved school, had many friends, and enjoyed crafts and sewing, often making dresses for Deborah. Pretty and blonde, she was the ray of sunshine in our household. More and more, I viewed Esther through the eyes of a mother, rather than a sister. I appreciated Esther's willingness to help. Mother was now often in bed for days as her chronic emphysema took its toll on her.

Now twenty, I was the oldest daughter at home and not only assumed mother's hostess duties at the parsonage, but took charge of her group of young girls at church as well. I had arrived at womanhood without any idea of what that implied. I was so totally absorbed in duty to my family, country and church, that I never thought of myself.

About this time, there was a growing awareness of Adolph Hitler and his new party, The National Socialist German Workers Party (Nazi Party) which had been organized in 1919-1920. The effect of the Treaty of Versailles coupled with the political unrest in Germany created a receptive audience for Hitler's fascist ideas. Although the Nazi party was actually started by an obscure toolmaker named Anton Drexler, Hitler soon became a leader. I was alarmed when I read about his radical ideas. They were certainly a far cry from my own loyalist leanings. He had been an obscure artist, a corporal during the war, and now was espousing great visions for Germany.

He said he wanted to bring together opposite sides into one great party for all the people. It would be a labor party of the brains and the hands, uniting the white and blue collar workers. His vision of new pride and loyalty struck a responsive chord in many. Although the whole world was reeling from the great depression, many Germans perceived our situation as worse, and Hitler's promises found a ready audience. As the National socialist German Worker's Party grew in numbers, Hitler boldly called for the union of all Germans in one Great Germany, along with sufficient land for the surplus population. His anti-Semitic ideas found a ready acceptance among those who had lost their property to Jewish businessmen. When he said that the Jews should no longer be allowed to corrupt the government or run businesses, he was touting a view that many already held. Others felt naively that since Hitler promised food and jobs, they could simply ignore his radical ideas.

I became increasingly uneasy about Hitler, because I found his ideas frightening. His promotion of a supreme Aryan race was like a soothing balm on Germany's wounded pride, but who could have expected that Hitler would eventually be bold enough to declare that only those of German blood should be citizens, and therefore no Jews could really belong to the nation?

Papa dismissed Hitler and often said, "This man does not have the experience or education to be a leader for Germany. The only way he could do it would be by persuading the lower class people to revolt." He never took Hitler seriously or thought he would succeed in politics.

Hitler's picture was often in the magazines. Mother said he looked odd with his cruel eyes and sloppy hairdo. She felt he was disgusting.

Like my parents, I did not really think he would amount to much and felt his ideas were a little crazy. Already Hitler was building a reputation as a fiery orator. Driven by curiosity, I went to hear him speak. His voice was demanding and to my dismay, I could remember his words, even though I disagreed with him. I never went to hear him again.

The year of 1925 was one of upheaval. President Ebert died and Paul von Hindenburg was elected in his place. When the economic pressures and hardships eased, my family and I felt that things were approaching normality and we would live as we had before.

After serving only nine months of a five year prison term for his role in the 'Beer Hall Putsch' in Munich, (a plan to overthrow the Bavarian government) Hitler was released. He found acceptance in political circles and rose in prominence. His party, now known as the Nazi party was revived with his release and invigorated by the notoriety prison lent to Hitler. He became a man the government could no longer ignore.

The Nazi followers of Hitler were indoctrinated and fanatical men who marched on the streets singing and carrying large red flags with a white circle in the middle and emblazoned with a black swastika. This became the Nazi party's official emblem. These men even marched into the churches on Sunday mornings, came down the aisles and positioned themselves around the altars during the services. They stood at attention and were quiet and respectful. Pastors saw no reason to object to their presence, since young people often indicated their devotion and commitment to the faith by assuming such positions. No one suspected that this was a ruse to wean religious people away from the cross to the swastika.

Papa was not fooled by the Nazi's pretensions and revealed his judgment when he said, "They want the church to hold the stirrup for Hitler when he mounts his horse."

My attention to politics was diverted by mother's increasing frailty and father's weariness. He worked long hours in the parish, but his age of sixty was revealed by his tiredness. Thus I had the full responsibility for my younger sisters. Deborah was helpful, while Esther had a steady stream of beaus calling at our door. I was concerned and told Esther that I disapproved of her staying out so late with her boy friends. Esther was quite casual and told me I was a worrier. "You ought to be out having fun instead of staying cooped up at home all the time. Then you wouldn't fret about me." Nevertheless, Esther still helped me with the stage productions for our party, the German Nationalists. Here Esther met a young man who was also one of her beaus. I felt uneasy about him.

Betty J. Iverson

PART TWO

War Years

Betty J. Iverson

CHAPTER FOUR: FAMILY CRISIS

There are certain days in life that evoke a vivid memory, and this was to be one of those Along with the post that day came a letter addressed to Herr Springer. The formal note was from Herr Werner Vogel asking for Liesel's hand in marriage. This was customary for a young man to ask a prospective father-in-law's permission to marry his daughter. Even though Liesel was now 28, the custom still applied. As Papa read the note, he grew pale and the letter slipped to the floor.

"What's the matter?" I asked, alarmed at his response. Wordlessly, he handed the letter to me. After asking for permission to marry Liesel, Mr. Vogel then stated that Liesel Springer would be declared "einselwesen," which means a person without a family. She was disowning us: her mother, her father and her sisters.

Papa appeared dazed as he murmured, "My little Liesel, my Liesel." I felt helpless not knowing how to comfort him, yet I was angry with Liesel. How could she have agreed to this? She'd grown distant from us involved as she was with her hostess duties for the Thomas Mann family, yet she was still part of our family. I resolved to visit her and learn first hand what she was thinking. I wrote her immediately and asked her to meet me in a small café in Hamburg.

I arrived early and did not have to wait long before Liesel swept in, a flurry of feathers and ruffles. She was dressed exquisitely in purple velvet with a plumed hat nestled on her auburn curls. As annoyed as I was with her, I couldn't help admiring her stunning appearance.

"My dear Tabea, it is so good to see you," she murmured, grazing my cheek with a cool kiss. "I hope you don't mind, but I invited Werner to join us."

Wasting no time with pleasantries, I got to the heart of the matter and said, "Papa received Werner's letter and he and mother are deeply hurt. How could you?"

A flush rose in Liesel's cheeks and she looked down. "I don't expect you to understand, Tabea," she began. "Your life is so different from mine. When I met Werner, he was everything I wanted in a husband and I loved him instantly. I would never do anything to displease him. He comes from a very distinguished family, you see, and is a lawyer with an important law firm." She grabbed my hand as she said pleadingly, "Please believe me, Tabea, I did not want to be declared einselwesen, but Werner insisted. He did not want to be the son-in-law of a pastor because he does not believe in God-he is a humanist. What could I do? He will give me what I want in life, and in return I must give wholly of myself and leave family behind. Oh Tabea, if you'd ever been in love, you'd know how I felt."

Her last remark stung, because Liesel knew I had never been in love. Unsure of myself I had always kept men at a distance. But I simply replied, "Liesel don't you have any love for us at all? Mother grows more frail every day, and Papa is showing his years. How can you so easily push them out of your life?" As an afterthought, I added, "And us, your own sisters."

Liesel looked up and her blue eyes were bright with tears as she said, "I'm so sorry but I have no choice." Hastily she added, "Please don't think I won't be in contact with you. I will find a way. And Werner has said that you may come to the wedding.

Just then a short stocky man in his thirties approached our table. Dressed conservatively in a dark suit, he exuded an air of wealth and propriety. But I noticed something else about him that made me want to laugh. He looked like a bull dog with his high stiff collar pushing his cheeks up, covering his neck completely. Liesel looked up and said eagerly, "Oh Werner, dear, I want you to meet my sister, Tabea."

He nodded politely, and sat stiffly on the edge of his chair, surveying me with cool gray eyes. I felt out of place, as if I didn't belong. I became keenly aware of my simple cotton skirt and blouse and low-heeled shoes. We exchanged pleasantries, but soon lapsed into an uncomfortable silence. When I made polite excuses to leave, Liesel repeated her plea, "You must all come to our wedding which will be in two weeks." While Werner nodded his assent, he did not seem to share Liesel's enthusiasm. I nodded and said auf Wiedersehen to Liesel and Herr Vogel, reticent to use his first name.

We did not attend the wedding, but Aunt Anna, who lived in Hamburg, attended along with her husband and five children. She reported that the wedding had been a lavish affair attended by many prominent people.

The gulf between Liesel and us widened even further when Papa accepted a call to Griez, Thueringia, late in 1927. Thueringia was a picturesque area of rivers and forests of oak, pine and beech trees. The Harz mountains nearby abounded with ski resorts. Papa was reconciled to the move, since he wanted to slow his pace as he approached retirement years. Mother, on the other hand, was apprehensive as she wondered how the climate and altitude would affect her health. She didn't dwell on her

Betty J. Iverson

concerns, however, but supported Papa, saying, "You know what is best, Hans."

For me, however, the move was painful, as Hamburg was full of enduring memories and many friends. I wondered how the small town of Griez would compare to the bustle and culture of Hamburg. Unfortunately, true to my fears, I found the hilly town of Griez quite dull, but I determined to make the most of it. I sought friends at the church, and registered with the local chapter of the German Nationalist party. I continued with my political activities.

The parsonage also took some getting used to. It was a huge three story stone house with high ceilings, almost like a castle. The enormous arched windows were draped with velvet: purple in the living room and light blue in the bedrooms. In each room there was a green or white porcelain stove in which they burned wood or briquettes for heat. The kitchen was dominated by a huge black coal stove. I discovered a hole in the middle that was perfect for baking apples. The house was named, "Pertelsberg", after the first owner.

Since the parsonage was near the church, Papa could easily check on mother during the day, as her health continued to decline. The swelling of her feet and ankles and shortness of breath were testimony to her failing body. Mother did not, however, dwell on herself, but instead asked each of us about our day. She looked over Deborah's art projects and encouraged her, and always got a glowing recitation from Esther about her classes and many friends at the gymnasium

I continued to feel at loose ends. One day my father was summoned for an audience with Princess Hermina, and I went along. Princess Hermina, now in her fifties, was

Kaiser Wilhelm's second wife, and she symbolized for
many of us the monarchy that was lost. Although the Kaiser
was in exile in the Netherlands, she chose to remain in her
castle in Griez, but visited him often. She never went in the
winter, however, as she detested the Dutch cold winters.
Her castle was one of four in Griez. The other three castles
had been taken over by the Communists and housed their
political offices, while the grounds were open to the public.

My heart was pounding with excitement as the butler
ushered us into an elegant salon, furnished with antique
chairs and tables. The princess greeted us warmly, and after
a few polite questions about the church, she turned her
attention to me. "Tell me about yourself."

I told her about the dramas I'd done for the German
Nationalists and hoped to do also in Greiz. Princess
Hermina listened intently, observing how pleased she was
that young people were still loyal to the old values. "Would
you like to teach these ideals to young girls?" she asked.

"Oh yes," I said eagerly. "I've always taught the young
girls at church, but never had any experience with them
politically. I'd very much like to do it."

"Then I will help you," promised the Princes True to
her word, Princess Hermina helped me establish a group for
young girls, who were called the "Cornflowers," and wore
bright blue uniforms. I taught them a love for the
Fatherland and a respect for the greatness of the Kaisers. I
never, however, spoke against Hitler, his ideas, or the Nazi
party, fearing possible reprisal

The German Nationalist party in Griez had two
divisions: "Konigin Louise" (Queen Louise) for the women
and the "Stahlheim" (steel helmet) for the men. We all

worked together in producing plays, much like those I had produced in Hamburg.

The production of the last play was not long in coming. I had written this play in poetic form with the title, "Germany Awake!" Sensing the changing political climate, I and the other actors were quite emotional and spoke our lines from our hearts. We berated our elders as young people have always done. "We did not sign those treaties after the war-You did. We are young and we want to forge our own destinies." Then very cunningly we said, "We do not want to be Socialist or Communist or Nazi, but German Nationalist. And we want our old flag, the red, white and black to fly over Germany." As soon as the curtain fell, I was whisked home by taxi because my father feared the Nazis might retaliate since we had been so bold in our statements.

Just as our country seemed to be getting back on its feet, the world wide depression deepened, and many were again unemployed, posing a threat to both our economy and government. In 1932, President von Hindenburg was reelected, but the Nazis won 230 seats in the Reichstag. Papa and I were alarmed because we, like others, had underestimated Hitler's power and influence. Soon he persuaded von Hindenburg to appoint him chancellor, but his appointment would have to validated by popular vote.

The election was a sham, and that day remained indelible in my memory. The polling places were in schools or restaurants. All citizens over 18 were eligible to vote. As I walked up to the door of my polling place, a school, I was appalled to see two Nazi soldiers standing outside. They greeted me in a friendly manner, and one of them pinned a metal "Ja" (yes) on my jacket. He then opened the door for me. I was too frightened to object because I felt they might arrest me. Inside, four men were seated behind a table with a list of all the voters lying in front of them. I stated my name and one of them shook my hand as he said, "That's a nice yes." He then checked the yes column after my name. I watched in painful silence. The vote wasn't mine but theirs. I'd been forced to vote for Hitler through mock friendliness covering a steel glove. I wasn't surprised that Hitler received an affirmative vote of 90%. The years since the war ended had brought us one humiliation after another. The future loomed ominous.

It was only a matter of time before Hitler gained control over the aging, senile von Hindenburg, and put his own policies and ideas in place. When a fire destroyed the Reichstag, (the government offices) in Berlin, Hitler blamed the Communists and used this as a pretext to ban that party. Soon he banned all political parties except his, the Nazis. This was the death knell to the German Nationalists. Soon the Konigin Louise, the Stahlheim, and my Cornflowers were all disbanded.

Hitler placed Nazis in key positions, so his programs met no resistance. To maintain control over the citizens, Hitler founded the Sturm-Abteilung, (S.A. brown shirts or storm troopers) and later, the Secret State Police, (S.S.) an intelligence and investigations troop, commonly known as the Gestapo.

The Fuhrer continued his endless speeches, almost fanatical in his quest to make Germany a powerful nation again. Since funds were limited, he asked everyone to volunteer and work hard for the glory of the Fatherland. He founded the Hitler Youth Movement and dressed the young men in brown uniforms with swastikas on their left sleeves. They were given Nazi flags and instructed to wave them at parades. Girls were also important, and for them, he founded the Junge Madchens, also dressing them in brown.

These youngsters were then assigned to arbeits dienst. (labor service to the country) Men, eighteen to twenty-one, worked nine hour days building the autobahn. They lived in barracks and spent the evenings in indoctrination and camaraderie singing about the campfire. A library of books espousing Hitler's ideas was always available. Hitler also wanted the farmers to increase production so Germany would be self- sufficient. Thus younger boys worked on the farms, as did the girls. The girls, however, took care of the children while the wives helped in the fields.

Since these youth programs were organized through the schools, parents had no control over them, and children joined because they feared they'd receive a failing grade if they did not. All school children were given intelligence tests and the most gifted were granted scholarships to the gymnasiums and universities. Those with lower scores were classified as slow learners and placed in special boarding schools where they were taught manual laboring skills. At age fourteen, these slow learners were sterilized, because Hitler wanted an intelligent race. Those parents bold enough to object, were arrested for being disloyal to the Fuhrer.

In general, educational standards were raised, but all schools from top to bottom were geared to the politics of the Third Reich, with an emphasis on youth. Anti-democratic concepts were taught, and all science and technology was geared to war. History was changed to validate Hitler's theories of Aryan superiority.

Papa was furious when he learned about this. "History must never be tampered with," he fumed. "History should

be factual so we can learn the truth about our ancestors—
their failings as well as their triumphs." He then hauled
down an immense encyclopedia from the shelf and
proceeded to teach my sisters and me the true facts about
our history.

The promise of a good life and safe streets, according to
Hitler, would be accomplished by simply getting rid of all
the criminals. Anyone who stole was quickly hung,
sometimes without a trial, to make a point. Camps were
established for the political education of offenders like the
Communists, or anyone who opposed Hitler.

While his promise of safe streets was fulfilled, we felt
as if we were rapidly losing control over our own lives. Not
one home in Germany escaped notice. Every household
could only listen to radio Berlin, which broadcast Hitler's
speeches and carefully censored news. To reinforce this
edict, the radio had a sign on it, "I listen only to Berlin".

There was no longer any trust between neighbors.
Landlords, known as Hauswards, checked on each home
and reported to the Blockward, who in turn, reported to the
Buergemeister. Each town was a designated Gau,
administered by the Kreisleiter, a Nazi. The Kreisleiters
reported directly to Berlin. We heard the rumors that if
anything was said against Hitler, he'd know it within hours.

Even school children were encouraged to report what
their parents said at home. I had heard about parents being
picked up by the Gestapo because of what they had said to
their children at dinner. Apparently a father had objected
when his children told him, "We belong to Hitler now, not
you." The father had retorted angrily, "Those Nazis aren't
teaching the truth."

Like bitter roots in a sweet spring, fear and distrust were rapidly enveloping our society, and I felt a growing uneasiness. Like all ministers, Papa had to be careful about what he preached, since there were always reporters at the services to note anything said which might be construed as critical of the new order. Some ministers, however, ignored the reporters and were bold in their criticism of some government policies. They soon disappeared into the anonymous void of the political education camps.

Papa never spoke openly against Hitler, but prayed that God would guide him in wisdom to rule in peace. Privately, he felt intimidated, noting, "My heart is heavy because I can't speak out. I'm handcuffed by the Gestapo." he often lamented to me.

Sunday mornings were chosen for the Hitler Youth activities, and they usually began with a march down the streets past every church in town, singing patriotic songs to the accompaniment of a loud brass band. Since the noise was deafening, drowning out his sermon, Papa made a pact with the organist that whenever the parade came by, he would play a loud vibrant hymn. The congregation soon learned to respond and, as if by rehearsal, they switched from listening to singing. Once the parade had passed, he'd resume preaching.

"I'm not willing to hand over the young people of this church to Hitler," he told me. "I plan to get to know each one personally." And he did, even arranging private services for them. I was surprised to see that most of them responded favorably, and came to see him or attended his services, furtively, reminding me of the early Christians of Rome. "I'm glad my own daughters are out of the reach of the Junge Madchens recruitment," he told me.

After Esther finished at the gymnasium, she learned the dress-making trade. My younger sister had grown into an attractive, precocious fun-loving young woman, with her blonde hair and flashing brown eyes. She enjoyed dancing and continued her pattern of staying out late. When I warned her not to become too serious about her current beau, a banker in his early thirties, reputed to be a wild bachelor, she shrugged and laughed, "Oh Tabea, you're such a house cat. I'm having a good time, and Erik is an enjoyable companion—nothing more! Besides, I'm old enough to take care of myself."

I was stung by the label, house cat, because it rang true. I had to admit that I'd devoted myself so completely to mother and my political activities, that I had no time for men or fun. I was never quite comfortable, anyway, on those rare occasions, when I was escorted to a concert by a young man. Shy with men, I usually discouraged any attention. Did I feel no one could measure up to my father? Did duty loom so large, that there was no room for anything or anyone else? I pushed such thoughts away, preferring to remain the dutiful daughter or sister.

One day I asked mother what was wrong with me. "I've never met a man I could feel emotional about." She was surprised about my concern, but admitted that she'd taken me so for granted, she never noticed. "Mother, will I ever get married like you did? Maybe I'm too ugly."

"Oh no, my lamb, you're a lovely young woman. You must be patient and wait for the Lord's bidding. If there is someone for you, He will bring him to you."

"But you, mother, how was it for you?" I persisted.

45

Mother smiled, with a far-away look in her eyes. "Well you know, it wasn't exactly a surprise when your father proposed to me. You see, after my sister, Elizabeth, died, I was like a mother to Liesel. I easily arranged my interior decorating appointments to take care of her. When your father came home to see her, I knew what was on his mind when he asked if Liesel would be upset by the separation when he took her back with him to Barman. I had no reply. And when he asked me to share his life with him. I couldn't answer right away, because I did not feel free. You see, I had been in love a few years before, but could not marry that man because he was Jewish. Yet he still had a place in my heart. While I liked and respected your father, I was not in love with him and told him so. I asked him for time to think."

I asked mother what made her decide to marry father. "I guess romance and love took second place to devotion to God and fulfillment as a woman. I felt this was my destiny. While I hoped I would fall in love in him, I couldn't be sure. I vowed to be a good wife to him whether or not I did. I knew he was a sensitive man who felt deeply. But very soon I did fall deeply in love with your father and knew such joy." I was encouraged by her words, and for the first time I began to hope that one day I too, would find love, someone to devote my life to.

In spite of Esther's continued light-hearted responses, I still worried about her, fearing she would be hurt as she obviously loved this young man. Esther had met Erik when they'd worked together on German Nationalist productions. Once productions ceased, they continued to see each other. While he was a pleasant young man and very polite, I had seen him several times with other women. When I mentioned this to Esther, she didn't believe me, but retorted, "You're just jealous because your younger sister has a boy friend and you don't."

One day Esther came home from work obviously quite upset. When I asked her what was wrong, she shook her head and said that she could never tell me. But the next day, our family physician, Dr. Sorger, called me in and told me what Esther could not: "Your sister is pregnant. I'm telling you, because I feel someone in the family needs to know. Your mother is so frail, that I fear this kind of news could have a fatal effect." I left his office with a heavy heart, not sure what I should do.

Matters were soon out of my hands when mother discovered Esther's pregnancy quite by accident one day when she went into Esther's bedroom while she was dressing. She left the room without a word, and collapsed into a chair, sobbing silently. I found her sitting at a small table in the hall, and tenderly hugged her, asking, "Whatever is the matter?" Mother raised her head from the table which now was a lake of tears and simply shook her head. I knew then that Esther's secret condition was no longer that.

Very soon, mother succumbed to a flu epidemic which was raging through town. She never recovered, and at the height of her delirious fever, she murmured to me that she felt so sorry for me. While I thought she was referring to the sacrifices I'd made for her, I also wondered if she was referring to the responsibility I'd soon have to shoulder for my sister. Mother slipped into a coma, opening her eyes for the final time when Dr. Sorger came. "Did you have a nice sleep?" he asked gently. Mother smiled weakly, looked around at her family gathered at her bedside, and then simply smiled, her eyes closing behind the curtain of death.

Although my mother was fifty-four, I thought she was still beautiful with her dark curls and smooth skin. Papa fell to his knees, grasping his dead wife's hands as he murmured soft prayers. Deborah also sobbed silently, but Esther ran from the room, sobbing loudly, "Oh no, don't leave me, mother. Oh no."

The ache and sorrow I felt at my mother's death was intensified by the fact that Erik refused to marry Esther, in spite of his parents' urging. (After he was drafted into the army, Esther never saw him again.) Dr. Sorger drew me aside, and told me that I should not share Esther's problem with Papa, since the shock of this news could possibly trigger a heart attack. "Aren't there relatives you could send her to for awhile?" he suggested.

An opportunity came at mother's funeral. I explained the situation to Aunt Anna, who was quite sympathetic and immediately invited Esther to come and stay with them in Hamburg. "Besides, your cousins will love having you around," she added. Esther gratefully accepted, as she was increasingly uncomfortable in Greiz. When Esther approached father with her plans to visit her aunt, Papa readily agreed, not suspecting that anything was amiss, in spite of the fact that Esther was six months pregnant. I wondered about his eyesight, or was it perhaps his grief. In any case, I was relieved that he agreed so easily to Esther's leaving.

When I saw her off at the train station, Esther hugged me tightly, saying, "You're like my mother now. You can't imagine how terrible I feel—as if I caused mother's death. Do you think she forgave me?" she asked in a quavering voice, her eyes showing the depth of her pain.

"Mother loved you very much, you were her ray of sunshine," I said. "She was disappointed, I'm sure, but she was not someone who held onto things. And even more important, the Lord is always forgiving." I hugged my sister comfortingly. There was nothing more to say. Certainly not that she'd broken her mother's heart. No, I could see that Esther had suffered enough, and there would likely be even more heartaches to come. Better to relieve her guilt and encourage her. The strain of my mother's death and being the sole person responsible for making all the arrangements for Esther had been exhausting. I felt a sense of relief as the train pulled away from the platform and away from Greiz, where people had begun staring rudely and whispering.

Esther wrote faithfully every week, telling of the kindness of Aunt Anna and her family. They had accepted her with open arms. In a few months, her son was born and Esther named him Hans Rudolph II, after her father. I felt like a conspirator not being able to share the news with him—only with Deborah, who was thrilled to be an aunt. In spite of the shame, I felt that my father would be pleased to have a namesake.

Liesel and her husband, Werner, had come to see her, Esther wrote, and they were very comforting. Liesel told her she was delighted to have a sister close by. Esther observed that Werner appeared to be a devoted husband, but was apparently quite possessive of Liesel and frowned on her entertaining friends. They told Esther about their extensive travels, even doing some mountain climbing. Liesel confided to Esther that she'd had a miscarriage, and the doctor told her she would never be able to bear children. "And you know what?" Esther ended the letter, "Herr Vogel told me I may call him 'Werner'. Isn't that nice?"

Nice indeed, I thought as I carefully folded the letter and placed it in my dresser drawer. With Esther and her son ensconced in Hamburg and no longer feeling the obligation to serve as hostess at the parsonage, I felt free of responsibility for the first time in years. I decided to pursue a long cherished dream: that of becoming a nurse. I made an appointment with the Director of Nursing at the State University Hospital in Greiz and was accepted for the fall class of 1933. I knew that I was entering a new phase of my life, one that would be a march toward my destiny.

CHAPTER FIVE: NEW DIRECTIONS

My pulse was racing with excitement when the day I had anticipated for so long finally arrived. I walked through the doors of the State University Hospital to begin my nurse's training. The hospital was on one of the highest hills in Greiz, surrounded by trees and lush gardens. I was proud to be part of this fine institution, reputed to have state of art surgery with all the latest equipment. I was not deterred by the fact that I would be older than most of the students in my class. I was tall and sturdily built and felt capable of meeting whatever challenges lay ahead.

I was eager to begin and absorb myself totally in my classes-to be a student. The days flew by, and I was fascinated by the nursing and science classes. But in the evenings I was required to attend the racial and political lectures taught by the Nazis. I was disgusted by their arrogant attitude toward anyone who was not healthy or pure Aryan. I thought this was clearly indoctrination. The propaganda was part of the curriculum I would have to endure in order to become a nurse.

Since I received my nurses' training at this hospital, I belonged to the Kaiserwerter Mother House. This was an evangelical order of which Florence Nightingale had been a member. We were expected to wholly dedicate ourselves to our patients, as she had. As for me, I felt that in nursing, I would be fulfilling my confirmation passage from Genesis, "I will bless you, and you shall be a blessing to others." I would not alter my beliefs to incorporate Nazi teachings. My three years of training passed by quickly. Graduation day was a proud day for me as well as Papa and Deborah. I easily passed my board examinations.

Betty J. Iverson

Mine was not the only significant event in our family that year. Like bulbs springing to life beneath the snow, a grandson cannot remain hidden forever. One day while Papa was sitting in his study, Nazis came with legal documents for him to sign concerning his grandson, now three years old. The shock of the news was great indeed, and he fainted, suffering the mild heart attack that Dr. Sorger had predicted years ago. I found it hard to believe that Esther had been in Hamburg with Aunt Anna for three years. I quickly explained to Papa where Esther was and what we had done at Dr. Sorger's urging. He now encouraged Papa to put the past behind. "Oh yes, yes," Papa responded. "I want to forgive my daughter and have her under my roof once more."   He sent for Esther immediately.

I will never forget the day Esther came home. Papa, Deborah, and I were at the station an hour early to meet the train, since Papa wanted nothing to go amiss. Deborah had a lovely bouquet of flowers. Papa stood trembling on the platform.   Tears slid down his lined cheeks as Esther alighted from the train, holding the hand of a small thin boy with large brown saucer-like eyes. Esther hugged us all in turn, crying, "Oh, it's so good to see you. I've missed you all more than I can say. Oh, Papa, Papa, can you ever forgive me?"

Papa Springer held his youngest daughter tightly and murmured through his tears, "That's in the past. We don't need to talk about it. You're back home again with us, where you belong." Then he straightened up and looked down at little Hans. "Well, young man, and what is your name?"

"Hans Rudolph the Second," the lad answered in a solemn high-pitched voice, as he shyly offered his hand.

Ignoring the hand, Papa swept the boy off his feet and enfolded him in his arms.

"Well, that's a fine name for a fine young chap. Welcome to your new home, my grandson." The expression of sheer joy on Papa's face was one I had never seen. This small boy had already captured his grandfather's heart. Perhaps here was the son he'd hoped for each time a daughter had been born.

Our household settled very quickly into a new routine. Esther found a dressmaking position, while Deborah continued to paint and do her art projects at home. She realized a modest income and was now a recognized artist in town. Deborah enjoyed being with Hans while Esther was at work. Papa, now retired, continued teaching Bible classes, so he had ample hours to spend with Hans.

My first position was that of a staff nurse on a medical floor at the State University Hospital. Quite soon I became aware of a unique group of nurses, known as brown nurses, who were also on the staff. These former Public Health nurses were reputed to have grown up in Hitler Youth Groups, and were loyal to Hitler's ideology and committed to carrying out his programs in the field of medicine. Alcoholics, the mentally retarded and patients with venereal diseases were sent into the hospital for sterilization, ostensibly to prevent birth defects.

As time passed, I noticed very few new cases of syphilis at the hospital. I was told the reason was that young adults were now strictly supervised and instructed to be morally pure. Also, the new treatment of Salvarsan (a yellow arsenical preparation) injections had proven to be effective.

A steady stream of patients from mental institutions was flowing into a restricted ward staffed only by the brown nurses. I never saw any of these patients leave the hospital. When I checked the charts of a few of them, I saw that the cause of death was listed as either pneumonia or heart complications. Rumors among the hospital staff, however, were that they were given overdoses of sleeping medication, usually Pantopan. The relatives of these patients were never notified of their hospitalizations, only of their deaths.

Hitler's philosophy was that it was better for the mentally ill to be relieved of their suffering since they were not cognizant of their existence anyway. "The money used to keep them in institutions would be better spent in feeding healthy children," he had said. Elderly people, too, were often accorded this same inhumane treatment and callously referred to as cemetery flowers.

The Fuhrer was decidedly in favor of motherhood and encouraged this by granting women with five children a monthly check. These women were given gold crosses on Mother's Day and instructed to always wear them. The sixth child born received a birthday gift from Hitler himself

Not content with increasing population by means of family units alone, Hitler established a Bund Deutsche Madchen (BDM) group for girls sixteen and older who were willing to present him with a baby. He would then adopt this child as belonging to the Third Reich. These BDM girls were sent to resorts where consorts were arranged. Once pregnant, they were kept in a home until the birth of their babies. After a time, they were sent to work for the Nazi party in various parts of our country, while the children were raised in special homes. I found this immoral. I had been told all this by a nurse who had worked at one of the special homes for children in

Konigsberg. She told me the home was spotless with shelves of toys and books, but these toddlers were being indoctrinated with Nazi philosophy.

I faced a new challenge when I was transferred from the medical floor to the surgical wing. I was excited about this new position and did not foresee any danger. Besides assisting the surgeons, I also learned to administer anesthesia. I then took care of the patients post operatively. I found administering anesthesia demanding since I did not have a monitor to keep me informed of the patient's condition. I relied solely on observation and vital signs. The usual forms of anesthesia were drip ether and chloroform. Occasionally I used Evipan intravenously (similar to Pentothal, but more potent). I would have to monitor the patients even more carefully then.

The chief surgeon was exacting and strict, expecting his nurses to be just as dedicated as he was. He would begin each surgery with a prayer. Later in the evening he often wandered through the wards, checking on his patients.

I also heard that this surgeon was not only concerned about the fate of the Jewish people, but actually involved in covert activities to help them. He often admitted Jewish patients to private rooms in the hospital with fictitious diseases listed on their charts. Quietly and suddenly they would be released to someone who would get them to England. All of us nurses maintained a wall of silence about these patients. I felt perhaps in a small way I was part of the underground fighting the Nazis. Even so, one young Jewish woman spat on me when she left, saying, "We'll be back. And when we come, we'll destroy Germany." Her fierce hatred stung me like a terrible insult. This incident haunted me.

One night a prominent Jewish surgeon collapsed while performing surgery, suffering a heart attack. He was admitted to the surgical ward and assigned to my care. I was pleased to take care of him, because I respected him and recalled his kindness to Deborah a few years earlier when he had operated on her ear. At 2:00 a.m. a Nazi doctor came in and ordered me to give two c.c.'s of Pantovan intravenously immediately. I knew that this was an overdose, so I did not give the medication. The Nazi doctor returned within the hour to see if his order had been carried out. "No, I did not give the Pantapon because a fatal dose had been ordered," I explained. "I assumed this was a mistake." The doctor glared at me and told me that it was not my duty to question orders. He turned on his heel and left abruptly.

He returned within minutes bringing with him a brown nurse. "You may leave now to your new assignment on the medical ward," he told me. I was disturbed because I imagined what would happen now. I was not surprised when the nurse giving the morning report said that the Jewish surgeon had suddenly expired. I was sick with anger and guilt.

I felt it was wrong not to fight such evil, yet my rebellious thoughts were squelched by the knowledge that camps were waiting for those who disobeyed orders or spoke against the Nazis. I had no idea what happened in these camps. Meanwhile no one wanted to acknowledge that Jewish people simply kept disappearing-almost like something you are sure has been misplaced or lost, or was never really there at all. The Gestapo reported that people were being sent away for political education, giving the impression they would return.

They never did-like the Jewish wife of one of our neighbors. One evening this man upset and in tears, came to see Papa. "They've taken away my wife. The Gestapo marched into our house and took Elsa to their headquarters. They told me they wanted to question her. What would Elsa know? She's just a Haus Frau. I waited up all night. When she didn't come home, I went to the headquarters in the morning. They told me they didn't know what happened to her. They wouldn't even look at me, but kept telling me that they didn't know about my wife."

He was so distraught. Papa prayed with him and advised him to see if the Red Cross could locate his wife. This proved to be fruitless. The neighbor came to see Papa a few days later. He feared that his children would also be taken away because their mother was Jewish. He was puzzled that the Nazis would treat him this way. "I own a textile factory and have always cooperated with the government. And now this." He shook his head sadly. "You can't imagine what a nightmare I'm living not knowing what happened to my wife. What do I tell our children?" In spite of inquiries and many trips to the Gestapo headquarters, he never learned the fate of his wife.

Events such as this were quickly overshadowed by the troops swarming out of Germany. On the pretext of regaining the Sudeten territory populated largely by people of German descent, Hitler's troops invaded Czechoslovakia. Using the excuse of liberating the free city of Danzig, the army marched into Poland in 1939 without a formal declaration of war. Not only that, some of the German soldiers were dressed in Polish uniforms. The German army swept through the country so fast and furiously that the invasion was known as the Blitzkreig. Newspaper accounts reported that the Fuhrer was so smart he knew in advance the Polish were planning war, so he beat them to it.

Although there were plots to assassinate Hitler at various times, they all failed, giving him an aura of invincibility. Of course, he was always surrounded by an impregnable entourage of body guards and had in place an elaborate espionage network.

In short order, both France and England declared war on Germany. From the number of wounded soldiers arriving at the hospital, I knew battles were in full swing. I had the premonition that I would not be a spectator for long. Two events rapidly occurred validating my premonition. First, the surgical wing was converted into a military unit. Then all the staff nurses, with the exception of the deaconess nurses, were drafted into the army.

My draft notice came totally without warning. I arrived for work as usual and was told to report to the army office. Inside I found all the other staff nurses there, looking as puzzled as I felt. A high ranking army doctor stood up and declared, "You are all in the army now. You are drafted because we need you. You will be in the Ninth Army Division, with your Mother House at Kassel." There was no handshake, just a brief nod as he left the room. I looked about at the other nurses, wondering if they were as stunned as I was. I thought immediately of Papa, and did not want to leave him because he was frail and elderly. But in that doctor's brief declaration, I realized that my future was not only uncertain, but completely out of my hands.

CHAPTER SIX: A SECRET MISSION

The brisk chill of the cold winter winds gradually gave way to the warmth of spring, and Griez came to life again. Thick patches of ice on the sidewalks and streets melted into rivulets, and the fruit trees swelled with buds. I was invigorated by the signs of spring all around me as I walked to the hospital. I felt that nothing could dispel my cheerful mood.

My supervisor met me upon my arrival, and without any explanation or further adieu, she told me to report immediately to the auditorium. "Your presence is required at a very important meeting." I entered the auditorium and met other nurses, doctors and paramedics, and watched as the rest of our army unit gradually drifted in. There were about one hundred-fifty of us.

A Nazi major-general stepped up to the podium and began, "Members of the Ninth Army Division, you have been chosen for a special mission. This mission is of the utmost secrecy, and I can't stress that fact enough! You will not be allowed to write home for at least two months; however, should an emergency occur, your relatives will be notified immediately."

He then paused, and I felt as if he was looking directly at me, although his words were spoken to all the nurses, "I want you to think of yourselves as soldiers now, not women. This will be a tough assignment with no room for sentiment. You are expected to remain calm in the midst of dangerous situations and at all times be aware that absolute obedience is your first duty."

He then announced that we would have twelve days leave in order to receive the necessary immunizations and be issued our field uniforms and equipment. Although the major-general had not been specific because of the secrecy, I felt we must be headed for a war zone. The looming question for me was where? Poland? France? Much as I disliked the Nazis, I was impressed by their ability to organize things quickly. I left the auditorium with one thought uppermost in my mind: how to break the news to Papa.

After dinner that evening, without any long explanation, I simply said, "Papa, the army is sending our unit on a secret mission in twelve days. I won't be able to write for awhile." I felt relief getting the words out in spite of the fact that Papa appeared very shaken.

Papa said thoughtfully, "I give your future into the hands of the Lord, Tabea." He picked up his worn leather-bound Bible and read from Psalm 91, "Because you have made the Lord your refuge, the Most High your habitation, no evil shall befall you, no scourge come near your tent. For He will give His angels charge of you to guard you in all your ways." These words gave me strength to face the unknown.

The days of my leave evaporated quickly. First, we nurses were issued uniforms ugly beyond imagination. The skirts were a drab gray and so long they reached our ankles. I felt like a scarecrow. Ignoring regulations, we shortened our skirts. This uniform was completed by heavy cotton underwear, knee-high laced boots and one dress (gala) outfit, which was also gray with a matching hat. Since I was a lieutenant, I was given a single silver bar to pin on the suit collar. A white silk blouse with pearl buttons relieved the drabness of the gala uniform.

Next I was given more ominous equipment: a gas mask, flashlight, sleeping bag and a knapsack. I needed a week of practice to learn how to march carrying all that equipment along with my luggage. "After all," I laughingly told the others, "We're soldiers now, and there won't be any gentlemen to carry our belongings for us." The paramedics watched us and applauded as we struggled to march with our loads. I suspected they had a few good laughs at our expense.

Papa insisted that a family portrait be taken prior to my departure. Although all of us tried to smile and appear happy, the picture clearly revealed the uncertainty we felt. I suspected Papa was having difficulty letting me go, but he never let on. Rather, he appeared quite confident. Perhaps the only words that revealed his anxiety were his frequent mentioning that God would protect all of us in the days to come. In private, he reminded me often of my vow to be a blessing.

When I was packing on my last day at home, I discovered an old diary that mother had given me when I was eighteen. I wasn't interested in keeping a diary then because I couldn't bear to expose my inner feelings where someone else might one day read about them. Now as I stood in my bedroom, turning that black leather book over in my hands, I thought the time had come to keep a journal. I didn't know what lay ahead, but if the war continued, I would surely be involved. Keeping a record would be important, not only for me, but for my family as well. How could I know what war really meant. The travel, the unknown heightened my excitement. I had no inkling of battles, front lines, or the full extent of what the Fuhrer was planning. I only knew duty to my country and to be a blessing.

My first journal entry was on April 19, 1941, a few days after my departure: Dark clouds covered the sun mirroring the many heavy hearts gathered at the train station. I felt that the whole town had come to see us off. Dr. Sorger was also in our unit and he said to Papa, "I promise you I'll look after Tabea." I thought how strange that a person like Dr. Sorger could be involved in my life again and again. He attended my mother through her long illness and was with her when she died. He had advised me when Esther was pregnant. And now we would be in the army together.

The cymbals of the military band interrupted my thoughts as they struck up a patriotic march. The Red Cross ladies handed out bags of candy, lending a festive air to this otherwise solemn occasion. The train appeared to stretch for miles. I counted seventy-five cars in all: five for the doctors and their equipment, three for the nurses, four for the paramedics, while the remaining cars held horses, straw, lumber and tents. There were two engines to pull this heavy cargo.

A shrill whistle ended the festivities, and Papa's calm exterior gave way as tears spilled down his cheeks. The look on his face reflected his fear that perhaps this would be the last time he'd see me, but he simply said in a husky voice, "I did not have a son to fight for the Fatherland, but I send, instead, a daughter to heal the wounds."

I kissed him good bye, hugged Deborah, Esther and Hans, and then quickly ran up the stairs for I too, had begun to cry. I wanted so much not to show any emotion, because I was a soldier now, yet Papa's words were heart-wrenching. I felt guilty because I'd promised mother I'd always take care of him. As the train pulled out of the station, I pushed those thoughts aside. I'd never been outside of Germany before, and the thought was both exciting and frightening. I smiled to myself as I recalled Esther's description of me as a house cat. No more.

As the train slowly moved along, the band struck up our national anthem, "Deutschland Uber Alles". Now I could not stem the flow of tears. I sank down in a seat and stared intently at the countryside as we rolled along. The train followed a zig zag route north, south, and east to maintain the secrecy of its destination. The engineer told me later that even he did not know our destination. "I am given my orders each day by phone from military headquarters."

As the Ninth Army Unit wandered toward an unknown destination, they were unaware that Germany was preparing to invade Russia, which was the reason for the secrecy. By this time the German troops had rolled across Denmark, Holland, Belgium, Luxembourg, and went on to Norway as well. France had already surrendered in June of 1940. Poland had been partitioned between Germany and The Soviet Union, with Stalin also swallowing up Latvia, Estonia, and Lithuania as well. Hitler's appetite for more land and more power seemed insatiable. The Nazi-Soviet non-aggression pact made in 1939 was about to be broken.

On the second day, the train stopped at Breslau, Germany (*now Wroclaw, Poland*) and everyone was given a pass for the day. I eagerly climbed down the stairs intent on wandering about and sightseeing. Since my only food had been cold snacks passed out by the Red Cross ladies at various train stations, I longed for a hot meal. Finding a small café, I ordered and quickly devoured a bowl of potato soup along with thick chunks of bread. I had chosen to spend the day alone, since I wanted to mail a letter I'd secretly written to Papa by flashlight at night to reassure him that I was fine. As I left the café', I asked an elderly gentleman passing by if he would mail my letter to father. (I didn't dare go to the post office since any correspondence had been forbidden) "Ja sure," he said, "I'll see that your father gets your letter, young lady."

The next morning the train crossed the border into Poland, and soon reached Warsaw. The city was a sorry sight, utterly ruined, with burnt houses and piles of rubble. It had been heavily bombed during the Blitzkrieg of 1939. I was astounded as I looked out the window at my first glimpse of the fruits of war. With the announcement of yet another day of travel, my hopes for a hot shower were dashed. I felt stiff and grimy after three days of travel.

Late the next afternoon, our train chugged into a small village southwest of Warsaw, and here we disembarked for our assignment at Fort Modlin, which had surrendered a day after Warsaw. Major Koslovski met us at the station and introduced himself by saying, "I am the Commander of the Sanitation Company #500 (a medical unit). I trust you had a good journey, and I welcome you here. The staff has been awaiting your arrival." After his greetings, a military band struck up a stirring march, and everyone climbed into cars and trucks for yet another journey of about twenty kilometers to the fort.

Seated on a bench in the back of a truck, I peered out at the flat desolate countryside. After the rolling green hills of Germany, this part of Poland was a terrain that wearied my eyes. Suddenly, very far in the distance, I saw a cluster of buildings. It was Ft. Modlin and so huge I could see it from a far distance away. The closer we came, the more immense the fort appeared. The place was a collection of acres upon acres of buildings enclosed by high stone walls punctuated by huge arched gates. Although I was curious and awe struck about the fort, exploring would have to wait. Foremost in my mind was a hot shower.

Once through the gates, we were driven directly to the mess hall and served dinner. The hospitality ended there. My dream of a hot shower and crawling between clean sheets on a comfortable bed was simply naive. Instead, we nurses were shown to cold empty barracks and told to stuff our own mattresses with straw, which turned out to be wet. I was consoled when I found the shower room, large enough for twenty people to shower at once. There was also an abundant supply of hot water. As the warm water trickled over my stiff body, my tension eased. Later I crawled into my sleeping bag stretched over the straw mattress, which was as hard as a board, thanks to the wet straw. I laughed to myself as I recalled the words of the Major-General, "You are soldiers now-not women." Amen, general, I thought drifting off to sleep.

APRIL 22nd In the morning, I strolled about the fort with a group of nurses. We had been told that the territory of the fort was so large it took four hours on horseback to ride around the outer walled perimeter. This was the largest fort in Poland, built by the Russians in 1812 when they ruled the area. The fort was surrounded by high stone walls on three sides with a low wall where it abutted the shores of the Weichel River. Massive buildings were constructed beneath six foot mounds of sod. Even deeper underground were the bunkers, all were connected by a network of tunnels. There were barracks enough for 3000 soldiers, brick houses for the officers, stables for the horses, and a collection of administration buildings. The largest building on the fort was as elaborate as a Rhine castle and had been built for the Polish ruler, Pilsudaki, who ruled from 1926-1935. His castle was now the headquarters for these medical units.

The fort appeared quite drab without a dash of color anywhere, not even a patch of grass, just mud and patches of snow. The streets were mired with mud and pock marked with deep holes from the bombing during the recent invasion. One of my first assignments, along with the other nurses, was to help fill those holes with stones so the roads could be rebuilt. I wondered why they used us nurses to fill the holes. Were they teaching us obedience or just short of men?

I wondered what we would be doing here, since such an enormous staff had been assembled from throughout the country. My answer came soon enough. One morning Major Koslovski called us together for the task of organizing. "Our mission here," he said," is to convert this fort into a place of mercy, an army hospital. We don't know yet how soon this facility will be needed, but we've got to be ready. Everyone must report for duty in the morning."

He began by dividing us into teams: two doctors, two R.N. nurses, four L.V.N. nurses and two paramedics. Each team was then assigned to a ward that would accommodate two hundred patients. I was assigned to a ward housed in a group of five barracks, isolated from the others and designated as the infectious disease ward. The nurse who would share the head nurse duties with me was a plump, matronly woman of about forty, who introduced herself as "Cissy." She was soft-spoken with a quick chuckle and a keen sense of humor. I liked her at once. We started by stuffing the mattress bags with straw, but this time the straw was dry. We had no beds for the patients yet. We continued our work, unpacking blankets, setting up emergency equipment, and completing all the routine tasks needed to provide care for the patients, who were expected soon. We speculated about the kind of diseases we would be treating, as we unpacked.

We worked in the mornings, but had the afternoons free to explore. Cissy and I usually wandered along the river bank where we were drawn to the blackened ruins of a castle on an island in the middle of the river. Curiosity finally got the best of us, and one day we rowed over in a boat to see it. All the walls lay in ruins, except for the tower. We had heard the rumor that in this tower was a trap door with a chute that led to the river. Political foes were often known to mysteriously disappear while visiting here. The only hint of this castle's former grandeur was a pair of huge carved doors standing starkly alone amidst the crumbled walls.

When Major Koslovsky got wind of our excursions, he reminded us that we were not at home, but on foreign soil. He told us that we must have a soldier escort on any such jaunts. We didn't mind at all, as the escorts were often interesting, especially Henry.

Henry was a history buff and told us about the castle. "This place was built in 1720 by King Augustus II the Strong of Saxony." I was surprised to hear this, because I'd learned about this flamboyant king long ago and knew he'd also been king of Poland, but had no idea he'd built a castle here. I could imagine the grand parties within these walls, for he was known to have spectacular festivities. "King Augustus II stood over six and a half feet and loved to adorn himself with diamonds and pearls and wear ruby buckles, buttons, or even broaches." He continued, "The most outlandish rumor was that he'd fathered over 300 children, an astounding feat for any man, don't you think?" he chuckled. Unfortunately, his castle now lay in ruins, destroyed by German Stukke bombers in 1939.

APRIL 24th Henry told me this morning that the men of the Sanitation Company #500, mostly paramedics, had been left at Fort Modlin after the invasion in order to occupy the country and keep the Polish citizens in check. Since they'd been here for two years and hadn't so much as laid eyes on a German woman in that time, they looked forward to our arrival.

Major Koslovsky, must have sensed how the men felt, because he arranged a dinner dance for us to celebrate. He told us we would be strictly chaperoned, and must be back in our barracks by 11:00 p.m. I enjoyed the evening, but felt more like a spectator than a participant, because I was so shy around men in social settings. I sat and watched the younger nurses enjoy the dancing and "gemutlichkeit," our wonderful German tradition that makes instant friends of strangers.   Some of these nurses were only nineteen, awakening my mothering instinct, a natural role for me. Since I'd promised a friend in Greiz to keep an eye on her nineteen-year-old daughter, Gudrun, a   friendly girl, I looked for her at the dance. I found her sitting alone in a corner, looking rather forlorn. "Gudrun," I greeted her, "Aren't you having a good time?"

"Oh Tabea, I'm so glad to see someone from home. I feel so homesick, and this is such an awful place," she burst out. I sat with her the rest of the evening and we talked about her family and Greiz. I told her about the castle to take her mind off her present unhappiness. She laughed about that and promised she'd come to see me often in my barracks.

APRIL 25th I received my first hint of the specific purpose for this hospital tonight at a private party at Major Koslovsky's apartment. He invited three other nurses and me for dinner along with three officers. Although his apartment was furnished simply, it seemed luxurious compared to our barracks with the damp floors and straw mattresses. I listened intently as he and the other officers talked about the inevitable march into Russia. "We must be prepared to receive the battle casualties from this invasion, because I think it will be costly." He looked at us nurses and said, "You will not only be nurses caring for these men, but you will need to be mothers and sisters as well." Then he and I played chess while the others danced. He ended our evening on a jovial note by reading some lines from the writings of the great German humorist, Wilhelm Busch. The evening was gemutlich.

APRIL 26th Part of the morning routine for Cissy and me and anyone else who wanted to join us was to exercise and jog over the mounds of the fort. High up on these hills we had a view of the countryside all around. On this particular morning, I was the first to reach the top and was stunned to see that instead of the usual flat monotonous countryside, there was a military convoy of tanks, trucks, and cars, heading in the direction of Warsaw. They stretched across the horizon like a long, green snake, slowly crawling along. "Look," I cried and pointed below. By now the others had joined me and we stood frozen to the spot. I pictured rosy-cheeked young men sitting inside those trucks, and wondered how many would come back to us mutilated or sent on to Germany in a box.

Adolph Hitler had plans to wipe out the power of Russia. He not only plotted to occupy the land, but to destroy the Red army in huge battles along the western border of Russia. He felt he could do this in only eight weeks by making deep thrusts with his panzer forces, and then following up with infantry and artillery to force the surrender of any isolated pockets of resistance. The troops seen that day were only a small part of the three million men and weapons being sent to the front stretching across Poland and East Prussia. In the South, the German army was using Hungarian and Romanian forces along with them, and in the North, the Finns had joined them in the hope of taking back land lost to Russia in 1939. This operation, known as "Barbossa", shattered the Soviet forces and might have succeeded if it were not for the harsh Soviet winter. In the meantime, Yugoslavia fell to the Germans.

APRIL 28th   We unpacked medical supplies today, including gas masks. We were then shown how to work during combat with gas masks on, and how to move patients quickly into the bunkers. Cissy, usually so pert and cheerful was uncharacteristically sober during this class. I felt a strange acceptance as the war was becoming more real to me every day.

In spite of all this, the balmy spring breezes belied the danger about us, and lured us to the river bank for evening strolls. It was now light until 10:00 p.m., and Cissy and I enjoyed the singing crickets, the gentle flowing river, and the glorious wild flowers along the river banks. In the midst of this quiet beauty, I could pretend there was no war. However, tonight we lost track of time and came through the gate after curfew. The guards gave us a stern lecture and reported us to the chief nurse. In spite of this, the call of spring overrode the fear of curfews, and we looked about and discovered a tunnel we could crawl through and avoid the guards and the reports.

APRIL 29th As Gudrun and I strolled along this evening, we heard a deep bass voice join us in our song. Turning around, we saw a nice-looking officer, clad in the usual green uniform, who was tall and blonde with a ready smile. He introduced himself, saying, "I'm Captain Reiter and a fellow lover of nature," he said. "May I walk along with you?"

We were delighted to have his company and his bass voice was just the harmony our songs needed. When we parted, Captain Reiter asked if we would like to meet him on May Day to celebrate together. "Oh yes," I responded without hesitation, while Gudrun nodded shyly in agreement. I could hardly wait for May first to arrive.

MAY 1st The sun shone warmly, ushering in the festival of spring. Back in Germany the school girls would be dancing the May Pole dance, and the Communists, if they were free and not banned, would be observing the holiday as a commemoration of workers.

Gudrun and I packed a lunch and headed for the river where we had arranged to meet Captain Reiter. Even though this was only our second meeting, we greeted each other like old friends "Isn't this a beautiful day, Captain Reiter?" I asked. He told me that I must call him Fritz, and wondered if he could call me Tabea—and my friend, Gudrun? We both nodded our assent. As we walked along, Fritz taught us some new folk songs. We stopped often to admire the tiny butter cups which made the grass in the distance appear to be spread with mustard.

In between the singing and collecting wild flowers, Fritz told us that he was a surgeon and had been drafted just as we had. He was quite philosophical about life and thought about things quite deeply as I do. "The world seems to be in harmony today, Tabea. There is beauty in nature around us, pleasure in the songs we sing, and now I have the added joy of your company." I felt my cheeks flush and could only smile in return. I wondered if he found me attractive. I had always thought of myself as rather

71

plain-looking. Was my nose too long for my thin face? Those speculations faded as I realized that what was even more important was that Fritz made me feel attractive.

Gently he took my hand in his and we strolled along hand in hand like two kindred souls. I could not express my thoughts as eloquently as he did, but I was happy to know someone who shared many of my ideals. When Gudrun ran ahead to join her young friends, we hardly noticed, we were so engrossed in each other. He wanted to know all about me, and I soon found myself babbling on about Papa, my sisters, and little Hans. I felt embarrassed because my life must surely seem dull to him. On the contrary, he appeared quite interested.

Although we tried to avoid it, the war inevitably crept into our conversation. "There is no doubt that the war will be extending very soon into Russia, but I don't think we'll win it all that easily." He then stopped and looked in my eyes as he said quite seriously, "And unfortunately, dear Tabea, we are not likely to see each other on another May Day." I must have looked quite sad, because he lifted my chin with his finger and said, "Come, I didn't mean to spoil this wonderful day for us. Let's see what's ahead."

We didn't return to the fort until dinner time, and found hundreds of people standing in front of the mess hall singing. I felt light-hearted and gay, and I thought that this had been the most perfect May Day ever.

MAY 2nd An ordinance (messenger) soldier brought me a letter from Fritz this morning. My hands trembled with excitement as I opened it. Never before had I experienced such an understanding with a man. Even though we'd just met, we were like kindred spirits who belonged together.

Over and over again, I read the opening words, written in elegant script, "Dear Nurse Tabea," before I continued:

"I remember with pride our time together yesterday and in my thoughts I walked again over the meadows and fields down to the river. While the wind played the song of the soul, we daydreamed, and the dreams became funnels for our lofty thoughts. Wave after wave washed over the soft sand on the beach and then disappeared as if to tell us that the thoughts which brought us close will soon disappear, too. Shadows of the future cannot touch the greatness of nature. For a moment we were still and listened, but the melody of nature covered the songs of our souls." The letter was signed simply, Fritz Reiter.

His words touched me! No one had shared such private thoughts with me before. I felt fulfilled to know a man who thought as I did about the Creator, the harmony and wisdom in nature, and the joy of music. For the first time, I felt confident as a woman and as young as Gudrun. I knew that a part of me that had been suppressed for years was now awakening. No longer stifled by commitments, my thoughts soared to romance, and I could not still my pounding heart. I pictured us again, strolling hand in hand along the river, sharing our deep thoughts as we watched the sunset. I felt like as young as a school girl. Yet a voice inside me said, "Don't get carried away with adolescent notions. To daydream, even for a moment, is foolish. There is a war that will swallow your future like a deep chasm. You are a soldier now, not a woman." Still the day dreams continued about Fritz and our day together, and I longed to see him again.

Two days later, Fritz rode over on a bicycle to the barracks where I was working. He looked so downcast that I knew immediately something was wrong. "I've come to say good bye, Tabea. I must leave within the hour." I asked him where he was going and tried to appear as calm as he was. Inwardly I felt shattered.

"They haven't told me, but I suspect I'm heading east. Maybe we will meet again, God only knows, but I surely hope so. I promise I'll write to you." And then he pulled me to him and kissed me lightly. As he pedaled away, I watched until he was out of sight, feeling hollow, completely empty.

(True to his word, Fritz wrote faithfully. His letters were laced with his wisdom and deep thoughts and always gave me a lift, words to ponder. I shared on paper with him things I'd never been able to share with another. Then, after three or four months, the letters stopped coming. My letters to him were returned, and I was left with the awful question of what had happened to him. A question that was never answered. I missed him terribly and resented the war, for not only taking him away, but even more for bringing him into my life, only to snatch him up. Would he be the first of many who would worm their way into my heart and then disappear?)

MAY 7th Today was inspection day, and General Zilmer, Commander of the Ninth Army, came from Konigsberg to look over Fort Modlin. He addressed all of us in an assembly, saying, "I'm very pleased with the readiness of this hospital, and I commend you for creating such a fine facility in the midst of this wilderness." From his speech, I learned that we were classified as an Army Reserve Hospital which apparently meant behind the lines.

The evening was reserved for gemeinschaft, and we were all invited to dinner with the general. Although his bearing was dignified, almost aristocratic, he was actually quite charming and friendly. He made it a point to meet as many of us as possible, shaking hands and smiling warmly. Later the doctors told us that he had confided in them his intense hatred of Hitler.

MAY 9th I was awakened this morning by the lilting voices of nurses softly singing, and suddenly they were in my room, chasing away the shadows of dawn with glowing candles and birthday greetings. Today was my thirty-eighth birthday and my first away from home. They brought me simple handmade gifts and spread them on my bed: book marks of pressed flowers, ribbon-woven doilies, and straw baskets of flowers. I was amazed at the gifts they'd crafted without the benefit of shopping, only using their creativity. But the best gift of all, I told them, was their wonderful friendship.

Later that day, a small band came by the barracks where I was working to serenade me with more songs. Apparently this was a gift from Major Koslovski. I was overcome by all these gestures. I'd even received cards and letters from home, since mail was now flowing freely back and forth, but all heavily censored—even birthday cards. I felt that this was a wonderful birthday, but, most of all, I thanked God for His constant goodness.

MAY 15th Polish peasants were added to our staff to handle the menial chores. Since there was no water in many of the barracks, it had to be carried in buckets from the kitchen. Two women were assigned to do the cleaning, and two men to fire the huge eight foot furnaces, which devoured enormous loads of wood. These Poles came from the villages in the hills near the fort and were polite and humble people, eager to please. The first morning they appeared for work, they knelt to kiss the hem of my uniform. I was embarrassed. Overcoming the language barrier as best I could, I motioned to indicate that they didn't need to adore me, just to do a good day's work. They seemed to understand. At least, the hem-kissing routine soon ended, and they did work hard.

Not all of the Polish men were peasants by any means, and in fact, some were obviously well educated, but had been forced into manual labor by the Nazis who closed the universities. Opportunities were almost non-existent for professional jobs. I felt compassion for these people, as their hardships reminded me of my family's plight during the last war. The men were very gallant, always treating Cissy and me like ladies, not allowing us to carry anything heavy. One problem we encountered, however, was theft, especially of food. I didn't consider this a crime, given the meager food rations the Nazis instituted for the Polish citizens. Whenever possible, I discreetly gave them food, which I knew was a dangerous practice.

JUNE 12th We admitted our first patients today when an epidemic of typhoid fever spread through the fort, affecting about two hundred people. The source of contamination was thought to be either the water or the Polish peasants, whose living conditions back in the villages were very unsanitary.

Soon the foul smell of watery diarrhea stools permeated the wards. We had to work around the clock just to keep the high fevers down. Then too, these patients needed special mouth care because their mouths were coated with white blisters, causing a foul breath. Their eyes became red and inflamed. Our treatments were both scientific and homeopathic. We gave antibiotics like Terramycin, as well as red wine with egg yolk to disinfect their intestines. Since all of us on the staff had been immunized, we were not afraid of contracting the disease. Nonetheless, we were careful to wear the special isolation gowns, masks and gloves. We soon became weary of the many long hours, and drank our share of red wine, too, to keep us in good health.

Within a couple of weeks the epidemic subsided, and all the patients were back on their feet again ready for duty within a month. Next came the arduous task of disinfecting the barracks by placing steamers of formaldehyde about filling the rooms with pungent, noxious fumes. My clothing reeked of the smell for days.

JUNE 22nd This evening began on a happy note, but ended in gloom and apprehension. The Sanitation Company # 500 decided to host a celebration party to commemorate their three years at Fort Modlin. I looked forward to this evening of festivity after the grueling weeks of work during the typhoid epidemic. I dressed in my gala uniform and an escort picked me up in a jeep and drove me to the Kommandantur, or headquarters. Here the banquet was served in one of the ballrooms, breathtakingly beautiful with hanging crystal chandeliers that sparkled on the white linen tablecloths. We dined to the strains of soft music and were laughing at the jokes of a humorist after dinner. An ordinance soldier approached Major Koslovsky, who was seated at the head table, with a telegram.

I watched closely as the major tore it open and quickly scanned the message. His face paled and he stood, motioning for silence. "My fellow soldiers, I have just received word that the battles will begin at two in the morning. We are to prepare for the imminent arrival of wounded men," he announced in a husky voice.

So this is how the war will finally come to us, I thought, feeling paralyzed in my chair. Where only a few moments before the room had resounded with the peal of laughter, there was now total silence. That silence followed us back to our barracks. The memory of that convoy heading for Warsaw flashed before me. Once back in our quarters, I gathered all the nurses together, and we prayed that the Lord would strengthen us for the ordeal ahead. We were very tense about the invasion of Russia. Most soldiers were unsure of victory—only the Nazis were confident.

Stretching from the Arctic Ocean to the Black Sea, 250 divisions headed to Moscow, Leningrad, and Kiev. This two thousand mile front also included divisions of Finns, Romanians, and Hungarians. Germany declared war on Russia by means of a simple note from Count Werner van der Schulenberg, the Ambassador, to Vacheslav Molotov, the Commissar of Foreign Affairs, in Moscow. The advance of the Nazis was swift, and the Red army so incompetent, that Stalin could not believe the swiftness of the invasion! Within three weeks, Brest, Litovsk, and Minsk had all fallen and Russian defense forces retreated further East as they suffered huge losses of men and equipment.

But the swift German advances began to slow once the Russians increased their resistance, and the Nazi brutality turned the people in the villages against them. Initially welcoming the Germans as liberators, they soon found them to be far worse than the Communists. Partisan bands were formed which followed Stalin's instructions to "scorch the earth." This invasion caused the Russians to forget their political differences and unite against the Germans as nothing else could have done. Add to this, an enormous Russian population with an endless source of manpower, harsh winters and the Germans' problems with moving supplies, Germany 's advances began to slow. In addition, Germany was suffering huge losses of men, eventually as high as 23% or over 700,000.

JULY 15th   Hardly anyone slept the   night before the wounded men were sent from the battle fields. All of us were up at five in the morning when the first of the wounded men began to arrive. Since there were no patients with contagious diseases, I was assigned to emergency care.

The men were brought directly from the field and the sight of open gaping wounds and faces shot half-away nearly gagged me. But I gritted my teeth, denied my emotions, and focused on the job to be done, pushing pity aside. I could always tell when a battle had been fought, because then we'd receive eight hundred to twelve hundred men at once, all flown in by U-88 ambulance planes. After that we would have a two week lull before more patients arrived.

The most memorable patient I took care of that summer was a 19 year- old boy. He had refused to allow the doctor to amputate his arm, even though gangrene had already set in. Impressed by his determination, I resolved to give this boy a chance, and began an old remedy of a continuous saline and Ravinal drip on the wound. I monitored the wound closely and within two weeks the black color and putrid odor began to fade, replaced by a faint pink, the sign of healing. Miracles of miracles. The other nurses and I rejoiced together in the saving of this boy's arm. I doubted that I would again have the luxury of providing such a time-consuming treatment.

The German army continued to push East, taking Riga, Smolensk, and even bombing Moscow. For a time, their advance was halted due to lack of supplies, exhaustion of the troops, and the increasing strength of the Soviet army. Then in August, the Germans took Novgorod and surrounded Leningrad, while the Finish troops surrounded the Russians at Vipuri.

Betty J. Iverson

SEPTEMBER 15th I was always rewarded by seeing half dead men come to life again and know that I had a part in their recovery. Over one-hundred-fifty soldiers were now stable enough to be transported back to Germany, and we decided to have a little farewell for them. Someone suggested that we bake cookies, which we all thought was a great idea until we realized that we had no cookie sheets.

One of the Polish men, overhearing our conversation, left and returned a few minutes later with large tin sheets which he had pulled from the roof. The chef was most willing to let us use his huge ovens, and the warrant officer gave us all the ingredients we needed. Cissy and I and several others stayed up most of the night baking cookies. We hardly missed our sleep as we chatted away like schoolgirls on a holiday.

As the front lines penetrated deeper into Russia, the more experienced doctors were sent to the field hospitals. Unfortunately, they were replaced by young inexperienced doctors from Germany who had never treated much of anything, let alone battle wounds. The one thing they knew how to do well, however, was to be arrogant and demanding. Most of the these new arrivals had absorbed the Nazi indoctrination at medical school, and I found them difficult to work with. They were not only condescending, issuing ridiculous commands, but they also practiced poor surgical techniques. I was especially appalled by their cruelty to patients. One doctor's habit was to rip off bandages stuck to wounds, rather than soak them loose with peroxide first. When a patient screamed with pain, he'd sternly berate him.

SEPTEMBER 20th Today during surgery an arrogant doctor persisted in grabbing sterile bandages without gloves on. When I reprimanded him for it, he shouted rudely at me. I was very angry, I calmly laid down the instruments on the tray and walked out of the room. Soon the rest of the staff followed, leaving the doctor all alone with the patient. A much subdued doctor came out into the hall and apologized. "We've never had trouble with our doctors before," I told him. "We are all too experienced to be treated like this, nor do we allow unsterile technique in the operating room."

Our treatment had exacted an immediate cure. While I was taught in my training to be respectful to doctors, I realized that many of these new doctors had passed their medical examinations more on the basis of their political persuasion rather than on their medical knowledge.

A second serious problem occurred when we began running out of supplies, especially the gauze bandages. We had to re-use them by washing and boiling the bandages. The patients then rolled the gauze strips after they were dry. This teamwork drew us together like a family.

SEPTEMBER 25th Whenever I became discouraged, I was cheered by the letters from Papa and my sisters. Often, too, there was a carefully written note from Hans, eager to share with me what he was doing in school. The news, however, was not always good. In her letter today, Deborah wrote,

> "Oh Tabea, strange things are happening,"
> she began, but the heavy mark of the
> censor's pen blacked out the next few lines.
> "We hear rumors that"—and again the lines
> were blacked out. "Father is upset, too,
> because young Polish boys, who were"——
> lines blacked out—— "are showing up here
> to work on the farms." I think Papa

imagines how we'd feel if that happened to
dear little Hans. There's so much suspicion
around, we don't even dare trust our
neighbors. But what am I saying? If we
cannot trust those we know and live with,
whom can we trust?" More sections of the
letter had been blacked out by the censor's
pen.

I wondered what else Deborah had to tell. Why was she
brave enough to pen the lines she had? Dear sweet
Deborah, who would never speak rudely or hurt anyone's
feelings. I was grateful she did not have to see the results of
war as I did. On the other hand, perhaps her own affliction
made her accepting of difficulties, and I could be wrong
about her inability to cope. Yet while I hated this war, I felt
that what I was doing was not only worthwhile, but
challenging. I had no idea what challenges lay over the
horizon.

CHAPTER SEVEN: EPIDEMICS STRIKE

OCTOBER 18th This day started out like any other until Cissy and I, and two paramedics from the isolation ward were called into Major Koslovski's office. Dr. Sorger was already seated there, looking apprehensive. What's this all about? I wondered.

"I've called you here to inform you of a special assignment in Johannesburg, East Prussia. I can't command you to go, but I hope you will volunteer. A staff is needed to care for about eighty or ninety typhus patients, so the current staff can have time off to rest and be immunized." The Major looked at each of us in turn, as if to gauge our reactions, before continuing. "I've asked you in particular to volunteer because, you not only have experience with contagious diseases, but were willing to be vaccinated against typhus two weeks ago. Because this disease is potentially fatal, I can only rely on your willingness to volunteer." He nodded to Dr. Sorger, saying, "And this fine doctor has agreed to be the commanding officer. With his maturity and experience, he will no doubt be a wise leader."

Dr. Sorger stood then and stepped forward, his dark brown eyes gazing at each of us in turn, "I won't minimize the risk involved in exposure to typhus, yet our skills are urgently needed. Lives are at stake, and I hope you will be willing to go with me to Johannesburg."

One by one, we nodded our acceptance without hesitation. Refusal was unthinkable, even for the paramedics who were young men with families back home. Our training had always stressed obedience without considering personal risk.

"That's fine," beamed Dr. Sorger. "The task before us is a formidable one, but we pray God will help us to fulfill it." He then shook hands all around and told us to be ready to leave very early the next morning.

As if by command, the facts about typhus learned long ago, came back to me. Typhus had taken many lives during the last war and was considered so hopeless that patients were often left untreated and set aside to die. The situation was slightly more optimistic now because of new medicines, but the disease was still often fatal and the name equivalent to a death sentence. This highly contagious disease, caused by the rickettsia organism, is spread by blood exposure as well as direct contact, being carried by lice, fleas, ticks and mites. Since the disease thrives in cold weather and crowded unsanitary conditions, many of our troops were infected in Russia. I had heard that it was not unusual for the soldiers to be so thickly covered with lice, their uniforms appeared white. Typhus was a miserable disease, causing extremely high fevers, as high as106 degrees F, severe headaches, deep comas, and rashes under the skin with bleeding, even gangrene.

Cissy and I talked about our impending assignment until late that night. We were more apprehensive about our lack of experience with typhus than the danger represented. However, I was always excited to learn new medical skills. "I'm so glad we'll be together, Tabea," Cissy said with a warm smile. "We're so used to working together, and we make a good team."

I nodded, for similar thoughts had risen in my mind. I felt a close bond of friendship with Cissy, and promised to remember her in my prayers as I bid her "Gute Abend."

When we boarded the ambulance the next morning, the staff at Ft. Modlin wept as if they never expected to see us again. I felt like a martyr on a journey to my grave. I shook my shoulders resolutely to rid myself of such morbid thoughts. This is a job I have to do-no more, no less than many others have been called upon to do.

The bitter coldness of the day was exacerbated by the fact that the ancient ambulance had no heater. The interior was bare with canvas covered windows. We climbed in the back and sat facing each other on wooden benches, wrapping ourselves in blankets in a vain attempt to stave off the cold. Dr. Sorger sat up front with the driver, and I wondered if he fared any better. A gusty east wind blew flurries of snow about, and there were often four foot drifts along the road. In some places, the road had been so badly bombed that whole sections had disappeared. The driver took off across open fields. The journey was a bumpy, cold nine hour trip, and the noisy engine made conversation impossible. Further, since we could not stop for fear of ambush, we snacked on chocolate bars. We were a stiff, sore and ravenously hungry bunch who tumbled out of that ambulance in Johannesburg.

Dr. Sorger insisted we have dinner and a good night's rest before reporting for duty in the morning. Cissy and I hastened to freshen up and change into clean uniforms. After the food and gemutlich, we planned our work schedule. Dr. Sorger indicated that the five of us would be responsible for everything: the cooking and cleaning as well as the care of the patients, since no one else would be allowed into the hospital. "Tabea, would you mind being the cook?" Dr. Sorger asked, and by way of explanation he added, "I've been a dinner guest at the Springer home many times, so I can attest to her culinary skills."

I beamed and nodded affirmatively. "I think we should have simple fare," I said thinking aloud. "The patients with high fevers will have high protein milk and red wine with egg yolk, while the convalescing patients will need high protein soups of meat and beans." The rest of the tasks were quickly divided: Dr. Sorger would do the laboratory work, Cissy, the medications, and the paramedics the cleaning.

OCTOBER 19th At ten in the morning, the commander of the army hospital arrived to drive us to the outskirts of town where the patients were isolated in an old mansion. As we drove up to a large three-story gray stone house, an eerie feeling came over me. I saw no sign of life about the place. Not only was there a barbed-wire fence encircling the house, but huge NO TRESPASSING signs were posted about. I couldn't decide what the house resembled most: a cemetery or a prison.

The commander did not even get out of the car, but sat and honked the horn repeatedly. Finally two nurses, smiling warmly, appeared in the doorway and beckoned us in. The commander couldn't leave fast enough, but muttering a gruff, "Auf Wiedersehn," he sped off the instant our baggage was out of the car.

I was relieved to find the house less forbidding inside. This house had formerly been the residence of a wealthy family, but was confiscated by the Nazis for army use. The rooms were large and bright, in fact, the dining room was large enough for twenty patients. A broad stairway led from the entry hall to the second story where former bedrooms were now patients' rooms. A small kitchen and dining room for the personnel were also on the second floor, while staff bedrooms were in the attic. An elevator connected the first and second floor kitchens.

After being shown the upstairs, Cissy and I immediately changed into our special isolation uniforms: pants suits, caps which covered our hair completely and rubber aprons. The nurses we were relieving then showed us around. Textbook pictures had not prepared me for the shocking sight of grown men shrunken to the point they resembled wrinkled children. Many were in deep comas, their eyes sunk back into their sockets and their skin stretched over their frames like oiled paper. Death was playing a gruesome game with them before snatching them away.

When the doctor in charge gave his final report. I was not surprised at the hopelessness he communicated, yet I felt there must be something that could be done for these typhus patients, besides watching them die. Since four or five had died every night, I wasn't surprised that the town feared the typhus house.

The nurses were anxious to leave since they'd been on duty here for over a month without immunization. I thought they were quite brave to assume this charge without protection. After a three week quarantine and vaccination, they would return. Once they left, Dr. Sorger called us together and said enthusiastically, "Let's not waste a moment," and we all agreed to start right in. We joined hands and he prayed simply, "We're starting a difficult task here, Lord. Help us to help these patients."

He quickly set up a laboratory in the house where Weil-Felix tests would be done. (This test both confirmed the diagnosis as well as determined the antibody level in the blood.) From the pharmacy, he ordered quinine, a heart stabilizing medication, and various antibiotics, including Aureomycin and Terramycin. Cissy and the paramedics separated the recovering patients from those who were comatose and began collecting blood samples.

I looked over the kitchen and called the warrant officer in Johannesburg to order supplies. I was only halfway down the list, when he interrupted with, "You don't need all that stuff! Anyway, according to regulations, I can't give you all that food you're asking for."

I was annoyed by his lack of concern about the serious situation and said heatedly, "I wish with all my heart that you got typhus so you could realize how dreadful it is. Anyway, General Zilmer is a friend of mine, and if you won't give me what I ask for, I'll call him in Konigsberg."

Within the hour, a delivery truck pulled up at the back door, loaded with everything I'd asked for. After that, I had no problems with the warrant officer. I was amused by the frightened expressions of the delivery men, who never handed any packages to me, but left them at the door, making a hasty retreat as if they were running away from a haunted house.

OCTOBER 20th During that first night, five comatose patients died. Dr. Sorger called us together in the morning and said. "These men are so weak, they must have more intense care with frequent doses of quinine to get them through the critical phase. I wonder if you would be willing to work continuously for 48 hours?" We were willing, of course, but I questioned how we could possibly stay awake that long.

"There is a drug, Perfectin, which was developed in France to keep surgery personnel alert, and it will keep us going for 48 hours," he responded.

I shrugged and said, "Let's do it." And, indeed, I was amazed what that little white pill did to us. We were so wide awake and alert, that we had difficulty unwinding after the two days. The results, however, were gratifying. With our intensive care, giving quinine doses every two hours, bottle feeding the lethargic patients and giving the Terramycin, the death toll reached zero. Dr. Sorger was quite pleased.

Those with high fevers were packed in ice, and we were on constant alert for lice that somehow had escaped our scrutiny, either on the men or crawling about the rooms. The paramedics not only shaved the patients' heads, but their bodies as well, rubbing them with Cubrex ointment to kill the eggs. They cleaned the walls and floors frequently with a Lysol solution, and used the formaldehyde steamers whenever possible. The work did not let up. It seemed that as soon as we transferred patients to the army hospital in Johannesburg, more typhus patients arrived from Russia.

NOVEMBER 10th The staff we had relieved were now ready to return, and we prepared to leave for Ft. Modlin. We had been told that plane loads of typhus patients were arriving there now, and we were expected to train the staff since we were now experts. Cissy and I laughed at this description of us, and thanked the Lord, who was the real expert. I recalled the many times that a recovering soldier told me he was grateful to God for sparing him. I was convinced that being near or around death gave people a greater sense of God.

Our success in handling the typhus epidemic in Johannesburg did not go unnoticed in the newspapers. Articles were written heralding the" strenuous efforts and intense nursing care of the staff at the typhus house." Relatives of patients sent letters of gratitude, and General

Zilmer himself wired congratulations, promising that we'd all be given lifesaving medals in a special ceremony.

NOVEMBER 21ˢᵗ We were all packed and ready to leave when the army commander who had beat such a hasty retreat upon our arrival, appeared on the scene and offered us the use of his staff car for the return trip. The honor of riding in this car was not nearly as important as being in a warm, comfortable cushioned vehicle. We were a jovial group and we sang carols to pass the time while driving through the snowy countryside.

Although it was late when we arrived back at Ft. Modlin, there was a crowd on hand to greet us. After hugs all around and much laughter, they led us into the dining room where a huge cake and a brimming bowl of punch were waiting for our welcome home. I was glad to be with friends again, but I was amused by the frequent comment of "How healthy you look!" I wondered what they expected.

The very next morning, Cissy and I inspected our isolation ward and were pleased at how well the staff had done in our absence using only the written instructions we'd sent. Already two hundred typhus patients had been admitted, and the pall of death hung over the ward like a lingering ghost. I often dreamed of crawling white lice, and in one dream in particular, my uniform was covered with those white creatures, and as quickly as I brushed them off, more appeared in their place. I woke up in a sweat frantically rubbing my arms and legs.

NOVEMBER 27ᵗʰ I awakened with such a severe headache and sore throat that I could not crawl out of bed this morning. Oh no, I thought, those typhus bugs have gotten me, too. Even Dr. Sorger was worried, but the blood test was negative and influenza, not typhus, was my problem.

Unlike the typhus patients, I was fully recovered after two weeks and sent home for a convalescent leave.

Meanwhile, the war in Russia and elsewhere continued unabated. There was no let up in the siege of Leningrad, begun in September of 1941. (The siege did not end until 1944 after a half million people had starved to death. With the city surrounded and the ice road of Lake Ladoga the only route for supplies, food became increasingly scarce.) Leningrad, founded as St. Petersburg in 1703 by Peter the Great as a Window on the West, was situated on the River Neva. The uprising of St Petersburg's industrial workers helped ignite the Russian revolution, and the city was renamed Petrograd and then Leningrad, reflecting the shifts in Soviet power. The people here were quite determined and did not relent during their nine hundred day siege as their five thousand gun emplacements withstood the German assaults.

Hitler hoped to capture Moscow, and almost did, his troops coming within twenty five miles. The Russian government had cautiously moved east to Kvibyshev, and scores of refugees also headed eastward by foot or by train, often overflowing the train depots. In all, two million fled. As the heavy snows began to fall, Hitler's generals asked that a winter line be established, but Hitler refused, making his generals and troops press on. Lines faltered, dissolved and fell to counter assault. Many Germans were taken prisoner while those left in the battle lines had inadequate uniforms to withstand the bitter cold.

The Nazi realm now stretched from Norway's frigid fjords to North Africa's hot deserts. Rostov, the gateway to the Caucasus and the oil fields, was captured, and on the Atlantic, the German U-boats were sinking Allied merchant ships and crippling Britain's defense capabilities. The

Germans referred to their success as Happy Time, but by mid year of 1942, anti-submarine techniques and air power ended the Happy Time, and by May 1943, the U-boats were withdrawn.

JANUARY 5th, 1942   Returning to Ft. Modlin after my leave, I found that little had changed.   Typhus cases continued to stream in from Russia, and the pungent smell of formaldehyde hit my nostrils as soon as I entered the ward.   After the confines of the ward, the winter wonderland of the snow that now covered the barren land was a delight. We often went on sleigh rides, walked on the frozen river or simply frolicked about like children, throwing snowballs or rubbing our faces with snow until our skin tingled.

FEBRUARY 4th Panic struck today when we found Cissy in her room, covered with the dark red rash of typhus from head to toe. When she didn't show up for work, we had gone to her room and found her just as she was lapsing into a coma. Once we moved her to the ward, I placed another nurse in charge and stationed myself at her bedside. Dr. Sorger soon joined me in my vigil. I remembered all our times together here and at Johannesburg and tears rolled down my cheeks. This wasn't just any patient–this was Cissy, my friend and confidante.

    In spite of my vigilant nursing care and all the usual treatments, Cissy's condition did not improve and she was still delirious with a high fever after three days. With her plump cheeks now shallow, and gray, she looked like a pitiful child. I was beside myself with worry, yet angry with Cissy because she'd contracted typhus when she carelessly drew blood from a patient without using gloves. "I could just shake you, you silly goose," I whispered to Cissy. "That's after this is all over, of course," I added.

But I was also disturbed that Cissy could have such a severe case of typhus when she'd been vaccinated.

When he found that the conventional treatments were not changing the course of the disease, Dr. Sorger told me he was going to try a new treatment. "I've selected a patient, who had a high Weil-Felix reaction with an obvious high resistance to typhus, to be a blood donor for Cissy. The patient, Lieutenant Kullen is a tall muscular man who never lapsed into a coma and is now in the convalescent stage. I'd like you to assist."

"Of course," I quickly agreed, but thought to myself that this was quite risky. But at this point anything, even an experimental treatment, was worth the risk to save Cissy's life.

That afternoon, Dr. Sorger gave Cissy an intramuscular injection of 20 cc of Lt. Kullen's blood, a common procedure known as self immunization that had been used often during epidemics in Germany. The next day Lt. Kullen was brought into Cissy's room on a stretcher and 100 cc of his blood was slowly given to Cissy in a direct transfusion, 10 cc at a time, replaced with 10 cc normal saline solution. The results were astounding. Within five hours, Cissy's fever dropped, she came out of her coma and began to drink some tea and soup. She looked at me and asked, "Where have I been?" I was too tearful to answer at that moment, but only bowed my head in thanks for another one of God's miracles.

FEBRUARY 18TH Lt. Kullen became a frequent visitor to Cissy, even offering to help with her care. He obviously took personal satisfaction in her recovery. He and I often took evening walks because we both needed a break. When Cissy had recovered enough to travel she left for her

Mother-House on a convalescent leave. Lt. Kullen was on hand to bid her Auf Weidersehen and thrust a small gift in her hand. I found it difficult to mouth the usual good bye words because I suspected I'd never see her again. We both shed a few tears and promised to write faithfully. I stood and watched the ambulance until it was out of sight. I thought that my life was evolving into a leaving pattern with people passing through my heart like soldiers who occupy a country but depart, leaving a fragment of themselves behind.

FEBRUARY 28TH I was still melancholy and missing Cissy when Dr. Sorger pulled me aside and said, "I was so encouraged by the success of the direct transfusion in Cissy's recovery, that I'd like to try it on a larger scale. Would you be willing to assist?"

"Of course," I said. "You didn't even have to ask." I was glad for the opportunity since this would keep me busy. He carefully selected donors, men with vigorous health and high antibody levels like Lt. Kullen. He had no trouble getting volunteers. Again, the transfusions produced astonishing results. Men came out of their comas in hours, rather than days or weeks.

The new treatment was widely heralded in medical journals, and Dr. Sorger became established as the bona fide expert in the treatment of typhus. His new method was soon practiced in army hospitals along the Eastern Front.

MARCH 12TH Lt. Kullen is leaving tomorrow for Germany and asked me to accompany him on one last walk along the river. As we strolled, we talked about the uselessness of this war. "The war has already taken so many lives," he said, "and men are nothing more than kindling to keep the bonfires of political ambition burning. Russia is no place to

fight a war, Tabea," he mused. "That country is too cold
for anyone to survive in the winter and then as hot and
damp as a stagnant swamp in the summer. I've been pretty
lucky, I guess, when I think of all those who've died from
mysterious fevers without names. You'd think Hitler would
have learned something from Napoleon's folly in Russia."

I nodded in agreement, although I didn't fully
understand all he said. "I hope when you're recovered,
Wilhelm, they won't send you back here."

He shrugged his broad shoulders and sighed, "I guess
when the army decides something, there's not much a man
can do about it." When we got back to the fort, he asked me
to come to his quarters where he had a gift for me. He then
presented me with a fine portable radio with a built-in
antenna. "With this, you can tune into the world."

I was overcome by such a generous gift, but he made
light of it saying, "It's too heavy for me to lug around. I
picked it up in Warsaw for a good price. I have the feeling I
may find myself in rugged places. Who would use a radio
in a muddy fox hole?" He then showed me how to find
London on the dial and told me to be sure to listen to British
broadcasts, since they were the only ones that reported true
accounts and not propaganda like radio Berlin.

Even though I knew that possession of a radio was a
grave offense, and anyone caught listening could be tried
for treason by the Nazis, I accepted the gift with excitement.
I had the feeling that this radio would be important to me
for the next few years. I began the very next morning and
stayed up to hear the 2:00 a.m. broadcast from London in
the German language. Some of the other nurses joined me
because they were eager to hear the "true news."

MARCH 20TH Today it was warm for the first time in months. The balmy spring breezes began to drive away the dampness and cold from the halls of the barracks. The number of patients arriving was diminishing and all was well, except for me. I had ignored a sore throat and dizziness that had plagued me for days. This afternoon I collapsed while placing a needle in a patient's arm for intravenous solutions.

Two Polish men carried me to my room. Dr. Sorger came quickly and examined me and then told me I had diphtheria. Apparently some other nurses were also ill with diphtheria. While children in Germany were immunized against diphtheria, adults were not. Dr. Sorger surmised that the most likely source were the Polish peasants who had brought it from their villages. I was given a potent dose of antitoxin. Unfortunately I was allergic to the serum and broke out in blisters all over my body, even inside my mouth.

Two days later my misery was compounded by kidney failure, and I swelled like a balloon. I couldn't roll from side to side. I felt like I was encased in a huge boulder. With my lips swollen and cracked, even talking was painful. None of the medications I was given relieved my pain or edema.

I recalled the story of Job and his trials and prayed, "Is this the end of my life? My work? If this is your will, God, please take me home quickly. On the other hand, Lord, you guided me into nursing and I've served such a short time. Couldn't I live a little longer? But Your will, not mine, O Lord." I lapsed into a dreamy state with no sense of time. I had a vague awareness of nurses tiptoes in and out of my room, either praying for me or bidding me farewell.

MARCH 27TH I had given up all hope when General Schmidt, the head of the Ninth Army Division Nurses, came to see me. When she walked into my room, there was no question of her position and rank, yet her touch was soft and gentle as she took my swollen hand in hers. She said, "Lieutenant Springer, I want to thank you on behalf of the German army for the fine work you have done both in Johannesburg and here at Ft. Modlin. I will do all I can to help you now, and I've brought along an allergy specialist, Dr. Heinz."

After she stepped away from my bed, I saw a thin, intense-looking young man standing behind her. He came forward quickly and asked me how I felt. "Oh doctor, I'm so grateful you're here. The pain in my muscles and nerves is unbearable. And look at me-all swollen."

He nodded and said confidently, "We'll fix you up and the pain will go away. You'll soon be as strong and healthy as ever and back on the ward with the other nurses, I assure you." How I wanted to believe him and watched anxiously as he drew up four cc. of Novocaine with his long slender fingers and slowly injected it into a vein in my arm. Within seconds, the pain began to recede, and I felt warm all over. After twenty minutes, I began to perspire so heavily that fluid ran from every pore in my body, soaking the sheets through to the mattress.

Dr. Heinz smiled, obviously pleased that his treatment was working. "Don't move now," he warned. "Your heart has much work to do." I continued perspiring profusely, and after two hours I could finally move my arms and legs. I felt as light as a cloud. Dr. Heinz then ordered a vinegar bath for me.

Dr. Sorger came in and was surprised to find me sitting up in bed. "It's wonderful to see you looking like yourself again, Tabea, he beamed. "I've written your father and told him to expect you home in a couple of weeks."

APRIL 5th I arrived home just as the fruit trees were blossoming and the spring air was laden with the sweet scent of lilacs. Although Papa had just turned seventy-seven, he appeared as robust as ever. "I'm a busy man now, Tabea, because so many of the young pastors have been drafted into the army."

Ministers weren't the only ones once exempt, who were being drafted. Single women, 20-35, were also receiving draft notices, and among them had been my pretty little sister, Esther. I was distraught. "How could this happen, Papa? Esther has a child."

He shrugged his shoulders as he recalled sadly, "The notice came in the mail one day for her to report to the City Hall. She went, of course, and when she told them about Hans, they said that Deborah and I could look after him. Isn't it amazing how they know all the details about your life? Anyway, she left the next week along with a group of five hundred women for the army base in Rendsburg, Schleswig-Holstein. She writes me that she's learning to operate large search lights, which will aid the ground artillery during the air raids." He put his hand on my arm, and said, "I didn't write you about this because I didn't want you to worry. Now I have two daughters in the war. I feel it's right that you should serve, after all, the wounded need care. But I do not like the idea of Esther being a soldier and learning how to shoot. They keep telling us that the front is growing larger and there aren't enough men at home to protect the citizens–so women have to do the job."

Try as I might, I couldn't picture my fun-loving sister as a soldier firing a gun or moving heavy search lights about. I was struck that the war was touching us more deeply this time. The shortages of the past paled in comparison to the kind of commitment being asked of us now as well as the imminent danger everyone was anticipating. Back then we were all together. And I worried about Hans. I felt they were wrong to take a young boy's mother away from him. I observed that Deborah was doing her best to be a substitute mother to Hans, not just a doting aunt.

Hans seemed even more solemn, and he followed me about asking if I thought the war would be over soon. There was no easy answer to this question, and a cheery "keep your chin up" answer would not have satisfied this thoughtful boy of nine. So I simply took him in my arms and said softly, "Dear Hans, I wish I could tell you, but I don't know. We can only pray that God will bring us safely through this time and then our family will all be together again."

Although Papa tried to get my mind off the war, he was obviously incensed by the Nazis' constant stamping feet in the streets, singing their hollow victory songs. Most people were like my father: acquiescent and loyal on the outside, but inwardly their teeth were grinding with anger and hatred. I guess we all felt the strong hand of the Nazis on our throats.

APRIL 20th On my last day home, a telegram arrived from Esther announcing that she was on her way home. Our time together would only be a few hours at the train station, but I was grateful for even that in this increasingly uncertain period. Even though I knew she was in the army, I was not prepared for the sight of the physically fit female soldier striding toward me with a stern expression, her body snug and lean in a dark blue uniform with brass buttons. A gun and gas mask hung from her hip.

She grabbed me in an effusive hug, crying, "Oh Tabea, I was so afraid I'd miss you." Papa stood watching proudly, as tears welled up in his eyes. We went into the cafeteria where we could talk. Esther took off her cap, and I was shocked to see her long curls gone and instead, her hair cropped short. Yet on her the style was becoming and softened her grim expression. Hans could not take his eyes off his mother in her uniform and appeared proud of her.

"How is it in the army, Esther?" I asked, a question I suspected that was uppermost in all our minds.

"The training is very demanding," she replied. "We are always running, exercising, and drilling–and then there is target practice. I'm not a bad shot, actually. There are five hundred of us living in my barracks, and I've been promoted to sergeant with twenty girls under my command. We've been told to expect heavy bombardments over Germany sometime in the future. Then it won't matter where anyone is, because the front will be everywhere."

And indeed, by May 1942, the Allied bombings began over Germany. Cologne was targeted, and one thousand bombers leveled a third of the city. Before long, Germany was being bombed day and night, because the B-17's and B-24's were equipped with Norden bombsights. Industrial targets were hit during the day, while the cities were bombed at night.

Esther looked about at all of us and changed the subject when she noted the anxious expression on Papa's face. "Oh I don't want to worry you, Papa. I'm sure it won't happen very soon." She turned to her son and said, "And Hans, you must tell me all about school."

As we attempted to make conversation, the uncertainty of knowing when we'd see each other again made our chatter uneasy. Deborah kept a bright smile fastened on her face, but tears welled up in her eyes, too. When we said our "Auf Weideresehens," Papa hugged me close and said, "You know we're all in the Lord's hands-no matter what happens."

I dozed on the long train ride back and looked forward to good night's rest in my room at Ft. Modlin. But this was not to be. Instead, nurses had decorated my room with bouquets of wild flowers and came by to ask about the folks back home. When I told them that women were now being drafted, they were astounded. "Hitler's using women to fight? I don't believe it!" exclaimed a young L.V.N. When I added that fourteen- year-old boys were also being trained to help operate the search lights, they were even more incredulous. "Isn't that ridiculous to send our men into enemy countries, only to have the enemy fly over Germany and bomb the women and children?" commented another. One after another agreed that being a nurse was perhaps the best way to serve during a war. I laughed as I said, "One of the doctors is always saying, "Let the horses do the thinking–they have bigger heads."

MAY 10th Since the sun was setting later, the guards relaxed the curfew and allowed us to attend movies in the small village nearby; however, they insisted on accompanying us. One particular night, a large group of us were walking back to the fort singing folk songs and bobbing our heads from side to side in rhythm as we joined in the chorus, "Hola Hi! Hola Ho!" Suddenly a shot rang out, and I felt a hot streak across my cheek. The guards shoved us to the ground while they searched the area, but found no one. Everyone gathered around me, appearing as stunned as I was. Apparently I was saved from a bullet hitting me in the middle of my forehead because I was bobbing my head as I sang. I knew that song would forever be significant to me.

Once back inside the safety of the fort, a doctor cleansed and bandaged my wound and told me the wound was superficial. The scar on my cheek was a daily reminder. As I sat and talked with the other nurses about the sniper attack, I wondered to myself if any of the Polish peasants on the staff were involved with the Partisan groups. We really couldn't know since they had always been polite and cooperative. Yet it was no secret that they resented the Gestapo's taking young boys from their families, even as young as eleven, and shipping them to Germany for political education and farm work. One of the nurses said she had heard that an altar boy was assisting with the mass when German soldiers burst in and dragged him out.

There were Partisan groups everywhere, not only in Russia and Poland, but in France, Denmark and the other occupied countries as well. There was also a small German underground, which included Ernest Reuter, (a future mayor of West Berlin) and Pastor Dietrich Bonhoffer, a well-known theologian. The underground was only mildly effective and by 1944 one of every 1200 Germans was arrested for political and religious offenses. Bonhoffer was arrested early in the war, and was one of the many ministers incarcerated and later executed.

I became aware that the Nazis had cut the food rations even more, because the Polish personnel were not only begging for food, but stealing it as well. Some guards overlooked this as they inspected them on their way out, while others searched diligently to find even the smallest packet of food.

MAY 14th Today a Polish maid begged me for food for her mother. "I don't ask for myself," she pleaded, "but for her. She is ill with pneumonia, and I have nothing to feed her. Is there anything you can spare?" I fixed a package of bread, butter and meat, and warned her to hide it carefully. Unfortunately, the guards found the food and she was promptly arrested. I was reported to the commanding general of Ft. Modlin and scheduled for a court martial the next morning.

CHAPTER EIGHT: THE HOSPITAL TRAIN

MAY 15th 1942 I did not know what to expect when I appeared the next morning at army headquarters for my court martial. I was nervous and my heart was pounding, but I managed to appear calm. I was ushered into a room where five officers were seated behind a long table. The officer in charge asked my name and told me to sit down. I felt the atmosphere was grim as he began the proceedings.

"Lieutenant Springer, on the evening past did you give food to the enemy, with full knowledge that this is strictly forbidden by military rules?"

"Yes sir, I did–but if I may speak in my behalf, sir, the woman's mother was dying. And I felt compelled to follow the command of my Lord to feed the hungry, even if that meant disobeying the rules of men."

The officers glared at me with piercing eyes and flushed cheeks. I felt their anger directed at me. One officer asked coldly, "Do you know the consequences of going against an order of the army?" I nodded meekly and said, "Sir, I am willing to pay for the food I gave to the woman. However, if I am punished, I will be compelled to report things I have observed some officers here doing that were incorrect to General Zilmer, a good friend of mine. For instance, I could make a list of those who have exchanged army goods for Polish valuables and trinkets to send home"

The air grew heavy with an uneasy silence. Angry expressions faded to anxious frowns. After a hasty, whispered conference, the commanding officer cleared his throat and stood up. "Lieutenant Springer, I'm sure you understand that there are always some incorrect deeds.

Perhaps what we should do here is forget what has happened in the past and keep silent about what we know. Now if you promise to do this, we are willing to dismiss your case."

I nodded in agreement. My court martial ended with smiles and handshakes all around. My knees felt like jelly as I walked out of that room. I wondered if the decision would have been as favorable if I had been tried by Gestapo officers.

The Polish underground continued to thrive, and many German soldiers lost their lives behind the front lines. Schools and universities were suppressed in an effort to stamp out the professional classes, but this only served to increase the resistance activities, including illegal presses to publish newspapers. The Polish underground proved invaluable to the Allies and escaped prisoners of war. Polish citizens were hung in the village squares in retaliation for every German soldier killed.

JUNE 1st I received a summons to appear at General Zilmer's office at the Ninth Army Headquarters in Konigsberg, East Prussia. My journey by train took six hours, giving me ample time to speculate In the past, General Zilmer had always met with us while making his rounds of the various Ninth Army Hospitals. I pondered what could be so important that he'd summon me to his office?

A car was waiting at the station. The driver took me directly to the post, an enormous walled army base which housed and trained thousands of soldiers. General Zilmer's office was in the administration building, and I waited in a small reception room until a secretary ushered me in. His office was spacious, but simply furnished with a huge desk and several straight backed wooden chairs. The required portrait of Hitler hung on the wall between the German and Nazi flags.

The General rose as I entered, and after we'd exchanged the usual "Heil Hitlers," he got right to the point. "Lieutenant Springer, I am assigning you to a hospital train as the head nurse. I felt you were well qualified for this important position because of your surgical skills and also your experience in managing the typhus epidemics." He paused for a moment to pick up a leather box from his desk. "It is also my pleasure to award you this medal of honor for your work in Johannesburg. We are proud of our brave nurses. I also congratulate you on your promotion to major," he said solemnly, shaking my hand. This was a proud moment for me, and I was sorry my family wasn't here to share it with me.

I asked the General about this hospital train, and he explained that the train traveled close to the front lines in Russia, picking up the wounded to transport back to the hospitals behind the lines. "Your staff will include fourteen paramedics and one licensed vocational nurse (LVN) to care for the train's capacity of two- hundred- fifty patients. The two doctors on the train with you will be Colonel Beckman, the chief of staff, and his assistant, Lieutenant Faber. The warrant officer is Lieutenant Preuss."

"And now, Major Springer, I would like you to meet Liesel Schmidt, the LVN who will be working with you." As he rose to call her in, he said softly, "She is only nineteen, so young to be close to the battle lines. I know I can count on you to look after her."

Liesel came in and offered me her hand in a shy handshake. She was a petite lovely girl with soft brown curls framing her face and a warm smile. I liked her instantly and knew I'd have no trouble heeding the General's request. I almost felt like a mother to her already.

I invited her to come back to Fort Modlin with me for the night, saying, "We'll have the evening in which to get acquainted before we board the train tomorrow." We were both excited about this assignment, in spite of the danger it posed. Neither of us had traveled much and we looked forward to seeing new places, even though the circumstances of war were daunting. We soon discovered that we also shared the same Christian faith and trusted our Heavenly Father to keep us in His care no matter what we faced, even death.

Then Liesel told me about herself. "I didn't have much of a home, so the army has become my family. You see, I was an illegitimate child, and my mother was never very interested in me. Perhaps she was ashamed or just too busy to be bothered. I was raised by my grandparents. They meant well, but they were very strict. I was almost relieved to be drafted and sent away. That made my leaving home a simple matter." Liesel told me this quite matter-of-factly I was impressed that such a sad childhood had not embittered her. On the contrary, she appeared to have a positive outlook.

Ft. Modlin was like a small town and in no time everyone had heard that I was leaving in the morning. Nothing would do, but that the staff had to have a party to send me off. Along with the toasts of good wishes for the future were the regrets that this was probably a final good bye. I looked around and saw many who I had worked with side by side. I found saying "Auf Weidersehen to Dr. Sorger especially difficult I couldn't imagine that I would ever see any of these people or this place again.

JUNE 2nd This morning a staff car took Liesel and me back to Konigsberg, where our train was being readied for the journey. Lt. Preuss, met us with a hearty, "Welcome aboard." He showed us to our compartments, which were surprisingly cozy. Red plush seats became our beds at night, and there were ample dressers and compact closets. "You may relax now, ladies," beamed Lt. Preuss, "but be ready in your gala uniforms at 2:00 p.m. to meet the commanding officer and the rest of the staff."

We quickly dressed in our gray suits and white blouses, and climbed down the stairs to look around on this balmy summer day. We strolled along the train which seemed to stretch for miles. As we approached the engine, we met the engineer who was checking the enormous wheels. He told us that he'd been on this train for over two years. Proudly he pointed out the two large steam engines with a coal tender behind. This was followed by five supply cars, the kitchen, the diner and four cars to house the officers and staff. Next the operation car, twenty-four sick bed cars, and finally, the Wagon master's car, thirty-seven cars in all. He beckoned us up the stairs at one point to show us the open gangways between the sick bed cars so patients could be moved quickly in case of an attack or a fire. I wondered how cold those open gangways would be when we traveled in fifty below zero weather in Russia. The size of the train was overwhelming, and I suddenly felt a stab of anxiety about being the head nurse.

Promptly at 2:00 p.m., Liesel and I joined the rest of the staff standing at attention in front of the train. We did not have to wait long for the arrival of Col. Beckman and Lt. Faber. As the Colonel delivered his welcoming remarks, I was struck by his noble appearance. His warm gray eyes imparted trust, and he smiled often. When he shook my hand in welcome, a feeling of security swept over me. Instinctively I felt that he was a man who could always be depended upon–no matter what. I liked him immediately.

Then Lt. Faber greeted us enthusiastically, vigorously pumping our hands in firm handshakes. His boyish grin made him appear even younger than his thirty years. The departing nurses gave us a brief orientation and that was the end of the welcoming ceremonies. We were then all given time off to see the sights of Konigsberg.

Konigsberg was a city overrun by different peoples through the centuries. The ethnicity of the city was unclear, because the people were neither purely Russian, German or Polish, but simply a Baltic -speaking people. The city was a Hanseatic league seaport. During the sixteenth century, Konigsberg was the capital city where German kings were crowned, hence the name. This was a city of grand opera, but also an industrial center. The enormous railway terminal housed twenty-eight tracks and was the main transfer point between Poland and Russia.

Liesel and I whiled away the hours rowing about in a boat, drinking in the serenity and loveliness all about us on the grounds of the beautiful castle. There were manicured gardens and sparkling blue lakes with swans drifting about like royal feathered princes.

In just three years, this pastoral setting would lie smoldering beneath the repeated bombings of Konigsberg, which would eventually be renamed, "Kaliningrad."

I found it difficult to fall asleep that night as my mind whirled about with the excitement of the day and the unknowns that lay ahead. At two in the morning, I felt a sudden jerk as the train pulled out of the station. Here we go, I thought. I suddenly wondered how Papa would feel if he knew I was headed for the front. No doubt he'd commit it to the Lord and remind me of Jesus's promise to be with us always. A feeling of peace covered me like a warm blanket and I dozed off, awakening at 6:00 a.m. when the train pulled into the station at the harbor of Pilau.

This harbor had been used advantageously by Hitler during the invasion of Poland. Large vacation vessels were docked here and used for Hitler's "Strength through Happiness Program," in which industrious workers of the Nazi party were rewarded with a two week vacation aboard ship. During the Polish conquest, German soldiers boarded the ships in colorful vacation attire, then quickly changed into uniforms, bringing out their weapons. They ambushed the Polish from the sea, overwhelming them instantly. Two of these ships, the Pretonia and the Robert Ley, remained anchored in the harbor. They had been converted into hospital ships and were used to transport wounded soldiers across the Baltic Sea to Germany.

JUNE 3rd We assembled in the diner at 8:00 a.m. for breakfast. Liesel and I ate our meals with the doctors and Lt. Preuss, while the paramedics ate in a dining car adjacent to the sick bed cars. Col. Beckman rose and greeted us warmly, wondering how we'd slept. Then, his eyes twinkling, he said, "I have a surprise for you ladies. You have been invited to be guests aboard the Robert Ley today." What a privilege! Liesel and I quickly assured him that we'd be happy to accept the invitation! I asked if he would be coming, too. He shook his head, saying regretfully, "I'm afraid I can't because of an important meeting. But you two go along now and enjoy your day."

As soon as Liesel and I set foot on the gangplank of the ship, sirens began to howl. The staff, dressed in immaculate white uniforms, lined the gangplank and saluted us as we were welcomed aboard by the captain and his officers. I was stunned by such a grand reception for simple nurses like us. The head nurse led the way to the dining room, softly lit by crystal chandeliers, for Mittagessen. I felt like I was entering a dream world of fine china and crystal, white linen table cloths and tables laden with platters of exotic salads and hors d'oeuvres. I was trying to take it all in, when the steward poured me a glass of golden Rhine wine. The captain proposed a toast to our health and safety on our trips into Russia.

After a feast of dorsch fish with cream sauce and potatoes, we lingered over dessert of assorted cheeses and pumpernickel bread. The conversation centered on Tristan and Isolde, currently playing at the Konigsberg Opera House. War and politics were carefully avoided, and for that brief interlude, ceased to exist.

After lunch, the captain showed us around the ship. The Robert Ley was spacious and elegant with carved landscapes on paneled walls and leather chairs in the lounges. The hospital section was spotless and well equipped, and I felt a tinge of envy for these nurses who worked in such luxurious surroundings. The sirens howled again as we left, announcing our departure. *Near the end of the war, the Robert Ley escaped to Sweden, carrying East German refugees, but the Pretonia was sunk.*

At dinner that evening, Col. Beckman told us that this would be our last meal on German soil for awhile. "We leave in the morning, and there will be difficult times ahead, but if we support each other our morale will remain high." I respected his wisdom and obvious concern for each member of the crew. He made me feel like I was part of a family. I had heard that he was a widower in his mid-fifties. He was

111

like a father to his crew. I thought that while the war separates families, it also creates new families of strangers.

Late that night the train left and sped north toward Memel on the Lithuanian border. Here the engines were replaced with more powerful ones, because three freight cars loaded with rocks had to be added behind the engines to act as a buffer for the potential land mine. A car with small cannons and missiles was also added near the middle of the train for defense against air attacks.

JUNE 6th After a two day journey, we arrived at Riga, the capital of Latvia, situated where the Duna River empties into the Riga Bay. Riga was a picturesque city, famous for an ornate opera house built in 1900. Since we would be here for three hours, Dr. Beckman gave Liesel and me permission to sightsee. I found the people here quite friendly and they spoke German fluently. I assumed they were of German stock, but they looked more like typical Swedes with their light blonde hair and clear blue eyes.

Upon our return, Dr. Beckman, his jaw firmly set, beckoned us to follow him. He led the way to train cars isolated on side tracks. He explained that certain citizens of Riga had been left to die in these cars by the Russians, who had planned to evacuate them to Siberia. Instead, they abandoned them when German troops advanced on the city. When the German troops discovered them, most had frozen or starved to death, still handcuffed in place on shelves. Peering inside through a small window covered with iron grating, I saw tiers of shelves five feet high. A scarf and a dirty rag doll lay on the floor. I imagined entire families being herded into these cars and shackled to the bare shelves, there to die huddled together. What an awful death! A wave of revulsion swept over me, and I despaired to think of such a waste of precious human life.

Within the hour we left for Pskov, our final destination. This city lay between Novgorod and Riga, about 350 miles northwest of Moscow. Lenin published a radical newspaper here in 1900, and in 1917, Nicolas II the last czar of Russia, abdicated at Pskov's railway station. In fact, many battles of the Russian revolution had been fought here.

Now the train rode on a single track across a flat open prairie. Dust clouds swirled about obscuring the sun and bathing the world in an eerie glow. We passed small villages of one room cottages where pigs and chickens shared the family living quarters, and the only furnishings were a table, a stove, and shelves on the walls for sleeping. I saw women in the fields with oxen, tending cabbages and other vegetables.

As we rode along, Liesel and I practiced walking through the train without bumping into the walls and maintaining our balance during sudden stops. By the end of that trip my arms were black and blue, but I could carry a cup of coffee from the diner to my compartment without spilling a drop.

As we drew near Pskov, the aroma of simmering stew drifted through the train, indicating that dinner was being prepared for the oncoming patients. Air raid sirens blared as we pulled into the station, and we quickly ran outside to the bunker. Within minutes, however, the all clear signal sounded, postponing my first taste of danger.

Ambulances soon arrived with patients from the field hospital, and within two hours we had boarded two-hundred- thirty. While the paramedics served dinner, the doctors, Liesel and I went through the train, welcoming the men. I carried a large basket of medicines for pain relief and antibiotics for infections, which I dispensed when needed as we went along.

JUNE 12th I developed the habit of sleeping lightly at night, dressed in my training suit, so I would be alert for sounds or groaning that might indicate hemorrhage. Not only was the train ride bumpy and jolting, but the men were heavily sedated at night, two factors which made bleeding to death a distinct probability.

One night I awakened uneasily. I sat up, straining to hear any unusual sounds, but heard nothing. Since I was fully awake, I decided to check on the patients anyway. In the fourth car down I found an amputee hemorrhaging from his stump. Quickly I clamped the vein and summoned Dr. Faber to suture the wound. Amazingly the patient, a lad of nineteen, slept peacefully through it all, unaware of his close brush with death.

The sick cars were very compact with three tiers of bunks on either side of the aisle. The windows at each tier of bunks had brown tie-back curtains and heavy black blinds which were drawn during air raids. Five gas lamps hung suspended from the ceiling over the center aisle. At the far end of the car was a corner for the paramedic, complete with table and chair, an instrument tray for emergencies and a linen cabinet.

I felt like a trapeze artist as I stood on the ladder to change bandages or to give an injection to a man in a top bunk. Once during a sudden stop, I was bounced off the ladder and grabbed one of the lamps to break my fall. As I swung back and forth like a monkey, a tittering of chuckles broke out and soon the entire car was engulfed in laughter. Those nearby apologized that they couldn't come to my rescue, and I certainly understood since they were all amputees. Hearing the commotion, the paramedic suddenly appeared and said, "What's going on here?" Then he spotted me swinging about and helped me down. I had a chuckle or two myself when I told Liesel later about my little escapade. She squealed with laughter, but added soberly, "I'm so glad you weren't hurt."

Liesel's sunny disposition and pretty face soon won the hearts of many a soldier, but she managed to keep them all at arm's length. Since she was a girl of obvious high moral character, I never worried about her. In fact, she was so interested in learning more procedures, that I not only taught her, but entrusted her with more responsibility.

Since we spent many hours with the men on the long journey home, I soon became aware that depression was even more of a problem than physical wounds. Often there were angry outbursts, "Why were we sent so far from home into God-forsaken Russia where we haven't a chance of winning?" Others muttered dejectedly that they could not see any reason for this war.

Encouraging them in my own way, I shared my experience of God's constant love and care. "God does not make war, men do." I declared. "But sometimes I think God lets things happen to show us what is evil. Even then, He does not abandon us, but gives us courage and endurance." This philosophy I had developed growing up in a secure home, strongly influenced by pious parents. Yet I was surprised by those who told me they had found God in the middle of a battle and learned to pray, as bullets whizzed over their heads. These men became quite important to me and nursing them back to health was rewarding. As always I found that when one gives love, it comes back.

JUNE 20th We knew we were back on German soil as soon
as the ride became smoother. Upon our arrival at
Insterburg, Junge Madchens and Red Cross ladies boarded
the train, handing out candies and magazines to the men
while they waited to be unloaded. After the last ambulance
had pulled away late in the afternoon, I relaxed for the first
time in days in a tub of steaming hot water.

*Insterburg, on the bank of the Inster River, was one of
the most beautiful towns in East Prussia, and famous for
horse breeding and race tracks. Herman Goring, one of
Hitler's generals and close confidante, lived here on a large
estate of lovely gardens and stables. Goring was the
Luftwaffe Boss, who enjoyed fame from his feats in aviation.*

*On one of our stops in Insterburg, Herman Goring
came to the station, Gestapo guards at his side, and
watched silently as we unloaded the patients. He then
indicated that he wished to speak privately with Dr.
Beckman. While some of the troops conversed with his
guards, the two men spoke quietly. Later Dr. Beckman told
me that General Goring was worried about Hitler's
increasing suspicions of everyone.*

After a two day rest, we left early in the morning. This
time we headed for an area close to the front lines. In fact,
our orders were to pick up men directly from the field and
we were likely to be under artillery fire. Dr. Beckman gave
us specific instructions: "In case of an attack, I want you to
lie on the tracks beneath the cars by the double wheels. Pair
off, two beneath a car, rather than all of you under one;
however, if there are patients on board, no matter what the
circumstances, your duty is to remain with them. I know I
can count on you to look out for one another."

He appeared so brave and so concerned about each one of us, that I felt my courage rise in response. That wasn't all I felt. I had begun to be as anxious about his safety as I was about mine. I began to realize that my deep respect for him was awakening romantic feelings that had been buried for a long time. These feelings had surfaced briefly when I met Fritz at Ft. Modlin, only to be buried again when he left abruptly and disappeared from my life. While I became ever more aware of my feelings for Dr. Beckman, I was extremely careful to never let them show. I kept our relationship on a professional level, and confided in no one–not even Liesel.

We traveled for two days across Lithuania. I had difficulty sleeping at night, not only because of the bombardments, but also because of the daylight. My day began with the sun streaming into my compartment at 2:00 a.m. The daylight often remained until 11:00 p.m.

There was artillery fire booming all around us as we neared Luga, but the constant movement of the train made us a difficult target. I felt very frightened, and Liesel and I looked to each other for encouragement.

As soon as the train pulled into the station at Luga, we began boarding patients. Wounded men were brought by everything on wheels from trucks to wooden carts. There had been heavy casualties the night before. Many men, who had received only minimal first aid in the tent hospital, needed immediate measures to stop the hemorrhaging. A few patients were ill with a contagious viral fever similar to malaria, and we isolated them in the last car.

Because of the likelihood of air attacks, we could only use flashlights, and thus surgeries had to be delayed until daybreak. Liesel and I assisted the doctors during the night stopping the bleeding and calming the anxious men with morphine. When the first rays of dawn pierced the dark curtain of sky at 2:00 a.m., we began operating and did not leave for Pskov until all the surgeries were done, since the train ride was so bumpy.

Once at Pskov, the critical patients were transferred to the field hospital there, and we continued on to Dorpat, Estonia to take on supplies. Dorpat (Renamed Ozero in 1945) was known for its fine beer, and Lt. Preuss bought an ample supply for both the patients and us-a treat we all enjoyed.

JULY 3rd Although it was 4:00 a.m., the sun was streaming into my compartment. The long daylight hours always made me feel as if the world was upside down, and often, as now, I could not sleep. I sat up to write a few lines in my diary and let down my window for a breath of fresh air. Suddenly there was a light tap at my door, and Liesel burst in, not waiting for me to open it. Her usual sunny face was clouded with worry.

"I hope I didn't wake you," she said breathlessly, "but I can't sleep. I feel something awful is going to happen. I just know it."

Her fears alarmed me, but I said calmly, "Why don't you stay with me for awhile. If something terrible is going to happen, we might as well face it together."

She seemed more at ease just being with me. We chatted about the trip, but Liesel always came back to her sense of impending doom, both trying to fight it, but also trying to pin point the source. Finally at 6:00 a.m., we decided to go to the diner for a cup of coffee to lift our spirits.

We sat at the window, watching the sun dance across the water in golden waves, as we traveled over the long bridge that spanned the Narva River. The church spires and squat buildings of Narva were just coming into view when suddenly there was tremendous noise that shook the train, throwing us out of our seats.

The train ground screeching to a stop, as we picked ourselves up off the floor and tumbled out of the train. As far as we could tell, the train appeared to be undamaged, but the bridge we had just crossed was crumbling and sinking into the water. Dr. Beckman hurried over to us, an anxious look on his face. "Are you two all right?" He asked.

"Oh yes, I replied, "Just a bit shaken up. What happened?"

"As near as I can tell, a bomb exploded when we went over the bridge. It was probably planted there by the underground. We made it to shore by a matter of seconds. Really a close call," he said, shaking his head.

Hardly anyone spoke during breakfast, yet I felt a close bond among us, that mixture of relief and good will that follows after a disaster. Only later in the privacy of my compartment, did Liesel and I allow our fears to surface and we began to tremble. We thanked God for sparing our lives.

CHAPTER NINE: LOVE REVEALED

JULY 5th, 1942 After such a close call, I was relieved to rest for two days while the train was being cleaned and restocked. I had heard that the oncoming patients had been recuperating in a field hospital for a few weeks, so they could be transported directly into Germany. I asked Dr. Beckman if Liesel and I could go sightseeing in Narva. He mulled it over for a few moments, and then said hesitantly, "I suppose it would be all right, but you must take one of the soldiers with you. This city can be dangerous. Look at what just happened when we pulled into town." I nodded, saying that we'd be very careful.

As we strolled along with our escort, I found Narva to be a disappointment as it was a large industrial city, with textile mills being the main industry. We walked past massive twelve- story buildings where two thousand employees produced material for German army uniforms. The huge waterfalls were the power source in the summer, but in the winter, when the waterfalls were frozen, coal was used. We were told that the frozen waterfalls of Narva were a magnificent sight.

This city is another that has never been its own master. It was ruled by the Danes until 1346 when the Germans seized it, used the fort as an academy for noblemen's sons, and established an order of knighthood. In 1558 the Russians overtook the city until 1581 when Sweden conquered it, but then lost it to Russia in 1704. After World War I, Narva was given to Estonia, only to be seized by the Germans on their march eastward.

JULY 12th This day shall always be one of the most meaningful days of my life. It was nearly two in the morning when we finished unloading the last of the patients. I had enjoyed a pleasant six day journey to Insterburg, since the patients required little nursing care. Most of the staff was now exhausted and had quickly retired, but Dr. Beckman asked me to stay up with him for awhile to relax and enjoy the warm summer night as we discussed the next assignment.

He set two chairs outside behind the train. I was surprised that he would arrange for us to be alone like this, since we all felt under constant surveillance, as if the eyes of the Gestapo were everywhere, searching for any infractions of the rules. The army strictly forbid any kind of liaison between men and women and even separated engaged couples. But for the moment I did not care. The stars beaming down reminded me of my heavenly Father's protection, and this man sitting beside me gave me a sense of security I had never known.

We raised our glasses of wine in a toast to our survival of the bridge explosion. "I felt like I'd been given a gift of new life." I said, my eyes meeting his. Suddenly a strong desire came over me, and I knew I wanted to spend the rest of my life with this man. I looked away quickly, struggling to keep my feelings under control.

Dr. Beckman must have known how I felt, because he took my hands in his and told me he knew of my feelings for him. "I adore you for it, Tabea," he said, "and I love all those little things you do for me–my laundry, bringing me a cup of coffee at night. I've been alone for so long, I forgot what it was like to be taken care of. Your love is deep and warm–like that of a devoted mother."

Once his quiet voice had put my feelings into words, there was no point in denying them any longer. And when he put his arms around me, I felt happy inside and knew there was more to life than giving myself for others. I wanted to tell him so many things about me and how much I cared for him, but the reality of the war stilled my tongue. Surrounded by death all the time, I felt like a person without a future.

When we went inside later, we agreed to keep our relationship a secret so we could enjoy each other's company without fear of being transferred or demoted. I looked forward to the many times he'd come to my compartment, and we'd discuss books we'd read or play a game of chess. Sometimes we'd allow ourselves to daydream about the future and he would always say, "When this is over, Tabea, we will have a life together. If my eye clinic is still there, we will return to Konigsberg and work side by side." He told me all about his ophthalmology practice there and how he longed to return-only this time, I'd be with him. I allowed myself to daydream and plan for a future with him.

While we respected one another professionally, he made me feel like a desirable woman. I loved him more each day, and on those rare occasions when we embraced, I wanted to hold him forever. I reflected that perhaps our love waxed strong and developed quickly because we were older. I hoped that this awful war would not steal my future away once more.

SEPTEMBER 14th We sweltered in the miserable summer as we traveled through northern Russia. The heat and humidity along with the swarms of mosquitoes so thick we had to wear shoulder-length veils, sapped me of my usual energy. When the commander decided to increase the train capacity by one hundred beds, we were all given leaves as this would take two weeks.

The front line continued to expand along with the ongoing conquest of Leningrad, and as a result, the numbers of wounded were mounting. For Hitler's summer offensive, he had obtained fifty-two additional divisions of Hungarians, Romanians, Italians, Slovakians and Spaniards. Hitler had two main objectives: take Stalingrad and the Caucasus mountains, and he ignored the warning of his generals that this was too much. The rapid advance began under the direction of General Fred Paulus. In the Ukraine, Kiev was surrounded by German Panzers and taken. General Runstedt, along with Field Marshall von Reichinau, overran all of the Ukraine, continuing on to Krakov, Rostov, the gateway to the Caucasus mountains. (Nikita Krushev was a Ukranian commissar.) In August, the Nazi flag was planted on Mt. Elbrus.

The Sixth Army was sent to Stalingrad and camped at the Volga River, surrounding the city on all sides, except for the 30 miles along the Volga River. They took most of the city, block by block while a Nazi division came to mine the buildings and burn out the town reducing it to rubble. But the ultimate victory was denied Hitler. In November, the Russians mounted a new offensive with huge reinforcements under General Georgi Zhukov. By the end of January, the Sixth army was exhausted and running out of food and ammunition. Trapped on a snowy bend of the Volga River and no longer able to fight both the winter and the massive offensive, General Paulus surrendered the Sixth Army to the Russians. There were only ninety-one thousand emaciated, ragged survivors out of three hundred-thousand. And of these, only five-thousand ever made it back to Germany. The myth of Hitler's invincibility was shattered with this defeat, and he became more reclusive, avoiding visits to the Front. This was not only a devastating blow for Germany, but a turning point of the war.

Elsewhere, German and Italian troops were trapped in Africa. General Erwin Rommel, even though hit hard and overwhelmed, was told by Hitler not to surrender. British and American troops were landing in Morocco and Algeria, and the Italians had already lost in Albania and Liga. The spreading out of his forces would be Hitler's undoing. The Americans were also fighting Japan throughout the Pacific from Guadalcanal to the Solomon Islands.

I was excited when I rang the door bell at home. Would everything be the same? Would Papa's great leather chair still be there by the fireplace? Hans opened the door and his eyes widened in surprise when he saw me. "Tante Tabea!" he cried as he went running down the hall, leaving me standing on the doorstep. I heard him shouting "Come Opa, come Tante Deborah."

Soon Papa appeared, shuffling down the hall, muttering, "What's all the excitement about?" Then he saw me and rushed to give me a hug. "I can't believe you're here, Tabea. Come inside," he said as he took my bag and ushered me in. Once inside, I glanced in the parlor and was relieved to see that nothing had changed.

Deborah came in then and hugged me, too, and told me that I looked tired. She wanted me to tell her about everything–once I'd rested. Hans came rushing back, his cheeks flushed with excitement. "Oh Tante Tabea, my mother is still in Rendsburg, and she's being trained for flak defense," he burst out with a mixture of pride, yet fear. I sensed he wasn't sure what it all meant, but perhaps that was just as well, I thought.

After I had briefly told Deborah about my life on the train, she told me about her latest success. She asked if I would go with her in the morning to the linen shop. Once we arrived there, she led me to a display of painted table runners and table cloths, all painted by her. There were beautiful flowers and colorful autumn leaves. I was proud of her. "Why they're lovely," I said. Deborah nodded, her cheeks aglow with pride. On our way home, Deborah talked about her plans for more painted linens, and the encouragement of the shop owner.

Once we arrived home, Papa pulled me aside and shook his head sadly, as he told me that since all the men had gone to fight, the women and young boys were taking on more and more. "I know the flak defense is needed to save the people. I just don't like the idea of Esther being in the army, and Hans here misses his mother. But we manage all right, don't we?" he said as he patted Hans fondly on his shoulder.

I found things surprisingly calm here in Griez. Although the bombings continued in certain cities, most people did not expect massive bombings. Nor did they expect Germany to be invaded, in spite of all the defense preparations. To most people, the German front was secure and the battles were being fought on other soil.

As I listened to the news reports from radio Berlin and to Hitler's speeches recounting our victories, I felt it was all so senseless, especially his theme, "If we remain united, we will conquer the world in a short time." Having seen the results of waging war in Russia and the toll it took on our young men, I was convinced that no army was a match for that vast country. I speculated about the wisdom of our generals leading our troops deeper and deeper into Russia. I had heard the rumor that Hitler, even though he had only been a corporal in the last war, usually did not listen to advice. When a general pointed out to him that he was spreading his troops too thin, he would respond in fury.

Father worried about the expanding Front line, too. "An army should only be used for defense, not aggression. This Hitler is power-mad, and not good for our people." Papa recalled the era of the Kaisers when honesty and patriotism were taught, and he felt a strong pride in the Fatherland. But now? I could see that he could not reconcile that era with what was happening.

I muttered uneasy good-byes to my family, knowing that our train would be penetrating deeper into Russia. But I also felt an uneasiness about them, too. I was not convinced that the war would stay on 'other soil'. Papa held me close, and promised he would hold weekly prayer meetings for the safety of the hospital train. He patted my hair softly and then looked me full in the face, as if to fix a picture of me in his mind. As Deborah and I embraced in a final farewell, she whispered, "Don't worry about us. I'll look after Papa and Hans." When the train pulled out, the sight of the waving hands of my family reminded me that we would all be praying and this averted the sense of doom I felt.

I had been instructed to meet Liesel at the Mother-House in Kassel, which served all the Ninth Army Division nurses by providing a place to stay, issuing uniforms, and communicating orders. Since it would soon be winter in Russia, we were given warm, heavy clothing.

I noticed that Liesel's usually sunny face was glum and she appeared so downcast that I asked immediately what was troubling her. "Oh Tabea, my grandmother made my visit miserable," she blurted out. "She kept warning me not to be like my mother. She doesn't seem to realize that I'm a different person. Sometimes she makes me feel guilty for being born." Tears welled in her eyes as she concluded, "Much as I love her, I'm never going home again."

I was stung to the quick to picture such an innocent girl being accused. I hugged her gently and murmured, "Liesel it's sad, but people often make wrong judgments not because of reality, but because of their own fears. I'm sorry she doesn't realize what a fine woman you are."

"Thank you, Tabea. While what you say may be true," Liesel responded, "I won't ever go back there. The Mother-House is my home now," she declared. "And when this war is over, I'll finish my training and become a registered nurse like you."

There was a light tap at the door, and we were told by the hostess-nurse that the Mother-Superior was waiting for us in her private dining room. The Mother-Superior was a petite woman in her sixties whose gentle voice bore traces of a French accent. Even though attired in the uniform of the Mother-House, a long black dress with while collar and cuffs and a waist length black veil covering her gray hair, she had the aura of an aristocratic lady. I was curious to know all about her, but it would have been improper to make inquiries.

She greeted us warmly, saying, "You field nurses always hold a special place in my heart. I worry about the dangers you face, and, of course, I am concerned that all the nurses remain morally upright." As Liesel and I described our work on the train, she was obviously pleased that we got along well together. "Continue to be brave. You nurses can do much to ease the cruelties of war," she said softly. "I will keep you in my prayers," she promised as we said "Auf Wiedersehen."

OCTOBER 18th We left by train this morning for Posen, Poland. I was curious about this town where my sister,

Liesel had been born years ago when it was German, because I had never been there. But there was no time for sentimental thoughts today as we pushed our way through the station crowded with throngs of soldiers. We had been given confusing directions to our train, and our suitcases, heavy with the winter woolens, were monstrous burdens. We clamored over tracks and dodged moving engines until at last we found our train hidden among some freight cars.

The paramedics greeted us warmly, quickly grabbing our suitcases, and welcoming us aboard like old friends. They had returned a few days ago to train their replacements and were leaving soon for new assignments. As we stood chatting, I realized how much I would miss them. (I also felt our work would be more demanding not only because they were being replaced with new trainees, but also because we'd be caring for more patients with less staff.)

I felt breathless and dizzy with excitement when Dr. Beckman strode in. He greeted Liesel and me with warm bear hugs and was eager to hear all about our vacations. He nodded sympathetically as Liesel recounted her unhappy experience. Then he turned to me and wanted to hear all about my family, too. I described their quiet lives: how proud Hans was of his mother, now a soldier, Papa's continued good health, and Deborah's latest art venture. Did this sound mundane? What I really wanted to share, but couldn't, was how much I had missed him. Not a day had gone by that I hadn't thought of something I wanted to share with him, or a place I wanted to show him.

He assembled the staff in the dining car for the usual pre-departure meeting. "As you are all aware," he began, "our work is going to be even harder now. We will not only be transporting more patients, but the harsh Russian winter will be upon us. I urge you to work together and support each other as you've always done. I know I can count on you." Around the dining car, heads nodded in agreement, and I felt a firm, though silent, bond among us, even among the new ones. Dr. Beckman then dismissed us with, "There will be dangers ahead, but I promise to provide as much protection for you as possible." The train left late that night, heading east toward Warsaw. At Pskov, on the Peipus Sea, we were ordered to Gatschina near Leningrad. I speculated whether this would be a dangerous area since it was close to Leningrad.

OCTOBER 20th We had heard artillery fire booming all day, but the sound was always safely distant from the train. Suddenly, at dusk, bursts of machine gun fire shattered the windows of the diner, spewing bits of glass all around. The sky lit up with red streaks of artillery fire, like bolts of lightning.

We quickly slipped into heavy leather coats and went under the cars, two under each car by the heavy wheels. The flames and smoke of the burning buildings of Gatschina, a few kilometers away, could be seen rising in the sky. Then the bushes along the track caught fire, causing us to swelter and cough from the heat and thick smoke. Tears rolled down my cheeks, and I tried to ease the burning in my throat by breathing through a handkerchief. I fully expected to burn to death any moment.

Around 3:00 a.m. the shelling stopped, and Dr. Beckman walked along the track, announcing that it was now safe for us to return to the train. Cautiously we crawled out, and I felt an ache in every muscle. We gathered in the dining car, marveling that no one had been injured. The only damage to the train had been the bullet strafed windows. I remembered the promise of prayer meetings for our safety.

Within the hour, we left for Gatschina, creeping slowly along the damaged track. Since the town was still burning, we could not stop but continued a few kilometers further to Babino, a small hut by crossroads which would now be used for a train station. There was three feet of snow on the ground, and the doctors and paramedics wore white coats for camouflage as they boarded the wounded. The toll had been high. In addition to three-hundred-fifty casualties in the sick bed cars, we placed additional wounded in the paramedics' compartments. After the wagon master had repaired the windows, we left for Pskov.

OCTOBER 26th I spent an exhausting trip since many men were hemorrhaging, others were moaning with pain and nearly every patient was depressed. Not only that, I found it unnerving to pass bombed and burned trains along the way, yet I refused to allow myself to anticipate a similar fate. At Pskov, we unloaded the critically wounded, along with a crew of reporters and photographers who had traveled with us briefly making a news film for viewing in the movie theaters back home. These men had lightened our depression, and also gave me some of their pictures. By now, I had become so used to all the sights and sounds of war, that the events hardly seemed like news to me. I realized then how far from a normal life I had come.

NOVEMBER 5th Our remaining patients were unloaded at Danzig in East Prussia, and we were given a three day rest while the train was being repaired. I was delighted not only for the break, but also for the opportunity to visit my Tante Magdalene, Papa's oldest sister, a widow, who lived here in an elegantly furnished apartment.

I reflected whether or not she'd remember me, but she welcomed me warmly, saying, "Tabea, what a brave woman you are. I'm delighted that we can have this visit." Her pleasant company and lovely surroundings were a refreshing change from the jostling train and grueling work. Tante Magdalene had always been an intellectual woman, being the first woman pharmacist in Germany in a day when few women had careers. She had married a college professor and raised two sons. Even now, at eighty-five, she was still very bright, and I enjoyed our stimulating chat. Tante Magdalene was the picture of aristocracy, with her silver white hair combed neatly into soft curls and covered with a dainty lace cap. She wore a long ruffled black silk dress, as all upper class women did.

We were both uneasy as we said our farewells, perhaps sensing that this was a final parting. I could not have imagined then the tragic end to her elegant life. *Near the end of the war, the Russians seized Danzig and left this beautiful city smoldering in ashes. Tante Magdalene perished along with so many others.*

NOVEMBER 12th We stopped briefly at Konigsberg for orders; then traveled along the coast through Latvia and Estonia. At Narva, Liesel and I made a special point to view the giant flowing ice sculpture of the frozen falls. Back at Gatschina, I was appalled to see that half the town was gone. The munitions factories had been flattened and only the jagged walls of building were left standing here and there. Since the munitions operations had been moved into the schools and field hospitals, the wounded were being treated in tents.

A group of soldiers, gathered at one of the tents, beckoned for us to come there immediately. Inside we found a seriously injured doctor and nurse. Apparently a grenade had exploded near the tent where they were operating, and the nurse's legs had been nearly severed, exposing the bones. We prepared her for surgery, and Dr. Beckman began the amputations. Meanwhile, the paramedics moved swiftly to board the other patients because of the bitter cold weather and danger of imminent bombing.

After the surgery was completed, I placed the nurse in my compartment, and assigned Liesel to stay with her. The young nurse's face was lined with pain and fatigue, and although she must have felt every jostle of the train, she never cried out. When Dr. Beckman came in to check on her, she smiled weakly and murmured, "Thank you for saving my life."

Dr. Beckman grasped her hand and squeezed it. Then he removed the iron cross from his uniform and pinned it on her shirt. "You are more deserving of this medal than me. I commend you for your bravery and willingness to serve the Fatherland amid the dangers at the Front." She left the train along with the other patients at Riga and from there was sent to her Mother-House at Marburg. I often thought about her.

NOVEMBER 22nd We were heading north toward Dno, when a furious blizzard struck. The heavy snow clogged the chimney of the engine and smothered the fire. The engine lost power and could not move. Within minutes, the train became so cold that we had to wrap ourselves in blankets and walk about to keep from freezing. The wind howled outside, and I watched as snowflakes froze on the cars, coating the train with a white frosting.

Working furiously, the engineers dug the engine out, cleared the chimney and started a fire again. Although the train began to warm inside, there was still not enough power to move. Not only that, the tracks were buried in deep snowdrifts.

When we did not arrive in Dno on schedule, the station-master sent out two engines and a freight car of twenty peasant women armed with shovels to dig us out. The rescue was timely as our oxygen supply on the train was running low. These Russian women were hard workers, and when they had finished digging us out, we invited them on board for bowls of steaming cabbage soup. They spoke German fluently and we enjoyed chatting with them. I respected the Russian women, and noticed that they were faithful to their husbands and did not become involved with our German soldiers as some women did in other countries. One of them told me that the Russians had mobilized all women from sixteen to forty-five, with the exception of students and mothers with young children.

We were towed into Dno by the two engines, but another day passed before we boarded patients because the ambulances had also been delayed by the blizzard. Snow had drifted over the roads, burying them under a thick white blanket.

The trip home was tedious due to the heavy snow, and the dreariness of only six hours of daylight. Because the gas lights in the sick bed cars were bright and a door opening would emit a flash of light, we could not have lights on while we traveled through Russia. Since the men were in total darkness most of the time, we carried flashlights and wandered through the cars after dinner to chat and joke with them, attempting to ease their boredom. We were all exhausted by the time we unloaded the patients in Gumbinnen in East Prussia, so Dr. Beckman ordered the train on to Konigsberg for the usual restocking, and for a rest for the staff.

I enjoyed marvelous evenings when Dr. Beckman took Liesel and me to an opera and later to a concert. I could almost pretend there was no war. He remarked again, as he usually did, that he wanted us to have a good time and forget about the Russian Front. For me, I was satisfied simply being with him and knowing that he cared for me. These happy moments made the hard work and uncertain future bearable. We were very discreet, but I couldn't help but touch his arm affectionately in the darkness of the theater.

DECEMBER 14th The beauty of this winter morning gave me no inkling of the drastic changes that lay ahead. The sun shone brightly on the glistening heaps of snow outside my window, and the trees sparkled with the ice ribbons wound about their branches. The train was in top shape, and I felt rested and ready to travel again.

When Dr. Beckman summoned the staff to the dining car, we anticipated the usual announcement of the next trip, but something was different this time. He walked in slowly, a troubled expression clouding his face. After a long silence, he began by expressing his deep appreciation for the way we had handled crises as a team and how grateful he was to have such a staff.

My heart sank. This sounded for all the world like a farewell. His eyes avoided mine as he announced, "I have been promoted to 'Oberfeldarzt', head of all the hospital trains in northern Russia. This is very sudden and completely unexpected, I assure you. I will be going with you only as far as the headquarters in Pskov. We are scheduled to leave tomorrow. Dr. Faber will be the acting chief, until a replacement is sent."

We sat in stunned silence. I could not find the words to congratulate him and watched passively as the paramedics shook his hand, expressing good wishes. Finally I could contain myself no longer, but ran to my compartment to shed my tears in private. Within minutes a very tearful Liesel tapped on my door, and we hugged each other like sorrowing widows at a wake. We were interrupted by footsteps in the corridor and a soft knock at my door. I quickly dried my eyes and opened the door. Dr. Beckman stood there looking at me quizzically, "Aren't you going to congratulate me?" he asked.

I looked down, shaking my head. "How can I? I cannot imagine living and working on this train without you." I wanted to say more but the words stuck in my throat. I felt my eyes must have mirrored my pain. Liesel, the tears streaming down her cheeks, quickly slipped away, perhaps embarrassed for her tears or sensing our need for privacy.

He came inside then and closed the door. Gently he put his arms around me and said, "I know my sudden promotion is a shock to you–it was to me, too. But now that I'm head of all the trains, I can order you through Pskov as often as possible so we can see each other."

"But I'll miss you so much," I blurted out. "I can't conceive of going on without you."

He nodded understandingly as he said, "I'm still your chief, and I'll make sure we keep in touch." His words brought only a small measure of comfort, but I felt I must congratulate him.

"You deserve this promotion, Dr. Beckman. You are not only a capable doctor, but you truly care about people. I'm very proud of you," I said as I remembered how often men on the staff had come to him with family problems. He never allowed ill feelings among personnel to develop, but always worked to resolve the issue. Even though he hid his tender feelings behind a reserved manner, we all knew he was warm and caring inside.

"Ah Tabea, your flattery will turn my head, but I thank you," he responded tenderly.

"I only said what's true, Dr. Beckman. Everyone on this train holds you in high respect."Strange as it may seem, and much as I loved him, I never once called him "Paul"–not even when we were alone. Was it this deep respect, almost awe, I felt? Or his wise fatherly ways? I didn't know. But what I did know was that I loved him enormously.

I finished my duties that afternoon in a trance, moving about mechanically. Liesel, too, had little to say to anyone. Lt. Preuss, noticing that everyone was downcast, announced, "Tonight we will have a celebration." He was a jolly fellow and a close friend of Dr. Beckman's, who could improvise a party at a moment's notice. So in spite of our heavy hearts, we celebrated.

But later in my compartment, my composure gave way to deep sobs as the heartache of losing him swept over me. I recalled the hours we'd spent together over the past six months, and how we had begun to know all the little details about each other. He never tired of hearing stories about my family. The uncertainty of knowing whether or not we'd ever be together again made the parting all the more painful. In my grief I asked the Lord for wisdom and strength in my loss. I drifted off into an uneasy sleep in the early morning hours.

DECEMBER 15th I determined to put my sadness aside today and appear poised and cheerful. After all, I would be near the man of my life for only a few more days, and I wanted him to remember me smiling. At breakfast I steered the conversation toward professional matters, and soon everyone was chatting. The morning passed by in a near normal atmosphere, and I could see that the others were as eager as I to make our beloved "Chief's" last days with us pleasant.

DECEMBER 17th Although it was 2:00 a.m. when the train pulled into the station at Pskov, everyone was awake. We gathered in the diner for our final good byes. The men were not ashamed of the tears that streamed down their cheeks as they shook Dr. Beckman's hand. When he took both my hands in his, I managed a trembling smile in spite of my aching heart. Then he turned abruptly and walked straight to the waiting staff car. The car sped off immediately, and I stood on the rear platform watching the tail lights fade in the distance. Was the most wonderful chapter of my life ending even as the lights were fading?

I came back into the dining car where Dr. Faber, our acting chief, was urging everyone to continue in the same spirit. He promised to help us in every way, especially emphasizing how important it would be to keep our morale high. I noticed that already his youthful air had matured. We shook hands all around, and once again a bond of fellowship enfolded us.

I returned to my compartment, but sleep eluded me, so I reached for my journal and put my grief into words:

"Der Ruf er kam, und nun bist du gegangen,
Der Zig ist leer, das Herz ging vonihm fort,
Und viele Traene der Belegschaftrannen,
Voll Dankes diesem treuen Herzen nach.

"Wir fahren weiter, aberwitzig Leben,
Wo bleibt die Kraft, der Inhalt, alles fiel
Uns drukt das Leid, und Stunden ohne streben,
Da warst uns Ansporn, edlem Ziel.
"Der Zug ist leer, das Innerste zerruetet,
Weil alle Herzens Guete hier verklang,
Noch merh, die edle Quelle ist verschuetter,
Der ein starker Kraftstrom uns entsprang.

"Die Zeit geht ja wohl ihren Gang so weiter,
Befehl und Tat, doch ohne Kraft aund Sinn,
Was stimmte uns denn wohl noch heiter,
Ging doch das Beste aus dem Zuge hin.

"Doch wenn wir leider non nich mehr erreichen,
Des frohen Kreises Jahre an der Zahl,
So soll das unverges'ne Einst uns leuchten,
Mit Wehmut sagen wir, "'Er war einmal."

"Und unser Wunsch? Moeg gutes dir begegnen,
Moeg Freude, Liebe and Zufreidenheit,
Dir weiterhin die Arbeitssteatte segnen,
Wir denken Dein in steter Dankbarkeit."

The translation of my poem into English is not word for word, and the rhyme is lost, but the thoughts expressed are something like this:

"The call has come, and now you have left.
The train seems empty, without a heart.
Tears have flowed down many cheeks
We love and thank you for all you have done.

"We ride on and will do our duty
But without your encouragement, your friendly word.
We are depressed, and pass listless hours
Remembering you, our inspiration, our guide.

"The train seems empty, the family circle broken.
Because the heart is gone, the pulse is still.
But more than that has left; the fountain of kindness
Who guided us each day is gone.

"But time will pass. There is work to do.
Orders, actions will be done, but without love, meaning.
What can make us enthusiastic again
with our inspiration gone?

"Now you and I are no longer together
To laugh, to love, to plan for future years
Must we forget all we were planning
And sadly say, "Twas once upon a time?"

Betty J. Iverson

"My wish for you, my love, is that
blessings from the Lord
Be always with you.
May joy and happiness follow you on your
way.
Thoughts of you fill me with love, hope and
gratitude."

My life stretched before me like the empty Russian
prairie, and I could not imagine then what lay ahead.

CHAPTER TEN: NEW DIMENSIONS

DECEMBER 19th. We often met other hospital trains on the way to the Front, and we looked forward to these chance meetings as an opportunity to exchange tales. Today we met a train between Dno and Gatschina. A paramedic from the other train told us how happy he was to be going home for Christmas. "I can't wait to see my wife and children again," he said, beaming.

He stepped out to connect a power line, and suddenly we heard a loud cry. Rushing outside, we found him lying unconscious on the ground. For almost four hours we worked on him, giving artificial respiration, but we couldn't revive him. Dr. Faber surmised that he had stepped on a wet track and was fatally shocked. How sad this Christmas will be for his wife, I thought. Her husband will be coming home all right, but there will be no hugs or words to greet her. Although we were all upset and shaken by this tragic death, we could not delay any longer, as we were expected in Gatschina.

DECEMBER 20th. As we drew near the tent field hospital, I was anxious about how we'd work without Dr. Beckman's leadership.   Having been warned of an approaching squadron of bombers, we hurriedly boarded over three hundred patients. Two engines were then added to the train because of the ice and snow, and we headed for the safer coastal route.

Perhaps it was the severe weather or the severity of the patients' injuries–I'm not sure which, but I felt uneasy. Most of the patients had frozen arms, legs, and some were losing even half their faces. Since the field hospitals were overcrowded, they had received little in the way of treatment. We promptly smeared Ichtiol, a thick black ointment, over the frozen areas. On the powder burns and frostbite wounds we used a cod liver oil ointment. Although we had huge barrels of these ointments on board, we nearly depleted our supply. Once we had applied the ointment, we bandaged the area, and did not remove these dressings for three or four days. We had learned from bitter experience that if we removed them too soon, whole pieces of flesh sloughed away. Unfortunately most of the frozen limbs, especially the feet, did not heal well and had to be amputated later. Facial wounds and missing ears were usually skin grafted.

Some of the patients described to me the icy winds from the northeast that made them feel like they were in a constant deep-freeze. Even if the sun appeared, the day continued to grow colder. "And we didn't even have the proper winter uniforms," one complained. "If a supply did come in, there was never enough for everyone. Did you see our boots? They gave us just ordinary army boots, which don't hold any warmth." He glanced down at his frozen feet. I shook my head sadly, knowing full well that those feet would have to be amputated, and I sensed he knew it, too.

When a nurse in an army hospital told me that the Nazi officers often accused the amputees of filling their boots with water so their feet would freeze and they wouldn't have to fight, I muttered in anger, "How typical of the Nazis. It's obvious they've never been to Russia in the winter." Since the temperature seldom rose above 58 degrees below zero, (Fahrenheit) it was always chilly inside the train. This was ideal for the frostbite patients, but we were always cold. The cold combined with the putrid stench of rotting flesh permeating the train, and I couldn't wait for the journey to end. I was enormously relieved to reach Tilsit and transfer these patients to the hospital there.

DECEMBER 24th By late afternoon the train was empty, and Liesel and I sat down wearily in the dining car with a cup of coffee. We both felt gloomy. Something clicked inside me and suddenly I asked, "Do you know what day this is?" She shook her head, murmuring that she'd just about lost track of what any day was. "Why it's Christmas Eve," I said. "I know it's wartime, but we must have some sort of celebration."

At that she perked up, and soon the two of us were strolling about downtown Tilsit, looking for a small tree. We also bought a few decorations, and decorated both the tree and the diner for a Christmas party. In spite of our efforts, the usual joy was lacking in our voices when we sang Christmas carols. Even Lt. Preuss, who could always be counted on to brighten any situation, was morose, and Dr. Faber appeared preoccupied.

My thoughts kept straying to Dr. Beckman. What was he doing this evening? I had received a note from him thanking me for the package of cakes and cookies that I had sent to him by way of another train. I felt let down that he did not express any personal feelings, even though I realized that the mail was often censored, so of course he couldn't. Still I longed for some precious words of affection.

DECEMBER 25th. Dr. Faber took Liesel and me to dinner at an elegant old hotel to celebrate Christmas. When we returned to the train, we were told by the Wagon Master that they would need a week to prepare the train for the next journey, so Dr. Faber granted us six day leaves. My heart leaped with joy–surely at home my mood would lift.

Liesel came in to help me pack, and said thoughtfully, "You need this leave, Tabea, but I will stay and help Dr.

Faber." I looked up in surprise, and she continued, "I really meant it when I said I'd never go home again." I nodded, thinking she was still smarting from her grandmother's accusations during her last visit. I suspected that Liesel would enjoy staying here anyway, as the men treated her either as a daughter or a sister. As attractive as she was, she managed to keep relationships platonic, as if she were fearful.

"I'll miss you, Liesel," I said as I hugged her. "I know the time off will do us both good." Since the notice was short, I could not notify my family that I was coming, so I surprised them again. We had a reunion, since Esther was home too on a Christmas furlough.

DECEMBER 28th. My little sister was still the picture of a disciplined soldier in her neat uniform and erect posture, only now she looked tired with creases across her forehead and deep circles beneath her eyes. I asked her if she was still operating the search lights. "Oh yes," she nodded. "Not only that, I'm now teaching other women and boys to operate them. This is often hard for the weaker ones, because the search lights are awkward and heavy to move about. Many of the women are scared because they've been told that the search-lights are often the target of bombs."

Esther got up suddenly and headed for her room. "I have something to show you," she said mysteriously. Upon her return, she proudly laid in my lap a certificate commending her for good marksmanship. I told her that she must have inherited her talent from Papa. We knew that as a young man, father had served with the Jager Company, an army unit of the finest marksmen.

Papa shook his head sadly. "I don't mind Esther learning to fire a gun. I just wish she didn't have to learn it as a soldier. It's a paradox to me: one of you is trained to wound and the other is trained to heal."

"Oh Papa, I would never shoot anyone unless I had to save a life," Esther insisted, tears welling in her eyes.

Hans came in just then and asked her to take a walk with him. Each time I saw him, he seemed to have grown more introspective and solemn. With his mother in the army, he not only had to be more independent, but was also missing the usual carefree time of boyhood. He spoke of the war so often, that it was obviously on his mind constantly. Yet Papa was proud of his little grandson. Deborah did her best as a substitute mother, although Hans confided to me once that he wished she wouldn't help him with his homework. "She really knows nothing about math, Tante Tabea. It takes me so much longer to finish my assignments when she helps me."

Friends dropped in to share holiday greetings. While I enjoyed seeing them, the conversation always drifted to the torment they were suffering under the Nazis. One man said, "I think these Nazis are bent on filling their political education camps, because they're avidly searching for people with even a remote Jewish heritage. Why I've heard they assign clerks to go through the files of all the churches." (The churches were the main source of family records, some going back as far as the twelfth century. All the births and deaths in a community were recorded in the church offices since they were considered a state institution.)

Nazi flags hung from the lamp posts, and pictures of Hitler were posted in all the restaurants. While I heard "Heil Hitlers" everywhere, I sensed a growing resentment and hatred of the Nazis by both the civilians and the soldiers. I often heard the remark, "When we finish with the Russians, we'll take on the Nazis." (I felt in my heart, that if Germany won this war, there will be a revolution.)

But there were also those who still supported Hitler because of his early successes, and thus patriotism flourished. Few dared to oppose his heinous practices from the incarceration of the Jews to the harassment of foreign citizens. There was no free press and a growing intolerance of religions. Even though stories about the Jews were told, few believed them, especially any reference to atrocities. It was essential to the Nazi ideology to keep alive the tale that the "evils of life" were due to the Jews.

When the time came for me to leave, our good byes were said with heavy hearts. Yet this reunion had given me new strength to serve. With the prayers of my loved ones going with me, I had the assurance of being in God's hands, no matter what happened. Sometimes I felt as if I had two homes. While I loved being with my family, I also looked forward to returning to the hospital train that had become my second home. But more than anything else, I lived in anticipation of those chance meetings with Dr. Beckman.

JANUARY 3rd, 1943. I met the train back in Konigsberg, and was told we'd be leaving in the morning. Dr. Faber, looking more rested, greeted me enthusiastically and said, "Wagner's opera, Lohengrin is in town and I'd like to take you and Liesel see it tonight." I accepted with pleasure, for anything cultural was a welcome break from the monotony of the train.

Lohengrin was quite dramatic and one of Wagner's most popular operas, even though it was a tragedy. The premiere, conducted by Litz on August 28, 1851, was held in the small town of Weimar, but ten years passed before Wagner saw a performance of his opera. Abounding in folklore, the story is based on the historical character of King Henry I of Germany.

The powerful music held me spellbound. As the tenor sang the soft lyrics of the king's prayer, I felt as if he were singing just to me:

"Oh Lord our God be with us now, give us Thy judgment clear and strong.

Before Thy word all men shall bow, that right may triumph over wrong.

Give strength to him whose heart is true, and give the guilty one his due.

Lord let Thy will to us be known, wisdom is found in Thee alone.

Show us Thy wisdom's holy light, do Thou O God defend the right.

O Lord our God, defend the right."

The tenor sang the song with such fervor, that the opera house seemed transformed into a heavenly scene, more moving than any church service I could recall. The entire audience sat transfixed like characters in a painting. I, too, was in a trance, transported back to my childhood where music was the heart in the body of our family. If one of us girls went into the music room, the rest would soon follow. Before long, we would have a concert going. Often father would join us on his zither, and mother sang in her operatic voice.

I felt Liesel shaking my arm and asking if I was all right. Abruptly I came back to the real world, a world that was badly hurting and I had a place in it. I felt strangely content, as I murmured, "I'm fine."

We walked back to the train in silence and sat in the diner until two in the morning discussing the opera over glasses of wine. Liesel who had seen very few operas, said she was nearly overwhelmed by Lohengrin. We were interrupted by the Wagon Master, who came in to announce our departure. Before heading for our compartments, we joined hands, vowing to work together as always. The stimulating evening kept me from sleeping, so I poured out my thoughts in a letter to Papa. The steady sway of the moving train finally lulled me to sleep.

JANUARY 12th. The mounting excitement among us grew until we were like children anticipating a holiday. We were nearing Pskov, the new home of Dr. Beckman. I inspected my face in the mirror over and over again, wondering if it was still "the kindest, most beautiful face in the world." And suddenly there he was standing on the station platform. My Dr. Beckman. After he had greeted us formally and handed the orders to Dr. Faber, he boarded the train for inspection. He commended us for managing the transport of such large numbers of wounded so well. "We were only doing what you taught us," I responded.

And then we had two hours alone together, and I felt the world slip away and time stand still. "I miss you terribly, Tabea, God only knows how much. And the others, too. Here I am surrounded by aloof officers who are business-like during the day and usually drunk at night." My heart went out to him. He was so lonely, and the dreary climate of Russia only added to his misery.

In his own unselfish way, he was more concerned about me. Taking my hands in his, he said reassuringly, "This will not last forever, Tabea. We will have a future together, but for now all we can do is wait." I nodded, wanting desperately to believe him-that we would have a future together.

"If only we weren't apart," I lamented. "Sometimes I think that separations are the cruelest blows the war deals us." When it was time to go, I felt I could not bear to leave him and only rushed to board the train at the last moment. As the train pulled out, he stood watching on the platform waving good bye with a fixed smile.

Liesel and I could talk of nothing for hours but our visit with him. "Wouldn't it be wonderful if he came back on this train?" Liesel asked brightly. But we both know this was idle dreaming, like a child wishing on a star.

JANUARY 15th. We were near Gatschina when numerous military transports on the track blocked our way. Dr. Faber told us it would be at least another day before we could enter the town. Not one to be idle, he arranged a tour for twelve of us to a unique castle nearby.

This enormous stone castle sat on the flat landscape like a long gray box. A Polish Baron met us at the door. He had been placed here as the manager by the German army. He ushered us into the green room; a small salon furnished with love seats covered in green velvet. Gold-framed mirrors graced the walls. He told us a czar had built this castle. His wife was a German princess, and she delighted in the elegant and pretentious furnishings of the 1800's.

The Baron, a short slender man with an aristocratic air, was obviously devoted to taking care of this castle. He proudly led us down long halls, carpeted with thick rugs, and pointed out the many paintings by both Russian and Italian artists. The banquet room was furnished with a long carved wooden table and tapestry covered chairs, ample for thirty-six guests. Heavy velvet draperies were hung at the windows, and crystal chandeliers sparkled brightly.

The Baron chose a small dining salon lit by candlelight for our dinner. He offered many toasts in fluent German, and we raised glasses of vodka in response. This experience made me feel again as if my world was a series of unconnected parts, very opposite, some almost unrealistic. This nineteenth century dream ended soon enough when we were back on the train.

Our train was then re-routed to Kirischia, a few kilometers from Leningrad. We traveled across flat, barren land with open fields as far as the eye could see. The day was bitter cold, too cold to snow, and I could understand why there were no towns here. Our pick-up point was simply a designated spot among the bunkers, and ambulances came from miles around to meet us. We stopped at a cluster of bunkers that the soldiers had built of logs and planks. Covered with snow, these bunkers looked like giant mushrooms, and only the machine guns protruding at each entrance lent a sinister air. In a tent nearby, boxes of hand grenades were stored, and mounds of cannon balls lay between the bunkers. I shivered at the sight of this. I was seeing first hand the life of a soldier at the Front.

We were not allowed to leave the train because of the danger, but always curious, I begged for permission to see the inside of a bunker and greet the men. I could not fathom how they managed to survive in such extreme cold. Dr. Faber finally consented, but insisted on accompanying me. We entered a bunker by way of a crude ladder, since the bunkers were built by digging deep round circles and standing logs up around the edge for walls. The bunker was quite dark inside, a gloomy place without light. When my eyes became accustomed to the darkness, I saw men resting wrapped in blankets on the dirt floor, while others gathered about an iron stove in the corner for warmth. The place felt like a grave.

The men appeared astounded to see me, and one said he'd never expected to see a German woman so near the front lines. Another grabbed my hand and said, with tears in his eyes, "Seeing you is like seeing my wife again." The uselessness of war struck me once again. These men were wasted to family, work, anything meaningful. The shadowy images of these men huddled in that bunker remained in my memory a long time.

Back on the train, we boarded two hundred-fifty six patients until three in the afternoon, loading the last ones in the dark. The men were happy to be in warm beds and appreciative of even the smallest service. One told me not to worry about any air attacks, because it had been quiet on the Front for two weeks. "It's strange," he went on, "I feel almost as if the war was suspended."

A wounded General was also among the wounded, and we placed him in the officers' car. Surprisingly, he was quite polite and behaved much like the ordinary soldiers, quite different from the arrogant, flag-waving Nazis at home who got medals simply for marching in parades. He had one special request, however, and that was for boiled potatoes. Apparently the field kitchens had been without potatoes for a long time. Dr. Faber ordered beef stew and boiled potatoes with butter for all the men. They devoured that stew like it was a feast.

Watching them eat such simple fare so lustily reminded me of the food shortages of the last war. I recalled eating potatoes and sipping black coffee which we'd made from barley grain toasted in our oven, and feeling like I'd had a grand dinner.

JANUARY 23rd. I always enjoyed the smooth ride across German tracks into Konigsberg. Since we were leaving the very next day, Liesel and I worked quickly to prepare. While the paramedics made up the beds, we sterilized instruments and cleaned the operating car. Meanwhile, Dr. Faber picked up the mail at the headquarters, and upon his return, invited Liesel and me to lunch. Since the day was warm and sunny, we took a streetcar to the castle. How beautiful it looked with its roof and turrets draped with snow. The lake was a sheet of ice, and the trees in the park glistened with iced branches. We walked briskly around the lake until our cheeks glowed, and I looked as young as my companions. I enjoyed my day with these two. I'd grown quite fond of them. Liesel, who was like a sister or a daughter and Dr. Faber, almost like a brother. We arrived back at the station just as the engine was getting up steam to depart for Riga to pick up patients.

JANUARY 26th. Our journey home from Riga was difficult since all three hundred patients were amputees, and needed far more than simply wound care. Once again I was at a loss for words when they spoke of the helplessness they felt when they looked at their useless stumps, where once there had been sturdy legs. Young men wondered if their brides would still want them, and fathers worried if their children could love a man unable to cross a street alone or run with them. While some men found God in the midst of this crucible, other lost their faith and nothing could convince them that "all things work together for good to those who love God." I had to speculate about what my own reaction would be if I lost my legs. And I remembered the young nurse we'd cared for. Would I be as brave and uncomplaining as she was?

At Loetzen, Poland, our drooping spirits were boosted by a reception for us. While a local band played and a children's choir sang, Red Cross ladies visited with the men, and wrote letters for those who requested it.

FEBRUARY 5th. We had a few days rest in Konigsberg after we had off loaded the patients. Then all too soon we were back on the train heading for Pskov. At the Duna River, the bridge had been bombed for the second time, and the army engineers had built a temporary railroad bridge by laying a single track over barges lined up side by side. The bridge looked so flimsy that we all stuck our heads out the windows like children on a school bus watching as the train moved slowly across. I thought we'd sink any moment, as the train swayed with the waves.

En route we passed through Pskowskoye, where the buildings were still smoldering from a recent bombing. Our train moved quickly into the open prairie. At a town, we could be the accidental victims of a bomb, and we had no flak car to defend us. Despite the Red Crosses painted on the tops and sides of hospital trains, the Russians often bombed them anyway since they suspected military equipment might be on board–and their suspicions were not unfounded. The German army often sent needed guns, radios, and electrical equipment to the Front in empty patient cars.

FEBRUARY 10th. We were all up early and dressed in our best uniforms to greet Dr. Beckman. When the train pulled slowly into the station, we all stood on the steps of the cars waving small German flags, and shouting, "Hail to the Chief!" as the train screeched to a stop.

Dr. Beckman's cheeks were flushed with embarrassment as he said gruffly, "It looks like a kindergarten class is having an outing." He then boarded the train for inspection and offered advice for coping with the relentless enemy—the Russian winter. His very presence among us was stimulating. Although we only had a half hour alone together this time to whisper our love for each other and our hope for a future together, those moments filled my empty heart. All too soon, he sent us on our way with an added flak car for protection.

The next day, we boarded over three hundred patients, most of them with frostbite. The temperature was again dipping to 56 degrees below zero, and the soldiers manning the flak car were replaced every two hours to prevent them from freezing. When they came inside, we'd give them soup and hot rum. On their long night watches, we took turns telling stories to keep them company.

FEBRUARY 17th. Konigsberg symbolized security and respite for us like a nest for migrating birds. We looked forward to our usual time of relaxation after we'd unloaded the patients and prepared for the next ones. This time our relaxation was cut short by a call from General Judal's office that he was coming for inspection this afternoon, and bringing with him our new chief. Suddenly everyone became busy from the Wagon Master checking his equipment to the cooks polishing their kettles.

At the stroke of two, we were all lined up in front of the train in our dress uniforms. We were not anxious about the inspection, but rather about the impression we would make on our new chief. Would he like us? Would he fit in with our family-like staff? These questions darted about in my mind as I watched them arrive. General Judal was the picture of a German aristocrat from his pencil slim mustache to his polished boots, but his smile was warm and his handshake firm.

Dr. Faber then introduced the staff, and General Judal presented the new chief of our hospital train, Oberstabsarzt (doctor-commander) Colonel Fritsche. In this moment, Dr. Faber, who'd done so well as our acting chief, became the assistant once more. Col. Fritsche was a short man, about sixty, with a fringe of gray hair about his balding head. His pale blue eyes blinked nervously behind rimless glasses as he greeted us in the cool polite manner of the German upper class. His cool manner made me feel uneasy.

As he toured the train, Gen. Judal commended us for the cleanliness and excellent surgery and emergency facilities. We'd made a good impression, but I was still concerned about my initial impression of our new chief. Reporters came in to take pictures during dinner, and when I saw my picture later, I was shocked by my sober expression. I had not realized the toll the war had taken on me. Without my prayerful relationship with my Heavenly Father, I was sure I'd have been in a far worse state.

Later that evening, Dr. Fritsche gathered the staff together, saying, "Let's get acquainted." He asked about our families, and when I mentioned that my father was from Saxony, his eyes lit up. "Saxonia is my home, too!" he exclaimed. As we chatted, he recalled being on the estate of my great grandparents, which was currently being used as a resort for the Hitler Youth Organizations. I thought how peculiar that little ties like this are so important. From that evening on, we regarded one another with mutual respect.

Dr. Fritsche announced that our next assignment would take us deeper into Russia to pick-up points near Leningrad and Moscow, where we would board members of the Blue Division, a Spanish Company. I wondered about these Spaniards.

FEBRUARY 25th. Our train moved north along the coast to Narva, where a flak car was added and guns and replacement parts were loaded in the patient cars. The highly sophisticated guns used by the German army were often useless because there were no replacement parts at the Front. The Russians, on the other hand, used less complicated weapons and could easily interchange parts if a gun jammed. When you added to this the Russian's advantage as skilled marksmen trained to aim for the head, the German soldiers were easy prey. The Russian soldiers often sat in trees camouflaged in white sheets, waiting for an opportunity to ply their skill.

As we turned south on the Leningrad-Moscow line, the artillery fire kept us awake all night long. When we reached Novgorod, the night sky lit up in a flickering sheet of crimson fueled by the fires of the shelling and bombing. Yet bombs continued to rain on the town as uselessly as matches on a bon fire. I could not believe how much of Novgorod had been destroyed since our last stop here. Houses lay in ruins, the streets were piled with rubble, and the field hospital was an empty shell. With trees broken off, power lines left dangling in midair, and the landscape pock marked with giant craters, it looked like an earthquake had struck. There were no people around, and I had an eerie feeling as if the world had come to an end.

This was a frightening sight, but I shrugged my shoulders and prepared for duty. The soldiers unloaded the dangerous cargo very stealthily before dawn, working by flashlight. Ambulances pulled up with patients and left with military equipment. Although only one hundred-eighty four patients came on board, they were a challenge from the start.

These soldiers of the Blue Company had been sent to fight on the Russian Front by Franco, who was allied with Mussolini and Hitler. While they had a reputation as good entertainers, they were poor soldiers and were quickly overpowered in battle. Since they understood very little German, we had difficulty explaining what we were going to do, especially to those who needed surgery. They wouldn't stay in their bunks in the patient cars, but were absolutely everywhere. I even found one on my bed in my compartment. I felt like a swarm of ants had invaded the train.

Their rugged, swarthy complexions made me uneasy, and I always felt they were plotting something devious. However, within a few days, we learned to communicate with hand gestures and a few basic words. Gradually my misgivings faded, and I began to appreciate their fun-loving ways and unflagging joviality.

One Spaniard resembled Mussolini and often loved to imitate him. When we pulled into the station at Luga, he appeared at an open window, his army cap perched squarely on his head, Mussolini style, and his hand held high in a salute. The word spread quickly among the civilians at the station, and soon a crowd gathered to greet the great Italian leader. Since he knew a few German words, he was able to carry off this impersonation convincingly–until Dr. Fritsche stopped him. Dr. Fritsche told me later that the man was so convincing he was afraid there could be repercussions.

The train inched slowly homeward over single track routes in the Russian plains where fierce winds howled night and day. We bid adieu to our jovial Spanish patients at Loetzen, Poland, and headed back to Konigsberg. What had seemed unmanageable became in fact a tonic of humor in an otherwise humorless war.

APRIL 25th. Today was Easter–but there was no sun, only a cold blowing wind, to welcome the glorious resurrection day. We were enroute to Gatschina and stopped briefly at Memel, where Red Cross ladies boarded the train with Easter greetings for us. We were used to the Red Cross receptions for the patients, but we were seldom the sole recipients of their attention.

They brought brightly colored Easter eggs, bouquets of spring flowers, and sweet buns and cakes. Their visit took away the dreariness of the weather, and I saw the joy of Easter in the faces of these simple Polish women. When Dr. Fritsche came into the diner, he was pleased to find us in high spirits and graciously invited the ladies to stay for breakfast. As they left, Liesel and I shook their hands warmly and I murmured, "God bless you, ladies. You have brought us peace and strength and made our Easter joyful."

We continued on to Pskov, passing flooded fields where the spring rain had melted the long winter's snow. Dams of hammered logs placed alongside the tracks kept the tracks from also being flooded, and in the villages logs were laid in the roads as tracks for the carts. As a precaution, Russian peasants and their animals were confined to their villages until the waters had receded. As far as I could see, the entire landscape was an ugly panorama of mud and murky water. Near Pskov, the rain stopped and the sun peaked through the dark clouds. Here the fields were dry.

Dr. Beckman was waiting on the platform to greet us and seemed excited about something. "Follow me," he said to Liesle and me as soon as we had greeted him. "There is something unusual here I want to show you." Leading the way to a remote corner of the terminal, he stopped before a huge cannon that spanned the length of three flatbed cars. I had never seen anything so immense.

"This is a "Dickie Bertha" which was shipped here yesterday from the Crimean Peninsula. I heard a rumor that it had destroyed the town of Sevastopol in one day." he explained. "They tell me that it takes sixty men just to maneuver it."

While its size and power were impressive, I was repulsed by the thought of such mass destruction. "Is there no end of ways to destroy life?" I muttered. Dr. Beckman also shook his head in disgust. I heard later that there were seven Dickie Berthas, used primarily in Russia and Sicily.

I waited, as every time before, for the little time Dr. Beckman and I would have alone. He looked tired and did not mention our future this time. Rather, he was apprehensive about the course of the war. "There are many, so many more wounded coming back from the Front," he lamented. "And I worry about you, Tabea–and all the crews going into Russia. Promise me you'll be careful and not take any unnecessary chances." I assured him that of course I would, but I thought to myself, what can I do about the falling bombs and strafing bullets? Our few moments passed quickly and ours was an uneasy parting.

APRIL 30th. As we traveled eastward from Pskov, Dr. Beckman's apprehension was borne out in the mounting destruction we passed the deeper we traveled into Russia. Where once the tracks had been kept clear and damage repaired, now trains of twenty or more cars were left burned out along the way like rusting metal corpses. Whole villages had been reduced to rubble as if unearthed from a previous civilization. All the while we continued to hear the continuous rumble of artillery, spreading the same waste with an unsatiable appetite. I felt this was no longer a war between armies of men, but rather a devastation. Like a ravenous dragon, the war continued to sweep through the countryside, munching cities and spewing out the rubble along its path.

Since stopping at Gatschina was not safe, we continued on to Pushkin, where the ambulances were waiting for us. Dr. Beckman's fears for my safety were not unfounded. Fighter bombers flew overhead dropping bombs while we boarded patients. Somehow they managed to elude the flak being aimed at them from the train. I focused on the ninety-first psalm in which God promises to give his angels to guard you in all your ways. In spite of the bombings, I felt secure in His hands. Soon I was so busy with the patients that I became oblivious to the whistle of the dropping bombs.

Several of the ambulances had been hit, but there were no injuries since the patients had already been boarded. When the very last man was on board, Dr. Fritsche ordered the train out quickly with the flak and freight cars in front for maximum protection. Under stress, Dr. Fritsche was a man who acted decisively and calmly made decisions and gave orders. Unfortunately, he did little else to help. Often complaining about his arthritis, he left most of the surgery for Dr. Faber to do. He was prone to be moody, so most of the staff stayed out of his way. On the other hand, he could sometimes be quite talkative and almost fatherly.

I felt relieved when the train began to move, for like a deer in the forest, in the war one is afraid to stand still for fear of being a target of your enemies. We proceeded very slowly because the tracks were bent in places and the road bed so torn up that derailing was a distinct possibility. After an hour, the engineer resumed normal speed, and I was glad to be heading for more familiar and safer places.

After five days, we unloaded the critically wounded at Narva. Darkness had fallen by the time we finished, and I noticed the falls shining like silver threads in the moonlight. Their rushing waters were a peaceful ode drowning the deafening cacophony of the artillery.

At Riga, we boarded more men to lower the census at that field hospital, and from there proceeded along the coast to Suwalki. These patients were well on their way to recovery and thus were cheerful company. Then, too, with the signs of spring all about us in the blossoming trees, the colorful wild flowers and the green hills dotted with sheep, I felt relaxed. We were beyond the danger of bombing, and I enjoyed the trip to our destination, an army base in Poland.

When our train pulled into the base, an army band struck up the Frederick Rex March. The hospital chief of staff and the director of nurses formally welcomed us to the base. She announced that there would be a dinner party in our honor in recognition of the dangers we faced. Before we knew what was happening, the hospital staff unloaded the patients and cleaned up the cars. Liesel and I were shown to our rooms at the hospital and were soon relaxing in hot baths.

At the dinner hour, clad in our dress uniforms, Liesel and I met the director of nurses in her office, and she then led the way to the dining room. As we entered, the band began playing military marches. I enjoyed an unforgettable evening of fine crystal, wines and elegant food, music and military escorts. I felt like the world had returned to that sense of order and gemutlich so common among us Germans. Promptly at eleven, the director of nurses stood, indicating the end of the party. I fell asleep later in a bed that didn't sway, and in a world that wasn't in crisis.

Betty J. Iverson

The strains of "Auf Wiedersehen" filled the air when we left the next morning, bringing tears to my eyes. A large group of doctors and nurses stood on the platform waving good bye, and I felt like I was leaving old friends. Back in Konigsberg, we were granted three week leaves, so that major remodeling could be done to the train.

MAY 4th This morning, Liesel and I boarded the vacation train, which transported army personnel on leave. Traveling to Germany from Russia and Poland, the train stopped only at Berlin and Frankfurt. Meals were served continuously, and Red Cross ladies handed out fruit and sandwiches whenever we passed through towns. While the ride was fast and pleasant, it was also risky, since this train was a frequent target of the Polish underground. Even on furlough, the dangers of war pursued us.

We went our separate ways at Berlin. Liesel headed for the Mother House at Kassel, while I continued on to Greiz, where I received a warm welcome from Papa, Deborah and Hans, who handed me a large bouquet of spring flowers.

MAY 10th. I felt restored being in quiet surroundings. While there were no bombardments in central Germany yet, precautions were taken to keep the town in darkness. Every home had black blinds on the windows, and curbs were painted white to guide the pedestrians at night. Since everyone wore luminous buttons at their left side, the night scene was a peculiar scene of white spots moving along the sidewalks. An unusual camaraderie developed among strangers as people exchanged "Guten Abends" in the still darkness. I felt no fear since crimes such as purse snatching or vandalism were unheard of and considered treason. Although the Gestapo was dangerous and feared, it did enforce law and order.

The Hitler Youth, fired by an almost mindless nationalistic spirit, continued working on the Autobahn, the farms and in special centers where they cared for the children of working mothers. The Nazi vision of the Third Reich stretching from Norway to North Africa was promoted in songs, marches and propaganda. I wondered how long the vision of victory could continue unchallenged. That vision didn't reconcile with the lack of military success I saw in Russia.

On this leave, I had the added joy of being home for my fortieth birthday. Deborah had ordered a special cake decorated with pink roses and a big 40 in the center. Friends dropped by to wish me "Herzlich Geburtstag Wunsche." (Hearty Birthday wishes.) I was grateful to God for the blessings of good health for Papa, who was still able to work at the church and visit the wounded, and the good health and safety of all the rest of us. While there was rationing, food was not scarce yet. Hitler had ordered that all the parks should be planted with vegetables, and school children be assigned to take care of the gardens.

Quite naturally, my friends asked how things were at the Front in Russia. I avoided answering when I could and was vague when I did answer. Back here where the war was white curbs and rationing, the war of rotted flesh, shattered limbs and destroyed towns would be incomprehensible.

I never really got used to bidding my family good bye during these uncertain days, but I was reassured that we committed each other to the Lord in prayer. As I headed to Berlin to meet Liesel, I speculated about the remodeling of the train. What lay ahead for us? All signs pointed to harsher times.

The Springer Parents

Father Hans
Rudolph
1865-1960
A clergyman

Mother Carla
1877-1930
A very devout woman who
suffered with asthma

The Springer Daughters

Tabea (left) and
Liesel (sister) circa
1920.

Tabea's sister,
Deborah
1955

Betty J. Iverson

Tabea Begins Her Nursing Career

Stae Hospital in Griez-Thuringen where Tabea entered nurses
training in 1933. As a graduate of this hospital, she belonged to
the Kaiserweter Mother House.

Tabea was drafted into the army in 1939, but continued on the
staff at the State Hospital until she left for Poland in 1941.

Two of the Sisters in Their Army Uniforms

Sister Esther with
son Hans – 1942.
She was drafted
despite having a
young son. She's
pictured here in her
sergeant uniform.

Tabea receives a
promotion to major
in 1942 because of
her outstanding
work in the
treatment of typhus
patients

167

Betty J. Iverson

Scenes from Ft. Modlin in Poland

Tabea sneaking out through the tunnel after curfew at Ft. Modlin.

A Sunday sleigh ride around the Fort,
pulled by a horse named "Olga".

1942
Isolation Hospital, Johannesburg, East Prussia

Cissy and Tabea in their isolation uniforms, used when nursing patients with typhus, a usually fatal disease.

Cissy (seated on the left in the dark uniform) recovered from typhus after an experimental blood exchange. This revolutionized the treatment of typhus.

The Hospital Train, 1942

From the left, Tabea, Dr. Beckman, and Liesel on the day they
reported for duty in Konigsberg.

Lt. Preuss in his compartment
chatting with Dr. Beckman on the platform.

Duty Begins on the Hospital Train

Tabea's first day on the Hospital train. From left, Liesel, the two unidentified nurses being replaced, and Tabea. In the rear from the left, Lt. Preuss and Dr. Beckman.

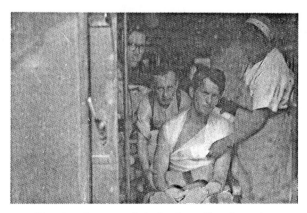

Treating the wounded after boarding the train.
Tabea is on the right.

Hospital Train Staff

Paramedics relaxing in their compartment

A group photo of paramedics

Wagon Master
checking the train
cars at Pleskau,
Russia

Scenes in Russia

German cemetery near Ljuben, Russia

Village near Pleskau, Russia.

Konigsberg, East Prussia, 1942

Liesel in her compartment on the Hospital train.

Tabea (second from left) and Liesel (far right) with visitors in front of the Hospital train.

Russians In Forced Labor, 1943

POW's repairing the railroad tracks on the Leningrad-Moscow
line in Vogorod, Russia.

Russian women preparing to shovel off the tracks after a blizzard.

Betty J. Iverson

Russian Children Who Came
to the Train for Food

Russian boy in
Podulsk, Russia

Russian child who
was fed from the
Hospital Train

Tabea with one of
the Russian
children.

Changing of Staff

From the left, Dr. Faber, Liesel, a sergeant, Dr. Fritsche, Tabea, Lt. Preuss, and a guest doctor.

Hospital Train staff and reporters socializing with POWs who were working at this stop.

The Transporting of Degraded Generals
February 1943

Generals degraded by Hitler because of disagreement with his war strategies. They are being transported to the Russian Front on the Hospital Train, guaranteed to meet their death in battle.

Tabea bidding-good by to the Generals. She was both sad and angry to see respected generals treated so inhumanely.

178

The Bitter Russian Winter

Loading patients at Ljuban, Russia in freezing weather—minus 75 degrees fahrenheit

Gatschina-Ladoga (near Leningrad). Russia children being fed at the train.

Betty J. Iverson

On the Russian Front, near Leningrad

The train station at Babino-Babagemo, the last station before
Leningrad.

A Spanish soldier imitating Mussolini
at the train station Luga, Russia

1944
Biala Podlaska, Poland

Tabea was head nurse of the kitchen.
Here she is with two of the cooks.

Taking a break from cooking for 1200 patients.

CHAPTER ELEVEN: THE WAR INTENSIFIES

MAY 27th "From the Steglitz station in Berlin, I headed for the Red Cross office to meet Liesel, who should have already arrived from Kassel. And there she was, looking rested and bright. She ran to greet me with a warm hug, and asked about my family, whom she'd gotten to know, as I had shared my letters with her. We chatted like two magpies, and I realized how much I had grown to love this young girl- as much as my sisters.

Since our train back to Konigsberg was not due until evening, we decided to see the sights of Berlin. With the bombings increasing, most Germans had adopted the attitude, "Get out of today what you can because it might be your last, and see those things you want to see because they may soon disappear." We knew that this lovely city had experienced some bombing early on and could only speculate about its future.

We took the subway to the Kufurstendam, an elegant avenue lined with exclusive shops and restaurants, similar to Fifth Avenue in New York City. We chose to have lunch at the fashionable Café Bauer, an exclusive restaurant with mirrored walls, five-course meals and wine poured as freely as water. I was amazed to see life carried on here as if there were no Russian, French or African Fronts. Seated nearby were stylish matrons with packages, probably their new spring wardrobes, and men in business suits conducting their business over lunch. Only the bomb shelter signs and the sprinkling of military uniforms in the streets were sobering reminders of the war.

Berlin, in the Brandenburg province and on the Spree River, has always been a popular city as well as being the capital of Germany. Founded in 1307, it had been the residence of all the rulers of Germany through the centuries, and was now also one of Adolph Hitler's residences as well. In the early thirties, the city was very hedonistic with nude and transvestite entertainers in the clubs. When Hitler assumed power, he touted Puritanism and banned jazz, homosexuality and prostitution. A bustling metropolis of over three million people, Berlin had everything: opera, a renowned orchestra, museums, night clubs and broad boulevards lined with blossoming trees and flowers. The most famous gateway into the city was the "Brandenburger Tor," a stone archway supported by six Doric columns at one end of the Avenue unter den Linden. (This gateway would survive the war intact and later be part of the wall that marked the division of the city into East and West Berlin.) The city was a transportation hub of Europe with four large airports, several train stations, the Autobahn, waterways for boats and an efficient subway system.

Liesel did not want to waste a moment, and after lunch we hopped aboard a subway to the charming Avenue unter den Linden, so named for the fragrant trees lining the street. Its beauty was extolled in popular songs, and on this spring day the air was full of the intoxicating fragrance of the tiny white Linden tree blossoms. We strolled along admiring the shops and lavish restaurants, and enjoyed a cup of coffee at a small café, sensing that this would be our last such excursion for awhile.

We arrived back at the station just in time to pick up our luggage at the Red Cross office. In a matter of moments, the charming scenes of Berlin were replaced with those of the harsh war. We were pushed and jostled about by such a huge crowd of soldiers that we could not even get near our train. Fortunately, some officers noticed our plight and cleared a way for us. Officers are usually nice to nurses, and I'm sure Liesel's pretty face was an added incentive.

The discomforts of war began immediately. We slept sitting up, crowded together for twelve hours, and our legs swelled in our knee-high leather boots. I couldn't wait to leave this packed train for my own compartment awaiting me on the hospital train in Konigsberg. But this was not to be. When we got to Konigsberg, the train was nowhere to be found and we were directed instead to the Red Cross headquarters. Wearily we lugged our suitcases into the office, and were handed orders advising us to stay at the Post Army Hospital barracks in Konigsberg until further notice. We waited there for two weeks before we were finally reunited with the train.

JUNE 14th A staff car took us to the station this morning and there was our train, looking bright and new, with every trace of battle hidden under a coat of paint. The biggest surprise was yet to come. Inside, additional tiers of bunks had been installed increasing the patient capacity to nine hundred. I was worried about the additional responsibility, since no more staff had been added. I shrugged and thought that more than ever now the ambulatory patients would have to help with the amputees.

I was not really surprised at this turn of events, since the siege of Leningrad was dragging on into the third year. The fighting on a larger scale resulted in many more casualties. Not only that, our trips into Russia were increasingly dangerous since well-trained Partisans were being parachuted behind our lines and blowing up bridges and railways. Since they dressed like peasants and lived with Russian families, they were difficult to apprehend.

JUNE 19th Our train pulled out that evening, and sped along the coast to Narva where the army engineer's makeshift bridge had been replaced for the third time. Gatschina was no more. I was shocked to see the civilians gone, and the tents of our army braced firm in the midst of a wasteland of broken cannons, bombed-out trucks and piles of debris. The seven hundred patients we boarded here had received little treatment and consequently their wounds were infected and foul smelling. We used gallons of peroxide to foam off the bandages which stuck fast to the wounds. The men had been given tetanus injections in the field, and some now showed the allergic reactions of swollen faces or rashes. I swept from one end of the train to the other, giving intravenous injections of calcium to counteract this. Since the solution had to be given slowly, I had an arduous and seemingly endless task on the bumpy train. I felt as if I'd walked a hundred kilometers by the time we reached Konigsberg. With so many patients to treat we depleted our medical supplies and would have to completely replenish our stock in Konigsberg. I wondered whether our government had been stockpiling medicines for years to prepare for this war.

JULY 2nd During the BBC news broadcast on my radio this morning, the announcer said that the Allies had invaded the island of Sicily, but four divisions of the German army continued to fight there.

The war in the Mediterranean was not going well for the Axis. As Italian troops failed in Greece and North Africa, Hitler sent more German troops to rescue Benito Mussolini from humiliation. The Allies maintained their advances in North Africa, taking Tripoli, continuing heavy counter attacks in the Kasserine Pass, and relentlessly fighting in the desert. Hit hard and overwhelmed by the Allies, General Rommel, known as the "Desert Fox" because of his cunning tactics, felt the wise thing to do was to retreat. He was forbidden by Hitler to surrender. Nevertheless, the Germans began to withdraw from Tunisia, and Italy lost Albania and Liga. Rommel left Africa in March 1943, and was succeeded by General Armin, who surrendered all the Axis troops in May, 1943. Greece had been liberated by the Allies by November 1944.

After he left Africa, Rommel supervised the army build-up in Europe in anticipation of an Allied invasion. Later, he was falsely implicated in the July 1944 attempt to assassinate Hitler. (Some of Hitler's officers attempted his assassination with a bomb in a briefcase. The bomb went off, only dazing Hitler. He ordered the shooting of the officers immediately.) Given the options of a trial or suicide, Rommel chose to take poison.

The Anglo-American campaigns continued in Sicily and Italy, weakening the southern perimeter of the Axis powers, while the Red Army was hurling Hitler's forces beyond the Soviet frontier. It was a slow, bloody climb up the Italian peninsula for Montgomery's Eighth Army which had entered at Taranto. Although there were air raids in Rome, the Germans continued to occupy the city until June of 1944. With the invasion of Sicily and Italy, Mussolini's prestige collapsed and there was much resistance to his regime. Known as "Il Duce," he had been a journalist, who espoused a radical form of nationalism, eventually founding the Fascist Party and becoming the Prime Minister. Unwilling to support Mussolini any longer, King Victor Emmanuel III ordered his arrest. In September 1943, Italy surrendered unconditionally although the Germans still occupied Rome and Northern Italy. There was much confusion as the Italian troops disbanded and either served under the Germans or reentered the war on the Allied side. (Italy had now officially declared war on Germany.)

Southern Italy, Sicily, and Sardinia were returned to Italian rule, while the Allies continued fighting the Germans in Northern Italy.

With the arrest of Mussolini, the Berlin-Rome Axis came to an end, but Hitler remained undaunted. He rescued Mussolini from captivity in the Abruzzi mountains, and made him head of a puppet government in Salo, Northern Italy. When Germany collapsed in April 1945, Mussolini was captured by Italian left-wing Partisans, who killed both him and his mistress, Clara Petacci, in a cottage on Lake Como. Historical accounts differ about the method of death, noting shooting and hanging. Perhaps it was both.

In the afternoon we watched as the private train of Adolph Hitler came speeding through the station at Konigsberg enroute from Russia to his headquarters in Rastenburg. I heard the Fuhrer speak on the radio that evening, assuring us that this invasion of Italy by the Allies would not affect our ultimate victory. "Our scientists are developing a new weapon and when it is finished, we will have all the nations of the world on their knees. My people, we do not have to fear an American invasion. With this weapon, I will have the world in my hands."

Hitler's speeches did not impress me, and I felt his assurances to the German people were not only unrealistic, but patently false. I had seen the casualties drastically shrink our army of trained soldiers at the Russian Front, who were then replaced with men as young as sixteen or as old as sixty. The wounded were neglected and consequently many were dying unnecessarily or not healing properly. Then, too, we had all heard the rumor that there would soon be an Allied invasion on our western Front. With the Russians advancing hard on our lines about Leningrad, swarms of Partisans all about us, and heavy bombardments along our route, we all felt an increasing danger to ourselves as well as the hopes of Germany.

We ate dinner that evening in an uneasy silence. Afterwards, Liesel came to my compartment and we talked at length about our future, which looked bleak indeed. I opened my Bible and read some passages from Isaiah, which spoke of God's redemption and that He calls us by name and we are His. The dangers sounded like what we faced. We knelt to pray, and in a halting voice I began, "Dear Heavenly Father, we place our lives in Your hands. And we ask, too, Lord that You watch over our loved ones back home where the bombings are mounting, bringing the same danger to them which we face–a danger for which they seem so unprepared."

JULY 6th The movement of the train awakened me early this morning. I lowered my window and the warm summer breeze caressed my face as tenderly as a mother's hand. The stars shone brilliantly, and I felt in that moment such a sense of quiet peace that I found it difficult to believe there was a war going on, filling the world with death. In that moment I felt that every nation was caught up in plotting and planning new ways to kill or destroy the beauty of nature, saturating the earth with the blood of millions.

Once again I was struck that this war had no good purpose. Did it make sense for fathers to leave their families to fight at the Front, while their wives and children were being bombed at home? Would this madness continue until the entire human race was destroyed? Why? Why?

My questions hung suspended in my mind. Yet gnawing at my consciousness like a stealthy mouse was the growing insight that as good Germans we never really asked questions-we simply did our duty. As the first morning clouds drifted across the horizon, I remembered a song my mother had sung with me when I was a child:

"Did you ever ask the clouds above why they are coming and going?
Why they move from South to North or from East to West?
Why? You ask. You know it just has to be so.

"Did you ever ask why you suffer so much, or why hate and grief are with you?
Why you are sick or feel without hope, left all alone?
Why? You ask. You know it just has to be so."

I had no answers to the "whys" of war, but in that moment, I knew that when I felt life was unbearable, trusting in the Lord would give me new life. As the sun crept over the horizon sending pink ribbons through the blue sky, I asked the Lord for a new spirit that I could nurse the wounded without asking "why?" The beauty of that sunrise gave me what I desperately needed: hope.

Liesel burst into my compartment looking as fresh and lovely as the newborn morning. "Did you see the sunrise, Tabea? Oh surely, this will be a better day for us!" Liesel took each day as it came, and once again, her youthful optimism shored up my new-found hope.

The next two days we were like trapped animals in the hot uncomfortable train cars, as we crossed the dry prairie. Because of the dust storms swirling about, we could not even open the windows, but sand seeped in anyway, covering absolutely everything. There was sand on our sheets, the floors, and even on our plates. The poverty and desolation of the Russian prairies was always depressing. The prairie was as unbearably hot now as it had been bitter cold in the winter. The people in the villages were as poor as the prairie, and most of them were glad to work for the German army since they could buy decent food for the first time in years.

JULY 8th   I was no longer surprised to see the once charming Gatschina now a dismal accumulation of hot, dusty army tents.   Once more we boarded patients but instead of heading back to Germany, we traveled north to Lagoda. Here a group of children approached, begging for bread. A tiny three-year old girl grabbed my hand, whining, "Madka. (Mother) Can I have some Hitler bread? It tastes so good."

I nodded and hurried to the kitchen. The cook not only provided hunks of bread, but gave out steaming bowls of soup as well. We watched silently while the children eagerly drained their bowls. They begged us to take them along, and I longed to gather them up in my arms and do just that.   I despaired over the poverty of these little peasants that would make them want to leave their homes. They were barefooted, for shoes were a rare luxury for children here. The boys wore drab loose fitting blouses over ragged pants tied at the waist with a rope.

The misery of those children haunted me, even though I was soon busy with the care of the newly boarded wounded. We pulled out quickly to escape the shells dropping all around. Our trip home was made even more tedious by the many stops to clear the tracks of wrecked trains or battle debris. By now I was so used to the sight, I didn't give it a second thought.

JULY 13th The day we pulled into Latvia, Liesel turned twenty-one, and we decided to make it an unforgettable occasion when we arrived at Riga. Another hospital train pulled in, and we invited that crew to our party, too. Lt. Preuss headed into town to buy a cake and a bouquet of flowers. The summer night was warm with soft wafting breezes, and we held our party outside. As Liesel came down the steps of the train, we all began to sing, and she looked very surprised, almost stunned. When Lt. Preuss placed the flowers in her arms, she appeared close to tears. She told me later that she was not used to such attention on her birthday. The canopy of stars and the moonlight were an invitation to romance that was wasted in the present circumstances. Still we enjoyed our camaraderie, telling stories and singing until two in the morning, long after the other train had left. I was delighted to see the glow in Liesel's cheeks and know she enjoyed her birthday. These light moments broke the tedium of duty.

JULY 29th Today, after boarding patients at Gatschina, we were ordered to proceed north to Pushkin, but were stopped because the tracks were demolished. We had heard reports that there were many casualties near Leningrad which would have to be brought to the train by ambulances and trucks. Dr. Faber and I offered to proceed further in one of the ambulances, under the protection of the Armored Division, to provide emergency care.

I enjoyed being alone with Dr. Faber. I had watched him mature into a fine surgeon and conscientious doctor. He never minded being awakened in the middle of the night, and could often be found wandering through the train talking to the depressed men. He never spoke of his family. I felt bold today, however, and asked how such a fine man had escaped marriage.

He laughed at my question and said, "I want to marry—and I hope to—when this is all over. I just think it is useless to make plans for things like marriage during wartime." He paused, and then asked, "And now I have a question for you. Why did you volunteer for this duty, knowing how dangerous it could be?"

I laughed and replied, "I guess my curiosity will be the death of me yet, but I just had to see Leningrad. I heard that the Front was shrinking so drastically that we would never be this far north again, so I felt this was my only opportunity."

I was disappointed, however, because we only got close enough to see the spires of Leningrad through a telescope. *While our troops appeared to be near enough to seize the city, they never succeeded because of the thinning ranks and the resoluteness of the people. By the time the siege was lifted in January of 1944, a half million citizens had starved to death. The additional troops needed for victory here were being shifted to the Western Front. Leningrad stood firm against assault, like a festering thorn in the hand of the Fuhrer.*

The journey home was nearly unbearable because of the intense heat and the flies and mosquitoes buzzing about. We passed out cloths filled with ice cubes to relieve the patient's discomfort, at least a little. One afternoon, when the train pulled into a small station to take on water for the engine, the gushing water spray was so irresistible, that Liesel and I slipped into our bathing suits and stepped under the spray. The water was so cold that it took my breath away and the force of it knocked me to the ground. But I didn't mind at all. I lay there chuckling and enjoying a delightful relief from the heat.

AUGUST 12th I was so excited when I heard that on our next trip, we'd go through Pskov. All I could think of was Dr. Beckman and how very long it had been since I'd seen him. Liesel was excited, too, and we went shopping for him. We looked for the foods which were scarce in Russia, such as puddings, sardines, herring, and fresh fruit. Lt. Preuss came along on our shopping expedition. Always looking for special treats for the men, he bought large boxes of tomatoes. We laughed as we remembered the time he'd gone into town to buy newspapers for the patients, and the train had left without him. "Ja–it took me two days to catch up." he recalled with a chuckle.

When our train pulled out in the early morning hours, Liesel and I stood outside on the platform to enjoy the ride through the Lithuanian countryside. Daylight was just breaking as we approached Pskov. Suddenly we saw to our astonishment that the beautiful skyline was jagged and broken. Gone were the huge cathedrals and onion domed churches, and almost worse than that, the train station had been demolished. The town was jumble of skeletons of burned-out buildings. Russian prisoners could be seen carting away the rubble.

My heart sank and I clutched the package for Dr. Beckman for reassurance. I hoped he would be there to receive it. Finally the train ground to a stop by a row of tents, and I saw him standing there, tall and dignified, amid the ruin. I nearly cried with relief when I ran to meet him. I hesitated as I drew closer when I saw that his eyes were empty of expression. Instead of a welcoming smile, his lips were set in a grim line. I searched his face for any sign of the love we shared, but saw instead exhaustion and despair.

He ordered a five hour stop for our train, explaining that he wanted ample time to prepare us for the days ahead. In a quiet matter-of fact way, he explained that our shrunken army was no longer holding the Front Line secure, and the bitter Russian winter was only a month away. "Gatschina and Luga will soon be lost and, as you can see, this place is a disaster," he said dejectedly, shaking his head. "We're losing in other places, too. The entire Sixth Army was captured at Stalingrad, but that crazy Hitler won't give up!" he cried angrily, pounding his fist on the table. "He just keeps pushing our troops, and if a general disagrees with him, he gets rid of him." (I wondered about the fate of these officers.)

I loved Dr. Beckman and cherished our moments together, but this time the moments were almost too painful to bear. I was grieved to see him so distraught, so hopeless, he, who could always cope with any kind of difficult situation. He had always been the comforting, inspiring person. Now he seemed unable to rise above his misery. For him, the war was lost, but for me, the war was destroying our love and stealing away our future. I had waited all my life for a love like his, and when our eyes met, I wondered if he read my thoughts. He only said softly, "The package you and Liesel brought means so much to me. You're still trying to take care of me, Tabea, and I'll never forget that."

"Do you think-," I began, but he interrupted me shaking his head and saying, "We cannot talk about the future. This Madman has stolen it away from us–from everyone." I wanted to hold him and shed my tears, but I simply told him that surely God would surely find a way. He looked up and said, "You have a faith in God, but I don't, Tabea. I only hope the end comes soon and stops this slaughter."

When the time came to leave, I trembled as he held my hand, but I managed a smile. Tears slid down Liesel's cheeks as if she, too, wondered whether this would be the last "Auf Wiedersehen." When the train pulled out, I wanted to jump off and stay with him, but instead I fell back with a prayer that God would be with both of us. After seeing the destruction of Pskov, we anticipated danger and four flak cars were added. Liesel and I slept in our uniforms, ready to move at a moment's notice.

We did not have to wait long for trouble to begin. First, I heard the shriek of a whistle, and then the train ground to a halt. I ran out of my compartment and the engineer told me that the car behind the engine had run over a mine and been demolished, but the engine was unharmed. Russian prisoners were brought quickly to repair the track, and in two hours we were on our way again. Liesel came in and we had our morning devotion together. She read from Jeremiah about the stirring of a great nation, cruel and without mercy, bringing terror on every side, causing anguish and pain as of a woman in travail. These words spoken to the Jewish people so long ago were startlingly a mirror of how I felt: surrounded by the enemy, but kept safe by the Lord's protection. I took Liesel's hand in mine and said, "Let's forget about ourselves and just try to be a blessing to others. At least, we're in this together."

AUGUST 18th I still felt the heat, even after we had arrived at Novgorod. There was a small lake nearby and I asked Dr. Fritsche if Liesel and I could go swimming. He assented, but warned, "Be careful not to swallow any water, because typhoid poisoning is a danger here." The water felt cool on my warm body, but the respite was brief. The alarm from the train pierced the quiet, and we hurried back. Dr. Fritsche met us on the steps of the train. He explained that he had sounded the alarm because he'd learned that the water was not only polluted but there was a large sea weed growing in this lake. It could wrap itself tightly about a swimmer's body if one Happened to be caught in it. Consequently, this lake was off-limits to us.

Soon the patients began arriving by U-88's, four place ambulance planes, and we boarded these patients until after midnight. Since the Front was quiet, we completed all the surgeries before heading back.

AUGUST 24th I was awakened by the movement of our train this morning and was surprised to be heading for another assignment so soon. In fact, Liesel and I had not even cleaned the surgery or replenished the medications. When I asked Dr. Fritsche where we were going, he only smiled mysteriously and said, "Wait and see." My confusion must have shown on my face, because he patted my arm and repeated, "Wait and see."

Since he obviously wasn't going to say anymore, I shrugged and left the diner. I was disturbed since he usually didn't keep things from me. I had always been informed of the orders. Because of the secrecy, we were all apprehensive and a mood of depression began to build among the staff. Since it was wartime, and the chief knew something he could not tell us, it must be dreadful. We ate lunch in an uneasy silence, that is, except for the two doctors, who were smiling mysteriously. I was frustrated because none of this made sense.

The train was heading north through East Prussia, when suddenly I saw the Baltic Sea glimmering in the sunshine. Soon we pulled into Seerappen, a seashore resort, and our train ground to a stop. Dr. Fritsche asked all the staff to assemble outside for an important announcement. We stood at attention as he announced in a grave voice, the corners of his mouth twitching, "You are here on a very important assignment for the next two weeks. I order each of you to rest, relax and enjoy yourselves to the fullest!"

We stood there like mannequins for a moment, not fully comprehending what he had said, confusion written on our faces. The doctors howled with laughter at our dumbfounded expressions. Finally, one by one, we grasped this incredible thing that was happening to us, and began to laugh, cry and hug each other, amid a storm of hoots and whistles. We smothered the chief with thanks, and beaming like a proud father, he explained, "I realized how hard all of you have been working, and I could see the strain taking its toll. These Nazis have a good idea in their strength through pleasure program. Dr. Faber and I talked it over and decided to plan this secret mission and use the program for our staff."

The engineer parked our train on a dead track at the shore, and we ate our meals at a nearby hotel, so the kitchen crew could vacation, too. Men, whose families were nearby, sent for their wives and children to join them. I could hardly believe that I was actually in a lovely village with white sandy beaches and a marina of sail boats and canoes.

That evening, as we relaxed around a campfire singing folk songs, I glanced at Liesel and noted with surprise there were big tears in her eyes. I asked her what was wrong. She shook her head sadly, "It's just that I was thinking of Dr. Beckman in that ugly place in Russia while we're here in such a beautiful resort." I hugged her and told her he would be pleased to know we were here–even if he couldn't be.

AUGUST 25th I awakened at six this morning to the sight of the sun glistening on the sea and the sound of waves softly lapping at the shore. I arose quickly, wanting to fill every moment of the day. Across the bay, I saw a two-story white stone hotel surrounded by manicured beds of red and white flowers and tourists milling about under the blue and white striped umbrellas on the veranda.

I plunged into the sea for an early morning swim and Liesel soon joined me. The men were up, too, and playing ball on the beach. Obviously no one wanted to waste a moment of this precious vacation. Soon we joined in, frolicking like children. Although we had our usual clean-up duties, I didn't feel like I was working in these surroundings. The hotel manager arranged for our personal laundry to be done, for which Liesel and I felt grateful since we both disliked this bothersome chore.

The sea was cold and on some days the tide was strong. One day I swam out farther than usual and panicked when a huge wave pulled me up, lifting my feet from the sand below. I struggled to stay afloat, waving frantically to the men on shore. They waved back amicably, misunderstanding my signal for help. Suddenly another huge wave pushed me forward, and I regained my balance and swam ashore where I fell exhausted on the beach. Only then did they realize that I had been in trouble and crowded about anxiously. Dr. Faber was adamant that I not swim out so far again.

Liesel had never been to a seashore resort before, and frolicked about like a young pony, swimming and relaxing on the beach most of the day. Typical of her free spirit, she persuaded me to swim in the nude with her in the early morning surf. I have always been modest, but agreed to try it and I enjoyed the freedom tremendously–that is until I spotted the men sneaking up to steal our clothes. We dashed out of the water just in time. In the past I would have been embarrassed, but today I found this incredibly funny, and we all dissolved in laughter.

Although Chief Fritsche kept to himself most of the time, he was concerned that everyone enjoy this respite. I played chess with him a few times and always found him a challenging and shrewd player. When we were on the beach, I would often look up and see him standing at the hotel, just watching all of us like a protective father.

SEPTEMBER 7th   On our last night in Seerappen, we planned a campfire, but different flames rose later in the sky. At eleven o'clock, the air raid alarms could be heard blaring in the distance, and we watched as a squadron of American planes headed for Konigsberg, not far away. Soon we heard a rumble in the distance and saw the tell-tale glow on the horizon. No one spoke a word, but I thought to myself that surely the United States would bring this war to an end. Now it wouldn't matter if you were at home or in the field, a civilian or a soldier–the war was everywhere, and no one could escape it. I knew there would be no more vacations like this.

SEPTEMBER 9th   As we were preparing to leave Konigsberg, Dr. Fritsche called us together and told us that a group of degraded high officers would be riding with us to Dno. He explained further that these men were generals who had either disagreed with Hitler or fallen from his favor in some way. They were now being sent to the Front to die with honor rather than being hung or shot at home. While most civilians were unaware of such happenings, soldiers knew about it and often referred to them as the Company of Heaven, an apt description, since they were always placed where they were sure to be killed.

Betty J. Iverson

We stood in respectful silence when the generals arrived accompanied by armed guards. Although they were dressed in the uniforms of common soldiers, having been stripped of rank or medals, everything about their bearing bore witness to their former status. They remained in their car during the trip, and we saw them again only when they left the train at Dno. I was sad when I bid them good bye, because unlike the uncertain fate for other soldiers, theirs was predetermined. I was outraged seeing such respected men humiliated like this.

SEPTEMBER 12th When we approached the Front lines, I heard the usual sound of artillery and machine guns firing all around us. I felt numb and went about my duties like a robot–without fear and without a heart. I was tired of the same ride, the same work, the same dangers and no longer even cared what happened to me. Life itself seemed purposeless. Towns disappeared overnight. Babies were born, who, if they escaped the bombs, died the next day in the fires, or the next week from starvation. With little shelter or clothing, those who survived these three beasts would face an even more cruel death at the hands of the approaching winter. I felt ashamed that I, a Christian, could feel like this. Yet here I was trapped in a situation that I could not control or even fathom. The "whys" would not be silenced. The more they forced their way into my mind, the more meaningless my efforts appeared.

Ambulances arrived with over nine hundred casualties, and my ruminations came to an abrupt end. I asked God for a sound mind for the tasks ahead. And I thanked Him for such a loyal and devoted companion as Liesel. I never ceased to be amazed that she didn't let the war dampen her vibrant spirit, but appeared almost casual about it. Perhaps when one is young there is so much future ahead that it outweighs the bad circumstances of the present.

SEPTEMBER 14th   Dr. Fritsche called ahead to Pskov, requesting permission to leave thirty critical patients in the hospital there. As dangerous as Pskov was, he feared the long train ride would be even worse for these men. When we arrived, Dr. Beckman was waiting along with ambulances. Although our time together was brief, this was a highlight in the midst of the void I was experiencing.

He appeared to have aged since I last saw him a month ago, and his uniform hung loosely on his once stocky but now thin frame. Although he tried to mask it, the despair deep within showed on his face as he lifted my chin and said tenderly, "It will be much harder now, dear Tabea. The Front is almost here and our army is being ravaged by the Partisans. Only those men too critically injured to move are being left in the field hospital here." I shuddered inwardly because he spoke and acted like a man under a death sentence.

Dr. Fritsche invited him to join us for a glass of wine in the diner.   When he told Dr. Beckman about the transporting of the degraded generals to Dno, Dr. Beckman shook his head sadly and responded, "How many more people have to die before that insane man does."

When we left that afternoon, Liesel and I both wondered if we'd ever see him again. Perhaps he felt the same way, too. But as we parted, he simply put his arms around our shoulders and said, "Be brave now, you two," as if this was a routine "Auf Wiedersehen" parting. We stood on the rear platform of our moving train, waving as long as we could glimpse him standing there, dignified and alone, amid the carnage.

This picture of him remained fixed in my heart. He was not only my love, but my strength and inspiration. I thought back on our six months together and realized they were the happiest of my life. I was grateful to snatch that little bit from the world that was going to ruin about us. I was determined that one day, somehow, I would see him again.

As we transported the wounded to the waiting gurneys, Liesel and I were busy chatting about what needed to be done for the next trip. We assumed that we would continue as before serving on the train together. Would there be other plans for us? We never anticipated any changes in the future.

CHAPTER TWELVE: LEARNING A NEW TRADE IN POLAND

OCTOBER 1st Liesel and I were finishing our usual clean-up duties when Dr. Fritsche called us into his office. His eyes blinked nervously while he fingered a letter on his desk. "I have orders here from General Judal for both of you to report to the Mother- House in Kassel on October 12th. You will be given new assignments." He paused and looked up at us, "I'm sure you've heard about the expected invasion in the west, thus many soldiers and nurses are being pulled back to establish a new line of defense there."

Turning to Liesel, he said, "Liesel, because Major Springer has commended your excellent work and skills on her reports, you will finish your training to qualify as a registered nurse. Later, you will be sent to France."

Turning to me, he continued, "Because of your experience at the Front, Major, you will go to Belgium to supervise a surgical unit there." A look akin to affection softened his pale blue eyes as he said, "I'm proud to send two such fine nurses where they are needed. On behalf of all the crew, I thank you for working so conscientiously during your seventeen months on this train." He shook hands with each of us, wishing us the best in our future. He then gave us a few days to pack and say our good byes.

Liesel and I were shocked at this turn of events and at such a loss for words that our mumbling of thanks for his kind guidance and our wishes for his safety must have sounded feeble and perfunctory. Foolish as it seems, we had never considered that we would be separated, even though we knew this was unrealistic.

We headed for my compartment and sat for awhile without uttering a word. The orders separating us had come so suddenly, so unexpectedly. I had never seen Liesel so downcast. I knew how much I relied on her bright spirit, but I had failed to recognize how much she depended on me. I took her hands in mine and said softly, "Liesel, you are a mature young lady now and well able to manage your life with the heavenly Father's guidance."

She looked up and murmured, "Oh Tabea, I will miss you so–but I know this has to be. I promise you I will be as dedicated to my duties and to God as I have seen you be." As we reminisced, we realized that there would be no more trips through Pskov and no more visits with Dr. Beckman. My last glimpse of him flashed before me and I said, "Let's write him a letter the men can deliver to him on their next trip."

The anticipation of new adventures soon overcame our gloom. With my love of travel, Belgium would be another country to see, and I'd heard it was quite picturesque. Liesel, on the other hand, could talk of nothing more wonderful than to realize her dream of becoming a registered nurse. We were both relieved that we wouldn't have to face another Russian winter.

One evening, Dr. Faber came by to invite Liesel and me to dinner. We accepted instantly, and looked forward to some time alone with him before we left. "Now Liesel, since we're disciplined soldiers who always obey orders, we must not let our emotions show," I warned. Liesel nodded in agreement as she hurried to dress and comb her hair one last time.

We met at a small darkened café. The menu was sparse. After we had placed our order, Dr. Faber looked up at us with sadness on his face. "I can't tell you how much I'll miss you both, not just as team members, but also as good friends. We've seen a lot of this war together."

Liesel nodded, as a tear slid down her cheek, and she burst out, "I don't know how we could have managed on the train without you. Oh, there were other doctors, but you were always so caring with the patients, and never too busy to answer any of my questions. I doubt I'll ever meet anyone like you again."

Dr. Faber looked embarrassed as he smiled, "Liesel, you flatter me. I'm sure there will be fine doctors in that hospital in Kassel where you'll be. And I know you'll be a top notch registered nurse." He turned to me and said, "Remember our trip to Leningrad that day, Tabea?" I nodded, savoring the memory, but not trusting myself to speak. "We only got to see it from a distance, but we were there. Yet much as I hate to see you leave, I'm glad you won't be exposed to the dangers of the Russian Front any longer," he said, seriously. "The hospitals in the west will surely be much safer." I nodded uneasily, doubting there were safe zones anywhere.

OCTOBER 11th On our last night in Konigsberg, Dr. Fritsche hosted a farewell dinner at a fine restaurant. Since food was becoming increasingly scarce, the fare was not only plain with few choices and little meat. The blackout blinds on the windows reminded us of the ever-present possibility of an air raid. At this time, almost half of the formerly beautiful Konigsberg lay in ruins.

Lt. Preuss, his dark eyes twinkling, strove to change the solemnity that was settling over us as the evening waned. Somehow he remembered every funny thing that ever happened from the time I fell from the ladder and swung about like a monkey to the time when the men caught Liesel and me swimming in the nude. Soon we were all chuckling. I gazed about the table in the dim light to capture pictures of these people, my second family: Liesel, the embodiment of hope, whose twinkling blue eyes implied that the sun was always shining; Dr. Fritsche, blinking nervously as usual, who appeared so cold at first, but underneath that facade was warm and caring; Dr. Faber, who was the epitome of gentleness and concern; and Lt. Pruess, a man of good cheer. How I would miss them–and all the rest too, from the engineer to the cook, who fed those Russian children, and, of course, the paramedics, who worked hard without complaint. I hoped our paths would cross again. So many people and places were already lost to me.

In the morning, the entire staff came to see us off at the train station, and sang "Auf Wiedersehen" as the train pulled out. When their voices faded, I glanced back at the hospital train for one last time, tears welling in my eyes.

When the train pulled into Kassel, I was struck by how much this city had sprawled since I'd lived here as a child over thirty years ago. The train station was still the same cavernous old building I remembered. Perhaps my fear that it would soon disappear under a rain of bombs like Konigsberg prompted me to want to show Liesel the city. When I mentioned my idea, she quickly reminded me that we were expected at the Mother-House. Still the memories came, and I sauntered along in a fog, wondering if the Wilhelmshohe Castle Park with those old monuments and the Lowenburg Castle were still the same. This whimsical pink granite castle had seen various residents from the King of Westphalia to the imprisonment of Napoleon III after his 1870 defeat at Sedan.

Most of all, I had loved the summers in Kassel when the Kaiser was in residence, because then we'd go to the colorful parades. As if it were yesterday, I heard mother calling, "Tabea, Liesel, are you ready to go? Will one of you see about Deborah?" I ran quickly to Deborah's room and helped her finish dressing. I was eager to go to the parade. And soon we were there at the parade route lined up at the curb. I heard the brass band playing as the Husar Cavalry came into view. Resplendent in their dark blue uniforms with two rows of silver buttons laced together with silver braid, their red capes flung over their left shoulders, they sat tall in their saddles on black stallions with silver bridles. Not only were they rumored to be the best cavalry in the Prussian Army, but Papa maintained that the Prussians had the best cavalry in the whole world.

But Kassel was also a time of difficulty for Papa. I remembered his frequent hushed conversations with mother, as he grew more and more quiet and preoccupied. Before long, we girls knew that he was having trouble at the church. "These Hessens well deserve their reputation for being hard-headed," he explained. "I can't interest them in reaching out to the community. They just want to keep their religion in the church building, and they don't want any changes there, either."

"Tabea, are you coming?" Liesel urged, looking at me with a puzzled frown. "Sorry," I laughed, "I was just reliving some childhood memories." I shifted my luggage and caught up to her brisk pace. We soon arrived at the Mother-House, which was nestled in the heart of a prestigious residential area. The Mother-House was an enormous three-story stone building surrounded by exquisite gardens and stone walls, with the air of a cloister. We rang the bell by the huge carved wooden door, and our ring was answered quickly by the Hostess-Nurse. She greeted us warmly, although she appeared to be a very business-like woman, attired in the customary black uniform and veil. Her main responsibility was to assist nurses passing through like us, and to take care of any who were ill. Graciously she showed us to our rooms on the second floor, the dormitory for the nurses. Classrooms, dining and the living rooms were on the ground floor.

Promptly at seven, the boom of a brass gong announced the dinner hour. Liesel and I filed into the dining room along with the other nurses. This spacious room was lit by crystal chandeliers and furnished with a massive buffet placed against one wall. The long table in the center of the room was set with fine china for thirty-six. The Hostess-Nurse led us to our places and then introduced us as, "Nurses from the Front who are passing through."

The other nurses, dressed in short, blue work uniforms, acknowledged our introductions with stiff smiles and brief nods. I had all I could do to keep from laughing at their formality. I had grown so used to the boisterous back-slapping ways of soldiers, who laughed, talked, and reached for the food as soon as they sat down, that these formalities were absolutely foreign to me. I bit my lip, gazing intently at my chair, not daring to glance at Liesel, who I felt must be having the same struggle. We stood for a few more moments in silence, waiting for the Mother-Superior. Finally she arrived, moving with such tiny steps that she appeared to be rolling on casters. She nodded for us to be seated, and then the Hostess-Nurse led us in prayer.

The Mother-Superior greeted Liesel and me warmly like old friends. She asked us to share our field experiences with the other nurses who were unfamiliar with army life. As we described the types of patients and the circumstances under which we worked, both during battle and on the bumpy train, I soon sensed a lack of interest, a cool politeness. Then I remembered that I, too, had such formal manners, but left them behind when the army beckoned.

After dinner, the Mother-Superior invited Liesel and me to join her for coffee in the living room to discuss our future plans. She turned first to Liesel, "You will remain here to complete your training. I will see that you are assigned a room and issued uniforms tomorrow." Then she said to me, "Major, you are to report to General Judal's office in the morning to pick up your orders for Belgium."

Alone in my room later, we giggled like school girls as we relived the dinner formality. "I'll have to watch myself," concluded Liesel. Then we talked seriously about what lay ahead for each of us. "Liesel, you may find it difficult to be taught procedures that you've already done many times before on the train. You may feel at times like you're starting all over again." I warned.

Liesel nodded in understanding. "I know what you mean. I've already thought about that, and I'm determined to be patient. Anyway, I'm looking forward to the welcome change of study and taking care of civilian patients again." Then we allowed ourselves to dream a bit about the future. For the first time, I shared with Liesel my hope of being with Dr. Beckman, and working alongside him in his ophthalmology clinic. "Oh Tabea, I suspected you loved him-that there was something special between you. I hope this will all end soon, so your dream can come true. As for me, I just want to follow in your footsteps." She leaned over and hugged me, saying, "We must always keep in touch, no matter what."

I vowed we would, and then told her, "I didn't realize how much Dr. Faber meant to you until that evening we had dinner with him." "Oh, it's really not anything," Liesel quickly responded, a faint glow rising on her cheeks. "It's just that he was so nice to me, and always treated me as an equal. No doctor has ever done that before. Usually they made me feel as if I was one cut above a scullery maid. And you did too, Tabea. You treated me like a partner, not someone beneath you."

In the morning, I reported to General Judal's office in the Kassel City Hall, which, like most city halls, had been converted into Army Headquarters. While my orders for Belgium were there, a change of plans was in the offing. The German Army, like most armies I suppose, is known for changing its mind. Dr. Judal greeted me warmly, and then fingering a telegram, he said. "This arrived this morning from a hospital in the Warsaw area, urgently requesting surgical nurses. Since you happened in today, I'm changing your orders from Belgium to Poland, and asking you to leave immediately." My cheeks burned hotly, but I merely nodded meekly, not trusting myself to speak. Inwardly, I was seething with anger. Why did they take me off the train only to send me back to Poland?

Back at the Mother-House, I glumly packed my things and said a final good-bye to Liesel, not lingering over our parting. The Mother-Superior sensed my disappointment and said softly in her lilting French accent, "The doctors are waiting for someone to help them. Perhaps you, with your Front Line experience, are the best person, and Warsaw, not Belgium, is where you should serve." So I went east again. At least it would be familiar.

OCTOBER 15th I felt strange returning to Poland, where the war had begun for me over two years ago. I had no idea where the Ninth Army Division Commander's office was in Warsaw, and I hesitated to hail a taxi because of the Partisans. I went instead to the Red Cross office. There I told my dilemma to a Red Cross worker, who offered to drive me to the office himself. In a matter of minutes, I'd been given my assignment, a field hospital near Biala Podlaska, about two hundred kilometers from Warsaw. I was told to proceed immediately. This kind Red Cross worker then called ahead to inform the hospital that I was coming so a staff car could be sent to meet me at the station.

During the train ride, I struggled with the apprehension and loneliness I felt. After the excitement and constant change of scene on the hospital train, I had a hunch that working in a hospital might be stifling, even boring. Would the surgeons be as arrogant and demanding as I remembered? How would I feel now taking orders from a head nurse instead of giving them like I was used to doing? I desperately wanted someone to talk to- but there was Someone. I poured my heart out, ending my prayer simply with, "God help me." And He did, in a most unusual way and certainly not one I would have chosen.

I arrived at dusk in Biala Podlaska, a little village of stone houses, churches, and cobblestone streets, surrounded by small farms and thick forests. Thanks to that thoughtful Red Cross worker, I was picked by a staff car. We left town immediately, the driver explaining that the Partisans were very dangerous here. While I rode along, I saw that the land was as flat as a table top and dotted with unkempt forests of scraggly trees and bramble bushes. After about six kilometers, the field hospital came into view, an enormous compound of one-story brown frame cottages and two-story stone buildings surrounded by a twelve foot high barbed-wire fence. Sentry guards posted at intervals about the fence bore grim testimony to the Partisans' strength.

We drove through the main gate after two guards had given clearance. The roads were cobblestone or dirt throughout the compound, with thickets of tall grass in the open spaces. This compound had housed cavalry regiments of the Polish Army, but had been converted into a field hospital early in the war, and retained the name, Cavalry Kaserne, which means cavalry barracks, the driver explained to me.

A rather plain woman, who introduced herself as Magda, the head nurse, came out to the car to greet me. She then placed me in the hands of another nurse, Ruth, who was warm and friendly and put me at ease at once. After showing me to my room, situated at one end of a patient's ward in one of those frame cottages, Ruth stayed awhile to see that I was comfortably settled. That night I prayed that God would take away my anger and use me where I was needed. Little did I know what I was asking for.

OCTOBER 16th This morning I met with Dr. Allanstein, the Commander-in Chief, in his office. Located in one of the cottages, his office was plain to the point of austerity with no rugs on the plank floor or drapes on the windows, except for the blackout blinds. Dr. Allanstein was short and balding, in his forties, with a round cherub-like face and rimless glasses. He was quite friendly and chatted amicably, taking a long time to get to know me. I guessed (correctly, as I learned later) that his degree was in psychology, judging from his skill as an interviewer. Halfway into the interview, he asked casually if I enjoyed foods and cooking.

"Oh yes," I said. "I learned to cook at a very young age because of my mother's poor health. I enjoy cooking and planning parties, and have even tried my hand at foreign dishes from Denmark and England."

"I see," he said beaming and nodding contentedly. "I have just the place for you. Tomorrow you will begin as Head Nurse of the kitchen. I could not believe my ears! Me-a former head nurse and skilled surgical nurse, work in a kitchen? I stood up and said stiffly, "I did not come here to cook, and I will not waste my nursing skills in a kitchen. If you do not put me in surgery where I belong, I shall write the Mother-Superior immediately for a transfer."

"Now, now, please sit down," he said patting my hand soothingly. He explained that when the request for surgical nurses went out, not only were several sent immediately, but the patient census dropped to eight hundred. There was no longer a need in surgery. "On the other hand," he said, "the patients have not had a decent meal for a long time because the kitchen is poorly managed. I'm not asking you to do the cooking–just manage and guide the staff."

I sat there silent and tight-lipped for a few moments until he leaned forward with a compelling appeal, "For the sake of all the wounded men and the morale of the staff, won't you please take over?"

His entreaty and my sense of duty won out. How could I say no. His gentleness and obvious caring also influenced my decision. He beamed and squeezed my hand, saying, "Wonderful, wonderful. I'll personally take you on a tour of the buildings tomorrow and will help you any way I can."

True to his word, the next morning, Dr. Allanstein took me though the buildings of the hospital compound, proudly introducing me as the Head Nurse of the Kitchen. The nurses I met appeared amazed that I would accept such a position, but he kept repeating, "You will see–you will see." I observed that each of the barracks housed about one hundred patients, with private rooms for nurses' quarters, a total of twelve hundred patient beds in all. Since there were over two hundred nurses on the staff, some were housed in a dormitory. The isolation wards were set up in the two-story stone buildings, along with separate units for the amputees and the mentally ill, while the large halls had been equipped for exercise and physical therapy. We toured over twenty buildings, which appeared clean and well-equipped. All of this I observed with the keen eye of a nurse. Finally we arrived at my new domain, the kitchen.

The kitchen was in a large frame building, and as soon as I walked in, I could see that it was not being used to the fullest advantage. Enormous brick ovens, centuries old, were standing cold and unused. They were heated by gas and large enough to hold pans of one hundred pounds of meat. When I asked why the ovens weren't being used, the men who were cooking explained that they preferred to fix soups and stews in large kettles on top of the cook stoves.

Dr. Allanstein then introduced me to the staff: three cooks, who had no previous experience; a group of twenty-two young Polish girls referred to as Paninkas, whose main duty was cleaning, but who now stared at me like frightened children; a sargent to manage the Paninkas; and two young Polish men to do the heavy kitchen chores, but who had the demeanor of educated men. The doctor then showed his stern side as he informed them, "Major Springer is now in charge of this kitchen. As a major in the German Army, she is to have your full respect. If there are any misunderstandings, they should be brought to my attention, and I will deal with them."

His introduction made it easier for me to step into the kitchen as the boss. After Dr. Allenstein left, the sargent showed me around. I could see at a glance many needed changes, especially ways to stop the obvious waste of food. I told the staff to carry on as usual until I had worked out the new program.

The Paninkas were so shy and subservient, that I called them in that very day in an attempt to set them at ease. These young women were dressed for work in simple hand-sewn cotton dresses and wooden shoes. My experience at Ft. Modlin two years ago had taught me how to work with Polish peasants. I felt they responded to my concern and were eager to please, as I assured them we would all work together.

That night I prayed for wisdom as I undertook this new task. While I considered myself a capable cook, I had never prepared meals for one hundred people, let alone twelve hundred patients and a staff of over two hundred including doctors with gourmet appetites. I would have a challenge! Yet I knew that no matter what I did, I could not fail. I had tasted the food and found it a colorless concoction of meat and vegetables all mixed together. Awful. As a matter of fact, the food was so bad, anything I did would be an improvement. This was a reassuring thought.

OCTOBER 25th   I spent a few days developing my program, and then took it to Dr. Allanstein, who was eager to hear all about it. "The first thing I considered was how could we replace the practice of chopping up all the meat into bits for stews and soups? Then I speculated that there might be some butchers among the ambulatory patients who could properly carve the meat." Barely pausing for breath, I forged ahead. "And I learned from the warrant officer that the meat is purchased at the army market. I would like permission to go there and select it myself." (The army market was about an hour's drive away on an army post where supplies were distributed to all the Ninth Army Divisions.)

Dr. Allanstein nodded affirmatively to all my requests thus far, but now I presented my most unusual idea. "Would it be possible to use the empty stables on the compound for four or five pigs which could be fed the scraps from the kitchen? These pigs would be another source of meat that could be smoked in an old smokehouse I discovered behind the kitchen."

"That's a fine idea," he said beaming happily. "I like all of your plans, and I can tell that our kitchen is now in good hands. Remember you can always count on me for support." While I knew he wanted to keep me happy in my new position, I was still quite pleased to find him so receptive to my plans. The organization of the kitchen was proving to be not only exciting, but a tonic for the heartache and loneliness I felt.

I sorely missed Liesel, and those occasional, yet poignant visits with Dr. Beckman. Although I had not heard from him recently, I had already received a letter from Liesel. She said she was enjoying her studies, had made a few friends, and the Mother-Superior was very kind to her. She ended her letter with, "I'm very happy here in Kassel, but I do miss you, Tabea–especially our talks." I was pleased to know Liesel was so well taken care of. As for Dr. Beckman, I continued to write him and to hope for our eventual reunion. After all, isn't hope the best medicine we have?

Soon the kitchen was running as smoothly as an operating room. Everyone knew his job and approached it with responsibility. The cooks learned how to use the ovens and the extensive array of huge roasting pans and trays. I not only found two butchers from among the patients, but two bakers as well. Somehow we managed to gather seven pigs, fifteen geese, and a flock of chickens which were all cared for by an elderly Polish farmer. In their spare time, some of the hospital staff had planted a vegetable garden and bordered it with colorful flowers.

I divided the Paninkas, who were now more relaxed, into two groups, one to do the cleaning and the other to help with the cooking. They alternated chores each week for variety. I learned much about cooking from these girls, for they were good cooks like most Polish women. I also let them bring pots from home for the leftover food, since the rations for the Polish civilians were very scant. Perhaps this simple act and the fact that there were no guards checking the employees as they left, contributed to our safety. Thus far, the hospital had not been a target of the Partisans.

One day, Dr. Allanstein brought in a large boar, weighing over one hundred pounds, and asked if I could prepare it. When I looked over the huge animal, I was flooded with memories. Wild game was sold in the fall in the open markets at home by the professional hunters, and mother had always bought wild boar meat. I recalled watching her carefully skin the boar, and then marinate it in wine and buttermilk for five days to dilute the strong flavor. "Well, I'll be glad to try it" I said, "but I will need a week to properly prepare it."

"That's fine, that's fine," he beamed. "I'm sure you'll fix a grand meal for the doctors."We began right away. The butchers skinned the huge boar, and placed the meat in a barrel, covering it with ten gallons of buttermilk, two gallons of red wine. They added bay leaves, cloves, garlic, onions and other herbs. After a week, the boar was ready to bake. I carefully rolled the boar in pigskin to keep the meat juicy and succulent and baked it in the oven. Then I watched over it like a doting mother and savored the aroma that soon filled the kitchen.

When the boar was ready to serve, I arranged the meat on large platters, garnishing it with all kinds of pickles. Accompanied by bowls of vegetables, roast potatoes, and burgundy wine, the wild boar was a gourmet feast indeed. The Paninkas wore their Sunday best clothes of beautifully embroidered blouses with full white skirts to serve the doctors in gracious style in their private dining room. After dinner, Dr. Allanstein insisted that I come into the dining room, so he could personally express his thanks. I smiled in response, beginning to feel like a real chef.

Soon my ambition knew no bounds. Once a week, I chose a group, such as the nurses or the amputees, and prepared a special meal for them. If a patient requested a favorite dish from home–he got it. When word got around, the requests poured in, and I was almost overwhelmed, especially by the many requests for potato pancakes. Now potato pancakes are a real favorite for most Germans. While they are not difficult to cook, the problem is that the potatoes must be freshly grated by hand. Since there was such a clamoring for them, and I was not one to go back on my word, I decided we'd have to do it.

I chose a Saturday for the pancake day since there were no scheduled surgeries then and some of the staff could help in the kitchen. The Paninkas brought hand graters from home and twenty patients came in to peel the potatoes. Benches were pulled into a circle in the middle of the kitchen, and while one group peeled potatoes, another grated them. The bakers then made the dough, and the Paninkas and I fried the pancakes. The hot pancakes were transported to each building in large aluminum kettles where they were served with bowls of applesauce. Dr. Allanstein came in to see what was going on and chuckled to see me standing over a hot stove, flipping pancakes. I turned to him and said, "I believe I remember you telling me that you weren't asking me to do the cooking, just to manage the kitchen." We both chuckled, contributing to the carnival-like atmosphere in the kitchen with the boisterous chatter, the singing of the potato peelers, and the antics of the men rushing in and out with the kettles of pancakes. When I finally sat down to eat my potato pancakes, I heaved a sigh of relief and vowed never to honor that request again.

DECEMBER 12th   The days were growing shorter and colder and a white mantle of snow buried the world outside. The flat white horizon here reminded me of the expansive white prairies of Russia. I had just received a short letter from one of the paramedics on the hospital train who said that the train had been bombed in Russia, but there were few casualties since there were no wounded on board. And I yearned to see, to touch to talk to Dr. Beckman. Although I wrote regularly, I had no word from him. But I continued to hope in spite of the fact that very little mail was trickling in from Russia anymore. Even letters from my family in Griez took weeks to arrive. My solitude was interrupted by a summons to Dr. Allanstein's office.

He began by asking how things were going in the kitchen. I assured him that everything was running smoothly, and he nodded approvingly. Then he shared the real reason for my summons. "Tabea, I would like for you to plan a Christmas dinner and program for the staff. Now one thing is very important," he said earnestly, "and that is that the food is served hot. Last year, the food was cold by the time it reached our plates and tasted dreadful."

I nodded understandingly. The good doctor, like most Germans, liked his food piping hot. The saying was, "Better a burned tongue than a lukewarm meal." "Remember the pancake day?" I reminded him. "The food will not only be hot, but we'll make some traditional Christmas dishes as well. As for the program, I'll be happy to plan it. I've done that many times before," I replied as I told him about my days as a Cornflower girls' leader and our patriotic dramas. He said that he knew he could count on me. I left his office thinking, here I go again–but I loved it.

Not wasting a moment, I went through the wards and found ten musicians, three comedians, two nurses with ballet training, and ten nurses for the Christmas drama, "The Ten Candles" which I had written ten years ago in Griez. Another patient volunteered to form a choir. The party would be held in the auditorium, a large cavernous building with a stage at one end and a piano, which was old, but in tune.

Soon the atmosphere of the hospital became electric with the excitement of Christmas preparations. Three pigs had been slaughtered and the butchers were busy making the traditional sausages, liverwurst and bloodwurst, to serve with sauerkraut at the party. Not to be outdone, the bakers were making creppel, a favorite holiday pastry similar to doughnuts, which is shaped into round balls, filled with jelly, and then fried and rolled in powdered sugar.

The Paninkas decorated the tables in the auditorium with white sheets, branches of evergreen and white candles in the auditorium. Some of the Polish men had rented musical instruments in the village, so the musicians were rehearsing Christmas carols. Ballet costumes were borrowed from Polish families, and I made angel costumes from sheets. Since the sheets could not be cut, I simply draped them toga style on the women.

Promptly at 7:00 p.m. the ambulances I had requested arrived at the kitchen to transport the food and staff to the auditorium where three hundred guests were waiting for the party to begin. I had trained some of the ambulatory patients as waiters and they helped the Paninkas serve the piping hot platters of sausages, bowls of steaming mashed potatoes and sauerkraut. By the time everyone was enjoying the creppel and coffee, I headed backstage to begin the program.

There were no Nazi officers here to protest a religious drama as there had been back home. Many in the audience had tears streaming down their cheeks when strains of "Silent Night" drifted across the room. I felt like Christ Himself was here among us, sweeping aside the divisive evil of the war. As I looked around the room and saw the mixture of Polish and German people singing together, a feeling akin to joy enveloped me. Dr. Allanstein was profuse in expressing his gratitude. "I will never know where you learned to do all the things you do. You are a nurse, you cook, and now I see that you have theatrical talent, too." I was embarrassed by his profuse compliment.

DECEMBER 25th What turkey is for the Americans, the goose is for the Germans. We began our preparations for the traditional Christmas dinner at six this morning, baking two hundred forty geese, forty at a time, in the large ovens. The butchers carved them, and kept the meat warm in a white wine sauce. Red cabbage which had been shredded and cooked the day before was now reheated. The Paninkas made large tubs of potato salad to accompany bokwurst, a customary meal for middle class families. I sent them home early that day with their pans full of food for their families' celebration. I suspected such days of feasting and plenty might soon end.

I was weary from baking all those geese, and left the kitchen early in the afternoon to relax in my room. I opened my mail which I had saved for this moment and found letters from home and a package from Deborah containing a miniature Christmas tree decorated with tiny ornaments and candles, fancy cookies and one of her hand-painted tablecloths. Papa's letter, filled with the hope and love of Christmas strengthened me, but suddenly I plunged into homesickness. The walls of my room closed in on me and I felt so alone, missing everyone who was dear to me, not only my family, but Dr. Beckman and Liesel as well. Then I found among the letters, a simple note from Liesel, which I had overlooked. She was still happy in Kassel and mentioned that she had heard from Dr. Faber. "I was so surprised, Tabea. He is being reassigned somewhere west, and hopes to drop by and see me on the way. Can you imagine? I will be happy to see him again. I wish you could be here, too." I smiled to myself knowingly.

I opened my Bible and read the Christmas story in Luke, reminded again of the wonder of the Son of God being born in human flesh, away from His Father. My homesickness faded as I remembered that everyone here was away from his or her family, too. I quickly left my room and joined a group of nurses strolling from building to building, singing carols to the patients. The joy of Christmas filled me once more.

JANUARY 1st, 1944 On New Year's Eve, all of us who were off-duty gathered in the auditorium to listen to the

Fuhrer's New Year's speech on the radio. Once more he assured us that we would be victorious in the war and assume our rightful position of superiority in the world. I felt sick listening to him. The seeds of hatred toward him had been sown when I saw the useless waste of men in Russia and then grew when I saw those generals stripped of everything, humiliated and then sent to their certain deaths. How could one man's evil unleashed upon so many continue unchecked? These evils were like a trickle flowing from a dam, but there would be full cognizance one day. Wary as always lest a Nazi spy be in the audience, I kept my feelings to myself.

At midnight, Hitler ended with the traditional "Sieg Heil," and Dr. Allanstein offered words of encouragement to us. We toasted the New Year with glasses of wine while a few men went outside to fire some shots in the air. That was the extent of our celebration. After all, what was there to celebrate?

JANUARY 4th I woke up with a temperature of 104 and a throat so sore I thought I had diphtheria again. A doctor came who assured me that I did not have diphtheria, but a severe case of tonsillitis and he admitted me to the ward for sick nurses. Dr. Allanstein was my first visitor. After asking how I felt, he sat with me for a long time. "I hope you didn't overwork yourself with all the Christmas preparations," he said worriedly. When I shook my head, he continued, "I really am grateful for all you've done with the kitchen. It is running quite smoothly now, and everyone is getting a decent meal." He leaned over and patted my hand. "Now I want you to have a nice long rest and not worry about anything." Since I could not speak, I merely smiled and nodded.

FEBRUARY 2nd I spent a month in bed and was still very weak. The infection had spread throughout my system, causing my joints to swell and ache. Dr. Allanstein decided that I should go home for six weeks and he sent a nurse along to accompany me on the trip.

Even though Greiz was in the grip of winter and the streets were icy, I felt warm and protected in the arms of my family. Hans was very attentive in seeing to my needs everyday when he came home from school. Since food was now scarce, he gathered vegetables for our family in the early morning hours at the farms. He had grown taller and, being a curious boy, was full of questions about the war in Poland.

After a few weeks, I felt well again and joined in the celebration of father's seventy-ninth birthday. Our house was crowded with neighbors and well-wishers from the church. This joyous occasion was marred only by the absence of Esther, who was no longer granted leaves. After our celebration ended, the phone rang and I answered it. To my delight, I found Esther on the other end. She sounded tired and totally immersed in her duties, but was happy to talk to me. Since she only had a few moments to speak, I bade her a loving farewell, and handed the phone to Papa so she would wish him a "Gemutlich Geburtstag."

MARCH 19th All too soon, the time came for me to leave, and an elderly friend of Papa's drove us to the station. Sensing as we all did that it was just not hardship but defeat that lay ahead, he assured me that he would look after my family. When I kissed Papa good bye, he said, "Tabea, I will continue to pray for you constantly. Remember we can go through anything with the power of the Almighty."

His simple words, reflecting his vast reservoir of inner strength, gave me the needed courage to face my uncertain future. Deborah hugged me tightly like a vise, expressing like all the others, that she knew there were dark days ahead.

Quite late that night my train pulled into the "Friedrickstrasse" station of Berlin, and the air raid sirens were wailing. I left the train quickly and followed the stream of people heading for the bunker in the basement under the station. Berliners had become accustomed to air raids since this city had endured heavy bombing for the past year. Although the bunker was huge, it soon became too crowded for anyone to move about and the air grew stale. Mattresses strewn on the floor were of little use in such a crowd, and the utter darkness was relieved only by occasional flash light beams. Surprisingly, no one worried about theft. The children were whimpering, some screaming, yet even above their cries, I heard the whistle of the falling bombs and the muffled explosions. I felt the tremors each time a bomb hit.

With each whistle, I asked myself if we would be the next target. I felt like I was waiting to be buried alive–which was much worse than what I had experienced on the Russian Front. At least there I could crawl under a train car and see the destruction coming. Here I was confined to a black hole underground where I could see nothing, yet hear the ominous noises. I hoped that the station above would be missed and we would be spared an entombment in rubble.

After thirty minutes, the sirens wailed again, signaling the welcome all clear. In contrast to the orderly way they had filed in, people now pushed and shoved to get out of the bunker and up the stairs into the cool night air. The sky was crimson from the many fires ignited throughout the city, and I heard the shrill siren of fire engines. Streetcars crept along in total darkness crowded with people going home to see if home was still there, while cars moved along at a snail's pace without their headlights on. Not even a match was lit, for fear the planes might return and see the light as a target.

I left the station and shivered in the darkness and cold night air. After a few minutes, I went back inside the station to the Red Cross office to inquire when the next train would be leaving for Warsaw. The office was so full of mothers and crying children that I could not even get inside. When I asked a passing conductor, he shrugged his shoulders and guessed the Warsaw train would not arrive for at least five hours. With the prospect of such a long wait, I determinedly shoved my way inside the office and passed the time by feeding the nervous, crying children, and soothing their mothers' fears.

MARCH 23rd When I arrived back at Biala Podlaska I felt like I was coming home, even though there was a strange grimness about the place. Instead of the usual car, I was met by an ambulance. The driver explained that ambulances were now necessary because the Partisans were blowing up all other military vehicles. "There are more Partisans showing up every day since the Russians are parachuting them into the countryside at night," he added. "Dr. Allanstein is not allowing anyone to leave the hospital compound unless it is of utmost importance–and then only with a guard." This is home? I thought.

Not only was resistance growing in Poland, but France as well, where the underground became more aggressive, blowing up bridges and trains. Hitler had begun to fortify on the western Front at the English Channel and on the south at the Aegean sea, but his defenses were uneven. He was expecting an invasion, but did not know where or when. The hoped-for victory that eluded him was due partly to his strategic mistakes, but even more so to the involvement of the United States both in terms of men and weapons.

General Dwight D. Eisenhower was sent to England in the spring of 1944 to plan and assume command of "Operation Overlord."

MARCH 24th This morning, Dr. Allanstein greeted me like an old friend, and I realized what a warm bond I had with him. He was anxious to know if I had fully recovered. When I assured him that I had, he said, "You know the kitchen continues to operate efficiently, and I realize that you miss nursing and would like to resume your duties in that area. It so happens that the head nurse of this hospital has been transferred, and I want you to take over."

I was genuinely surprised, since I had really not thought about where I would be assigned upon my return. "I'll be happy to take over," I responded quickly, "and will do my best."

"Good-good." said Dr. Allanstein, beaming broadly. "I am also sending in a recommendation that you be promoted to colonel." He then showed me my office, a small room adjacent to his. It was also simply furnished with a large desk and bookshelves lining one wall. There were the usual flags and picture of Adolph Hitler on the opposite wall. As I glanced about my new domain, a picture of the kitchen with its huge ovens came to mind. While I saw this new position as a great opportunity, I felt I would probably have only half the challenge and nowhere near the fun I had when managing the kitchen.

We discussed briefly the dangers outside the compound but did not dwell on them. All of us now expected a bitter end to the war, and the slogan circulating about was, "Enjoy the war–you don't know what peace will bring." The Front was creeping upon us like a menacing snake. We felt it, we watched it, and we drew closer to each other.

APRIL 16th Every week, trucks brought in more wounded men and the recovering patients were flown back to Germany in huge transport planes. Surgeries were performed night and day, sometimes continuously for days on end. Nurses had to be led from the operating rooms when their legs became swollen from standing for hours, and I often stepped in when they were too exhausted to continue.

Trapped as we were inside the hospital compound, we desperately needed spiritual and emotional support. When I asked Dr. Allanstein for a chaplain to minister to both the patients and staff, he readily agreed, and somehow managed to get a young Catholic priest. Tall, blonde and smooth-shaven, the priest appeared much too naive to be an effective chaplain, but he soon changed my initial impression. He was not only mature, but open-minded and a good counselor as well. I offered to help and together we set up the auditorium for Sunday worship. Since both of us knew many hymns by heart, we printed a small hymnal, and I played the piano for services.

Worst of all, and strange to any but those who have had the experience, boredom was setting in. To counteract this, I found teachers among the patients who were willing to lecture on a wide range of subjects from philosophy to Russian. A group of actors offered to stage dramas. Although the war was closing in on us, we felt a peace and serenity that kept at the bay our sense of impending doom.

MAY 9th Today, my forty-first birthday, was an unforgettable occasion. When I entered my office, there were vases of wild flowers on my desk, gathered by nurses from the garden early in the morning. Dr. Allanstein, not to be outdone, had ordered a bouquet of carnations from Warsaw, which also adorned my desk, along with a note.

Anton Bertel, one of the patients and an actor who had worked diligently on the dramas, came by to congratulate me and inscribed this beautiful poem in my book:

"Wenn Menschen einer Liebe leben
Und treu wie gold im fuehlen sind,
Dann kennt nur gutes all ihr Streben,
Sie stehen fest, in Sturm und Wind.

"Die Einsamkeit ist ihre Starke,
Ihr Geist erkennt der Tugend Wert,
Sie meistern jede Lebensharte,
Nur Freunde stets ihr tun verklart.
"Ihr Selbstvertrauen preist das Leben
Und achtet keiner Wunder Schmerz
Sie tragen still und Gott ergeben,
In sich ein starkes, eines Herz."

"Mit herzlichen Gruss, und zur freundlichen Erinnerung, an unsere Front Buhne."

His poem expressed his philosophy that only a deep feeling for humanity and a love for each other that is anchored in the love of God can overcome the cruelties of life and bear the painful wounds of the body and heart. Virtue is a value acknowledged by the human spirit and shown in self confidence, and a strong heart.

Like all of his poetry, this one was very uplifting, and I felt myself rise above the pathos of war and its bitter fruits. With his writing and acting, Anton did much to relieve the meaninglessness we all felt. A recognized actor and poet in his thirties, he had suffered a leg injury in battle, but was now recovered and walking about.   He was a slim, handsome, yet very intense man, who often followed me about like a romantic suitor. Although I was teased by the other nurses, I really didn't mind his attentions. In fact, I found him fascinating and his devotion flattering.

A small party was held at the end of the day in the doctors' dining room and in spite of the festive mood, a spirit of brooding overshadowed us. We all sensed that we would not be having days of celebration anymore.

CHAPTER THIRTEEN: THE DEVASTATION

May 14, 1944   Each morning I made rounds with Dr. Allanstein through the patient wards at ten o'clock. Often I did not see him until then. Today, however, he called me in as soon as I arrived. The minute I set foot into his office, I knew something was up, as he wasn't his usual jolly self.

"Tabea," he began glumly, "I have received orders to send you and six other nurses to the Reserve Hospital in Stenzica. Apparently they have received many patients with typhus fever who are not responding to treatment, and they have asked for experienced personnel."

I understood why I had been ordered to go there, because I was familiar with the usual typhus regime and the new treatments. I resisted going because it was clear from the orders that we wouldn't be back. Dr. Allanstein was not pleased with the order and said disgustedly, "I called General Judal at his headquarters in Konigsberg and explained that I have no one to replace you as head nurse. He was adamant that you should go to Stenzica. Nothing I said made any difference."

"It will be hard to leave here," I began, but bit my lip as I choked back tears. To cry would be embarrassing since "good soldiers do not show emotion." I was beginning to feel less and less like a good soldier.

Dr. Allanstein knew me so well that words were not needed. He gently took my hand in his, and said softly, "Tabea, we are grateful for all you've done for the patients here, but apparently the need in Stenzica takes precedent over ours. Now, take the morning off, so you can choose the nurses to go along with you."

Without hesitation, I sought out Ruth Shefler, and was delighted when she agreed to come. This soft-spoken woman of twenty-two was not only strong and capable of working long hours, but she was a pleasant companion as well. Ruth had been drafted into the army as a Nurse's Helper, the equivalent of an L.V.N. Well educated in literature and journalism, she spent her spare time reading and corresponding with friends and teachers back in Germany. Her father was an officer in the German Army and her mother, a writer. Hers was a family of culture. Ruth often told me she felt her army service was her patriotic duty, a temporary interruption in her journalism career.

After that, I simply chose five nurses who told me they wanted a change of scene. We were only given twelve hours to pack, and that was that. We'd all been vaccinated for typhus, since this was now standard practice for all army medical personnel. I stole away to my room to reflect on yet another change in my life. I struggled with God, asking Him what He was up to moving me again–and so soon. I mulled the matter over and realized that I had not wanted to leave the hospital train, but on the other hand it had been bombed on the very next trip. I wondered about the fate of this hospital where so many people had come to mean so much to me. I ultimately realized that God had always taken care of me, often in peculiar ways. So why should I question Him now? He was not doing anything to me, but likely for me.

Dr. Allanstein arranged a farewell for us that evening in the doctors' dining room, offering toasts to our safety. Anton Bertel read some of his poems, evoking touching memories and I knew I would miss this fascinating young man.   I looked back on my seven months here as challenging with that spice of variety, beginning in the kitchen and ending in the head nurse's office. Reluctantly I bid Dr. Allanstein "Auf Weidersehen," expressing the hope that our paths would cross again. I'd grown quite fond of this gentle man, whose warmth and good will made him an atypical army doctor.

The ambulance bearing us seven nurses left early the next morning for Stenzica. It was a small village nestled among farms between Deblin and Lublin in eastern Poland about two hundred-fifty kilometers away. The road wound along the Wieprz River, through a fertile valley of pastures dotted with grazing sheep and goats. I watched a woman in the field guiding her crude plow pulled along by the family cow. The small one-room houses illustrated the poverty of these peasants.

While I enjoyed the pastoral beauty all around me on this balmy spring day, I also saw the scars of war in the ruins of the towns we passed through. Even worse was the sight of the throngs of emaciated, tatter-clothed children playing amid the broken shells of buildings. I was shocked to see how much of Poland had been destroyed in the three years since I had left Ft. Modlin. I asked the driver if we could picnic by the river, but he shook his head, saying it was too risky and we might be ambushed. Instead we munched our sandwiches in the safety of the ambulance.

By late afternoon we pulled up at the hospital, about twenty kilometers from Stenzica. This Polish Civilian Hospital had been converted to a German Army Reserve Hospital early in the war. The large two-story white stone building, surrounded by a high barbed wire fence punctuated with guard towers, looked like a prison. We were stopped at the gate by grim-looking soldiers bearing machine guns, who not only searched the ambulance but me and the other nurses as well. They would not allow us to pass until their inspection was completed and our orders had been thoroughly examined. While I realized there was a reason for this frightening reception, nonetheless I felt like an enemy.

I was relieved when we finally received clearance and proceeded through the gate to the hospital entrance. There a tiny, bird-like woman was waiting to greet us. "My name is Berta Klein and I'm the head nurse here. Who of you is Major Springer?"

I stepped forward, and she grasped my hand, exclaiming, "We are so glad you and your staff have come. We've heard that you are quite experienced in the care of typhus patients. Our men are gravely ill and are not responding to the treatments. We hope you can help us." She looked around at our group and said warmly, "I welcome you here, and now I will show you to your rooms."

I was pleased that Ruth and I were given a room together. As we unpacked, we shared our uneasiness about the place. The guards' reception at the gate underscored the danger in this area. "There are Partisans around us here, that's obvious," I concluded. Ruth nodded and observed that soon we'd be so busy we wouldn't notice it. Besides, she conjectured, how could anyone get by those guards?

Berta introduced us at dinner to the two doctors in charge of the isolation unit. They told us about the sixty typhus patients, new cases from Russia, who'd been ill for about a week. Although the usual routine, including intravenous feedings and antibiotics was being followed, the doctors said that most were still comatose with high fevers, and only a few had regained consciousness. I described the new treatment of direct transfusions from the recovering patients to the comatose ones. The doctors listened intently and, after mulling it over, concluded that they'd like to try this technique in the morning.

Before we began our duties the next morning, Berta took us on a tour of the hospital. The main building had a capacity of four hundred patients and was clean and well-equipped. Patients here were primarily being treated for influenza and dysentery. There were several barracks behind the main building being used as dormitories for the nurses and the isolation ward for typhus patients.

Once in the isolation ward, my staff and I slipped into the isolation gear of hooded suits of heavy beige material and rubber gloves. The outside dangers slipped away as we concentrated on the tasks before us. Weil-Felix tests were done to determine the best donors. Many of the men had the look of death about them with sunken eyes and thin corpse-like bodies. I was reminded of the pitiful men at Johannesburg. Quickly we separated the comatose from the conscious patients and prepared them for the direct transfusions. As done previously, the blood from a convalescent patient was withdrawn, ten cc at a time and then injected slowly into a comatose patient until a total of two hundred cc had been transfused. We watched closely for adverse reactions.

The recovery was remarkable as before, and the doctors were astounded when the men awakened from their comas in just five hours. "This is amazing, just amazing. I was somewhat skeptical, but felt we had to try it–and just look," one doctor said. "Without this, I'm sure these men would be dead." Tongues long silent began to mumble words. I thought of Cissy, the pioneer patient from three years ago, when she had first opened her eyes. Because we had taken a chance with her, men like these now had a chance. Soon the patients were sitting up and sipping the high protein liquids of egg yolk in red wine and beef broth. Within two or three weeks, most had recovered enough to be moved to the convalescent ward.

"Everyone is talking about the dramatic improvement in the typhus patients," Berta told me one night at dinner, as she pressed me for more details. I explained to her how Dr. Sorger, my family doctor before the war, had first tried the transfusions as a last resort on a dying nurse.

I soon learned that although Berta appeared delicate and petite, she was quite strong and totally dedicated to her patients. In her late thirties, Berta wore her blonde hair parted in the middle and pulled back into a bun, giving her the air of a no nonsense woman. We had become good friends in the way that war creates instant friendships.

JUNE 9th I heard on my radio this morning that the Allies had invaded France on the Normandy coast and I wondered if the end was near. I was grateful to still have my radio since I felt so isolated here in Poland. Depending on rumors or announcements for news, was frustrating since both were unreliable. If the end was near, I wanted to know about it.

The road to victory for the Allies in Europe began with D-Day, "Operation Overlord" on June 6, 1944 and was a complete surprise to the Germans. Over 155,000 Allied troops, the largest amphibious force ever assembled, landed on the Normandy coast at Utah, Gold, Juno, and Sword beaches, taking eighty square miles in twenty-four hours. Even though the losses were heavy, the American and British troops had gained a foothold in German-occupied Europe. Although Hitler expected an invasion, he didn't know where on the coast or when. The Allies had fooled the

Germans into thinking it would likely be in the Pas-de-Calais area, thus the German High Command kept the 15th Army there for the main attack. Plodding through the hedgerows and villages, the Allies fought a laborious trek eastward to Paris. (This city was finally liberated on August 25, 1944.) Meanwhile, the bombs continued to rain on London (V-1 or buzz bombs) and also in Holland, even though the British tanks were rolling in.

As the Allies pushed eastward from Paris, the Russian troops were pushing west. Germany was now waging battles on three fronts and soon lost Rome. Hitler withdrew his troops to the west along the German border. Surrender was hoped for, but instead the Fuhrer planned a massive counterattack in the Ardennes a few days before Christmas. Germany's plight was further heightened by Romania's and Finland's change of allegiance to the Allies.

In Poland, the Germans felt the noose closing about them, too, as the Partisans, stimulated by the invasion, became more aggressive by planting bombs and storming German positions. The Polish Home Army boldly attacked the German troops in Warsaw in August 1944, but were overpowered. Sadly the Russian Army was camped across the Vistula and watched as the S.S. troops ravaged the Polish citizens and razed the city.

That evening, Ruth and I sat quietly in our room and listened to the Fuhrer's speech, anticipating his reaction to the invasion. He kept repeating that "we would win the war." I was annoyed that he said nothing about the invasion.

The rumor mill was circulated that Hitler shouted at his generals that he knew the best strategies. Yet very soon Hitler would move his headquarters from Rastenburg to his bunker in Berlin, since he didn't want his whereabouts known. He would still broadcast on occasion. In the last speech that I heard, he repeated that threat of, "Don't' fear– we are going to win when the secret weapon is finished. We only need to drop one over America and the war will be over." While I felt our scientists were capable of great feats, I hoped they would not succeed with this weapon. The Fuhrer was a madman.

JUNE 12th The staccato sound of machine gun fire in the distance gradually became as constant as the ticking of a clock. The tremors and exploding bombs kept us awake at night, and our hospital was now part of the front line with machine guns poking out of the windows on every side. We sent as many patients as possible back to Germany. As ordered by the Fuhrer, the chief doctor instructed us to carry a syringe and an ampule of morphine in our pockets to inject ourselves and die, should we be ambushed by the enemy. I had no intention of carrying out such an order and dropped the ampule of morphine in my pocket with disgust. I was willing to take whatever came, feeling that suicide was not only unChristian, but cowardly. I had heard that the Nazi officers carried strychnine. As if things weren't bad enough, the Nazis kept the hatred inflamed against us by hanging civilians in the city squares in retaliation for each Partisan attack–ten Polish citizens for each German killed.

JUNE 14th I now saw many wounded German Army civilian employees brought to the hospital. The secretaries and technicians were victims of the Partisan attacks. While I felt that the Nazis' cruel methods would be ample reason enough to turn the Polish people against us, I still wondered if there weren't other reasons why the Polish people here hated us so vehemently while they had been pleasant and cooperative at Biala-Podlaska. My answer was not long in coming.

One day when I was scrubbing up with two doctors before surgery, I overheard them jokingly refer to the bars of soap as "Esau, Abraham, and Levi." I was baffled, but I was cautious about asking for an explanation. I waited until I was alone with Berta that evening. She appeared frightened by my question, and tried to change the subject, but I persisted. Reluctantly, she agreed to tell me what she knew. "You must never discuss what I am about to tell you with anyone else, as it will place you in grave personal danger."

"Not far from here," she began, "is a factory which uses the bodies of Jews from the camps to make soap and other items like skin lampshades. Before their bodies are burned, however, the Nazis remove any jewelry and pry the gold out of their teeth. I've heard there are storage rooms filled with gold and jewels." The room reeled about me, and I felt waves of nausea. I was horrified.

I asked where the camps were and how people got there. "Oh I'm not sure," said Berta, "but I've heard that there are several in this area. I've been told that Jews are shipped to these camps from Russia and other countries and are packed so tightly in cattle cars that many are dead by the time they arrive. Others are beaten or starve to death once in the camps."

A picture of those empty train cars in Riga flashed into my mind, and I recalled how cruel we thought the Russians had been. Now this! With so many Polish and Russian Jews being slaughtered in the camps, I could easily understand why we Germans were hated so bitterly here. As the Jews had disappeared early in the war back in Germany, even our neighbor's wife, I had a vague awareness of Jewish and other citizens in the camps, but had accepted the political education explanation.

Back then I did not dwell on it. I felt uneasy since I had no idea what I could do about it. Soon I forgot all about it once I became involved in taking care of the wounded. I'd seen a lot of war casualties, but this horror was the ultimate of all the cruelties of war. Suddenly an unexplained phenomenon fell into place. Since my arrival at Stenzica, I had noticed a constant repugnant odor of burning material similar to scorched meat. Now I realized that I was smelling the combustion of human flesh. How could I enjoy a meal with this going on nearby.

I left Berta without a word and went into the chapel where I sat for hours like a heavy stone. Patients came in for their evening prayers and left, but I sat there so numb I could not even lift my voice to heaven. Finally I opened my heart to God and this time there were no whys. The proof of God's existence had been shown to me time after time, and I knew He would not allow this evil beyond all evils to continue.

It was not until 1945 when the Allies overran Germany and liberated the concentration camps, that the world became aware of the atrocities committed. Nazi ideology had focused on the Jews as being responsible for the "evils of life" as well as Germany's economic plight. "Endolsung", the final solution in which over six million Jews, and others such as protesting ministers, gypsies, homosexuals and Communists were killed in thirty or more of these death camps. Some of the more notorious camps were at Auschwitz, Buchenwald, Dachau, Bergen-Belsen, and in the east: Lublin, Maidaier and Treblinka. Some were designated as extermination camps, including Auschwitz and Treblinka.

Hitler had killed our crippled people, but he had inherited from this war more crippled men than he could take care of. He had sought to destroy the Jewish people, but, in turn, his own golden Aryan youth, his pride, had been maimed and killed, his beautiful Fatherland was being smashed and destroyed and with it the dream of the Third Reich. I recalled an old German proverb, "God's grinding is slow, but it is thorough and good."

I felt it impossible that God could ever forgive this wickedness and I, as a German, felt guilty and ashamed. Finally my eyes gazed up at the dying Savior extended on the cross, a typically Roman Catholic crucifix, with bleeding wounds, which seemed so appropriate in this moment. I felt the Lord's presence in that chapel and my heart began to stir again. Forgiveness from men does not come easily, but God forgives freely.

It was very late when I walked into my room. Ruth looked up questioningly, but I simply said that I had been in the chapel. A sensitive woman, she guessed that I did not want to talk further. She did not ask me any questions.

Like most of my fellow countrymen, I was intellectually and emotionally numb. The days of continuous battle noise melted into weeks, and I no longer felt it was extraordinary to carry a syringe and morphine in my pocket. Imminent danger was my constant companion and I fully expected shells to come crashing through the walls any moment.

JUNE 29th A jeep driven by hysterical paramedics swerved through the gates early this morning. Hearing the commotion, I ran out and found two medics from Biala - Podlaska crying incoherently as they mumbled the horrible news that the hospital had been ambushed by over a thousand Partisans. "It was a gruesome battle as the staff and patients fiercely resisted with whatever they could lay their hands on once they ran out of ammunition." They began sobbing hysterically, describing the sight of slaughtered nurses lying in pools of blood on the floors of the wards.

I choked back sobs, and when I could finally speak, I asked, "Dr. Allanstein? What happened to him?" One paramedic told me he didn't know. He shook his head and said he didn't see him anywhere.

Soon an ambulance arrived from Biala-Podlaska bringing a few of the patients who had escaped the ambush. Some of the Polish staff had hidden them under the straw in their farm wagons. They repeated the same story, but also did not know anything about Dr. Allanstein. They added that they saw surviving personnel being led away, presumably to prisoner-of-war camps.

I looked around at the other nurses who had come with me and they were as stunned as I was. We felt at once the unspeakable horror of the fate of our friends and yet gratitude that we had been spared. We bathed in tears the events of the day when we gathered that evening. The priest held a special mass for those who were lost in the massacre and added a prayer that the Lord would strengthen all of us in these times of fear and terror, keeping our souls in His hand should we be brought to the point of death. Thank you God, I prayed silently, once more you have spared me.

The chief doctor at the hospital in Stenzica, convinced that a similar massacre was likely to occur here, ordered ambulances to transport every patient medically stable back to Germany. The other nurses and I went through every ward, bluntly informing the remaining patients of our dangerous situation.

The suspense of waiting to be ambushed in a building from which there was not only no escape, but was also surrounded by barbed wire was dreadful. It was like being tossed into a deep well and waiting to slowly sink under the water. The fence seemed inadequate to keep the Partisans out, but strong enough to trap us in. Again I thought of the Russian Front where I could at least run from crater to crater or crawl beneath the train to dodge the artillery fire. Ruth and I talked of our predicament for hours, and concluded that this was a time of God's punishment upon the Nazis. All of Germany would have to suffer, innocent and guilty alike. Yet each day we remained alive we saw as a gift of God's mercy. "I don't care if the chief doctor tells us a thousand times to inject ourselves, I never will." Ruth said adamantly. I nodded in agreement. I told her I felt like I was standing on a cliff, but I was uplifted just being with her.

CHAPTER FOURTEEN: ON THE MOVE AGAIN

JUNE 30th Berta called me into her office at noon today to tell me that orders had just arrived from General Judal's office. I was to report to the Mother-House in Kassel on July 2nd for reassignment to a surgical unit in Brussels, Belgium. Again? I thought, will it really happen this time? I certainly did not mind going. In fact, it would be a relief to leave Poland, but it would be difficult to leave such good friends as Ruth and Berta. I felt a pang of guilt, knowing I was heading for a safer place. At least so I thought.

Ruth wrote a short farewell message in my book, which said in part, "When the guns have already turned brown with rust, you will still remember that you were here and left your heart in the east." In the midst of this hell, friendships were planted, blossomed and bore fruit quickly. Ruth's wisdom, which was great for her young years never ceased to amaze me, and I hoped she'd survive to tell her story of the war.

Suddenly my own war years passed before me like flashing scenes. The hope that I had clung to, that I would be reunited with Dr. Beckman began to fade. Oblivion, like a thief, kept pace behind me, swallowing up the people and places of my past. I wondered if my life would ever return to normal, where friends could be cherished and enjoyed for years.

I learned later that at the time of the massacre at Biala-Podlaska, the German lines had been pulled back and the hospital trains ceased going into Russia. In spite of my inquiries, no one could ever tell me what happened to those men on the train. Suddenly there were no letters from them, as if they too, had disappeared from the face of the earth.

While I hoped that they had somehow escaped to Germany, I thought it was more likely that they were either killed or imprisoned in Russia. And Dr. Beckman, always a conscientious doctor, would have stayed with his patients to the end. Had he been killed? Captured? The questions hung there waiting for answers that I would seek when this ordeal was over.

JULY 2nd I arose early this morning and went to pray in the chapel. As I knelt before the altar, I felt God's love, like arms around me, bringing a sense of peace which eased the dread of parting. Ruth walked quietly near me as I bid farewell to the patients and nurses on the wards. The priest then held a private communion mass for Berta, Ruth, and me. Afterward, Berta handed me a poem which reflected how we both felt:

> "I ask you Lord for just one blessing,
> That's all I want for my happiness.
> Teach me to understand my brothers,
> Give me an eye for their distress.
> O let me know, let me have feeling
> For the hurt in another soul
> Let me find words of comfort
> To soften the pain, heal the wounds.
> For the errors of others
> May I show forgiveness.
> Move my soul within with love
> To help the heavy laden
> And to be merciful of heart.
> May I forget my selfish needs
> When others are suffering pain."

Everyone was standing in front of the hospital when the ambulance arrived that was taking me to the train. Tears slid down Ruth's cheeks as she gave me a final hug, and I suspected she'd like to be going west, too.

The train I boarded at Stenzica was a small local train with fifteen cars. It only went as far as Warsaw. When we approached Warsaw, I could not believe my eyes, because even more of this former bustling city was gone. Big hotels had been reduced to rubble, and only part of the train station remained standing. Every time I passed through Warsaw, less of it was left. I wandered about seeking information on trains heading for Berlin, but no one seemed to know when the next one was due. A soldier passing by said he'd been waiting several hours and was about to give up hope.

Finally after six hours, a train pulled in from Lublin, and my hopes rose only to be dashed because the train was already jammed with passengers. I could not imagine how I could possibly get on and stood there in a quandary. Suddenly two soldiers lifted me up and pushed me through a window. Then they handed up my suitcase as they hoisted themselves up. We were packed in the car like herrings in a barrel. I glanced around and saw soldiers everywhere–on the stairs, in the aisles, and lying flat on the roofs of the cars. Sadly, some of these men were knocked off when the train passed through tunnels.

We rode nonstop to Berlin, a six-hour trip. By the time we arrived, my feet were so swollen from standing in one spot that I had to be helped off the train and into the Red Cross office by two young soldiers. I was so exhausted I didn't care if I ever reached Kassel. After all I thought, the war will go on without me–I'm certainly not that important. I stretched out on a hard couch in the waiting room and slept for twelve hours straight. The next morning I left for Kassel.

The Mother-Superior greeted me fondly and wanted to know all about the situation in Poland. She was obviously aggrieved to hear bout the deaths of so many nurses. "I am so worried about all our nurses who are still so close to the battle lines," she lamented, shaking her head. "I pray this war will end soon." Then she opened my orders, noting, "Before you go to Belgium, you are to be trained in the latest surgical techniques and anesthesia."

"Here?" I asked hopefully, thinking that then I could see Liesel. "No, you are to report to the Army Hospital in Rudolstadt, Thueringia. Since you were under stress in Poland, you may have a week with your family before going to Rudolstadt."

I was grateful for the chance to go home again, yet I was also eager to see Liesel. "May I visit Liesel Schmidt?" I pursued. The Mother-Superior shook her head and told me that Liesel was away at the Maternity Hospital on the other side of Kassel for her obstetrics training, and there was no way for us to get together. She was sorry, but added that I would be pleased to know that she was a fine nurse. While I was glad to hear that Liesel was well thought of, I was disappointed that I couldn't see her. I missed her, and in these increasingly uncertain times, didn't know when I'd have the opportunity again.

The ride to Greiz went twice as quickly as the trip from Poland, even though it was farther. Deborah's eyes opened wide with surprise when she opened the door and saw me standing there. She hugged me as Papa came up. He hugged me too, saying, "I'm so thankful Tabea, to see you alive and well–and to have you here with us." He stepped back and looked me over from head to toe, adding with a twinkle in his eye, "In fact, I'm amazed that you've changed so little after all you've been through."

When I told him that I'd be at Rudolstadt for awhile, he was relieved. "We've heard how dangerous it is now in the east. I'm glad you will be near by." Papa then shared Esther's letters, observing that she was still in Rendsburg. "I'm still operating the searchlights, but I'm quite weary of working nights. How I long to come home as I miss all of you, but especially Hans. He's growing up without me and that worries me very much."

Just then Hans came in from school and wanted to know what was happening in Poland. Like all German boys, he had been required to join the Hitler Youth Corps the prior year when he turned ten. He was being taught that the Germans would win the war and rule the world. But Hans' training had been undermined by my father who had explained to him that the Americans were now in Europe and would not be easily conquered. Papa spent long hours with Hans, just as he had with us daughters in the past. He taught him the real history of Germany from his vast library. The Nazis had rewritten the textbooks going as far back as the time of the Roman Empire, misrepresenting the truth. They made the Teutonic race appear superior over all others, giving them a more prominent place in history and larger land areas, then they had, in fact, enjoyed.

Hans was more influenced by his grandfather than by his teachers, but he knew never to speak up in school because that would have been dangerous for the entire family. With wisdom beyond his young years, I could tell that Hans was able to digest what he learned at home, yet present the picture of a model obedient student at school. Papa saw in him the future of our family, as well as our country.

I asked Hans what was being taught about the Jews. "At school, they set aside time for racial education," Hans responded. "My teacher told us that the Aryan race must be kept pure because it is the dominant race. He said that the Jews were a people apart from the Aryans. They actually belong to Palestine, not Europe, and should be taken out of Germany. Our teacher even has a slogan written on the wall, "Germany is for Germans." Hans shrugged and added, "We aren't allowed to ask questions."

I asked Hans what he meant. "Well what happened to the Jews in town? All of us know some Jewish students who haven't been to school in a long time. The only explanation the teacher gave us was that the Jews were removed in order to be politically educated and to prevent them from having any power."

I nodded, aware that Jews were still disappearing, but now I had an inkling about their fate. I still had no idea where the camps were located in Germany. When I became bold enough to share what I knew about the fate of Jews in Poland with friends in Griez, they would not believe me. They insisted that the Nazis were their German brothers and would never do anything as cruel as I described. The Nazi version of the camps being established for the political education of potentially subversive people was still readily accepted.

But when I told Papa, he believed me and his eyes flashed angrily as he said, "I've always considered the Jews the beloved people of God and we are the children of Abraham only by adoption. These Nazis embody all the evil of the Anti-Christ, and Hitler is a tool in the hand of the devil."

JULY 13th Since I seemed to be on the move so much these days, and the radio was cumbersome to carry, I gave it to Papa when I left. I showed him where to find London on the dial and warned him to keep it hidden. "I know, I know."   He said, "I'm grateful I will be able to listen to reliable news now."

I arrived in Rudolstadt in late afternoon.   It was   a picturesque town surrounded by mountains and forests. The huge hospital complex was set in an upper-class residential area in the heart of town. I reported to the Head Nurse's office as soon as I arrived. Bianka, the Head Nurse, welcomed me and wasted no time showing me around. The hospital was five stories high and admitted both civilian and military   patients.   Gardens,   untouched   by   the   war, surrounded the complex.

The next morning, I was introduced to the head physician, Dr. Whitman, who was reputed to be an excellent surgeon. He appeared to be in his fifties and let me know immediately that he was strict with his staff.   His introductions were stiff and formal, and I felt the atmosphere in that surgery cool and professional. I watched the various surgical procedures and methods of anesthesia. On the second day I was allowed to assist with anesthesia, which I had done many times before on the hospital train. Here chloroform was used and the patients's vital signs' were closely observed since there were no skin color changes, as with ether, to indicate when the patient was being too deeply anesthetized.   I was pleased that Dr. Whitman trusted me immediately with responsibility.

I often stole back to the operating rooms at night to handle the various instruments so that I could become more familiar with them.   The techniques were new to me, especially for chest and plastic surgeries. Each day brought a new challenge. With thoracic surgery, the patient's life depended on the speed of the surgeon, and I had to work quickly and be ready with four or five needle holders at once. Often chest walls were torn by shell fragments and lungs were punctured and diaphragms were ripped loose.

In contrast, the plastic surgeon's skill was slow, delicate and creative. He worked like a sculptor taking the skin from the forehead and fashioning new eyelids and noses. Jaws were restored by using the round edge of the hip bone. Since this surgery was done under local anesthesia, the surgeon often joked with his patients, and I appreciated this more relaxed atmosphere.

Air raid alarms interrupted us night and day, and we had to move the patients quickly down to the bunkers in the basement. If operations were in progress, however, the surgeons continued on, taking their chances. Strange as it seems, I noticed that Dr. Whitman always appeared to know when the bombers were coming and ordered the patients downstairs even before the alarm sounded. After giving the order, he would smile coyly, saying, "I have to go." Then he would leave town. While he ultimately saved many lives, some of the staff suspected that he had a contact in London who warned him.

The basement bunker was immense and well-equipped, including operating rooms, delivery rooms, generators for light and power and an ample supply of food and water. There were radios and card games, even a pool table. The walls were lined with bunk beds in this spacious room. I was told that this comfortable bunker had been set up according to Dr. Whitman's specifications.

Rudolstadt was the frequent target of bombers because of a large munitions factory there which manufactured guided missiles. I sensed insecurity at this hospital in spite of the Red Crosses painted on the roof. Many people were quite vocal about the foolishness of having both a missiles factory and a hospital in the same town. Because of the heavy bombings, the hospital began filling up with injured civilians I was in the operating room almost continuously. The welcome interludes between alarms became shorter and shorter.

Children are always the saddest victims of war, and among the most pathetic were those children who had been buried under the rubble and, when finally dug out, were withdrawn and mute. They were so afraid, they shied away when I tried to hug them or just touch them. Other children were in a constant state of agitation and screamed hysterically any time the alarm sounded. Soon, the alarm shrilled so often that no one could sleep at night. Many families begged to be allowed to spend their nights in the hospital bunker.

SEPTEMBER 14th Fall arrived with the usual panorama of glorious colors, as the leaves turned shades of red and gold. The seasons were ignoring the war. On this warm afternoon, several of us were strolling through the gardens around the hospital admiring the colorful trees, when suddenly we heard a roaring sound like that of many loud motors. Looking up, I saw in the sky a huge formation of planes heading for the town. The sight was spectacular, like thousands of silver sparrows gleaming in the sun. The sight was so stunning that for a moment we forgot the danger they represented. We stood like birds spellbound by an approaching snake. Finally one of the doctors shouted, "Run for cover–it's a carpet formation."

As we ran to the bunker, we watched while one plane outlined the town with a yellow streak and a plane in the middle dropped a yellow flare. Then, as if by signal, all the planes released their deadly cargo simultaneously. We darted into the bunker just in time. The detonation of the many bombs landing at once was so powerful that the ground shook like an earthquake, and we had to hold onto each other to keep from toppling into a heap. Then, just as suddenly, it was still–a foreboding silence. We stood like statues, hardly daring to breathe and waiting expectantly for more to come.

Still in a state of shock I instinctively rushed upstairs as did everyone else. The first wounded civilians were being brought in when I arrived. I was not prepared for the sight of a human body destroyed beyond description. A woman staggered in with jagged pieces of glass stuck in her back, splitting open her torso, her kidneys hanging loose. Others had crushed arms or legs, which had obviously been pinned under heavy beams. And again, I was deeply touched by the sight of the little ones, some with abdomens torn open, spilling out the intestines. The sight was more horrible than anything I'd seen at the front.

There was no let-up in the surgeries, even after twenty-four hours. As soon as one operation ended, another began. We were all exhausted. One of the nurses administering anesthesia suddenly began to act strangely, joking and talking loudly with the surgeon instead of quietly counting the respirations as usual. Even more alarming, I noticed that she had become glassy-eyed. All of us had been too busy to notice that she had been sipping a solution of novocaine from a can of local anesthesia. While we summon within ourselves the strength to withstand the abuse of war on our bodies and minds, there is a limit to what a human being can endure. The nurse had numbed herself.

When we finally got beyond the human damage, we walked outside to see the loss in our surroundings. The main hospital had not been hit, but the supply buildings around were flattened. Over half the town had been reduced to rubble. As I walked along I saw men with shovels digging out both the living and the dead from under heaps of bricks, boards and mortar. The factory had been totally wiped out. We all secretly rejoiced and hoped that now the town would be left alone.

NOVEMBER 23rd Our hopes were not realized. There was no let-up and the bombings continued as before. These American bombers were different from the Russians who seldom hit their targets. We ran from the American bombers, who were always precise, but we would brazenly wave at the Russians.

One night was particularly endless and the bombs were dropped in a solitary stream all night long, one by one, like dripping rain. Hundreds of bombs must have landed near the hospital, because the building shook constantly. We worked the entire night in the bunker operating rooms. For the first time, I questioned that I could hold onto my sanity. Only God's love kept me from despair.

I seldom heard from my family because the mail trucks were either bombed or blown up. There were neither parts nor time between the raids to repair them. Since Griez was not far away, I worried that this city might also be bombed, but I had no way of knowing. I simply committed my family to the Lord's care. I felt strangely comforted to realize that there was no need for the army to send me anywhere else–the war was everywhere. Once again I was wrong about the army.

The Allies advance had gained momentum, giving the German troops little time to organize counter-attacks. General George Patton, American 3rd Army, and General Henry Crerar, Canadian 1st Army, led the troops and the

Avranches were taken by the end of July. Their advance was bolstered by the second Allied invasion forces moving north through France from the Mediterranean coast. The Germans quickly withdrew, but prevented the Allies from cutting off their large forces. By September, however, these two Allied forces were joined, and fifty thousand German soldiers were captured. The push continued into Belgium, Luxembourg, and Alsace. The Allied Front now stretched from the Vosges Mountains along the Siegfried Line of Germany and across the southern border of Holland. The Allied advance was now slowed by German resistance, and Hitler prepared to launch his bold plan.

During the fall, he had secretly gathered Germany's resources for a counterstrike. The Third Reich still had ten million men, and by expanding the draft ages and converting all services to infantry troops, Hitler was able to create another twenty-five divisions. Although the Allies had intensely bombed factories, weapon production continued.

And strike the Germans did, in the vicious "Battle of the Bulge." In mid-December German armored and infantry divisions struck the thin Allied lines in the Ardennes sector of the Front, and the six American divisions holding this area retreated. Reinforcements were quickly sent, however, and the Allies stopped the Germans east of the Meuse River. It was not until January of 1945, that Hitler realized his bold plan had failed and ordered his troops to withdraw. This had been a costly, bitter battle for both sides: the Germans lost 100,000 men and the Allies 76,000.

Although Hitler ordered a second offensive to the south, in the Alsace-Lorraine area, this also did not succeed since Allied reinforcements were sent there too. The Germans were halted before they could take the Saverne Gap, the main pass through the Vosges Mountains. In the meantime, Russia continued to close in from the West.

Defeat looked inevitable, but the leaders of the Third Reich dug in their heels, and continued to call up men between sixteen and sixty to form a Home Guard (Volksstrum) and "fight to the last man."

CHAPTER FIFTEEN: THE WAR ENDS

DECEMBER 9, 1944   Dr. Whitman called me in and handed me orders that had come from the Mother-House in Kassel, which directed me to report to Bad Liebenstein, a health spa and resort village about eighty kilometers away. "I can't afford to lose you," he said. "I called Kassel to protest this order, but nothing I said made any difference. You may as well pack and leave in the morning."

I nodded in resignation, feeling like a barrel rolling down a mountain stopping here and there but always tumbling on again, never seeing the end of the journey. Moving had become my way of life, but the stops were briefer now. Yet with all the blood being shed around me, I was grateful to still be alive. I had found working here with this excellent surgical team an invaluable experience.   I secretly hoped that in Bad Liebenstein, I would get away from the constant bombing and pitiful civilian casualties.

I read the orders and was surprised at my unusual assignment to convert one of the hotels into a surgical facility specializing in second stage amputations.   Since limbs were often amputated hurriedly in the field hospitals, a second operation was necessary later to reshape the stump.

Our good byes were brief, and soon I was on the train, anticipating a journey of a couple of hours. As things turned out, this was not to be. The train was filled with country folk and stopped at the villages along the way. I leaned back against the cushions and gazed out the window at the farmers working in the fields. Suddenly from out of nowhere, planes swooped down and began strafing them and dropping bombs. A piercing alarm shrieked, as the train shook with the tremors of the detonating bombs, and I was thrown out of my seat. When the train screeched to a stop, we all lunged out and headed for cover under the bushes alongside the tracks. Although bombs were dropping and bullets were flying, the passengers were quite matter-of-fact as if this were an everyday event. I was amazed. From my vantage point under the bushes, I watched the planes swoop low over the fields again and again, strafing the farmers. Some of the bullets found their marks, and those able to walk pulled the others to the shelter of a grove of trees. I was puzzled by this attack since the farmers were elderly. The army had long ago claimed all the young and able-bodied men.

As abruptly as they had appeared, the planes vanished into the clouds. It was ominously silent. Still we continued to lie under the bushes, fearing the planes would return. After what seemed like an eternity but was probably only five minutes, we crawled out to survey the damage. Fortunately, no one was wounded, but some of the children were hysterical Once we had calmed them down, we turned our attention to the train, and saw that it had been reduced to a smoldering hulk of twisted steel and broken glass. Even worse were the deep craters in the road bed, and the tracks now strewn about like broken match sticks.

Obviously there was no choice but to walk the ten kilometers to the next village. I hoped to board another train there. I picked up my suitcase and started walking, and soon the other passengers followed. We must have been a curious sight trudging along. By the time I reached the village, I was exhausted, but my spirits picked up when a train arrived within the hour.

Arriving in Bad Liebenstein at twilight, I was astounded to find not only the station intact, but the entire town as well. Wonder of wonders. Here was a picturesque village untouched by the ravages of war. Every hotel, shop and home stood proud and elegant. The trees and bushes were lightly dusted with snow, like a scene from a Christmas card. As I walked along, I was enthralled with the grandeur of the hotels I passed, where the wealthy had come in years past to enjoy the hot mineral baths, hoping for cures. The evening was so quiet and peaceful, that I felt as if I'd stepped back in time. People were casually strolling along the narrow streets and I joined them, rather than hail a taxi. After all, I thought, I've carried my suitcase ten kilometers already, a few more won't matter.

As I passed by an old stone church, the strains of a Bach prelude drifted out, and I sat on my suitcase to listen to the music and collect my thoughts. Churches and Bach preludes belong in a world apart from bombs and bullets. Gradually, the narrow escape from the bombing faded as well as the memory of the destruction of people and buildings in Rudolstadt. My taut muscles relaxed, and I felt at one with my Maker. I might have sat there longer, but the oncoming darkness nudged me back to reality, where music and steeples do coexist with death and destruction. I asked a passing gentleman for directions to the Hotel Kaiserhof where I was expected. He looked me over, perhaps taking in my tired eyes and dusty uniform. He grabbed my suitcase and said, "Come with me, Fraulein. I'll take you there."

The Hotel Kaiserhof was named after Kaiser Wilhelm II, who had been a frequent visitor. A four-story building with ornate balconies and terraced gardens, the hotel's handsome exterior gave no hint that anything but the vacationing rich had checked into the rooms. However, all too soon I would learn that the beds were now occupied by two hundred, very ill soldiers with diseases ranging from pneumonia to nephritis. The large banquet halls and ball rooms were now the settings for lectures and rehabilitation, rather than parties and formal balls.

Perhaps it was the relief that I had finally arrived or simply the exhaustion that I refused to acknowledge until now, but as soon as I walked into the hotel my knees began to buckle. I barely reached the nearest couch and sat down before I collapsed. A tall stocky brunette with a square jaw and prominent nose hurried up and asked, "Are you all right? Are you Major Springer?"

When I nodded wearily to both questions, she went on, "We've been expecting you. I am Colonel Meier–Elsbeth, the supervisor of all the nurses here in Bad Liebenstein. I had planned to show you around as soon as you arrived, but I can see you are very tired. Perhaps it would be wise for you to retire early, and I'll see to it in the morning." I nodded gratefully.

Elsbeth than introduced me to Benita, a nurse who had just walked up. Her birthplace in Riga, Latvia might have been guessed from her fair skin and golden blonde hair. Benita showed me to my room and arranged for my dinner to be served there. I drifted off to sleep with a prayer of thanks for my survival and for being in such quiet surroundings.

DECEMBER 11th Elsbeth came for me this morning and took me across the street to the Hotel Herzogin Charlotte where I would be the head nurse. As she outlined plans for setting up operating rooms and training staff, I perceived her innate ability to put things in order.

Once inside the hotel, we found large boxes of supplies stacked in the entry hall: operating tables, lamps, linens, all the instruments and equipment needed to set up an emergency room and aseptic and septic surgery areas. "Everything must be ready to go by the end of the month," Elsbeth declared, "since there are large numbers of wounded expected in January."

Strolling through the vast empty Hotel Herzogin Charlotte, named after the German Princess, I admired its grace and charm. The walls in the entry hall were lined with huge gold-rimmed mirrors and portraits of the various royal persons who had been frequent guests. A broad winding staircase led from the entry hall to the two upper stories. As I walked along, I began to jot down where I would place the patients. (I'd been told to plan for one hundred.) I decided to place them on the second floor and the staff on the third floor. I would use the large banquet rooms and lounges on the first floor for surgery and receiving rooms.

We relaxed for a moment on the second floor balcony, and once more I was enthralled with the serenity. "It is so still." I remarked. "After the constant bombing of Rudolstadt, I feel like I'm in a dream world here."

Elsbeth turned to me, surprise written on her face. "You mean your hospital was bombed?" When I nodded, she continued, "Why I assumed that all hospitals were safe. I've been in Bad Liebenstein for nearly two years, and we've never been bombed. Since it is considered a hospital town, it is supposed to off-limits to bombers."

Elsbeth then pointed out the various hotels lining the street. "All of these grand hotels, each one is more grand than the next, catered to the whims of princes and kings. They now serve a different kind of guest. Over there are the brain surgery patients and the general surgery patients are in the next one. See that small hotel down the street? We've placed the patients with contagious diseases there. They are sent to us primarily from France, Russia and Africa. The elegant Hotel Kaiserhof houses very ill medical patients. We use the large banquet and ball rooms for lectures and rehabilitation.

I thought to myself that this was quite an appropriate place for the sick to heal. When we parted, Elsbeth kindly advised, "Why don't you relax for a couple of days and look over the village before you begin your assignment?"

DECEMBER 15th Elsbeth called a meeting of all the nurses and asked for volunteers to staff the newest facility. There were about one hundred twenty nurses working in ten hotels, with an RN heading each staff of LVNs. Even though she was our supervisor, Elsbeth offered to train as an anesthetist. The others who chose to work at my hotel were: Benita, who felt an immediate affinity to me because I had spoken fondly of her people in Riga; Herta, a soft spoken young woman who had been drafted into the army in Theuringia; Hummel, a very cheerful girl; and Erica, who was friendly and attractive with curly brown hair framing her face, but had a mischievous gleam in her eye that made me curious. They were young and eager to begin, and so we did.

Tearing open the boxes in the entry hall, we set up the surgery rooms first. Our amiable chatter made the work go quickly and by the end of the week, we had transformed the hotel into a hospital. Then I began their surgical training. Strange as it seems, I felt peculiar working undisturbed by bombings-a strangeness I relished. The occasional alarm set off by a plane straying off its course, I hardly noticed.

DECEMBER 20th Our staff was soon enlarged by the arrival of three paramedics, two cooks and a supply officer.

All that was missing were the surgeons, and we anticipated their coming with a mixture of excitement and anxiety. After all, some surgeons well-deserved their reputations for being short-tempered, aloof and demanding. They could be young and fresh out of medical school, or mature and experienced. We did not know what to expect.

At noon, an inspection team consisting of a doctor and a nurse suddenly appeared, announcing that they had come to survey our hospital. They swept through the hotel like a whirlwind and asked few questions before pronouncing the arrangements satisfactory. As quickly as they had come, they left.

At long last the doctors arrived. Dr. Hubenthal, a colonel and the designated Chief of Staff, was in his fifties, a neat trim man with pleasant manners and an affable smile. With him were two young assistants: Dr. Herman, a friendly man with a warm smile, and Dr. Holman, who was a lion of a man with the air of one out to conquer the world. From the outset, I felt wary of Dr. Holman and wasn't surprised to learn later that he had trained under the Nazis. I soon observed his cool manner toward the patients and sloppy technique in surgery.

DECEMBER 24th Since my arrival at Bad Liebenstein, I had begun to receive mail from home again and was relieved to know that Griez had not been bombed and my family remained well. Papa wrote with resignation, however, that they knew defeat was near. He hoped the army would leave me in Bad Liebenstein, because the town appeared to be safe.

Even the war and the prospect of defeat could not prevent a Christmas celebration. The patients and staff at the Kaiserhof were rehearsing for a Christmas Eve program, and I wrote to Papa requesting a script I'd written years ago in Hamburg. It was a poetic reading about the bravery of the German soldiers in World War I who sank with their ship in the Scapa Flow. I read this melodramatic script accompanied by the piano. Many others spoke or sang of their love for the Fatherland along with our singing of carols. There were hundreds of us, ambulatory patients and staff, gathered in the banquet hall at the Kaiserhof for our Christmas dinner. That special glow of Christmas continued as we strolled through the patients' rooms singing carols.

Later alone in my room, I read the only letter I'd received, which I saved to read until now. I felt such a yearning for Dr. Beckman on this night-and Liesel as well. I had not heard from her for many months. With each passing week, I felt as if Paul, my Dr. Beckman had been swallowed up by the vast prairies of Russia. Yet I continued to savor the memory of our love and cling to my hope for a future with him. But, no, my letter was from neither of them, but from Papa. He was happy that I was away from the bombings and reminded me that the birth of the Christ child was more significant than the wars of men. Although his words were comforting, I felt very alone.

DECEMBER 27th Dr. Hubenthal was very excited today when he asked me to come with him to a site he felt would be a good bomb shelter in the event our safe status changed. After a ten minute walk, we arrived at a spacious wine cellar carved into the mountains that surrounded the town. We stepped inside, and I was amazed to find myself standing in a huge cavern two stories high that could easily accommodate hundreds of people. The barrels lining the walls were now empty, but I imagined that at one time they were filled with mellow wines. I could see the tourists strolling here in the cool of the evening, sipping the wines and enjoying the gemutlich. "And look," Dr. Hubenthal pointed out as he flashed his torch about, "This cave is still wired with electricity. Isn't this wonderful?" He was as enthusiastic as if he had just stumbled across a treasure. His words tumbled out in excitement as he outlined his plans for converting the cavern into a bunker that would include an emergency surgery and a storage area for valuable medical equipment.

Not one to dawdle, he immediately hired a group of civilians and within five days they had emptied the cave of the wine barrels, painted it and put in place straw mats and emergency equipment. I advised the nurses to secret their valuables here, which proved to be a wise move that later kept their belongings from falling into Russian hands. I placed in the cave my most prized possession- my photograph album.

DECEMBER 31ˢᵗ A New Year's Eve celebration was held at the Kaiserhof, and most of the younger nurses went, even though the war was a dour chaperone. Elsbeth and I were not in the partying mood and chose instead to bring in the New Year quietly. We went to worship at a small village church and then talked until the bells tolled at midnight. We both agreed that the war was grinding to an end, probably within the new year. But our hopes for peace were intertwined with anxiety, since we had no idea what peace would mean for us Germans. Our families were foremost in our minds. We both speculated if we'd ever see them again.

Realizing that victory was in sight, the Allies began meeting in February to coordinate the final offensive and determine the fate of Germany and Poland after the war. British Prime Minister Winston Churchill, American President Franklin Roosevelt and Josef Stalin, General Secretary of the Soviet Union, met at Yalta. The Red Army was given control of Bulgaria, Romania, Poland and East Prussia. The Russian army already occupied most of Poland anyway, and Stalin had even recognized the provisional Polish government at Lublin. In the end, the Allies agreed to a Soviet-Polish border west of the pre-war border, with Poland being promised part of eastern Germany.

The three powers agreed that Germany would be divided into four separate zones of occupation with the south to be administered by the United States, the north by Great Britain and eastern Germany by Russia. A section along the French border was carved out of the American and British zones (in the Palatinate, Baden and Wurtemberg areas) for France. Since Berlin lay within the Soviet zone, it would be administered by all four powers. It's no wonder that at this point plans for the eventual unification of Germany were left undecided. The seeds of conflict sown here continued to grow. Stalin proved to be a shrewd diplomat who not only won considerable concessions at this conference, but future Allied conferences as well.

Russia continued to push westward toward Berlin, while the Allies pushed eastward all along the Rhine River. (General George Patton led his troops across the Rhine in late March.)

JANUARY 3RD 1945   Dr. Hubenthal announced that patients would arrive today, and we should be prepared to operate at a moment's notice, beginning with the most critically wounded.   He had barely finished his announcement when the ambulances drove up and within the hour we had filled every bed. We worked continuously at two tables, concentrating first on those patients who were hemorrhaging and then proceeding to the second stage amputations. It was well after midnight by the time we finished. I was pleased to see that everyone had remained calm and worked well as a team member. I was proud of my staff.

FEBRUARY 1ST Since we had only small field sterilizers, I usually stayed up until two in the morning sterilizing the linens and instruments. Dr. Hubenthal often kept me company during these lonely morning hours, chatting about his family, who lived nearby in Plauen. "I look forward to the day when I can return to my practice as a general surgeon. My wife is a good woman, and she misses all of us. Not only was I drafted into the army but my three sons were as well. We've both very worried, since we haven't had word from any of them for a long time. The youngest is only nineteen." He shook his head sadly. "I hope the end isn't too bad for us. How about you, Tabea? Where's your family?"

I proceeded to tell him all about them, mentioning Esther being in the army, too, and operating the search lights in Rendsberg. "Drafting a young mother? It doesn't make sense." He declared.

I couldn't have had a better staff if I had handpicked them, myself. Benita was so fascinated with surgery that she often talked to me about becoming an RN after the war. She had been drafted at fifteen when the Germans took over Riga and was deported to work on a farm in Saxonia. After a year, she was trained as an LVN and sent to Bad Liebenstein. Since the Latvians had been treated so poorly by the Russians, Benita asserted that the German seizure was a liberation, and thus felt loyal to us.

Hummel worked as hard as a farm maid, and possessed that innate ability to change even the saddest situation into a happy one. We called her "Sunshine." While Erica was reliable, she was also flirtatious with the doctors-much to their enjoyment. Only she could hand them the wrong instrument with a smile and never be reprimanded. Quiet and shy, Herta was unassuming, yet very conscientious and efficient. I entrusted her with more responsibility.

While the nurses were superb, I quickly realized that the two young doctors were not only inexperienced in doing amputations but easily flustered when they had to work long hours. Since Elsbeth proved to be a capable anesthetist, Dr. Hubenthal often used me as his assistant rather than one of the doctors.

Dr. Hubenthal was a master at removing shell fragments embedded very deeply in wounds. This surgery was done under x-ray plates so the metal pieces could be seen. This was a risky procedure, because the x-rays could burn our hands, but there was simply no other way to locate the buried metal fragments. This operation was challenging, but the numerous amputations were depressing, especially when the patient was young or had lost both arms and legs. If our eyes met by chance during such a surgery, Dr. Hubenthal would shake his head sadly. The irony of it often struck me that these men, now ruined for life, had been exhorted by Hitler to "Keep fighting until the war is won."

FEBRUARY 15TH In spite of all our efforts, not all the patients recovered. We were without Penicillin, and the other drugs being used to fight infections were useless. Consequently men died, often five or six a day. There was no way for the relatives of these men to either claim their bodies or come to the funeral because of the bombings and unreliable transportation. The funeral was usually conducted by either the Catholic priest or the aged Lutheran minister standing alone at the graveside reciting a brief eulogy for a man who was a total stranger to him. We nurses were struck by the pathos of this situation and began attending the funerals at the cemetery. Soon we formed a group to six to sing hymns. If the funeral was held in a chapel, I accompanied them on the organ. We all felt it was important that these men have at least a simple service to mark their passing.

Week after week as I watched these men being buried with so little honor when they had given their lives for the Fatherland, I became outraged. One day I decided to do something about the situation and went to the Nazi commander's office and asked to speak to the Kreisleiter in charge of our section. The Kreisleiter received me very cooly, but I ignored his lack of interest and asked boldly, "Why don't you attend our soldiers' funerals? After all, they died for the Third Reich and are deserving of some recognition. Perhaps the Hitler Youth could be there as an honor guard."

He shuffled through papers on his deck in a bored manner, and did not look up as he muttered, "I have nothing to do with the army. Anyway, there is no order from Berlin about any speeches in graveyards."

"Well," I snapped angrily, "I hope for your sake there won't be any such order from Berlin soon!"

He stood up, his face flushed and shouted, "I'm going to have you arrested!"

I glared back at him and shouted just as loud, "You just told me that you have nothing to do with the army. Keep it that way!" I stormed out of his office, not looking back.

This Kreisleiter was a Nazi to the very core of his being, as I supposed most of them were, and I had heard the citizens were afraid of him. When he ordered all boys fourteen years-old and men over sixty-five to report for training in order to protect the town from the American army, the mayor did not interfere. And when he overheard a woman say, "We're not going to win the war," he made her report to his office everyday and tell him, "We will win the war."

MARCH 17TH Our food supply dwindled to the point where we were subsisting on meager portions of vegetables and a watery potato soup which the cooks made from potatoes stolen from the fields at night. We had an occasional sip of wine to relax us when we took Perfectin to keep us awake during the long tedious hours of surgery. Life became an endless succession of surgeries and funerals. Although I was weary and often in despair, the Lord gave me the strength to carry on. I knew that God would determine the resolution of this war. I longed for the Front line to overtake us. Lines from one of Paul Gerhardt's hymns winged their way into my mind and lodged there like a homing pigeon:

> "Give Lord this consummation
> To all our heart's distress.
> Our hands, our feet, e'er strengthen
> In death, our spirits bless."

Long after midnight I was suddenly awakened by a knock on my door. "Come quickly," urged the paramedic. A man is hemorrhaging." I followed him and quickly found the tell-tale red stain of oozing blood through the thick gauze bandage on the patient's neck pinpointing the site where his severed right carotid artery had been sutured. I applied firm pressure until Dr. Herman came to re-suture it.

The man had lost a lot of blood, but we were able to save him. A bright spot in an otherwise melancholy night.

APRIL 2^(ND) I have never had a vision before, but today a terrifying scene flashed before me. As I came down the stairs, I saw the entry hall suddenly filled with screaming, bleeding soldiers, writhing in pain, some crawling up the stairs toward me. I broke out in a cold sweat and would have fallen if I had not grabbed the railing to steady myself. As abruptly as the vision appeared, it vanished. I continued on down the stairs and sank speechless into the nearest chair.

Herta came over and asked anxiously, "Tabea, what's wrong? You look as if you've seen a ghost!" She brought me a glass of water, watching as I sipped it. When I felt composed enough to speak, I told her about my vision and said it was like a revelation. A look of alarm stole over her face and she commanded, "Sit right here. I'll get Dr. Hubenthal."

He came quickly and listened intently while I described my vision. "It is entirely possible that you did see a vision, Tabea. Sometimes when a person's nervous system is overworked, they become psychic." His words were encouraging and what I desperately needed to hear, for I feared that I was losing my mind. "We know the Front is drawing closer every day," he continued, "since we're hearing the artillery fire booming constantly. Frankly, I wouldn't be surprised if we did receive large numbers of wounded soon."

I went back to my room to rest for awhile. I wondered if my vision had been prompted by intuition or if, in fact, I had experienced a revelation. I asked God to preserve me from a mental breakdown. My thoughts strayed back to those times on the train in Russia when we boarded scores of wounded men, and the only thing that we could do immediately was relieve their pain. I called the staff together at once and instructed them to have morphine ready, should many wounded arrive simultaneously.

APRIL 3RD The rolling thunder of the artillery increased to a constant roar. Early this morning the injured began to arrive in ambulances, trucks, carts, anything on wheels. The men were mutilated and covered equally with blood and mud. Some were so badly burned and their faces scorched so black, that only the movement of their eyes indicated a spark of life. Within two hours, my vision became a reality. Not only the hall and the stairs, but every room on the first floor was filled with groaning, bleeding men. As I walked through the rooms, I felt Christ there beside me, looking at the pitiful men with compassion.

APRIL 4TH This day was both an end and a beginning. Nurses and paramedics from the other hotels swarmed in to help us and by one thirty in the morning, we had the situation under control. We were most shaken by the pitiful charred bodies of men, still breathing, yet their moaning indicating that the morphine had barely touched their excruciating pain. The odors of ether and chloroform hung heavily in the air.

After the last patient was settled, we sat down together, congratulating ourselves on a job well done. But our chatter gave way to an uneasy silence as we realized that the Front, now two hundred kilometers away, would soon engulf us. Perhaps Hummel expressed the worry deep inside all of us when she softly murmured, "Have we worked so hard to save patients only to see them die?"

Then Dr. Hubenthal spoke slowly and deliberately, "I've thought the matter over and am convinced that the only thing to do is to surrender. I will go with an ambulance with a white flag on it to the American line and surrender in peace, so there will be no fighting here."

We all nodded in silent agreement, and there was absolutely no opposition. Dr. Hubenthal called the mayor and asked him to stop the Kreisleiter from resisting with his pitiful collection of teenagers and old men. The mayor also told the Kreisleiter to move the farmers' wagons which were blocking the streets. I though that was a silly idea anyway to attempt to stop American tanks with farm wagons.

Dr. Hubenthal left at eight in the morning, his hopes high that the white flag would provide safe passage to the American commander. I assured him that I would pray for him constantly. I deeply admired this man for his courage and wisdom. As a precaution, we moved as many patients as possible into the basement. When I saw that everything was under control, I stole up to my room to be alone.

Strange, but often when I face a crisis, the many blessings in my life pass through my mind like a joyful procession. Today was no exception, and I felt more keenly than ever the protection of my heavenly Father. I knew He would be with us now at the hour of surrender. But I was forced to acknowledge other uncomfortable feelings, too—the pain of my country's loss. The Fatherland had stood staunchly for over a century, and I knew it would never be the same. The last war had ended the era of the Kaisers, and I anticipated even more drastic changes from this war. Even though five generations of my family had been born here, I suddenly felt as if my roots were being ripped out of the soil, and I was left dangling. The Fatherland I knew and loved did not exist anymore. In that moment of despair I could not imagine that my roots would ever again find a new repose.

At ten o'clock the mayor called to say that he had just arrested the Kreisleiter. "That man kept shouting that we must all fight to the last man," quoted the mayor, "but I told him that there was no Hitler anymore and we were all through with fighting." The mayor's call filled us with relief, because we knew that now there would be no resistance.

A soldier stopped in to share an anecdote. It seems a certain general had sought refuge in Bad Liebenstein because it was a safe town. The general, however, did not want to be caught in a surrender, so he ordered an ambulance to drive him across the mountains. A young man volunteered to drive him, saying he knew the way, but instead of heading for the mountains, he drove the general to the American Front.

I was convinced that the American army was an instrument in the hands of God designed to stop the cruelties of Hitler, whose lust for power had destroyed so many people and countries. The ravage of Poland remained a vivid memory, one I could not easily forget.

At four o'clock in the afternoon, heavy armored tanks rolled through the streets of the village, and we heard instructions in German broadcast through bullhorns, "Close your windows. Stay in your homes. Keep the streets free." The Americans were here. They had arrived without a shot being fired. We had surrendered and the war was over–at least here. I felt dizzy with relief and went into one of the lounges where a stately grand piano, long silent, stood in one corner. I lifted the lid and with tears streaming down my cheeks, began to play, "Now thank we all our God."

We had survived–we were free of Hitler. I did not fear the Americans, but on the contrary felt confident that if we were cooperative, they would not harm us.

Hugo, the supply officer, Herta, Elsbeth, Benita and I were in the entry hall when the door opened and three American officers walked in. "Guten tag. Wir sollen sehen, was sie brauchen," (Good day. We will see if you need anything.) one said in perfect German.

Without thinking, I responded automatically, "Heil Hitler!" Our official word of greeting. Hugo shoved me aside with a scowl that warned me to be mute. I looked at him and said, "Well, that's what we've been ordered to say for ten years."

One of the American officers put his hands on my shoulders and said, "That's all over now, lady." Then he asked again if we needed anything.

"We don't need anything from you!" Hugo answered harshly.

I glared at him and said, "What do you mean? You haven't fed us decently for weeks." Then I asked the Americans to come with me and I would show them our patients. When they saw the severely burned men and the amputees, they appeared genuinely moved. The American captain gave me twenty four ampules of Penicillin for the burn patients and promised to provide more. He told us that the hotel was now under guard and no one would be allowed to enter or leave. We were officially prisoners-of-war.

One of the soldiers who had searched the hotel for ammunition gave Herta and Benita some chocolate bars and told them with a grin, "Put on some weight."

While all this was happening, Dr's. Holman and Herman were strangely absent. I felt they were probably hiding somewhere, so I gave the order to the nurses to give the Penicillin injections to the burn patients. I had felt uneasy about Dr. Hubenthal all day and was relieved when he finally returned late in the evening, escorted by American guards. He told me that he had been in conference with the American officers for hours. "They wanted to know what supplies and additional staff we needed," he said wearily. "I told them how low we were on food and medicine, but I felt our current staff was adequate since we wouldn't be admitting any more casualties."

I nodded in agreement. I mentioned that our two young doctors were strangely missing, and he was not particularly surprised. "I don't know where they could've gone, but it's not too likely they'll be as free as they might hope." (I suspected that we might not see them again or know their fate.) We then speculated about what lay ahead for us. While our fate was as yet undecided, we hoped we would be released soon to return to our families. All of us hoped to be reunited with our loved ones.

The kindness and concern of the Americans impressed me deeply. Peace had tiptoed in so softly, so mercifully that it was like a dream. How could I adequately express the gratitude I felt later as I fell asleep without the noise of battle in the background?

My sleep was short lived. At four in the morning I was awakened by the rumble of trucks, heavy steps in the hall and boisterous shouting in English. I hurriedly dressed and followed the sound of voices to the kitchen. There in the midst of food I had not seen in ages: butter, eggs bacon, white bread and jelly, were two American soldiers setting up a field kitchen. I stared in open mouthed astonishment. One of the soldiers looked up and asked politely in German, "We'll have breakfast with you this morning, Fraulein. Is it all right to use your kitchen?" I nodded without hesitation and managed a weak, "Ja." It was more than all right with me. The breakfast they served us two hours later was a feast.

The American cooks were not only angels of mercy for us, but for the town as well. They set up stoves on street corners and fed the hungry children. In our hotel, they planned the menus and did most of the cooking, allowing our German cooks to assist. The Germans were rather disgruntled at being relegated to assistants and dish washers but eventually adjusted. The bountiful meals now being served to the patients made up for those weeks of near starvation.

APRIL 6TH Since we were confined to the hotel, we could not attend church this Sunday but gathered about the grand piano for a morning devotion. In the afternoon the nurses and I were sitting on a balcony folding bandages when we noticed a convoy of American trucks pulling up to the Kaiserhof Hotel directly across the street. Quickly but courteously, the Americans led recovered German soldiers to the trucks. We all knew they were headed for prisoner-of-war camps. As the scene unfolded before us, we became increasingly anxious about our fate."We have been declared prisoners-of-war, but what this really means has not been clearly explained to us," said Elsbeth, frowning.

"I know," I nodded. "The Americans are kind to us and allow us to carry on our work as usual but for how long?"

Then Hummel, in her own cheerful way, observed, "Perhaps we won't be sent to the camps because we are medical personnel and not infantry. Maybe they have another plan for us."

APRIL 15TH We began English lessons this evening, taught by a patient who had formerly been a gymnasium teacher. The English I had learned years ago, I rarely used and consequently forgot most of it, so I welcomed this opportunity. Other courses were offered including one in anatomy taught by Dr. Hubenthal. These intellectual endeavors kept us from dwelling on our prisoner status.

Ingenuity came to the fore since it was difficult for all the amputees to be mobile when we only had one wheel chair. A paramedic nailed wheels on boards so the men could sit on them and roll themselves about. Since the amputees were now in the healing stage, they began to focus on their future as handicapped persons. We all knew Germany was bankrupt, so it was doubtful they would receive any disability pension. One rather optimistic amputee, who had adjusted remarkably well, got books from the town library and studied to prepare himself for an occupation. "I'm determined to carve a life for myself and support my family," he often told me. I watched him as he wheeled himself about on his board, talking to the others, trying to convince them of their value, since many felt utterly worthless.

In mid April, the Soviets prepared their final assault on Berlin. The British moved onward to Hamburg and Lubeck, while the Americans headed toward Munich and the Czech and Austrian borders. Hitler, now in his bunker in Berlin, continued to push nonexistent German divisions about on his map, calling on his Nazi officials to destroy resources.

By April 20ᵗʰ, the Soviets entered Berlin and the Soviet and American armies met at Torgau on the Elbe River on April 25ᵗʰ. Realizing the end was near, Hitler along with his mistress Eva Braun committed suicide in his bunker on April 30ᵗʰ. The Germans signed an unconditional surrender on May 7ᵗʰ at Reims. Stalin insisted on a formal ceremony in Berlin on May 9ᵗʰ.

Since President Roosevelt had died on April 12ᵗʰ, Harry Truman had been quickly summoned to the White House to succeed him as U.S. president. After Hitler's suicide, Admiral Donitz assumed political authority for Germany.

APRIL 30ᵀᴴ   From people passing through town, we learned that the Americans had met the Russians at the Elbe River and they had marched into Berlin together. Rumors were circulating that Germany would be divided, but no one was sure where the division would be. I dismissed these rumors, feeling certain that the Americans would never allow the partition of our country.

We were gathered in Dr. Hubenthal's office listening to the news, when the announcer said that Adolph Hitler and his mistress, Eva Braun, had taken their lives in his bunker in Berlin. Soon many hearsay tales circulated about the death of Hitler. Some said since his body was burned beyond recognition, it wasn't really him. Others distrusted the story of his suicide, feeling Hitler was too cowardly for that. I must admit I found it difficult to believe that he was really dead. While the fate of the Fuhrer remained a mystery to me, I hoped most of all for the death of the Nazi party which had reared its ugly head of hatred and evil. I never wanted to see another swastika again.

MAY 9ᵀᴴ   Yesterday Admiral Donitz negotiated the capitulation of Germany. I felt little emotion when I listened to the news broadcast, since I had acknowledged my personal loss a month ago. Today also marked another year of life for me. I was forty-two and speculated that probably half of my life was behind me. The years had winged by as swiftly as a darting hummingbird. Early memories of adventures with my sisters, hikes in the forests, feeding little pigs and picnics in the parks of Hamburg. My heart ached as I relived those special moments with Dr.Beckman and the love we shared. Tears sprang to my eyes. Many people and places had enriched my life, and I felt like the Psalmist, David, that my cup had indeed run over.

I opened my window to breathe in the fragrant spring air laden with the sweet scent of lilac blossoms. The garden below was aglow with colorful flowers, a myriad of purple, blue and white competing in beauty. My heart was filled with the simple joy of living. The greatest gift of all, the love of friends, was on the threshold. Suddenly I became aware of soft steps in the hall, as though they were trying to conceal their approach. The gentle strains of "Jesus Lead Thou On" drifted into my room, and I opened my door to be greeted by the loving smiling faces of my nurses. Erica, beaming her usual coy smile, thrust a large bouquet of lilacs into my arms and handed me a framed poem, signed by all of them.

MAY 13TH   A new American commander arrived today, who was as kind as his predecessor, but more lenient. He allowed us to attend church and the movies, but kept the curfew from eleven at night to six in the morning. The citizens of Bad Liebenstein were friendly to the Americans and felt secure under their protection. The children followed the soldiers everywhere always hoping for chocolate bars or a jeep ride.

JUNE 16TH The number of patients at the Hotel Kaiserhof dwindled to eighty and the doctor in charge asked the American commander for permission to hold an evening of entertainment to relieve the boredom and homesickness. The commander granted permission, but insisted that the event be supervised, since it was an assembly. The commander himself assumed this task, and I noticed that he enjoyed himself immensely. Six patients put on a comedy show, and from somewhere a band materialized and played music for dancing. While the evening gave us a big lift, our anxiety about the future hovered over us like an ever present cloud. I felt a twinge of sadness, too, as I thought of the men back at the Hotel Herzogin Charlotte who would never dance again.

CHAPTER SIXTEEN: LIFE UNDER THE RUSSIANS

JULY 1ST Today was a very dark day. I heard on the radio that the Americans had given Saxonia and Thueringia to the Russians. Didn't they know that these were two of the most important states where the scientists had been working on Hitler's secret weapon? Worse than that–Bad Liebenstein and Griez were both in Thueringia. I was devastated as I, indeed none of us, wanted to live under the Russians. The announcer went on to say that the Allied powers were continuing to confer in Berlin, but I barely listened. I felt as if all was lost. The news filtered down to us in bits and pieces, and Germany's future looked more unsettled every day. I was like a child on a teeter-totter.

 My anxiety was increased by the fact that there was no way to get letters to or from home because mail delivery stopped when the Americans assumed control. The only way to get word to anyone now was to send a letter along with refugees passing through and hope it would be delivered. Unfortunately, few were going east and in the direction of Griez these days.

With peace had come a multitude of problems regarding reparations and the division of Germany into what eventually became the Soviet and Western zones. The boundary between these zones would follow the Elbe river. Since Berlin would be under a joint four-power control (as was Vienna) but lying within the Russian zone, Roosevelt had asked for a corridor to link it to the West, a request which Stalin ignored. Poland, to make up for its loss of land to Russia, was given territory in eastern Germany, expelling all the German citizens. Cities were taken block by block, with people being given only fifteen minutes to gather their belongings and leave their homes.

JULY 3RD Since Bad Liebenstein was near the western border of Thueringia, the exodus of refugees on the streets swelled to a continuous stream of people, pushing carts piled high with belongings, a stream that never ceased day or night.   I watched whole families, elderly couples and solitary individuals.   I was reminded of the exodus of the Israelites from Egypt.   Soldiers, whose units had been disbanded, shed their uniforms and took their places among the fleeing throngs.   Soon the creeks all around became clogged with discarded army uniforms.   Over and over again, the refugees recounted tales of mass evacuations of people to Russia.   Not only that, they reported that railroad tracks were being ripped up and whole factories disassembled to be shipped East.   Russian soldiers confiscated food from the people and openly raped women in the streets.

I felt more vulnerable than ever.   There were still ninety-six patients in our hotel, who needed care, and it was only a matter of time before we would be given over to the Russians.   I prayed fervently for courage and direction, more keenly aware now of the critical and irrevocable decision that lay ahead.

Events transpired in rapid succession, beginning with Dr. Hubenthal calling me into his office.   With the American commander present, he explained that this section would soon be released to the Russians.   The distress must have shown on my face, because the American put his hands on my shoulders and said firmly, "Don't worry.   I will be back to bring you and your patients to the West.   Just be brave and don't cause any trouble for the Russians."   While I wanted to be reassured, having heard the stories of

Russian cruelty from the refugees, I entertained the thought that we might not be here when he returned for us. But I told him that we would be waiting. I hoped he'd return for us soon.

Then a second blow fell, more devastating than the first. Dr. Hubenthal handed me a letter from my original Mother-House, Kaiser-Werter, which had recently been closed by the Russians. With trembling hands, I opened the letter to read:

"The head nurse, Tabea, was a nurse of our Mother House during the war. She has proved to be very efficient in field hospitals and has been working from April 1941 to the end of the war. She has always nursed the wounded faithfully and with great ability and acquired special knowledge in nursing spotted typhus fever patients and also in surgical procedures. Because of the closing of our nursing association, we must dismiss those nurses who are far away. We wish nurse Tabea the best for her future and in her profession."

The letter was signed by the Mother-Superior. While the letter was complimentary, it meant the end of my membership in a nurses' association. Would this jeopardize my professional credibility? Once again the feelings of rootlessness enveloped me. My heritage had been snatched from me by the war, my home was under the red flag and Dr. Paul Beckman had disappeared from my life. Now I had lost my professional identity with the closure of the Mother-House.

But there was more-much more! Dr. Hubenthal shifted uneasily in his chair and avoided looking at me as he spoke. "Tabea, I'm placing you in command of this hospital. The other doctors have gone, and I am leaving now to join my family. Since the Americans have released us, we are no longer under obligation. I'm sorry to leave so quickly, but I want to be gone before the Russians arrive. Would you be willing to stay with the patients until the Americans return?"

Before I could sort out my thoughts and fashion a reply, a paramedic stepped in and announced, "Your ambulance is ready, sir." With that, he got up and left the room. I was so shocked, I sat there speechless. I could not fathom how he, who had been so devoted to his patients, could leave without a backward glance. I was disillusioned and in that moment was convinced that there are times when women are stronger then men. So be it! Let the doctors flee to their homes. I would stay and take care of the patients to the best of my ability.

I walked to the ambulance for a final but unenthusiastic good bye. I noticed that many of the nurses and doctors from the other hotels were leaving, too. Dr. Hubenthal shook my hand and promised to contact my father and let him know I was well and remaining with the patients here. With that, he left.

I went back inside and Elsbeth and the others were standing in the entry hall, looks of disbelief clouding their faces. They apparently knew the situation and were as dumbfounded as I that Dr. Hubenthal had left so abruptly. I explained to them that we had been released by the Americans and they could leave too if they wanted. "I plan to stay with the patients, but I won't command you to remain." My words were bold because I felt in my heart that they would not leave me.

My faith in them was justified when Hummel, speaking for all of them said softly, "Of course we'll stay, Tabea." We decided to be candid about the situation with our patients, assuring them that in an emergency we would get the civilian doctor to come. (Although we didn't know he would.) I was most concerned about the seven burn patients who remained critical and called the civilian hospital to see if they would take them. The doctor at the hospital refused, saying we were prisoners-of-war, and he would need permission from a military commander.

It's funny how in a desperate situation, one can always find something to be grateful for, and for us it was our cooks. They chose to remain with us. The Americans had left an abundant supply of food, so at least we'd eat well.

Shortly after noon, the last of the American troops left, and immediately a mass exodus began. Businessmen, families, more nurses and those patients who could walk took to the roads heading west. Once again the streets were jammed with refugees, only this time they started from Bad Liebenstein. No one wanted to fall into Russian hands or be taken by them as a prisoner-of war.

JULY 6TH The town was preparing to welcome the Russians. Banners were hung across the streets, and pictures of Lenin and Stalin appeared everywhere. Long red streamers hung from windows and cascaded down the walls of the hotels. A man even came into our hotel and hung a Russian flag from the balcony. The sight of it disgusted me. I couldn't imagine where in the world all those flags and posters came from so quickly–like seeds that sprouted overnight. The Russian zone was about to engulf us. I hoped desperately the Americans would keep their promise to return.

In the afternoon, a Russian officer came into our hotel and asked how many patients we had. He was polite, spoke German fluently, and informed us we were free to attend the movies. Little by little, the streets became clogged with divisions of Russian troops, and I watched as they shoved and elbowed the civilians. They were as brash and abusive as the Americans had been well-mannered and compassionate.

During the night, I was awakened by the screams of women and the drunken shouting of Russian soldiers from the street below. I arose and looked out the window, but saw nothing unusual. Except for a knot of soldiers gathered under a lamp post, the street was deserted.

The next morning, a nurse from the Kaiserhof came over and confirmed our worst suspicions–Russian soldiers had come in during the night and raped some of the nurses. The victims were so ashamed and upset that they remained secluded in their rooms. While we were indignant about it, we concluded that reporting the incident would do no good. In fact, it might make matters worse. The security we had known under the Americans had abruptly been replaced with a feeling of helplessness. We felt as if we were at the mercy of the Russians.

We decided we didn't want to chance a similar occurrence at our hotel. Elsbeth suggested that we lock the front doors securely by late afternoon and ask a patient to stand guard. Then Erica came up with the ingenious idea that the six of us should sleep in one room and disguise our whereabouts by placing a wardrobe in front of the bedroom door, covering the opening completely. "We can leave and enter the room by removing the back wall." she said. She was always clever as now. This idea along with the support of each other boosted our sagging spirits.

JULY 8TH We were in the midst of changing dressings on our burn patients, when two American officers came in and told us to have the patients ready to leave the next day. I was happy and relieved to see them, until I remembered the critical patients. I took the officers to examine these men, and they agreed that the trip would be too strenuous for them and they should be transferred to the civilian hospital. As they left, the officers explained to us that if our families were in this zone, we were free to go home after the patients left.

We all came from homes in areas now under the Russian flag. Each of us faced a difficult decision. Should we go with the patients who still needed us, or go home to our families? For me, this was not just a crucial decision, but the most critical decision of my life. I and I alone must decide what to do. There was no doctor, no army, no Mother-House to order me anymore. To go west or to stay east was my difficult choice. Since the mail had ceased, I had no way of knowing if I even had a home to go to. If my family was still alive and I went west, it would appear that I had turned my back on them. On the other hand, if I stayed in the Russian zone and they were dead, I'd have chosen oppression for nothing. And then there were the patients. I felt they still needed me, even on the other side of the border. Wordlessly each of us pondered our choice. I prayed for guidance as never before and drifted off into a fitful sleep.

CHAPTER SEVENTEEN: MOVING WEST

JULY 9th   I stood on the balcony watching the Russian soldiers milling about on the street below. The red banners hanging from every hotel balcony waved a symbolic welcome in the gentle breeze, but the sight of them chilled me to the bone. Only last night I recalled how uneasy I felt when the German civilian doctor came to check the patients at my request. He told me that the Russians would not recognize our discharge papers, but would consider us deserters. "And you know what happens to deserters?" He asked mischievously, pointing his finger at me as if to shoot.   While I didn't believe him, his words were unsettling.

I went inside and called Herta, and we began preparing the patients for the trip. Those men in traction whose bones were wired together we took to surgery.   While Herta administered a light anesthetic, I worked swiftly to remove their external wires and then immobilize their limbs in plaster casts. The men displayed compete trust in us, not one protested that we were not doctors.

I was still in a quandary about what to do with the critical patients. I stood at the bedside of one and said hesitantly, "Erik, I really feel it would be best for you to go to the civilian hospital here. The trip is terribly risky."

"Oh no!" He responded with all the strength he could muster. "Please take me with you. If I am going to die, let me die on the journey west rather than at the hands of the Russians." All around the room, one after another, each man echoed the same sentiment. Reluctantly I agreed to plead their case with the American transportation officer.

Betty J. Iverson

At the stroke of ten just as promised, the Americans arrived with an entourage of eighty ambulances and several large canvas covered army trucks. Obviously well trained, the drivers moved the patients into the ambulances with expertise and gentleness "You've prepared the men well for the trip, Ma'am," one told me. I took the American officer to see the critical patients, who again begged to be taken along. Although three of them appeared near death, the officer consented and ordered them placed in the ambulances behind our vehicle.

In the end we found it difficult to be candid, but each of us sensed that we had reached a common decision to go west. To be sure we felt an obligation to our patients, but more than that we feared what life would bring under the Russians. Not one of us wanted to acknowledge the greatest fear of all: perhaps there was no home or family to which we could return.

After the last patients had been boarded, Herta, Benita, Hummel, Erica, Elsbeth and I climbed into our ambulance. We had no sooner gotten settled, then some Russian soldiers came up and demanded our watches. The American officer sent them away and placed a guard with us. I was disgusted to see the Russian soldiers standing around glaring and hurling insults at the Americans as if they were enemies rather than allies.

As the convoy prepared to roll, a group of civilians approached some black soldiers who were loading boxes of food into the trucks, and asked to be taken along. Without hesitation, the soldiers threw out a few boxes to make room for them, and the civilians scrambled in. When the convoy finally began to move, I breathed a sigh of relief feeling as if I were being delivered from a dire fate.

After a few hours the convoy stopped, and the soldiers helped Elsbeth and me out of the ambulance to check our critical patients. Amazingly, they were not only tolerating the trip, but some were actually better. While the patients were fed lunch in the ambulances, we shared field rations with the soldiers, who had spread a blanket under the trees alongside the road. I relaxed in the sunshine filtering through the trees and the warm company of the Americans. We were in the west and free, leaving anxiety and fear behind. This was an unforgettable moment.

After a journey of six hours, we arrived in Laubach, a village on the Lahn River in Hesse. The American officer told us that they planned to set up a hospital here for most of our patients, but for now he would take them on to Giessen, twenty kilometers away, to a large German military hospital. The critical patients would remain there. I was amazed to hear later that all seven had recovered.

Our driver then took us to our quarters which turned out to be an old villa on the outskirts of the town tucked away in a thick forest of the foothills. Apparently this villa, Shunk, had been a hunting club before the war, quarters for the German officers during the war and was now occupied by medical staff. As we drove through the huge iron gates, I felt like I was slipping back in time. We passed neat gardens along the winding driveway before pulling up to the entrance of an old stone two-story lodge that blended into the forest as if it had always been there.

No sooner had we climbed out of the ambulance, stretching our stiff muscles, then the huge carved wooden door opened, as if on signal. Standing there was a tall elderly and robust couple waiting to welcome us in. "Come in, come in," said the man who was deeply tanned with blonde hair and a thick mustache. "I'm Willie and this is

Olga, my wife." She nodded and smiled graciously, her blue eyes twinkling. Clad in a simple cotton frock and apron, her gray hair pulled back into a bun, she hastened to usher us inside while the soldiers brought in our luggage. Olga told us that they were the caretakers and would do all they could to make us comfortable. She added that she knew we must be tired, but asked if we'd like to see the villa before Willie showed us to our rooms.

I don't know what there is about us Germans, but we always love a tour, so naturally we eagerly agreed. From where I stood in the entry hall, I could see a fire blazing in an immense stone fireplace in a large room off the hall. Paintings of hunting scenes hung on paneled walls, and I could picture the hunters lounging about on those heavy couches in front of the fireplace with their schnapps, exchanging stories. Olga led the way to the basement, where she proudly showed us their apartment, the kitchen where she cooked for all the guests, and the large dining room. Once more I viewed a room for sportsmen with hunting scenes carved into the paneled walls as well as on the furniture. Colorful beer steins and pewter plates stood on shelves about the walls. The long wooden table could easily seat fifty for those sumptuous feasts that were spread here long ago. Today, however, I guessed the meals were simple, if not sparse.

Later alone in my small bedroom, I sank to my knees in relief and gratitude. "Oh Lord, how can I adequately thank you for all you have done for me. Here I am– no fear, no more bombs, no prowling soldiers. And yet my heart longs for my family: Where are they? How are they? Papa, Deborah, Esther and Hans. Has Esther come back to Griez? Are they still in our home? So many unanswered questions, Lord Jesus. I can only entrust them to Your loving care and wait for the day when we will be reunited. And Dr.

Beckman and Liesel–bless them wherever they are. As for me, my new life here is just beginning and in Your hands."

As my feelings of relief and thankfulness spilled out, I tried to convince myself that somehow they had survived and I would see them again. I almost felt guilty about my new-found security. I drifted off to sleep without any premonition that there would ever be casualties besides the war wounded in my charge.

JULY 10th We had to have a hospital for our patients. The Americans were taking over the hospital in Giessen, where our patients were temporarily housed, for their wounded. We had to set up a hospital here for the German wounded. Dr. Herman Gattig, a German army doctor serving under the Americans, called and asked me to go with him to inspect the Laubach courthouse to see if it could serve the purpose.

Converting this courthouse is going to be a challenge, I thought as we strolled beneath the high ceilinged rooms. We noticed first of all that the main sources of water were the hall drinking fountains. In the end, we decided that we could make a hospital out of the courthouse. Without further adieu, the six of us nurses started in, moving out the desks and files and scrubbing the walls and floors. The Americans provided all the necessary equipment and furniture from beds and tables to bed pans and linens. We strung sheets on wires for privacy and placed small portable lamps about the rooms for light. A downstairs office was chosen for the meal preparations. The Americans set up a field kitchen there and provided a cook.

After three days we had the wards ready to receive one hundred patients, and a small minor surgery was in readiness. Dr. Gattig, who'd been helping us all along, now announced that a Dr. Witting, an easy-going German surgeon from Laubach, had been assigned by the Americans as the chief physician for this hospital. Dr. Gattig would continue on as the over-all commander.

JULY 16th Dr. Gattig called me into his office and told me that he was appointing me as the head nurse of the courthouse. Why not? I thought. I have been a head nurse in a fort, on a train, in a cavalry barracks and at a hotel. Maybe the next time I'll be the head nurse on a boat or at a park. But I simply nodded and said I'd do my best. "The five nurses who came with you may be assigned at your discretion," Dr. Gattig said. Then, almost as an aside, he added, "Now Major Springer, I am also appointing you head nurse of the other hospitals."

As I asked about these other hospitals, I must have had a blank look on my face. Dr. Gattig hastened to explain. "There are five schools within walking distance of the courthouse that were converted into hospitals at the end of the war to take care of the heavy civilian and military casualties. The head nurse who has been serving there is leaving to return to her family."

My appointment had to be confirmed by the American army, and a soldier in a jeep came for me the next morning. "Hold on, lady, I drive fast," warned the freckle-faced young man. I did as I was told and found the bumpy ride to Giessen rather exciting.

JULY 24th I was officially installed as head nurse today, incredible to me since I only got here two weeks ago. We celebrated at the villa this evening, yet beneath our gaiety was the common anxiety that as more and more patients were discharged, we would be increasingly unnecessary. For the moment, however, the thought of being unnecessary was the farthest thing from my mind as I chased around from the courthouse to the five schools. Each of the schools housed about seventy-five patients and was staffed by townspeople. I placed Elsbeth and Erica in charge of the medical wards, Hummel in charge of the courthouse patients and Herta and Benita to manage the minor surgery.

Almost immediately I encountered a problem with the carelessness of the town nurses, who were not as thorough or dedicated as I was to the patients. This had always been stressed in my training. The more strict and firm I was, the more they rebelled. If it hadn't been for Elsbeth's wisdom and tactful advice, I might have totally failed. "Tabea, you will have better results if you show a personal interest in the girls and try to understand their problems". She advised. "As things stand now, they're scared to death of you."

I hadn't realized I had become so rigid, and I took her advice to heart. But advice is one thing–applying it is another. After much thought, I decided to have personal chats with the nurses on my daily rounds and listen to their problems. I also set up weekly staff meetings. Gradually the tension between us faded, and   I understood their situation better. In turn, the nurses became more competent.

AUGUST 5th   The delightful month of August arrived, stimulating the flowers in the parks to bloom profusely and the roses to contribute their color and fragrance to the gardens. Summer has always been my favorite season, not only because of the beauty in nature, but also because of the daily concerts in the parks. The American guards allowed us to take evening strolls until eleven, even though we were still considered prisoners-of-war.   Often they would accompany us, and we'd have interesting chats. They loved to talk about their families back home and what life was like in the States. I remember especially two, Willie and Walter. The war lingered vividly in their minds, like a sketch on a blackboard that defies erasure. I was touched by these men whose language I barely understood, whose country symbolized hope and whose feelings were so easily stirred by the sight of the many fatherless German children.

Walter was a relaxed, friendly man, who treated me gallantly on our walks and made me feel like I was his friend. He appeared to have accepted his role in the war. Willie, on the other hand, was troubled. "Whenever I see these kids, I ask them where their father was killed," he would say huskily. "And I always hope they will tell me it was a place I wasn't. I just couldn't stand it if I thought I'd taken some kid's father away from him"

"All soldiers feel that way, Willie, I said. "Germans, too, felt bad about the many fatherless Polish children. That is the tragedy of war. A man is commanded and he goes to fight for his country, because he is loyal and obedient, but the reality is terrible." My words sounded so prosaic—even to me. Yet I wanted desperately to console him, because he was obviously struggling with personal guilt about his participation in the war. He worried me, especially his bouts of depression.

"I'll never forget mowing down line after line of Germans with my machine gun," he'd tell me many times on our walks. I always pretended I'd hadn't heard it a hundred times before.

"Willie, you must realize that there was no other way to stop Hitler from destroying the world except by killing the men who were sent to fight for him." Every discussion of war made my answers seem more inadequate. He was such a thoughtful, but troubled, man. Compassion-especially for the children- was a characteristic of the American G.I.'s that deeply impressed me. I watched them as they constantly plied the youngsters with food and candy, laughing and playing with them. In turn, the children obviously adored them.

Times were tough for the civilians. It was not uncommon for three or four families to share one apartment, especially in the heavily bombed cities. Most had lost all their money in the war, and food was so scarce, almost nonexistent. Even I had lost over six-hundred marks in savings at the Kaiserwerter Mother-House. I recalled my mother's sacrificed silver pieces and the lion-footed dining set as I saw many who now traded in their heirlooms and jewelry for food and essentials on the black market, which was thriving because it was the only supplier. I couldn't decide whether to despise those who profited in the black market or be grateful that they were supplying what people needed. I do know that I felt rich by comparison to those around me. The American army fed and housed me, and I had a job. One would have thought I could finally be at ease, yet a gnawing uneasiness like a growing cancer threatened to consume me. What about my family?

Since the Russians were not allowing mail between the east and the west, I could only rely on messengers to communicate with my family. I had paid a repatriated German soldier one hundred marks to take a letter back with him to Greiz, but thus far I had heard nothing.

The Potsdam conference held in July found Churchill, (being replaced in the middle of the conference by the new Prime Minister, Clement Atlee) Stalin and Truman meeting. While some issues were still not fully resolved, harsh peace terms were laid on Germany. The Allied leaders called for an unconditional surrender of Japan. When Japan did not respond, Truman made the decision to drop an atomic bomb on Hiroshima, August 6ᵗʰ, followed by a second on Nagasaki August 9ᵗʰ. Japan surrendered on August 14ᵗʰ.

Nearly six years after the Nazi invasion of Poland, the Second World War had come to an end, the most destructive and widespread conflict in the history of the world. The toll of human deaths was mind boggling: seventeen million soldiers, six million Jews plus others in concentration camps and thirty million civilians. For some countries the civilian death toll was greater than that of the military. Some historians have speculated that this war was an echo of the "other great war with an armed truce in-between." In other words, was this war part of the same conflict?

The East and West Zones were administered quite differently. From the outset, the American, British and French allowed elections and the revival of political life and the parties that preceded the Nazis, while the Russians extinguished non-Communist parties in their zones. There was not only political disorganization but economic prostration. Industry and agriculture were impaired, and communications and railways crippled. Germany faced a bleak outlook, which was only exacerbated by the growing antagonism between the U.S. and the USSR. Eventually there would be three blocks of power: Western, Communist, and Neutral.

AUGUST 18, 1945   Today we were processed and then released as prisoners-of-war. An army truck arrived early this morning to take us three hundred kilometers to the POW camp at Alsfeld. We were crammed onto benches in the back of the truck along with fifty other people. This was a sample of what it was like to be a prisoner-of war that we had not experienced before, but soon would.

The POW camp was a dismal sight. Several acres of parched open field on the outskirts of Alsfeld were encircled by a barbed-wire fence. A group of tents had been set up to house the American Army Field Division, while the prisoners-of-war obviously slept in the open with only blankets for protection. Holes had been dug in the ground for sanitation.

I was shocked at the sight of thin, gaunt men in dingy uniforms milling about, some obviously men of high rank. When I inquired about these conditions, I was told quite tersely that not only were there no other facilities to house them, but it was taking a long time to process the over two thousand who were waiting. For some inexplicable reason, the Americans here were not as friendly as the ones in Laubach. Did they consider us Nazis?

We were escorted to a huge tent that served as the headquarters. What we anticipated to be a routine procedure of completing papers and answering a few questions actually turned out to be a grueling four hour cross examination that delved into our whereabouts during the war, our family backgrounds and even our political views. The American officer who interrogated me in very fluent German was the first I'd met who was cold and cynical. His attitude confused me. I kept thinking of the Americans who had liberated us, evacuated us and who were now accompanying us on the streets and in the parks of Laubach. None were like this man. Only when my eyes focused on his name tag, which revealed a Jewish surname, did I understand. I longed to say to this Jewish American, "But I'm a German—not a Nazi." His cold demeanor stilled my tongue.

We left the camp that day as free women. We could return to our duties without restrictions or curfews. While our new freedom felt good, we all concurred that we'd never been made to feel like prisoners until today. Hummel suggested that we spend our forty marks, ($10) given by the German government to each released prisoner-of-war, on a fine dinner in Alsfeld. And celebrate we did, perhaps knowing that this would be our last time together. With men being discharged every day, we'd probably close the courthouse and schools soon. Our conversation dwelt on the future.

Elsbeth began by saying, "I'm going back to Hamburg and apply for a supervisory position. I certainly think I've had some experience along that line," she chuckled.

"That's wonderful," I said. "I know you'll do well." The other four talked about completing their education, and were very hopeful and optimistic. If nothing else, the army had given them a future and a career path. I alone remained silent and fortunately no one noticed. What would I do? I had no idea.

SEPTEMBER 1st Dr. Gattig summoned Dr. Witting and me to his office for the inevitable announcement that the hospital at the courthouse would be dissolved this week and return to its former function again. However, there were plans in the offing for the five schools. "Herr Witting, you will be free to resume your practice here in Laubach, and Major Springer, we would like you to stay on as head nurse," he continued.

How could I be a head nurse when the hospitals were all closed and the patients gone home? My confusion must have been obvious, because Dr, Gattig hastened to explain, "Only the courthouse will no longer be used as a medical facility. The schools will continue to function as hospitals–

only with a different kind of patient." I asked him what he meant by a different kind of patient.

"Well, it seems there is an urgent need for a treatment center for women with venereal diseases," he said simply. "Such a center will be established here, and you are to head the staff. We hope most of the nurses will stay on. There is a doctor on his way, who is a venereal disease specialist, and he will be the administrator. You will continue under the supervision of the American army."

He spoke very matter-of-factly, as if he were discussing chicken pox, but I felt like someone had punched me in the stomach. My ears were ringing. I could not believe that I was being asked to take care of prostitutes. Was this how my army career would end? I had always had compassion for my patients, but now I felt resentment. I did not want to take care of "that kind of girl." I made no attempt to hide my distaste, vigorously shaking my head.

Dr. Gattig appeared not to notice as he went on to explain that these women had been civilian employees of the German army, such as secretaries and clerks, who had nowhere to go when the war ended and were literally starving. A group of G.I.'s had taken them under their wings and set them up in tents in the forest. "Unfortunately, they passed on to these girls the venereal diseases they had contracted in France," he said. "Three months had passed before they were discovered by an American army commander, and by then the diseases had reached epidemic proportions."

I shook my head again, groping for the words to refuse, when Dr. Gattig reached across his desk, patting my hand. "Major Springer, where will you go if you don't take this position? While it may be difficult for you, I don't think

Betty J. Iverson

you have any choice. Besides, the Americans appointed you because they felt you were capable." He continued to reassure me, stressing that the specialist coming was very good, and I would get used to this kind of nursing. "After all," he said, "venereal diseases are contagious–just like measles. These illnesses need treatment and control, too."

Then he took my hand, saying, "This hand has done so much in the operating room and is now being called upon to care for the black sheep who are God's children, too." His persuasive tactics were successful, and I numbly nodded agreement. He was right about one thing–I had no choice.

Dr. Gattig stood, indicating the end of the interview as he shook my hand in a final farewell. He too, was leaving in the morning to resume his civilian practice. Both doctors gave me certificates commending my work and that was that. As of this moment, my food rations were reduced to that of a German civilian: meager quantities of bread, potatoes and vegetables, a half pound of meat and one stick of butter each week. I was now a civilian nurse employed by the Americans and working for a German doctor. My dream of a new life was following a thorny path. I hoped that my nurses wouldn't quit, although I expected that some might.

With their new function in mind, I inspected the schools and at the same time broke the news to the staff. Of the five who had come from Bad Liebenstein, only Herta was willing to remain. Fortunately I did better with the rest of the staff, all of whom indicated that they would stay on.

I returned to the villa to be alone with my tortured, frustrated soul, as I contemplated this turn of events. I prayed earnestly, fighting the anger that was churning inside me, because I had been coerced into nursing girls like that—girls with a disease they shouldn't have.

Suddenly I saw myself as the Pharisee who stood so proper and pure in the front of the publican at the temple, lording his superiority over others. Who was I to judge what they had done? After all, I had been protected and fed by the American army, while they were bereft of food, homes and husbands to take care of them. I was overcome by a sense of shame and humiliation. These girls needed me as much, perhaps more, than any patients I'd ever nursed. I begged God to forgive me and change my proud heart and open my eyes to see His ways as I undertook this new duty.

He not only opened my heart, but also my memory. I wandered back to the days of Papa's ministry in Hamburg. Strange, but I had forgotten that he had worked closely with the Salvation Army in founding a midnight mission in the St. Pauli district of Hamburg, a section frequented by prostitutes. They hoped to save the young runaways, who came to the city in hopes of finding a job or to change their luck. Instead these young girls were lured by the syndicate women to work in the houses of pleasure, and the young boys were nabbed to satisfy the homosexual desires of older men. All these activities made the Port of Hamburg infamous. Papa helped found this mission, hoping he could stop this waste and bondage of human beings. He was especially upset that the girls were often shipped to Argentina under the guise of being given governess positions, only to wind up in bordellos. It was a slave market.

Whenever Papa approached the owner of a bordello to release a girl, he would be told, "She owes me a big debt for room and board. When she pays up, she can go." Since prostitution was legal in this section of Hamburg, it was quite difficult to secure the release of anyone, unless they became ill with venereal disease. Then they were left on the streets to die. Life there was degrading and dangerous. My father often remarked that the police gave them protection around the mission. I wished he were here now so we could talk things over, because he would be understanding, and full of mercy–without any misgivings. In this moment I felt so proud of him and hoped I could develop the same love and concern that he had always given.

There were many farewells at the villa this evening. The American guards were leaving, too, as well as Elsbeth, Erica, Hummel and Benita. The peace I had made with my new assignment made the farewell easier than it might have been. Yet these good byes, like so many, were final as it was difficult, if not impossible, to keep in touch. Elsbeth was leaving for Marburg in the morning where she'd been promised a supervisory position. Unable to locate her family, Hummel had decided to join relatives in Bavaria and work in a kindergarten. Erica was going to Darmstadt, where she'd heard there were openings at the civilian hospital.

I asked Benita, what she would do. Of them all, Benita was the most adventuresome, but that was hardly surprising. She'd been on her own since age fifteen when she had been deported to Germany. "As long as the Russians are in Riga, it won't be home to me. And it has been so many years since I've heard anything from my family there that I have lost all hope that they are still alive. But if they are, we will meet again one day. For now I must build a new life." Her blue eyes sparkled as she spoke. "Last week I went to the American Center for Foreign Affairs in Giessen, and they were encouraging when I asked about emigrating to the United States. They said my nursing experience and my desire to continue my education gave me a good chance to realize my goal." The war was over, but the partings went on unabated.

CHAPTER EIGHTEEN: THE FALLEN ONES

SEPTEMBER 2nd Nature has always been my tonic in times of melancholy, and it certainly was on this day. I looked out at the vibrancy of fall in the yellow birch leaves glinting in the sun and forming a patchwork forest of reds, greens and yellows. I watched out my window as the jeep bearing Willie and Walter pulled away. I was sorry to see them go, for they had been more like companions than guards to me. The mother in me hoped that once back home, Willie could shed the guilt that plagued him. After the last jeep had pulled out, the villa was quite silent. I would face tomorrow in the morning.

SEPTEMBER 3rd This morning, Dr. Julich, the venereal disease specialist, arrived. He was a handsome man in his thirties with neatly trimmed dark brown hair, attired in a worn, but pressed suit. His kindness and tolerance were obvious to me from the outset. He greeted Herta and me with an easy smile and his twinkling brown eyes put us at ease at once. "It's important that you think of venereal diseases as illness, and not as a punishment for immorality," he stressed, as he briefly oriented us. "Try to see these patients as girls in need, rather than social outcasts." He had a knack for making the work seem urgent. The viewpoint and urgency he stressed were designed, I'm sure, to rid us of our misgivings. He was successful.

He then introduced us to the two L.V.N.'s he had brought along who would work in the examining rooms. Trained by him, they shared his positive outlook, as did the two laboratory technicians who would work in the laboratory set up in the unused basements rooms at the villa.

When I took Dr. Julich on a tour of the empty school buildings now ready for the new patients, he radiated that same enthusiasm to the nurses there. I felt that if anyone was harboring ill feelings toward the incoming patients, he certainly did his best to dispel them. Unfortunately we had not considered the patients' feelings.

That afternoon they began arriving. The first group of twenty girls were brought in an army truck under heavy guard to the villa. They screamed, shouted obscenities, and bit the guards who had to forcibly bring them into the examining rooms. The girls made it quite clear they were not interested in treatment. My misgivings returned–they were animals. But I mustered as friendly a manner as possible, greeting each girl and explaining what would be done and why treatment was important. My words were heeded about as much as leaves blown away with the wind.

One particular woman, disheveled and grimy, showered me with foul phrases I'd never heard before, not even in the army. Then she shrieked at me, "Save your pretty talk, old witch. Just get me the hell out of here! This is what I think of your treatment," she said as she spat in my face. Now I was furious, but I gritted my teeth and resolved to meet the challenge. However, I wasn't sure just how and stood there in a quandary until Dr. Julich arrived. He spoke softly to the women, and they began to calm down and cooperate.

While the examinations were being done at the villa, the American guards went to the schools and wound barbed-wire fences, twelve feet high, about each one. Armed guards were then stationed at the doors and along the fences, making the treatment centers look like prisons.

SEPTEMBER 15th With such difficult and unruly patients, the staff needed constant encouragement. More patients arrived every day, repeating the same ugly arrival scene, until all five centers were crammed full. Since most girls did not want to be here and were convinced that treatment was not necessary, they tried to escape. The Americans answered by placing more guards around the schools. Some girls appeared nude at the windows, attempting to seduce the guards. One even went so far as to jump out of a second story window, but she was promptly shot before she could reach the guard. That settled things down considerably.

Before long our hospitals became an international center. There were more women infected than I could have possibly imagined. They were brought here from Poland, France, Italy and the Baltic countries. Some had had syphilis for over a year with chancres as large as cauliflowers. These chancres were extremely painful and difficult to heal. We used a mercury solution, Salversan, which was effective. Penicillin was the primary drug used to treat both syphilis and gonorrhea. Once a week, I was taken by car to the American supply headquarters in Darmstadt for the Penicillin. I was responsible for the drug and instructed to keep an accurate record as Penicillin was often stolen and sold on the black market, where it traded like gold. We kept our supply locked in a cool dark room, and took a daily count.

OCTOBER 14th Although the days were trying, our evenings were filled with pleasant camaraderie with the new contingent of American guards, Dr. Julich, and his staff. We oftn sat around the fireplace chatting and singing. Dr. Julich was eager to learn all about the United States, spoke English fluently and got along well with the guards. In turn, they respected him. Always a charming man and curious about others, I never heard him say much about himself. In fact, I did not know if he was married. On the other hand, Martha, one of the lab technicians, and I, always found much to talk about, and chatted between songs. She was about my age and also had family in the Russian zone. With so much in common, we became good friends.

Willie and Olga often joined us about the fire. When Willie brought out his zither to accompany our German or American songs, I was reminded of my childhood when our family drew together like moths to a lamp for our family time. In the lingering twilight hours of summer, we would sit outside chatting with neighbors and singing along with an accordion or a zither.

This companionship helped to fill the void when Herta came to me one afternoon to tell me that she was leaving. Always so loyal, yet quiet-spoken, she simply announced, "I'm so sorry to tell you this, Tabea, but I am leaving soon." My heart skipped a beat when I asked her if it was the work.

"Well, partly," she returned hesitantly. "But I've been thinking a lot about my future. I am anxious to finish my R.N. training, and I want to search for my family. I've been to the Red Cross twice, and they haven't found so much as a trace of them–but I will keep trying."

Her words struck a responsive cord in me. Should I be doing more to locate my family? The letters sent with messengers and my trips to the Red Cross office had also produced nothing.

On her next day off, Herta left for Giessen, and did not return. I never saw or heard from her again.

NOVEMBER 1st This morning when I opened the back door to get the newspaper, I found a freshly killed deer lying on the steps with a note attached:

Dear Head Nurse, Tabea,

> Would you be so kind as to make a good
> meal out of this deer for about fourteen
> Americans? We will bring you everything
> you need.
>> Staff Sergeant J.P. Messiano

Staff Sergeant Messiano was the commander of the guards and had his office at the villa. He treated all of us Germans with respect and seemed to understand that only the Nazis were his enemies. I smiled to myself thinking that all those hunting scenes around the villa must have inspired him.

I called Willie to help me bring in the carcass, and his eyes lit up with delight as if he'd shot the deer himself. "It has been such a long time since I've skinned a deer," he said enthusiastically. "In fact, if my memory serves me correctly, it was back before the war began." I watched as he began the task, deftly cutting up the leg and down the stomach, wielding the knife like a surgeon.

That afternoon, the sergeant brought boxes of food for what apparently was going to be a banquet and invited all of us at the villa to join them, too. We appreciated his gesture, since he obviously knew about our rations. I took the day off from the treatment centers to cook, and Martha and Alma, the other lab technician, offered to help. Soon we were up to our elbows in potato dumplings. Meanwhile, the deer had been cut up into roasts and was marinating in wine and butter in heavy cast iron pans, until just the right time to roast. We gathered colorful fall leaves and decorated the long table and the shelves on the walls of the dining room, making the room look very festive.

Finally the Americans arrived, and what a jovial group they were. As they walked into the dining room, one said, "It looks just like Thanksgiving." How nice, I thought, an occasion just to give thanks. What would these Americans think of next? I felt less strange everyday to be working with, and now eating with, Americans in peace and friendliness. No war, no fear, no suspicion.

After dinner, Willie brought out his zither, and we sang. The Americans taught us the song "Getting to know you." The room was bursting with such warmth and happiness that I wished the whole world could be like this.

NOVEMBER 27th As the weeks went by, the girls became more receptive to counseling when I spent time with them, and some even showed an interest in finding a different life. Once cured, they were discharged to refugee camps at Giessen or Darmstadt where they stayed until they found employment. Sadly, there were always more to take their places. The American Military Police kept finding the girls everywhere: in empty freight cars, garden cottages on abandoned estates and in the unused bunkers. The treatment centers continued to run smoothly under Dr. Julich's excellent direction. From the number of admissions, it was apparent that the schools would remain hospitals for some time to come.

DECEMBER 9th This week began on an ominous note. The Americans decided to transfer control of the treatment centers to the Germans, with the promise that they would continue to supply the Penicillin and the guards. Today the German officials sent a committee to the centers, comprised of a two officious women, a timid secretary and an arrogant doctor, who introduced himself as the "New chief of staff."

311

Dr. Julich and I were both shocked and resentful. We did not know what to expect when they summoned us to meet with them. They treated Dr. Julich in a demeaning and disrespectful manner, and never mentioned what a remarkable job he had done. He stormed out of the room in disgust, his face flushed with anger. "I'm resigning immediately to return to private practice," he announced bitterly. "There is obviously no longer a place for me here."

My heart sank at his words, because I had not only come to depend on him, but would miss him terribly. Not only that, but Dr. Jocksel, the newly appointed chief, was obviously a rude and callous fellow. He would get no respect from me. Back at the villa that evening, Dr. Julich came to tell me good-bye. "Tabea, I must warn you that Dr. Jocksel as well as some of the committee members are Nazis. You must keep a sharp eye out." I nodded numbly, for I knew, like most Germans, that the Nazis, like leopards, did not change their spots, but simply hid their allegiance under a thin veneer. One thing they could not disguise, however, was their hatred for the Americans. And then Dr. Julich was gone.

The four staff members Dr. Julich had brought along were staying on, but only until he had established himself and could send for them. His abrupt departure was followed by that of Sgt. Messiano. He wrote me a nice farewell note, which said in part: "With people like Tabea in Germany, it won't be long before we can leave Germany to the Germans."

I was only mildly reassured that Dr. Julich's staff was remaining, because I felt it was only a matter of time before Dr. Jocksel would bring in his own people. The surprise, however, was how quickly.

DECEMBER 14th Today a new lab technician was added to
the staff by Dr. Jocksel. While both he and his new
technician, Elsa, stayed at the villa, they kept to themselves
and were unfriendly. Not to be outdone by this Nazi, Olga
and I conspired to keep him on German rations, not sharing
with him the extra food often provided by the Americans.
The oppressed I have fed, but I felt no obligation to feed the
oppressive.

The ritual of showing a new doctor around has always
been one of my delights. In Dr. Jocksel's case, however,
the tour of the treatment centers was tedious. Everywhere
we went he issued orders to the staff in a sharp gruff tone,
and I felt embarrassed to be with him. He neither looked at
the American guards nor acknowledged their greetings.
When I stopped and spoke with them, he glared at me.
Later when we were alone, he ordered me to ignore the
Americans. I chose to disregard this order, which didn't
ingratiate me in his favor.

December 24th The first snow of the season fell softly
during the night, and I awakened to a world shrouded in
white. While only last week I had been looking forward to
Christmas and would have been delighted by the snowfall,
today the Christmas setting had arrived but not the
Christmas spirit. Perhaps the holiday reminded me that I
was not only away from home, but still did not know if
there was a home and family. The warmth of the people at
the villa was at best a partial substitute.

When I lamented to Willie that we had no money for
simple decorations, not to mention a tree, his face lit up and
he told me slyly to wait and see. Within the hour, he called
me down to the dining room, and there stood the most
beautiful pine tree I had ever seen. It was lovely and full
with its top branches touching the ceiling. "Oh, it's the

loveliest tree I have ever seen," I cried. "Where did you get it?"

With a slow grin, Willie pointed to the forest. "There are so many out there. We had always cut one for the villa before, but I guess Olga and I got out of the habit during the war."

Even unadorned, the tree was festive, but the American guards would not leave it bare. They made silver bells by wrapping foil from their gum and candy wrappers around paper cups and then cut out paper stars to nestle among the branches. For the final touch, they hung striped candy canes. The sight of this decorated tree finally unlocked my spirit to Christmas and the joy of Jesus' birth.

That night we gathered round the tree to sing Christmas carols in both German and English and the songs sprang from my heart. This was Christmas after all, and the joy of Christ transcended everything, including the bleak landscape of my soul. On this special night, I don't know why, but I expected Dr. Jocksel and Elsa to join us. Of course, they didn't.

JANUARY 10th, 1946 Another year had rolled around, and I had been too busy to ponder what lay ahead. Most of all, I hoped for word from my family. Dr. Paul Beckman and Liesel remained as shadows in my memory. Meanwhile, I was disheartened about the drastic changes which had taken place the past two weeks at the treatment centers. The staff was constantly on edge because Dr. Jocksel continued to be critical and domineering to the nurses as well as abusive to the patients.

I became aware of his actions last week when I saw him strike a girl in the face when she complained that the examination hurt. I suspected that he was not so upset that the girl had a venereal disease, but that she had been infected by Americans, whom he despised. Slapping the complaining girls became his routine pattern, but it climaxed for me today when he struck a patient so hard the sound could be heard through the closed door. I brusquely opened the examination room door and left it ajar so the American guards could hear Dr. Jocksel's abuse. He was infuriated by this and shouted at me, "You have no right to interfere with examinations. Don't ever come near this room again!"

Since then, he adopted a sullen attitude toward me and spoke only when necessary–and then in terse monosyllables. I overheard him attempting to persuade the Americans that Elsa, rather than me, should be in charge of the Penicillin. The Americans refused his request, noting that there had never been a bottle missing.

JANUARY 16th Highly agitated, Martha called me to the lab to look over the order book for Penicillin. She pointed out that Penicillin was still being ordered for patients who had been discharged several weeks ago. After careful study, I discovered that fifty bottles had been ordered in this manner and all of them were now missing. I strongly suspected that they were destined for the black market where a bottle of Penicillin now fetched fifty marks. Since Elsa had signed for them, she was the obvious culprit.

While I felt that Dr. Jocksel was also involved, I had no alternative but to bring the matter to his attention since he was the administrator. When I showed him the pages, his eyes bulged and his lips twitched furiously like a madman. In a rage, he shouted at Martha, "You had no right to tell her!"

Then he glared at me, his eyes blazing with such hatred that I thought he was going to hit me like he did the girls, but instead he said icily, "This hospital is under German authority–my authority. I order you to keep your mouth shut! If you know what is good for you, you will forget the entire matter. A loyal German does not report to the enemy American." He then dismissed us with, "Carry on as before–as if nothing has happened."

That did it! As I left his office, I vowed that I would not be badgered by the Nazis anymore. Nor would I stand by and watch profits, for a drug my girls needed, go to line the pockets of a man like him. Blinded by loyalty, we had all cowered before the Nazis for the past ten years. The fear of them had shut us up even before there was a war. No more. Even if I seemed like a traitor, I was going to report the matter. That night at the villa, I spoke with Sergeant Ferrero, the new commander of the guards. He promised me he would explain the situation to the American commander.

JANUARY 18th The German committee, along with the American commander, came to Laubach today for an investigation. The only evidence of the theft was the pages from the book which showed fifty bottles of Penicillin unaccounted for. The committee concluded that since there was no proof of what had happened to the drug, no charges could be filed. The American commander appeared unconcerned, and in fact, intimated that I had made up the entire incident. Missing bottles of Penicillin were apparently not high on his priority list, and he appeared anxious to dismiss the matter. On the other hand, the German committee said they wanted to avoid further problems and decided to fire Martha and me, giving us three months' salary.

Within two hours, I had in hand a brief reference from Dr. Jocksel and had joined the ranks of the unemployed. Thus ended a job I had not relished, yet had come to find rewarding, perhaps even enjoyable. I was not as angry about the dismissal as I was about the injustice and unfairness of the decision. Yet I shouldn't have been surprised. After all, the committee had to protect their doctor. The decision, however, made me fear that things could revert back to the Nazi regime we all thought was vanquished. I had mourned the loss of my country, and now I mourned the rising again of Nazism. What kind of Germany was left for me?

As I looked ahead, I was filled with hopelessness. I had no job, no Dr. Beckman and no word from my family. Soon I would be without housing or the support of the Americans. My future loomed as empty as the vast bleak snow-dusted Russian prairie.

CHAPTER NINETEEN: A NEW DESTINY

JANUARY 16th   I awakened to a Christmas card world outside my window. I   lingered in bed and enjoyed the sight of icicles hanging from the eaves, glistening in the sun like crystal spears. I thought back to yesterday, and I felt no remorse about leaving.   After all, whom would I miss? Certainly not Dr. Jocksel. Willie and Olga had already left last week because of his constant complaining and rudeness. I heard that they were now managing an apartment building here in Laubach.

A soft tapping at my door nudged me out of bed. Martha stood on the threshold, tears streaming down her cheeks. She looked so pathetic that I pulled her inside and hugged her tightly. "Martha, Martha, I'm so sorry to see you hurt. You always did a good job here."

She shook her head, saying, "Oh, I'm not sorry that I was fired, or that I'm leaving here. It's just the unfairness of it all–to both of us. I have come by to say good-bye and to tell you how much your friendship meant to me. And I have good news, too. Dr. Julich has a position for me." She paused, a troubled expression clouding her face as she said, "But you, Tabea, what will you do?"

"Me? Oh something will turn up, I'm sure. I always manage to find a job," I said with a confidence I did not feel. I not only did not want her to worry about me, but I was ashamed of the hopelessness I felt deep inside.

She had been gone only a moment when there was a second knock at my door. This time I found Sergeant Fererro standing there. He offered to send a jeep for me at one o'clock to take me anywhere I wanted to go. "Thank you, that's very kind of you. I'll be ready." I said, even though I didn't have the slightest idea of where I would be going.

As he turned to leave, he said, "Tabea, I really appreciate how kind you've been. You have made me feel at home here. I think it's just rotten what they've done to you." Those few words of his were like a balm that soothed the hurt and bewilderment I felt. I was impressed that once again I was encouraged by an American who offered help and expressed support for me.

There was another knock on the door. I thought, is there no end to the visitors this morning? A messenger stood there with a note from Willie and Olga. I tore it open eagerly and read, "Tabea, we've just heard about what happened to you, and we want you to come and stay with us as long as you like. Our spare bedroom needs an occupant." Directions were included. I sent the messenger on his way with my glad acceptance.

As I dressed I mulled over my situation. I had a place to stay and a way to get there, but no job. The thought struck me that I had not had a vacation in over two years— why not take one now? After all, I had three months salary in my pocket.

I watched from my window as the driver drove up his jeep to the villa promptly at one o'clock. I walked out of that villa with my head held high, feeling like a queen leaving her castle. Dr. Jocksel, was nowhere to be seen, so I presumed he was in his room. Although he made no obvious move to bid me good-bye, I liked to think that he saw me leave proud and undefeated.

The driver helped me out of the jeep at Willie and Olga's apartment, and handed me a package from Sgt. Fererro. As I thanked him for his courtesy, I felt a sudden regret that I would not be around these fun-loving Americans anymore. I hoped that my face did not betray my feelings. There was no time for me to dwell on this as Olga opened the door and wrapped me in a warm hug, welcoming me like a sister. When we opened the package, we found a week's supply of food. I felt once more God's loving care through the kindness of people. I was uncertain-yes, but worried-no.

MAY 22nd The gray days of winter reluctantly yielded to warm spring rains, and the fruit trees responded with swelling buds. While the months spent in the warm abode of Willie and Olga had restored and refreshed my spirit, I felt the time had come for me to join a nurses' organization, and get back to my career again.

I had not been without a job—on the contrary. The hospital in Laubach recruited me to work as a mid-wife and baby nurse. Since the hospital could accept only emergency patients, all the babies of the German women were being delivered at home. I usually spent two weeks taking care of the mother and baby after a delivery.

I made an appointment with the Mother-Superior at the Mother House in Bad-Homberg, about two hundred fifty kilometers away. Since this Mother-House had been affiliated with mine, (Kaiserwerter) I felt confident that she would help me find a position. At the very least, I assumed she would offer me shelter until I was settled. This was not only traditional, but I had received this benefit many times at the Mother-House in Kassel.

Willie drove me to the station, handed me my suitcase, and squeezed my hand encouragingly as he bade me good-bye. "No matter how things turn out, you will always have a home with us." I was reassured to know I had a place, even if it wasn't home. Would any place ever be home again?

The train ride took about five hours, with a short layover in Giessen. I stared unseeing out the train window, and my thoughts wandered back to other train rides when I'd felt anxious and alone. When I was on the train to Bad Liebenstein, I'd felt resentful and angry leaving Rudolstadt so soon. I'd hoped for a reprieve from the bombing, only to have the train bombed. While I had worries then, lack of work was not one of them.

As the train pulled into Bad-Homberg, a small resort town, I noticed all the posters advertising cures for kidney and stomach ailments in the mineral water baths. There seemed to be no end to the number of sanitariums, claiming cures. Struggling with my suitcase, I finally found the Mother-House at the edge of town, a cold, forbidding-looking structure.

The Hostess-Nurse directed me to the Mother-Superior's office, with a greeting as cold as the exterior. In fact, the Hostess-Nurse barely said a word and the Mother-Superior greeted me perfunctorily, as if I was an unwelcome interruption. I sat erect and silent while she looked over my discharge papers and certificates of reference. Finally she glanced up, peering at me with steel gray eyes, magnified by her thick glasses.

"I see you've spent most of the past few years as a head nurse or supervisor. There are no positions like that open right now, and I'm sure you would not be satisfied working under someone else's direction. Also, I noticed that your family is in the Russian zone. I think it would be better if you joined them there. After all, I'm sure nurses are needed in the east, too." She spoke each sentence firmly and crisply, chopping off her words.

"But I don't want to leave the west," I protested. "I have no idea if my family is still alive, but even if they are, I can provide for them better from here." How I wanted to tell this woman that when the war ended, all German army records had been sent to West Berlin. While the Red Cross attempted to reunite soldiers with their families, there were many like me, who did not know if their families had survived the bombings or were evacuated. I felt it could take years for us to find each other again, or, in the worst scenario, we never would. I had not been able to obtain any word about them, nor Dr. Beckman nor Leisel Schmidt. Not only that, having experienced living under the Russians for just a brief time convinced me that I would not want to do that again. But her coldness kept my tongue silent.

She shrugged her shoulders and said, "Well, I'm sorry but I really have nothing for you." She handed my reference papers back me. Without rising or speaking another word, she turned her attention back to the stack of papers on her desk. The interview was over. I had spent five hours, traveling to an interview that lasted less than ten minutes.

Without knowing quite how I got there, I found myself back on the street. I felt ridiculous, as I walked along with my suitcase because she had not even offered me shelter. Nor did she bother to phone any hospital to inquire on my behalf. I was humiliated to be dismissed so abruptly. I smiled to myself as I speculated that it was possible to be an orphan at the age of forty-three. I was more alone now than I had ever been in my life.

I left Bad-Homberg on the next train out. On an impulse, I decided to stop at Giessen. Much of this town had been leveled by bombs, and until now I had no desire to see more ruins. However, for some inexplicable reason, I wanted to see the town today. I walked past block after block of shattered buildings. Bricks and stones lay scattered about like children's blocks. Finally I came upon a large pile of rubble that had been a children's hospital. I had heard that thirty nurses with babes in their arms were entombed here, in one of the war's many makeshift graves. I sat down on a broken wall. But instead of tears, I felt ashamed. How could I feel morose and futile, when I was still alive? Through all the bombings, God had spared me. Surely He would not abandon me now.

Suddenly I heard a cheerful voice call out, "Tabea! What in the world are you doing sitting down there?" For a moment I thought my mind was playing tricks on me. I had been so distraught and absorbed in my thoughts that I had failed to see a jeep drivel up to the curb only fifteen feet away. I recognized the voice as that of an American, but the voice was not familiar to me. I looked up then and recognized this man as one of the officers who had come to the deer banquet at the Shunk Villa. I was amazed that he remembered me from that single meeting.

My face obviously showed my feelings, because he insisted that I climb into the jeep and tell him what was bothering me. Like an obedient child, I recounted every detail of my firing to my rejection today by the Mother-Superior, including her advice that I go east. I was going to say more, but he interrupted me, exclaiming, "You're just what we need at our hospital here."

He didn't offer any further explanation or even seem concerned that I had no idea what he was talking about. He drove to the train station, talking the whole time, a mixture of English, throwing in some German, as if I couldn't understand. My emotions and his words were tossed about in a jumble by the pitching, lurching jeep. At the station he jumped out, dragging me by the arm, saying we had to get my suitcase. In a whirlwind, we were back in the jeep and driving to a hospital. Before I knew what was happening, I was sitting in a chair in the personnel office of the American Army Hospital. Within minutes he had summoned the nursing supervisor and the chief surgeon. I was hired on the spot–for what I wasn't certain. But they were going to pay me a salary and also provide room and board. The nursing supervisor said she would meet with me in the morning and explain all the details.

It was a miracle! Only hours before, I had been a nurse with no job and no prospects. I had been fired from my former job and humiliated in my efforts to find a new one. I had sat forlorn by the entombment of pediatric nurses, feeling totally alone in the world with no future in sight.

Now I was seated in this hospital office surrounded by the welcoming faces of Americans. People who needed me and valued what I had to offer. I would be given shelter and a salary. And all because of a strange and wonderful coincidence. I had once prepared a deer banquet for an American soldier and his friends, and he remembered me. The Lord works in mysterious ways. I felt my ripped out German roots easing into a new home. It was American and would eventually have a new name- Kansas.

EPILOGUE

Tabea worked for the American army at the hospital in Giessen, as the head nurse of the German nurses on staff. She grew fond of the American army nurses, as well as the doctors and chaplains. She felt increasingly drawn to them and the country they represented.

Tabea eventually established contact with her family. She paid a man going east 100 marks to deliver a letter to her father. She then received a reply from him by messenger. He reassured her that they were all alive, but struggling in poverty under the Russians. He wrote that Esther and Hans lived in a small apartment, and she was forced to sew army uniforms for the Russians. Once mail was allowed between the east and west, Tabea sent them needed items, but her letters were censored and her packages examined.

She did not give up on her efforts to find her vanished friends. At the Red Cross office, she again sent letters of inquiry about Dr. Paul Beckman and Liesel Schmidt. The replies always trickled back, "Person cannot be traced-missing in action." Tabea felt strongly that Dr. Beckman had not survived the war. While that was a sad prospect, she considered that being a prisoner in a Siberian labor camp a far worse alternative for him. This was the fate of many German army officers. East Prussia had been transformed by Russia, and Konigsberg was renamed Kaliningrad, to reflect its new allegiance. Dr. Beckman's home and clinic were surely gone.

Esther and her son, Hans, eventually made their way to the west. They were helped across the border by a resistance group, who were primarily East German farmers who had banded together. They were very cautious and gave Esther only the name of her contact in the next town. She was taken as close as twenty kilometers from the border. The closer Esther got to the border, the more Russian patrols she saw. She and Hans had been instructed to appear like local residents. They walked along the railroad tracks, stopping at houses along the way and purchasing produce from the farmers.

Early one evening they were stopped by a Russian soldier on a motorcycle. He questioned them, but let them go when Esther told him they were going to visit her sick mother. She and Hans then walked up to a house nearby, and the Russian watched as they entered. Fortunately, the elderly couple there welcomed them inside. Later that night, the man took them in his wagon to a field on the border. They ran into the woods and from there crossed the border. Esther was relieved that there were no fences here. The area was secured by Russian soldiers, who patrolled the border on motorcycles.

Esther and Hans appeared at the gate of the hospital in Giessen one evening, and Esther asked the guard to summon Tabea. After a tearful reunion, Tabea met with the American commander, who disregarded the rules and allowed Esther and Hans to stay with Tabea until they could be settled in a refugee camp nearby.

She said that Papa Springer had reluctantly agreed to her plan to escape for the sake of Hans. The Russians had closed the gymnasium and began to assign young boys to work in Griez or sent them to Russia. Papa did not want that to happen to his grandson. He chose not to come because of his age. Deborah did not want to leave her father or Griez.

Surprisingly, Esther told Tabea, they recently heard from Liesel, whose husband was killed in the war. Her home in Hamburg had been destroyed in the bombing raids. She now wanted to reconcile with her family. Apparently, Papa Springer was so excited he could talk of nothing else for days.

Tabea felt great joy being near Esther and Hans, but she also felt a piece of her heart leave whenever an American, of whom she was particularly fond, returned home. The feeling that she belonged with them became more pronounced until she was convinced that she, too, should go to America. Tabea felt suspended between the two countries: the country of her birth which had given her life and heritage, but ultimately shame and despair; and the other country which had lifted her up and given her hope and a glimpse of freedom. She knew she would never have the same love for Germany again. She felt her future lay across the sea. After ten years of working for the Americans at the Army Hospital in Giessen, Tabea emigrated to the United States. Papa Springer understood and wrote to her, "Every fifty years a Springer emigrates to America."

Betty J. Iverson

ABOUT THE AUTHOR

Betty J. Iverson feels strongly that World War II was the event of the century and we must write the stories which will preserve the history of that era before the people slip away. She met Tabea Springer in Marina, California and realized hers was a unique story and agreed to write her memoir. After the first draft, Tabea told her, "Now I like my story."

Betty is a skilled interviewer and often her specific questions opened the floodgates of Tabea's memory and incredible events spilled out. Betty has researched and conducted many interviews to write this book. She has continued this process to write her second book, *A Time To Flee. (Unseen Women Of Courage)*

Betty is a nurse case manager with a B.S. from California State University at Hayward. She has had poetry and health articles published in the Monterey Peninsula Herald and has taken writing courses through the years. Writing is her first love. She feels privileged to be entrusted with Tabea's Story as well as those of the other women. She is active in her community and counts European immigrants among her many friends.

Printed in the United States
961200001B